Heir
to
Sevenwaters

Also by Juliet Marillier

THE SEVENWATERS TRILOGY
Daughter of the Forest
Son of the Shadows
Child of the Prophecy

Wolfskin
Foxmask

THE BRIDEI CHRONICLES
The Dark Mirror
Blade of Fortriu
The Well of Shades

For young adults:
Wildwood Dancing
Cybele's Secret

Heir to Sevenwaters

JULIET MARILLIER

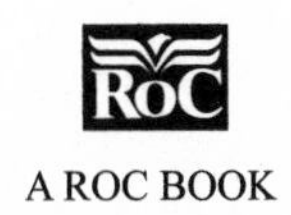

A ROC BOOK

ROC
Published by New American Library, a division of
Penguin Group (USA) Inc., 375 Hudson Street,
New York, New York 10014, USA
Penguin Group (Canada), 90 Eglinton Avenue East, Suite 700, Toronto,
Ontario M4P 2Y3, Canada (a division of Pearson Penguin Canada Inc.)
Penguin Books Ltd., 80 Strand, London WC2R 0RL, England
Penguin Ireland, 25 St. Stephen's Green, Dublin 2,
Ireland (a division of Penguin Books Ltd.)
Penguin Group (Australia), 250 Camberwell Road, Camberwell, Victoria 3124,
Australia (a division of Pearson Australia Group Pty. Ltd.)
Penguin Books India Pvt. Ltd., 11 Community Centre, Panchsheel Park,
New Delhi - 110 017, India
Penguin Group (NZ), 67 Apollo Drive, Rosedale, North Shore 0632,
New Zealand (a division of Pearson New Zealand Ltd.)
Penguin Books (South Africa) (Pty.) Ltd., 24 Sturdee Avenue,
Rosebank, Johannesburg 2196, South Africa

Penguin Books Ltd., Registered Offices:
80 Strand, London WC2R 0RL, England

First published by Roc, an imprint of New American Library,
a division of Penguin Group (USA) Inc.

First Printing, November 2008
1 3 5 7 9 10 8 6 4 2

Printed in the United States of America

In memory of my mother,
Dorothy Scott (Johnston)
December 1911–July 2007.
All her life she practiced selfless love.

ACKNOWLEDGMENTS

This book could not have been what it is without the assistance of my family. I thank Ben for brainstorming the original story with me, and Elly and Simon for reading the manuscript and helping me with plotting. My writers' group gave me useful feedback along the way and kept me working through the difficult patches.

I'm immensely grateful to the three editors who have worked on the book: Brianne Tunnicliffe at Pan Macmillan Australia, Anne Sowards at Roc, and Stefanie Bierwerth at Tor UK. Heartfelt thanks to Gage Godfrey-Nicholls for her beautiful Sevenwaters family tree. A special thank-you to my Australian copyeditor, Julia Stiles, for an excellent job. Cate Paterson at Pan Macmillan has continued to be a source of great support.

My agent, Russell Galen, has assisted me during the planning and writing of this book with his usual blend of professionalism and common sense.

Heir to Sevenwaters is dedicated to my mother, who died in mid-2007. Mum, thank you for reading my handwritten childhood sagas with such patience, and for always saying nice things about them! Thank you for teaching me the value of storytelling. You encouraged me to dream.

CHARACTER LIST

Sean		chieftain of Sevenwaters and Glencarnagh
Aisling	*ash*-ling	his wife
Their six daughters:		
Muirrin	*mir*-in	a healer; married to the Inis Eala healer, Evan
Deirdre	*dair*-dreh	
Clodagh	*kloh*-da	
Maeve	mayv	fostered in the household of Liadan and Bran
Sibeal	shi-*bayl*	
Eilis	*eye*-lish	
Niamh	*nee*-av	(deceased) Sean's elder sister
Fainne	*fawn*-yeh	Niamh's daughter, now custodian of a sacred island
Liadan	*lee*-a-dan	Sean's twin sister

Bran		Liadan's husband; formerly an outlaw mercenary, now chieftain of Harrowfield in Britain
Johnny		eldest son of Liadan and Bran; leader of fighting men and heir to Sevenwaters
Coll		his youngest brother; fostered at Sevenwaters (between Johnny and Coll are two other brothers, Fintan and Cormack)
Johnny's personal guards:		
Gareth		Johnny's best friend
Aidan		younger son of Lord Murtagh of Whiteshore
Cathal	ko-hal	
Mikka		
Sigurd		
Conor		Sean's uncle; chief druid at Sevenwaters
Ciarán	*keer*-aun	Conor's half-brother, a druid
Doran		Sean's senior man-at-arms
Nuala	*noo*-a-la	Doran's wife; cook at Sevenwaters
Eithne	*eh*-nyeh	Aisling's personal maid
Orlagh	*or*-la	serving woman
Cronan		a man-at-arms from Glencarnagh
Lughan	lu-aun	steward at Glencarnagh
Illann	ul-an	a chieftain of the southern Uí Néill (ee *nay*-ill) clan
Eoin	ohn	chieftains of the northern Uí Néill
Naithi	no-hi	
Colman		
Willow		a wandering storyteller

Firinne	*feer*-in-yeh	(deceased) Cathal's mother
Rathnait	ro-nitch	a girl of good family
Mac Dara	mac *da*-ra	a prince of the Fair Folk
Albha	*al*-va	a lady of the Fair Folk
Saorla	*sayr*-la	her half-human daughter
Mochaomhóg	ma-*khayv*-og	legendary clurichaun ancestor

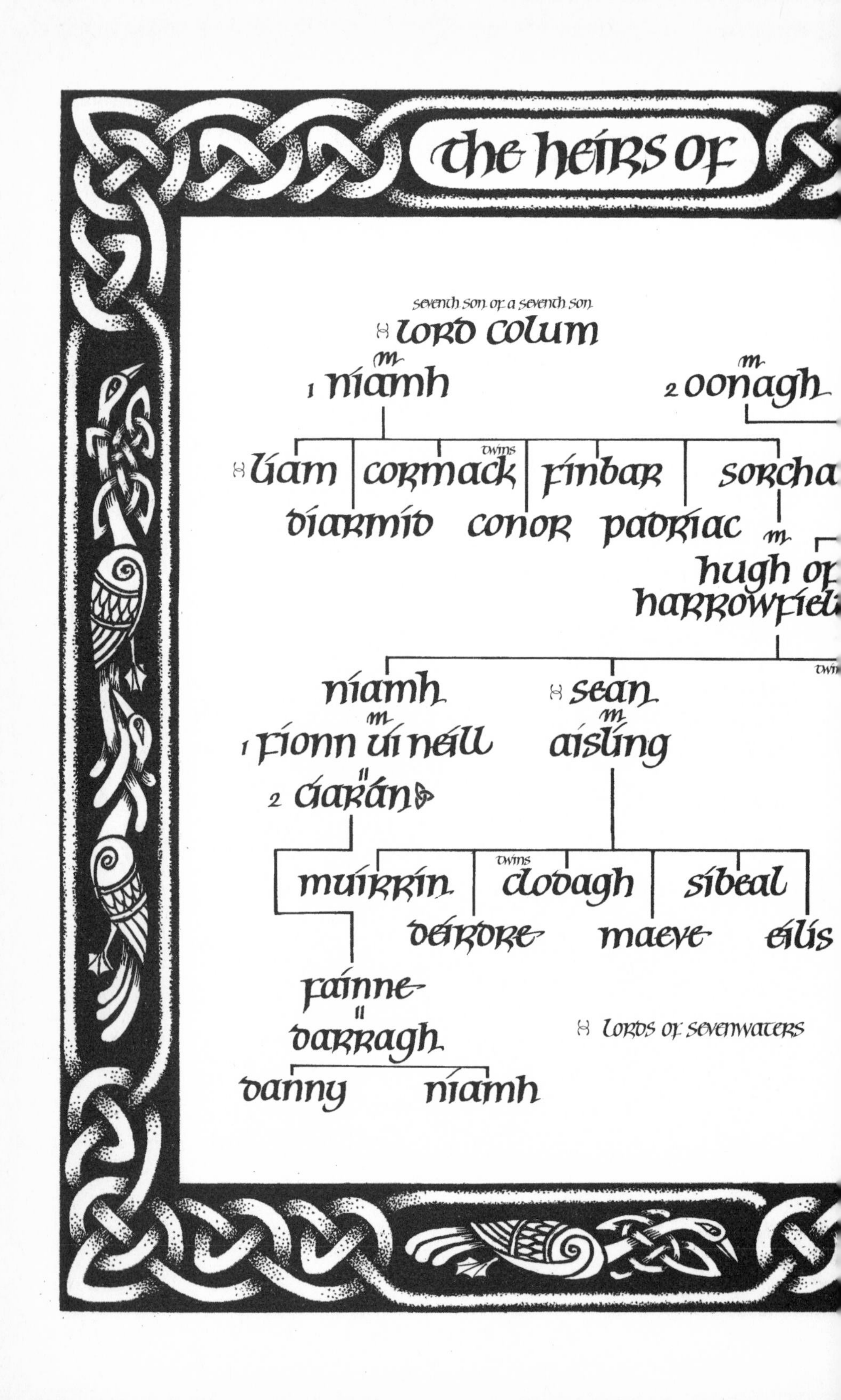
The Heirs of
seventh son of a seventh son
Lord Colum
m
1 Niamh
m
2 Oonagh
Liam
Cormack
twins
Finbar
Sorcha
Diarmid
Conor
Padriac
m
Hugh of
Harrowfiel
Niamh
m
1 Fionn Uí Néill
2 Ciarán
Sean
m
Aisling
Muirrin
twins
Clodagh
Síbeal
Deirdre
Maeve
Eilís
Fainne
Darragh
Danny
Niamh
Lords of Sevenwaters

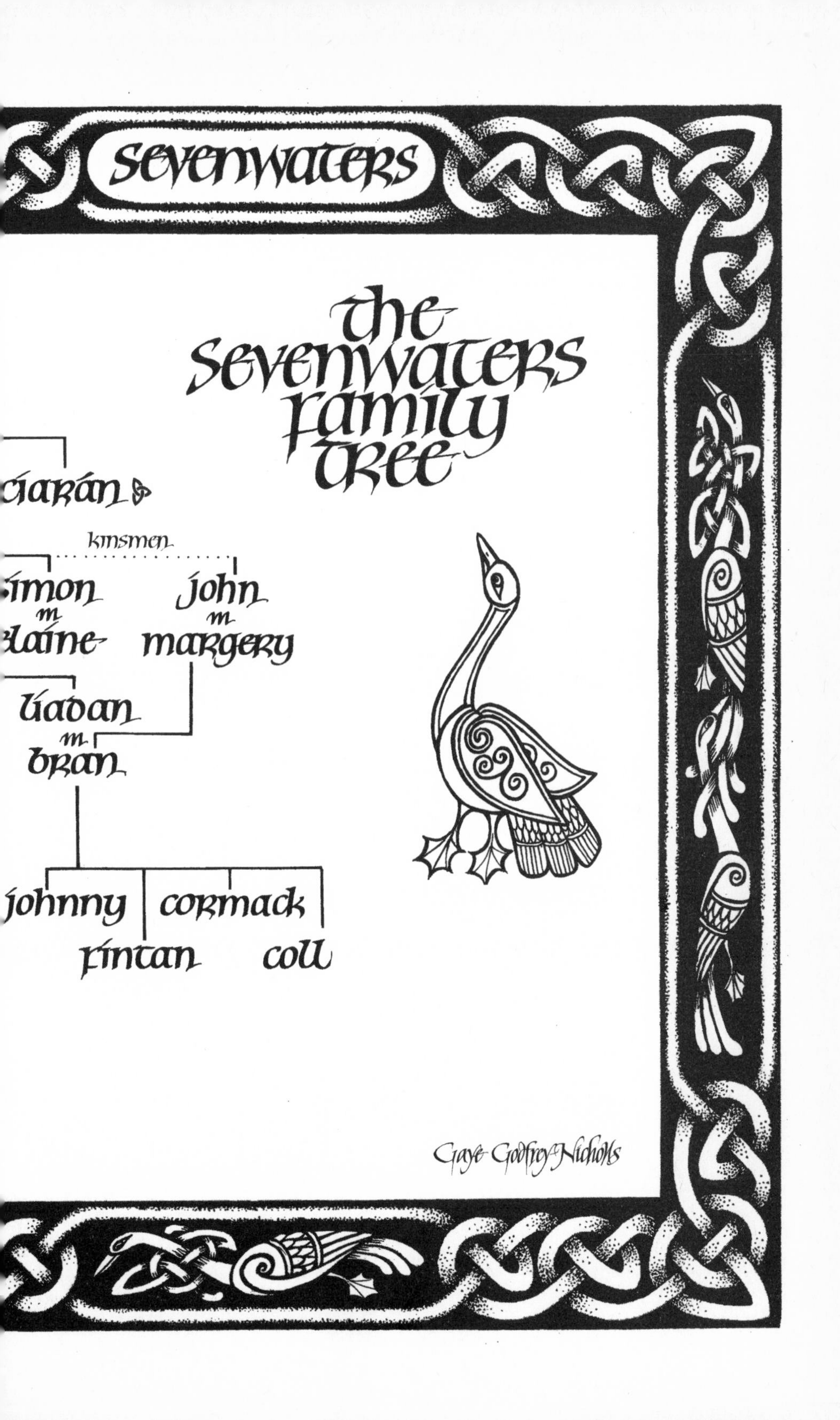
Sevenwaters
The Sevenwaters Family Tree
kinsmen
john
m
margery
líadan
m
bran
johnny
cormack
fintan
coll
Gaye Godfrey-Nicholls

HEIR
TO
SEVENWATERS

CHAPTER 1

My fingers numb with cold, I fastened a length of gold-embroidered ribbon around the hawthorn and murmured a prayer to whatever spirits might be listening. "When it's time for the baby to be born, please don't let my mother die." Another ribbon, higher up in branches burgeoning with spring's fresh green. "And please let the child be healthy." A third, slipped between twigs that scratched my skin, drawing bright blood. "And if you can, make it be a boy. Mother wants a son more than anything in the world."

I thrust my hands back into my sheepskin mittens and closed my eyes a moment to gather my thoughts. The lone hawthorn, which stood in a clearing within the great forest of Sevenwaters, was hung about with many offerings: ribbons, laces, scraps of wool and strings of wooden beads. Such solitary thorns were known to be gathering places for spirits. Until my mother had grown so heavy with child that she could no longer walk here safely, she had come every day with a token to place on the tree and a prayer that she might at long last be granted a healthy son. Now I carried out the ritual in her place.

It was time to head for home again. My sister was getting married in the morning and I had a lot to do. Deirdre and I were twins. She was slightly my elder, but I was the one who had inherited the household responsibilities Mother was too tired to deal with any longer. It made sense. Deirdre was going. Tomorrow afternoon she and her new husband, Illann, would be riding back to his home in the south and she would have her own household to manage. I was staying. For the foreseeable future my life would be taken up with supervising serving people, ordering and checking supplies, solving domestic disputes and keeping an eye on my two youngest sisters, Sibeal and Eilis. I hadn't expected this, but then, nobody had expected Mother to conceive another child so late in life. Now we were all on edge. Mother called this a gift from the gods. The rest of us tiptoed around the subject, fearful of speaking the unpalatable truth. Women of her age did not deliver healthy babes. Like as not, within two turnings of the moon she and the child would both be dead.

"Thank you," I said over my shoulder as I walked away from the hawthorn and into the shade of the forest. It was best to keep on the good side of the Fair Folk, whatever one's opinion of them. The forest of Sevenwaters was as much their home as it was ours. Long ago, our family had been entrusted with the task of keeping the place safe for them. This was one of the last refuges of the ancient races anywhere in Erin, for the great forests were being felled for grazing and the Christian religion had spread widely, displacing druids and wise women. The old faith was practiced only in the most protected and secret pockets of the land. Sevenwaters was one of these.

The path home wound its way through dense oak woods before descending to the lake shore. On another day I'd have enjoyed going slowly, drinking in the myriad shades of green, the delicate music of birdsong, the dappled light on the forest floor. Today I must make haste, for by nightfall our house would be full of guests and a long list of tasks lay before me. I owed it to my parents to ensure the domestic arrangements went as smoothly as if Mother herself were supervising them. I knew Father would have preferred Deirdre's wedding to be later, perhaps in the autumn, and not just because Mother was so frail right now. But once Illann had set eyes on my twin he'd wanted to marry her without delay, and Father had judged the alliance to be too valuable to be put at risk by insisting they wait. Illann was a chieftain of the southern Uí Néill and a close kinsman of the High King. It was the kind of match people called brilliant. Fortunately, Deirdre seemed to like Illann almost as much as he liked her. She'd been bubbling with excitement since the day she first met him.

The oaks towered over me, their mossy boles glowing in the filtered sunlight. My feet were quiet on the soft earth of the forest path. Between the trees, on the very edge of sight, moved evanescent beings, gossamer fine, shadow swift. In the rich litter of debris that lay around the roots of the great oaks tiny creatures stirred, scuttling, creaking, whispering. The forest of Sevenwaters was home to many. Badger, deer and hare, beetle, warbler and dragonfly lived side by side with the more otherworldly inhabitants of the wood. It would be strange for Deirdre to leave all this. Her new husband's holding, Dun na Ri, shared a border with the southwestern part of Father's land, but I knew nowhere could be like Sevenwaters.

As soon as I got back to the house I would make sure my younger sisters had their gowns ready for tonight's feast. I'd find an opportunity to speak with Father alone so I could see how he was; I knew Mother's tiredness was troubling him. I hoped I could reassure him. And I'd ease Mother's mind by letting her know that everything was under control. I should speak to my two druid uncles as soon as they arrived. Conor needed to be asked if the plans for tomorrow's spring ritual and hand-fasting suited him. Ciarán would want a place to retreat to. He came to our home quite often to work with Sibeal on druidic lore, for she would almost certainly join that community herself in a few years' time. Tutoring his young student in the garden or in the peace and quiet of an isolated chamber was one thing; facing a house full of visitors was quite another. Ciarán was acutely uncomfortable with crowds. Besides, he sometimes brought his raven with him. Folk found the bird unsettling.

The path narrowed, snaking between groves of closely growing elders whose narrow trunks formed graceful, bending shapes like those of leaning dryads. The foliage stirred in the breeze and I felt suddenly cold. Someone was watching me; I sensed it. I glanced around but could see nobody. "Who's there?" I called. There was no reply, only the whisper of the leaves and the cry of a bird passing overhead. My flesh rose in goose bumps. Our home was extremely well guarded; Father's men-at-arms were expert. Besides, the forest protected its own. Nobody came in by stealth. If a member of our household was out there, why hadn't anyone answered when I called?

Something moved under a stand of massive oaks about a hundred paces from the track. I froze, eyes narrowed. Now nothing was stirring. I took three more steps along the path and halted again, my skin prickling with unease. Something was there. Not a deer or a wild pig—something else.

I kept very still, peering into the shadowy depths under the trees, but I could see only patterns of light and shadow. Under the broad branches of the oaks vast distances seemed to open up, as if there existed doorways to a realm far wider than the expanses of the forest might allow. It was said, of course, that within the woods of Sevenwaters were portals of a very special kind: openings to the Otherworld. Traveling through such a doorway would be both wondrous and perilous, for time passed differently in that place. A man or woman might spend one night there and come back to find a hundred years had flown by in the human world. Or one might tarry for half a lifetime among the Fair Folk and return to one's own world with less than a season gone. It was wisest not to stray into such corners of the forest unless one placed the desire for adventure above all else.

Something caught my eye, not a movement, more of a . . . presence. Was that a man standing against the trunk of a great tree, a man wrapped in a hooded cape of shadow gray?

"Who's there?" I called. "Come out and account for yourself!"

Even as I spoke it occurred to me that if anyone obeyed I was ill equipped to deal with the situation. I had no skills in combat and not so much as a vegetable knife on my person. I picked up my skirts and ran.

For some time the only sound was the thud of my footsteps on the soft path. Or were there two sets of footsteps? I ran faster, and whoever was following me sped up to match. My breath was coming in gasps now, and behind me someone else was breathing too, in and out as he maintained steady pursuit. My heart jumped about in my chest; my skin was clammy with fear. The trees seemed to jerk and spin, and the spaces between them to widen as if inviting me to leave the path and stray at random. "I won't have this," I muttered to myself. "I just won't." It didn't seem to help.

A voice spoke right inside my mind. *Clodagh! Clodagh, where are you?* I tripped over a rock and sprawled full-length on the path, my head swimming with panic. A moment later I realized this had not been the taunt of a pursuer, but the familiar voice of my twin sister. I sat up, brushing the hair out of my eyes, and knew immediately that if someone—otherworldly presence or human miscreant—had been following me before, that person was now gone. The forest around me was peaceful. Birds sang. Leaves rustled in the slight breeze. The path led straight onward. Above the canopy of tall oaks the sun shone on a perfect spring day.

I took several deep breaths before I answered. My skirt was badly torn and my right knee had a bloody graze. I screwed my eyes shut for a moment, willing what had just happened into a closed corner of my mind. It was a complication I could not deal with right now. I was simply too busy.

Deirdre? I answered my sister's call, using the skill possessed by the twins of our family, a link that allowed us to communicate silently, mind to mind. My father had this ability. His twin sister, Aunt Liadan, lived over the sea in Britain. The two of them had been able to share their thoughts and their news since childhood. *What's wrong?* I asked my sister, making myself get up and limp toward home.

My hair! I put chamomile in the water, and now it's dried out looking like a furze bush! I can't get married like this! Where are you, Clodagh? I need you!

I reminded myself that my twin was leaving Sevenwaters tomorrow to embark on a completely new life in an unfamiliar home. *It'll be fine, Deirdre,* I told her. *I'm on my way back from the hawthorn. Don't panic, we'll think of something.*

I picked up my pace again. Soon the high roof of the stone keep where we lived could be seen in the distance above a soft shawl of trees. Our home was a stronghold built to keep out invaders.

The uncanny forest that surrounded it and the broad lake that lapped at its feet were in themselves deterrents to armed assault. My father had established fortified settlements in strategic areas of the forest, each headed by a freeman with his own complement of men-at-arms. This was necessary, since Sevenwaters was situated right between the two warring factions of the Uí Néill clan.

My mind went back to the figure I had half seen under the trees. Could a spy have succeeded in coming right into the forest unchecked? What could such a person hope to gain by that? I shivered, imagining myself abducted and held as a hostage, the price of my safe release Father's agreement to relinquish control of his lands, or something even worse. Perhaps it was not a good idea to go for long walks on my own. People did get kidnapped. I could remember a terrible story about a girl who had been taken in that way. By the time her family had decided to comply with the captors' demands, she had been killed. The tale went that her severed head had been thrown back over the wall of her father's house.

My mind on this, I walked out from under the trees and straight into a big man in a gray cloak. A pair of strong hands gripped my shoulders hard. I screamed.

The man let go abruptly. I stepped back, ready to bolt past him for the safety of home.

"Ouch," said someone in a lazy drawl, and I saw that there was a second man standing behind the first with his fingers in his ears. "That was loud. You've evidently lost your touch with the ladies, Aidan."

Aidan. I drew a shuddering breath and looked up, realizing that the man who had seized me had been the very one whose arrival at Sevenwaters I had been keenly awaiting since my cousin Johnny had sent word that he would be here for the wedding. I could think of better circumstances under which I might have met him.

"Aidan!" I said, smiling awkwardly. "Welcome back! I was thinking about something else and you scared me. So Johnny's arrived?" I'd been really foolish. All of Johnny's men wore gray cloaks, the better to blend in with the hues of the forest. Both Aidan, whom I knew, and the other warrior, who was a stranger to me, wore them. Both had the facial markings, tattoos around the eye and nose suggestive of particular creatures—Aidan's a lark, the other man's a fox—that were worn as both mark of individuality and badge of brotherhood by every member of Johnny's war band.

"We got here not long ago," Aidan said. He was regarding me quizzically, and I wondered if he had actually forgotten me since last spring, when he had come to Sevenwaters as part of my cousin's escort and had seemed to take a particular interest in me. "I didn't mean to startle you. Is everything all right?"

He was just as good-looking as I'd remembered: tall and broad-shouldered, with a strong-boned face, well-kept brown hair and friendly eyes. He was by far the most handsome of all Johnny's men, I thought; at least, all of them whom I'd met. My cousin was a leader of elite warriors. He ran an establishment that offered training in all aspects of combat, and his personal guards were the best of the best. As my father's heir, Johnny spent part of every year with us at Sevenwaters and always brought a complement of five or six guards with him. The other man was staring at me. I must answer Aidan's question. I opened my mouth to do so, but the dark man spoke first.

"This has to be one of Johnny's multiplicity of female cousins—the blinding red of that hair confirms it. Now, which one is it? Not the baby; not the seer; not the eldest, whom we already know. And the crippled one's at Harrowfield. This can't possibly be the young lady getting married tomorrow. I deduce it's the one you've mentioned more times than is altogether appropriate, Aidan. What did you say she had a talent for? Oh, that's right, housewifely skills, washing and cooking, that kind of thing." He gave an ostentatious yawn. "Forgive me, but I can't imagine anything more boring."

He might as well have smacked me in the face. I struggled for a response.

"Cathal!" Aidan had flushed scarlet. "Please ignore my friend," he added, turning toward me. "I keep trying to train him in the social niceties but thus far he's failed to grasp them."

"We're warriors, not courtiers." Cathal spoke with studied weariness. "One doesn't need social niceties on the battlefield."

"You're not on the battlefield, you're a guest in the home of a respected chieftain," I snapped, unable to control my annoyance. "We do maintain a basic level of good manners here. Perhaps my cousin was so busy giving you a run-down of our personal characteristics that he neglected to mention that."

Cathal looked through me.

"Clodagh, I'm mortified by my friend's rudeness," Aidan said, offering me his arm. "His name is Cathal and, like me, he's from Whiteshore. Johnny left him back on the island last year, and perhaps that's where he should have stayed. We're so sorry if we've upset you."

"Speak for yourself," said Cathal.

I wasn't sure I wanted to introduce myself to such a disagreeable individual, but I was the daughter of the house, and if this was Aidan's friend, unlikely as that seemed, I had better at least go through the motions. "I'm Clodagh, third daughter of Lord Sean and Lady Aisling," I said tightly. "Welcome to Sevenwaters. I'm surprised to see you down here." The lake shore was at some distance from the keep, at the foot of a sloping sward with the forest to either side. If they'd only just arrived, they should surely have been unpacking gear and settling in.

"Cathal wanted to walk by the water," Aidan said. "You're still looking upset, Clodagh. I assure you, Johnny speaks nothing but good of you and your sisters, and we're fully conversant with the rules of Lord Sean's household. I apologize on Cathal's behalf for his ill-considered words. It's all sound and no substance with him."

"Such a comment seems somehow inappropriate from a bard," Cathal said, gazing out across the lake as if he were not even marginally interested in the conversation.

Last spring and summer Aidan had once or twice been persuaded by his fellow warriors to play the harp for us after supper. He was a talented musician, which had struck me as surprising. Johnny's men were fighters by profession. The essence of a bard's art was creation, a warrior's destruction. It seemed to me that doing both might leave a man's mind full of conflicting questions.

"I hope you'll play for us again while you're here," I said.

Aidan smiled, revealing the dimple at the corner of his mouth. "Only if you play too," he said, brown eyes dancing.

"I might," I said, thinking of all the reasons why I had so looked forward to his return and deciding that his presence at Sevenwaters would, on balance, outweigh that of the obnoxious Cathal. "My sister's betrothed, Illann, has arranged for musicians to come from his own household for the celebrations. But I imagine you're here for a while; there should be plenty of opportunity."

"If you look at Aidan like that, he'll certainly perform for you," Cathal said. "He's all too ready to woo likely women with a well-crafted love song or two. Just don't take him seriously, that's my advice."

"In the unlikely event that I think your advice may be useful, I'll ask you for it," I said in what I hoped was a quelling tone. "And you can keep your personal remarks about my sisters to yourself. If I hear such comments from you again I'll . . ."

"You'll what?" His brows arched. "Tell your father? Slap me on the cheek? Run off and cry?"

"Stop it, Cathal!" Aidan looked mortified. "He doesn't mean a word of it, Clodagh. Now, may we escort you back to the house?"

"In a moment," I said, then turned back toward Cathal. "I'll ask Johnny to send you away immediately," I told him, though I knew I could not actually expect my cousin to accommodate such a request. There were always strategic reasons for the deployment of his men. That applied even if they were accompanying him to a family wedding. "I know what high standards he sets for his personal retainers. It's not just skill in weapons or tracking or observation. It's the way you live your whole life. If you're as rude as this to everyone, I can't imagine why he's kept you. You must have some quality that's completely invisible to an outsider such as myself."

I expected a barbed retort, but Cathal simply shrugged. As we walked back to the keep and Aidan engaged me in a conversation about music, his friend fell into a deep silence.

Deirdre was in the chamber the two of us had shared since we were little girls. Although our house was a keep, its interior was comfortably fitted out, with many private rooms. Sibeal and Eilis shared the bedchamber next door. After tomorrow I'd have this one all to myself.

My twin was sitting on her bed, her head in her hands, crying. She'd been absolutely right about her hair. She and I had inherited our mother's flaming curls, which could be striking if tended with care, but had a tendency to go wild at the least provocation. I could see that the chamomile had not been a good idea.

Deirdre sobbed out something about Illann thinking she was ugly and deciding he didn't want to marry her after all, which I took to be her worst fear about tomorrow.

"Nonsense," I said, sitting down beside her and putting my arm around her shoulders. "We have almost a whole day before the hand-fasting. There's plenty of time to fix your hair." The long list of other things I had to do flashed through my mind, but for the moment I ignored it. "A sprinkle of lavender water, some careful plaiting, that's all it needs."

"We don't have a whole day," Deirdre pointed out. "There's the feast tonight, and the dancing. And now Johnny's here . . ."

Perhaps the tears were not all related to her appearance. Deirdre did tend to make everything into a drama, but she was genuinely upset.

"Deirdre," I said firmly, "come and sit by the mirror. The sooner I start working on your hair, the likelier it is you can be your beautiful self for tonight's festivities."

"I can't possibly make an appearance for the feast," Deirdre muttered as she settled before the mirror. She pinched her cheeks in an attempt to redden them. "I look completely washed out. I should never have chosen green for the wedding gown. I wonder if it's too late to—"

"Morrigan's curse!" I exclaimed in horror, catching sight of myself in the bronze mirror over my sister's shoulder. Cathal's comment about my obviously not being a bride made complete sense now. My hair was even frizzier than Deirdre's and had leaves and twigs in it. After my headlong sprint in the cold, my cheeks wore the flush my sister was aiming for. My eyes were red too, and so was the tip of my nose. The rent in my gown showed not only my grazed knee but also a considerable length of leg. It was no wonder Aidan had given me a funny look as I came out of the forest.

"What?" demanded Deirdre, diverted from her woes. "What's wrong?"

"Nothing," I growled as I used the comb to separate my sister's hair into sections. It would take a great deal of work to get her mop under control, but then I'd had plenty of practice. "Unless you count the fact that I just bumped into Aidan looking like *this*." He and Cathal were probably laughing about it together right now.

"Oh, so Johnny did bring him again? That's wonderful news, Clodagh. I know how much you like him. I bet Aidan asked if he could come. He seemed quite keen on you last year. And he's so suitable. I mean, Aidan doesn't quite have the pedigree that Illann does, but he is a chieftain's son, and I know Father would like an alliance in the west. Just think, Clodagh, we could both be married in the same year!"

"Aidan may be suitable husband material," I said grimly as I pinned up a strand of Deirdre's hair, "but I won't be marrying him any time soon. Or anyone, for that matter." For a moment I had basked in my memories of last year, when Aidan had walked in the garden with me and played the harp with me and generally gone out of his way to talk to me. That had been before Mother conceived her child. Now everything was different, and it didn't matter whether I liked Aidan or he liked me, because I knew I would not be free to marry for a long time, if ever. "I'll have to stay here, Deirdre, you know that. Even if everything goes well for Mother, she'll be weak and tired for a while. She'll need me. And if things go wrong . . ." There was no need to spell it out. "Never mind," I said with forced cheerfulness. "I've certainly wrecked my chances of making a good impression on Aidan today, anyway. He had the most awful friend with him. The rudest man I've ever had the misfortune to clap eyes on. I can't imagine where Johnny got him from. He must be losing his touch."

Something had changed in Deirdre's expression. I met her eyes in the mirror. "You can't have been crying just about your hair," I said. "What's really wrong? Is this about Johnny?" This was a topic on which even I had to tread warily.

"Why would it be?" Deirdre's response was a little too quick.

"You know why, Deirdre. For years and years there's only been one man you liked, and it wasn't Illann. The fact that first cousins can't marry doesn't even come into it. It wouldn't be fair to Illann if you took him as second best."

"That was ages ago. I was a child. You don't imagine I've been harboring a secret passion for Johnny all these years, do you?"

I knew that was exactly what she had been doing, but I would not upset her further by saying so. I pinned up the last section of her hair before starting to comb and plait. "Are you feeling nervous then? About . . . well, about the wedding night and all that?"

"A bit," Deirdre said. "Ouch, that hurts, Clodagh! But not nervous enough to cry over it. It's not as if Illann and I haven't . . . That is to say, there have been certain things . . . I'm pretty sure I'll like it, once I get used to it."

"You're lucky," I said, combing steadily. "The most advantageous marriage Father could ever have dreamed of for one of his daughters, and you actually like Illann enough to want to share his bed."

"Your time will come."

"I expect Father will choose some ghastly old man for me, someone who happens to be useful as an ally." As an attempt at humor, it sounded unconvincing even to me.

"He wouldn't do that, Clodagh," Deirdre said seriously. "You know he wouldn't have insisted on my match with Illann if I didn't like him. And given what Illann's connections can do for Father, that was remarkably good of him."

"True." I didn't think Father would be needing to deal with prospective suitors for me. Whatever happened when Mother gave birth, she would not be able to resume her duties around the house for a while. If the worst occurred, I must be prepared to take on the domestic management of Sevenwaters for my father's lifetime. Although I was one of six daughters, there was no doubt that this particular job would fall to me.

My eldest sister Muirrin was married and lived at Inis Eala, headquarters of Johnny's warrior band. Deirdre would be handfasted and gone tomorrow. Our next sister, Maeve, had suffered severe injuries in a fire four years ago and now lived in my aunt's house in Britain. Aunt Liadan, Johnny's mother, was a healer of unparalleled skills. If anyone could help Maeve regain movement in her poor twisted hands and come to acceptance of her scarred face, Liadan could. Cathal had been right: my sister was a cripple. But none of our family ever used that ugly word.

As for my two youngest sisters, Sibeal was a scholar and a seer, destined for higher things, and Eilis was only nine. Mother had been training Deirdre and me for years in the expectation that each of us would marry and need to perform these duties capably in our husbands' households.

"What's the matter, Clodagh?" Deirdre's gaze sharpened as she watched me in the mirror. "You look sad suddenly."

"I'm going to miss you so much," I said. "Thank goodness we'll still be able to talk to each other when you're gone. I don't know how I'd manage without that. I mean, you've always been here. It's like part of myself going away."

Deirdre said nothing.

"You'll want to know what happens when Mother has the baby," I went on. "I'll be able to tell you straightaway." That wouldn't be easy if Mother and the child both died. My mental link with my twin meant news was delivered rather baldly, without the possibility of asking a third person to be present, or getting the recipient seated, or ensuring privacy before coming right out with it.

"She's going to die, isn't she?" Deirdre's voice was oddly flat now. "After tomorrow, I'll never see her again."

My own eyes stung in sympathy. We hadn't talked about this, not properly. We'd skated over the surface of it rather than admit to ourselves, or to each other, what we knew was most likely to happen. "She might get through it," I said. "The baby might survive too. Mother certainly believes that."

Deirdre had bowed her head. Her hands were tightly clasped in her lap. She did not speak.

"Maybe Illann could bring you back to visit before the baby's due," I said, putting down the comb. How terrible for my twin if what she had said came true, and she never got the chance to say goodbye.

"I don't even want to think about it!" Deirdre snapped. My twin had always been volatile, her emotions as tumultuous as an autumn storm. I was the calm one; in general, I simply got on with what needed doing. "I hate the idea of being here when it happens," my sister went on. "Just imagine seeing her die right in front of us and not being able to do anything about it. If she has a boy and it lives and she doesn't, I'm going to hate that child more than anything in the world." She was crying again, her face crumpling with miserable fury.

I hugged her, blinking hard. "That's nonsense," I told her, though I had felt something dark and cold pass over me as she spoke. "People never hate babies, they only have to look at them to love them. And Mother may not die. Perhaps she's right about this child being a son and a special gift from the gods. Perhaps all those offerings have worked for her at last."

"You don't really believe that, Clodagh." Deirdre glanced up and I met her eyes in the mirror. I was shocked at the look in them; it was almost hostile. "I meant what I said. If Mother dies, I never want to come back here. I'm going to put Sevenwaters behind me and concentrate on being the best wife to Illann that I can possibly be."

I had thought I knew Deirdre better than anyone, but she had shocked me. The thought of her turning her back on Sevenwaters and her family hurt me. I could think of nothing to say, but I had the curious sensation that I had suddenly grown much older. I picked up the comb and set to work again. Neither of us could afford to appear before the rest of the household looking as if we'd been crying. Deirdre must shine at tonight's feast and I must put on a convincing pretense of happiness, for my father's sake in particular.

As chieftain of Sevenwaters, Father was juggling a far more testing set of challenges than I was: not just Mother's uncertain future and that of her unborn child, but the fact that Deirdre's marriage was likely to create resentment amongst certain powerful leaders of the northern Uí Néill. They would at the very least be suspicious of this new tie between Sevenwaters and the southern branch of their feuding clan. On top of those things, disquieting rumors had been heard in the district. People had begun to blame the Fair Folk for stock losses, for accidental fires, for crop failures and storms, as if that wise and noble race had almost overnight become mischievous and meddling. Talk of that sort troubled Father, since our land had long provided a haven for the Tuatha De. It was no wonder he was looking so tired. Deirdre and I must smile and hold our heads high tonight. We must celebrate tomorrow's hand-fasting with every appearance of joy and hope.

"Clodagh," Deirdre said, "there's something I have to tell you. You won't like it."

"Oh?"

"I'm really, really sorry about this, Clodagh. I know it's going to make you unhappy, but I have to do it."

I put the comb down, completely mystified. "Come on, out with it then," I said. "Whatever it is, it can't be as bad as all that."

She dropped her gaze. "Clodagh, we can't do it anymore. When I'm gone, when I'm at Illann's. It won't be appropriate."

"Can't do what?" I had no idea what she meant.

"Talk, the way we do. I'm so sorry, I'll miss you terribly, but . . . Once I'm married, it would be—it wouldn't feel right, Clodagh. Don't look like that, it's not the end of the world. Be practical about it. What if Illann and I were lying together and suddenly you were there between us? Not actually there, of course, but it would be the same. We just can't do it anymore."

Something cold and hard lodged itself in my chest. "You can't mean that," I whispered, knowing that she must or she would not have said it.

"I'll have a new home and a new family." Deirdre's voice wobbled, and she set her jaw. "I have to concentrate on that. I'm sorry to hurt you, Clodagh. But I do mean it. I'm not going to let you in anymore; I just can't. And please don't argue about it. I've made up my mind. It's not only because of Illann and me. I need to learn to stand on my own feet and face my own problems. I've become too used to asking you for help and expecting you to fix things, and now I'll be a married woman with my own household, and . . . Here, give me the comb." She was battling not to shed more tears. "You should change your gown, it's all ripped," my sister said shakily. "What were you doing out there, climbing trees?"

I usually spent time with my father every evening in his small council room, talking over the day's events. I would bring him up to date on the domestic affairs of the household and he would tell me about his discussions with neighboring chieftains, his decisions in relation to our outlying settlements and their free tenants, his purchases of cattle or his plans to travel to councils and gatherings. Sometimes we'd talk about the conflicts that beset our region, usually involving the warring branches of the Uí Néill clan. We'd been doing this since long before Mother's pregnancy. In the past she had often made a third in our conversations. Now that she was so unwell she had neither energy nor inclination for such talk, so it was just the two of us. Deirdre had never been interested in such matters.

Father often told me I had a good head for strategy. It was not especially common for chieftains to consult their daughters on weighty issues, I knew, but then Father was no ordinary chieftain. It seemed to me that even if I had had brothers, Father would still have trusted me and valued my opinions, as he did Mother's. Perhaps it came from his having grown up with a twin sister who had been unafraid to make bold decisions in her own right. Perhaps it was partly because he had become chieftain at the age of sixteen, and had relied heavily on my mother's support—she had been his childhood sweetheart and they had married young.

Knowing there would be no opportunity for our usual talk tonight, with the celebration supper to be followed by music and dancing, I seized a chance to speak to him in midafternoon, waiting until the two southern chieftains he'd been talking to left the council chamber, before slipping in.

Father was sitting with chin on hand, a document before him on the table. He was staring into space, his eyes distant. There were gray threads in his dark hair now, and lines on his face that had not been there before Mother conceived her child. Father was known as a strong, wise leader, a decisive man who knew how to be tough but was always fair. Right now he looked exhausted and despondent. His two wolfhounds provided silent companionship, one with her muzzle resting on his knee, the other lying across his feet. They lifted their heads as I came in, then lowered them again.

"Father," I said, closing the door behind me and shutting out the sound of chattering voices from the hall, "I wanted to see if there was anything else you needed done. All the arrangements are in place for tonight's feast and for tomorrow's ritual. Most folk have arrived now. Muirrin and her small escort will be here in the morning, Johnny says—apparently she was called to attend to a sick child in our northern settlement as they passed through, so Johnny left three men with her and came on with the rest. All the guests are accommodated. The horses have been seen to and Doran has found space for the grooms and attendants. But there's no sign yet of the two northern chieftains you invited, Naithi of Davagh and his cousin, Colman."

"Mm," murmured Father, and his lips tightened.

"You think they're not coming? Not even sending representatives? That would be extremely discourteous."

"I hoped they would come, Clodagh. I extended the invitation to those two because, of all the leaders of the northern Uí Néill, they seem the most open-minded and fair. And with their influential neighbor, Eoin of Lough Gall, away from home, I thought that Naithi and Colman might be prepared to sit at table with Illann just for the two days of the festivities. It seems I was wrong. They're unhappy about the marriage. Angry, most likely."

I could see he was deeply troubled, and decided I would not mention shadowy presences following me in the forest, or indeed rude young men insulting me; not while he had that look on his face. "Father, this is very serious, isn't it, this difficulty with the northern chieftains?"

He motioned to the bench beside him and I sat down, realizing that I had been on my feet all day and was tired.

"I'll deal with it after the wedding," he said. "Yes, it's serious, but Johnny's here now and we'll devise a strategy. You look a little tired, Clodagh. This is a busy time for you. And you must have mixed feelings, with Deirdre going away."

"I'm fine, Father." I managed a smile. "I'm getting used to all this. It's one less worry for Mother if I make sure everything is the way she would want it to be."

There was a short silence. The unspoken thought hung between us: that Mother might never again take up the reins of the household; that she might not be with us for very much longer.

"I wish the wedding could have been later," I said, remembering how pale and weary Mother had looked when I went up to see her earlier. "She gets tired so easily. I suggested she might leave the supper early."

"I'll be glad when Muirrin gets here and can give us her expert opinion on your mother's condition," Father said, rubbing his eyes. "I have to say, Clodagh, that although this is a wonderful marriage for Deirdre, I, too, wish the timing could have been different. It's too much for Aisling right now, even with you handling the arrangements so efficiently. She seems . . ." He broke off, unwilling to put his thought into words.

I laid a hand on his shoulder; he covered it with his.

"I know, Father," I said quietly. "But the festivities will be over by tomorrow afternoon. And Muirrin should be staying until after the baby is born." My eldest sister was a healer; this was the job she and her husband carried out at Johnny's establishment on Inis Eala, where combat injuries were frequent. We were lucky she had been able to come to Sevenwaters.

"I'm sad that Maeve cannot be here," Father said. "I know she shies away from such gatherings, but she'd want to see her sister married. I miss her, Clodagh. You girls are all precious to me in your different ways. I hope you know that."

"I do, Father." I heard what he was not saying: that Mother's fervent desire for a son—she was unshakeable in her belief that she was carrying a boy—could all too easily be taken to mean that she cared less than she should about her six daughters. I had heard my youngest sister, Eilis, say that Mother did not love her as much as the child who was coming. Sibeal had hushed her, telling her that mothers love all their children equally, always. I did not really think this was true. "And we love you. You're the best of fathers. It will feel odd, won't it, when Deirdre is gone? Once Muirrin leaves again you'll only have three of your girls left. And Coll, of course."

Father smiled. "You asked me if there was anything else I needed done. I suppose I should ask if I can be sure my nephew will be on his best manners before our distinguished guests tonight."

"What Coll may not be prepared to do for me," I said, "he'll do for Johnny. He worships his big brother. I think we'll have perfect behavior for a little while at least."

"Perfect? From that child? I doubt it." Father's tone was affectionate. Coll was not a wayward boy, simply adventurous. He and Eilis got in and out of trouble together regularly. It made the household livelier, which I thought a good thing.

Someone tapped on the door. When I opened it a chink, there was a chieftain waiting to speak to Father. At least I could snatch a few moments' rest in my chamber, I thought. For Father, the day's business had begun at dawn and would not be finished until the feast was over and all the guests safely abed.

Nobody would have known, at suppertime, that Lord Sean of Sevenwaters bore such a weight of anxiety. My father's strong features were calm, his smile convincing as he presided over the festive meal. To accommodate our many guests we had four tables laid, one for family on a dais at the side of the hall, the others set crossways in the main part of this chamber, the biggest and grandest in the keep. Embroidered hangings decorated the walls; lamps cast a warm light over their bright colors. A fire crackled on the hearth, for the spring evenings could be chill here.

When Johnny was with us he generally sat at Father's left hand, with Mother on the right. This was in recognition that he was Father's heir and would one day be chieftain of Sevenwaters. Tonight he had ceded his place to Illann, the new son-in-law, and was sitting beside Deirdre, opposite me. It was easy to like Johnny. He was a sturdily built young man with close-cropped brown hair, steady gray eyes and a swirl of facial tattooing that was subtly suggestive of a raven's plumage. He had always been kind to us girls, though we were slightly in awe of him. Johnny was older, of course; a year or two the senior of our eldest sister, Muirrin. He was a seasoned battle leader and greatly respected among fighting men.

The chieftains of the region did not view Johnny with quite such universal admiration. As the closest male kin—eldest son of my father's twin sister—he was the rightful heir to Sevenwaters. But his father, Bran of Harrowfield, had once been a fearsome outlaw, and the local leaders had long memories. Aunt Liadan had been abducted by Bran's warriors when she was about my age, so she could tend to their injured comrade. From that unlikely beginning had come Johnny, and a love that still shone as bright as the stars in the eyes of Liadan and her grim-looking husband. In fact, a prophecy had foretold that my cousin would one day be chieftain of Sevenwaters. That was common knowledge. It was plain to me that Johnny would do the job extremely well, and I knew Father shared my opinion. Of course, should my mother have a healthy son, things might change.

My gaze moved from Johnny to Deirdre, who was seated beside Mother. My twin looked lovely. There was no trace of her earlier tears. I had persuaded her to let me put her hair into a braided, upswept style, and it made her look at least three years older and quite elegant. Illann couldn't take his eyes off her, and the glances she gave him from under half-lowered lashes showed how much she liked his admiration.

Mother was pretending to eat, but she didn't fool me. Father kept glancing at her, no doubt seeing what I did: the shadows under her eyes, the waxen pallor of her skin, the strained smile as she tried to concentrate on something Illann was telling her. Aware that Illann's sister, seated on my other side, was looking at me oddly, I plunged into conversation. "Your household musicians are very good," I said. "The fellow on the whistle, especially."

"Illann only hires the best." His sister cast an assessing look around the hall and paused as her eyes fell on Aidan, who was seated with several other men clad in the blue and gray of Johnny's personal retainers. Her expression warmed; I could see she found his looks as pleasing as I did. "My brother understands that most households in these parts haven't the resources to keep a permanent band. I suppose Lord Sean needs to fall back on the wandering bards. It's a matter of luck whether you get a good one or some fellow with no talent at all."

"Of course," I said, swallowing my irritation, "we do have two druids in the family. They're handy for a little storytelling after supper." I saw a smile pass across Conor's face. My father's uncle was chief of the brotherhood and spiritual leader of our community. He maintained a keen interest in strategic matters and came to Sevenwaters regularly to advise Father. Ciarán, his half-brother, had excused himself from tonight's festivities as I'd expected. I had housed him in the little chamber next to the stillroom and I knew he would be there alone, absorbed in meditation or study.

"As for wandering bards, my cousin has a talented musician amongst his men," I went on, glancing at Johnny, who had his close friend Gareth, an amiable, sandy-haired man, standing on guard behind him. He had one warrior stationed by each door as well. Even in this place that was his second home, Johnny took no chances. What he did made him desirable as a friend to the wealthy and powerful. It also made him a target.

"Oh?" queried Illann's sister.

"We might prevail upon Aidan to sing and play later," Johnny said. "Our bride-to-be loves the harp. She plays well herself."

This was a slight exaggeration, since my twin had never worked hard enough on the exercises required to build up her technical skill. Johnny's compliment had brought a blush to her cheeks. She did look lovely. Since we were almost exactly alike, I'd been careful to dress plainly tonight so Deirdre could be the one to shine. My gown was a smoky blue with a gray overdress embroidered in white. My hair was braided into a single tight plait, its only adornment a blue ribbon.

"Thank you, Johnny." Deirdre's smile was a touch tremulous. Whether our cousin had ever quite understood the depth of her long devotion to him, I did not know.

I coaxed Mother from the hall and shepherded her up to bed as early as I could. Her maid, Eithne, went off to brew a herbal drink, and I sent another serving woman to fetch warm water.

"I'll stay until they get back," I told Mother as she sat down heavily on her bed and shook off her shoes.

"Thank you, Clodagh. In fact I'm happy to have a little peace. This one's restless tonight." She took my hand and laid it on her belly. The infant kicked me hard, and a thrill went through me at the wonder of it. But I was afraid. This child was so strong already. For a moment I saw it as an adversary, a ruthless being that would take my mother's life without hesitation in order to secure its own.

"He's eager to get out and join the celebrations," I said. I had become practiced at hiding my fear in front of mother, a skill I had, ironically, learned from her. I had watched her dealing calmly with one household crisis after another over the years and I had picked up her knack of covering up any unease she felt with a look of cheerful competence. "Mother, you didn't eat anything at supper. I'll have some bread and fruit sent up from the kitchen for you."

"There's no need to fuss, Clodagh." There was a trace of her old briskness in her tone. "The gods want this boy born safely; I've known it from the first. Why else would they give me another chance now after all these years?"

"You should rest, all the same. Would you like me to keep you company until you sleep? It's not as if this is the first time I've ever heard a band, after all. And it's Deirdre's night, not mine."

Something must have shadowed my face or darkened my tone.

"Do you wish it was yours, Clodagh? Are you unhappy about being left behind?" She settled obediently against her pillows, but her eyes were shrewd as they examined my face.

I sat on the edge of the bed, looking down at my hands. "The fact that Deirdre and I are twins doesn't mean we want the same things in our lives, Mother. I am happy to stay at home for now. There's plenty of time."

"You're close to the same age I was when I wed your father," Mother said with a faint smile. "But, of course, Sean and I had known each other since we were children. There was a time when I thought we would never be together, and my heart almost broke, Clodagh. Some folk say that kind of love burns itself out, that it can't endure the trials and tests of ordinary life. But that isn't true."

There was a faraway look in her eyes now. I knew what she was not saying aloud: that her longing to give my father a son had cast a shadow over their life together, and that now, at last, she believed it was about to be lifted. "I hope Deirdre and Illann will find the same kind of happiness in time," Mother went on. "They do seem very fond of each other already. Now here's Eithne back, so off you go, Clodagh. I see that charming Aidan is in Johnny's party again this year. He wasn't the only young man who had his eye on you during supper, and that despite the fact you've dressed so plainly. You're very considerate of Deirdre. I hope she appreciates what a good sister she has in you."

I returned to the hall just as the meal was being cleared away. I slipped in the back, scanning the crowd to see where my sisters had got to. Deirdre had risen, her hand in Illann's, ready to lead the dancing. She looked every inch a lady with her piled-up hair and dark russet gown. Father was in a corner talking with a group of men. Johnny, Gareth and Conor were all there, along with two of the invited chieftains, and they didn't look as if they were discussing weddings. As I glanced at them I met the dark eyes of the unpleasant Cathal, who was standing on the fringe of the group, looking out over the hall. His gaze passed over me as if I were of no more interest than a piece of furniture, and a mightily boring one at that. I was mortified to feel my face flush, and turned away to look for my younger sisters.

It seemed one of Illann's musicians was also a juggler. As the hall was prepared for dancing, this man kept the crowd entertained by tossing his five colored balls in the air while performing an increasingly challenging range of acrobatic tricks. Coll and Eilis were at the front of the group watching him. My youngest sister was looking uncharacteristically tidy in a gown I had sewn for her, pine green with an edging of rabbit fur around the sleeves. Her face was fierce with concentration. I knew Eilis well enough to recognize that she intended to master the art of juggling as quickly as possible, and in particular to be better at it than Coll.

Sibeal stood further back, her midnight blue gown helping her fade into the shadows. It was not so much that Sibeal was shy. With the right person, Ciarán for instance, she conversed fluently on any number of erudite matters. Like me, Sibeal loved stories and music. But she had always been different. Her abilities as a seer made her ill at ease in the company of folk like Illann's family and the visiting chieftains, who would expect her to have the interests and opinions of an ordinary girl of twelve. Conor wanted her to wait until she was at least fifteen before she committed herself to the druidic life. I was happy that Sibeal would not go away for a few years yet. She was mature beyond her years, at times quite startlingly so, and made a good confidante. With my twin gone, I would be glad of her presence.

Under instructions from Deirdre, folk were moving the furniture to make room for dancing. Gods, I was tired. No wonder I had fallen victim to my own imaginings out in the forest earlier; I'd probably been walking along half-asleep. There was a little door not far away leading to a set of stone steps that went up to the roof. In summertime that was a good retreat, with a broad view over the forest of Sevenwaters and only passing birds for company. I slipped through and shut the door behind me. All I needed was a few moments' respite, and then I'd go back and smile for the guests.

It was not quite dark. A lamp had been placed on the bottom step and the sound of music floated down from above, a slow air I had played myself, though not so well as this. I followed the sound up to the first turn of the stair, where I found Aidan seated with harp on knee and a little frown on his brow. He was dressed up for the festivities in a tunic of dark blue wool with a snowy shirt beneath it, plain good trousers and well-polished boots. His hair was neatly tied with a ribbon at the nape. He looked, if anything, still more handsome than he had earlier. I recalled the way I had hurtled out of the forest like a screaming banshee, and felt quite awkward. It was a long time since Johnny's last visit here, and I wondered if I had misremembered the degree of interest Aidan had shown in me then. When he saw me he put a hand across the strings and the tune came to an abrupt halt.

"Please don't stop on my behalf," I said. "It was lovely."

Aidan made to stand, tucking the harp under an arm.

"Don't get up, please. I'll go if you want to be alone." Gods, I sounded like a flustered thirteen year old.

Aidan's cheeks reddened. "I'm just practicing. Johnny expects me to play later. I want to get it right."

"It sounded fine." I settled myself three steps below him, tucking my skirt around my legs. "That's the tune I taught you last year," I could not help observing.

Aidan grinned. "Ah, you remembered! Would you listen while I run through it again? Perhaps you'd rather get back to the dancing."

"The dancing can wait," I said, fully aware that it was improper for me to stay here alone with him, but suddenly not caring a bit.

His fingers moved over the strings, and as the tune rang out again I had an odd sensation, as if I were the harp and felt the touch of those hands on my body, gentle but sure. My thoughts shocked me. I must put such foolish notions out of my head and concentrate on the music. As soon as he was finished I must go straight back.

"Excellent," I said as he reached the end and looked at me with a question in his eyes. "You've improved a lot since last year." I hoped my blush was not visible.

"Really?" There was a sweet hesitancy in Aidan's smile.

"Really," I told him, smiling in my turn. "I've got my own set of embellishments for the second verse—you could use those for contrast. Shall I show you?"

He passed his harp to me without a word and I demonstrated what I meant, biting my lip in concentration. I was not nearly as able a musician as he was, and it was awkward playing on the steps. But Aidan listened intently, then took the instrument back to try out what I'd suggested.

"If you fetched your own harp, we could perform together," he suggested.

"Maybe another time." This was Deirdre's night to shine. It would be unfair to her if I made a show of myself. "I'm expected to go out there and dance. I think I'd better do so before people notice I'm missing."

"Will you dance with me, Clodagh?"

"Oh." Ready words vanished again. "I wasn't hinting—I didn't mean—"

"I know that. Actually I'm not much of a dancer. You didn't get the opportunity to find out when I was here last time, but I would certainly tread on your toes."

His honesty was disarming. "I'll wager you dance as well as you play," I told him. "I did visit Inis Eala once, you know. Everyone dances there." Johnny's island community was inhabited by grim warriors and energetic women. The folk of the island worked hard and they put the same vigor into enjoying themselves.

"True, but most do it with more enthusiasm than grace," Aidan said wryly, descending to my level and offering his free hand to help me down the steps. "If you're willing, I'll give it my best try."

Back in the hall the juggler still held the younger ones spellbound, but the music had begun again and folk were already dancing. Deirdre had her head high and her hand in Illann's as they stepped forward and back, circled and passed under the joined hands of other couples. Aidan set his harp in an alcove and we attached ourselves to the end of the line. I caught Deirdre's eye. She, at least, had not missed the fact that I had come back into the hall from a secluded area in company with a young man. Well, let her think what she wanted. As Aidan offered a rueful apology for stepping on my toes, I let my troubles go and was happy.

I stayed with Aidan for a second dance. We didn't talk much—he needed to think about the steps. The third was a jig, requiring such concentration that we didn't exchange a word. The hall was getting noisy. A long chain of folk was forming around the perimeter of the dancing area and spilling out into the courtyard where a bonfire had been lit at a safe distance from the house. We were wary of fire at Sevenwaters, for it was only four years since the hideous accident that had scarred Maeve for life. But we had learned to deal with this, since fire formed an essential part of major celebrations such as weddings and seasonal rituals.

The chain of dancers snaked past us. Coll and Eilis were in it.

"Clodagh!" my youngest sister shouted. "Come on!"

Then Aidan and I were in it too, whether we liked it or not. With one hand in my sister's and the other in Aidan's, I found myself dancing out the door into the courtyard, where wild shadows were thrown high on the walls by the changeable light from the great fire. Our forms were transmuted into immense prancing deer and owls and hares, or mysterious creatures that were half human, half something quite other. Aidan was laughing. His hand in mine was warm and strong. My heart beat faster. The drummer from Illann's band came out after us to stand by the main steps, picking up the pace as we moved away from the house. The line went right around the fire now, down as far as the stables and back again, and people were starting to sing.

"All right?" I saw rather than heard Aidan ask me. I nodded, answering his smile with one of my own. Proper conversation was impossible. The singing was robust, the dancing undisciplined. The line lurched along and we had to grip hard to avoid being pulled right over. Eilis was laughing hysterically. I hoped she could not understand the words of the song, which were getting progressively bawdier with each verse. Perhaps it was time for me to take her indoors. But I was enjoying myself, and so was Aidan—he squeezed my hand, grinning madly. The drum hammered away. Now the whistle player had come out too, adding a high, true version of the melody to the erratic one the singers were bellowing.

Down by the stables Eilis tripped, pulling me hard. I stumbled, letting go of her hand and Aidan's. Before I could so much as blink, someone pulled me out of the line and into the darkness by the steps to the harness room. He had my arms in a powerful grip; he knew exactly how to hold a person so she couldn't fight back.

"Let me go!" I shouted. It was as ineffectual as my efforts to free myself. The singing drowned out everything. If someone wanted to abduct me, this was the perfect time.

"Stop struggling, then." An unmistakable voice spoke right in my ear; I could feel the warmth of his breath. Cathal. "Believe me, I have no desire at all to molest you. I just want to offer a friendly warning."

"Friendly! I'd hate to see how you treat your enemies. Let me go, Cathal! You're hurting me." *And you're frightening me.* I would not give him the satisfaction of hearing me say that.

His grip slackened marginally. I made to pull away and he tightened it again. He'd chosen his spot well—the corner of the stable was between us and the riotous company. I couldn't see any of them, and nobody in the courtyard would be able to see us.

"What in the name of the gods is this?" I hissed. "How dare you manhandle me?" As soon as he let me go I'd bolt back inside and tell Johnny just what kind of mistake he'd made in hiring this uncouth bully.

"Planning to rush in and tell on me?" Cathal murmured. "You won't do that. You wouldn't want to spoil your sister's wedding party, would you? Now listen. A good girl like you doesn't dance all night with the same man unless there's some kind of promise between them. I don't believe there's any such undertaking between you and Aidan. Take my advice. Leave my friend alone. Appearances can be deceptive, Clodagh. He's not for you."

This was the reason he had seen fit to assault me in public? It defied belief. "Finished?" I asked, squashing the urge to ask him what he meant or to make the obvious retort that it was none of his business whom I danced with.

"Clodagh!" Aidan's voice came from not far away, its tone concerned. "Clodagh, where are you?"

"He's smitten," Cathal said, removing his hands abruptly from my arms. At that moment something stirred behind him, a shadow, a figure perhaps twenty paces away, hardly more than a slight disturbance in the many shades of gray between here and the gates. I blinked and it was gone. "Make sure you're not," Cathal went on. "There's nothing but harm in it. Now you'd best go before my friend gets entirely the wrong idea. Ah, Aidan, there you are. We thought we saw something, a little stray dog maybe, but it's gone."

"A dog." Aidan's tone conveyed complete disbelief. His sunny smile had vanished. His eyes judged first Cathal, then me.

"Excuse me," I said, and passed between them with my chin up and my heart thumping. I headed straight for the house, collecting Eilis on the way. I did not report to Johnny or to my father. Cathal was right: I would not spoil Deirdre's party by making accusations against one of my cousin's trusted warriors. I would simply stay out of both men's way. Cathal was devious. Everything about him set me on edge. I had liked Aidan when he came to Sevenwaters last spring, and I liked him even more now. But I had not liked that look of jealousy and doubt in his eyes. Let the two of them sort this out between them, whatever it was. For now, I had had quite enough of men.

CHAPTER 2

On the day of Deirdre's wedding, the household at Sevenwaters also observed Meán Earraigh, the ritual for spring's balance point. Ciarán had taken no part in the previous evening's festivities, but he emerged to help Conor conduct the rite. This druid uncle of my father's was tall and pale, with hair of a deep fiery red and intense mulberry-colored eyes. Ciarán was a man who seemed solitary even when in company. Although he was Conor's half-brother, he was much younger, of an age with my father.

Meán Earraigh was one of my favorite feasts. Down on the grass by the lake shore we marked out a circle with leaves and flower petals. There the ritual was celebrated, with family and guests joining the chanting and the sharing of mead and herbs. We bade farewell to winter and greeted the new season's warmth and promise. Sibeal played the part of the maiden, wearing a circlet of blossom as she danced in the circle. She was exactly the right age this season, just barely come to her monthly bleeding. She danced without awareness of self, her dark hair rippling down her back, her eyes distant, her features gravely composed. For as long as her part in the ritual lasted she was not a reserved girl of twelve, but the embodiment of the goddess in her youthful, budding form.

Alongside my sister danced the young son of one of Father's freemen, representing the sun in its nascent power. The whistle and drum, the reed pipe and harp set my feet tapping, though the pace of this measure was contemplative. Conor made an imposing figure in his white robe and golden torc, with his snowy hair bound into many small braids. He watched the young dancers with pride, but there was a shadow over Ciarán's features, as if the pair's very freshness and innocence touched a secret sorrow in him. The dance drew to a close. The boy put a sheaf of spring flowers in Sibeal's hands, representing the burgeoning growth of the season, and she dipped a little curtsy.

Unlike some of his Uí Néill kinsmen, who had turned to the Christian religion, Illann was steadfast in the old faith. This had strengthened his suitability as a husband for Deirdre, and it meant the hand-fasting that followed the spring ritual could be conducted with a full druidic ceremony. I had never thought Deirdre especially beautiful; to do so would have felt a little like admiring myself—vain and wrong. But my twin looked lovely today, her happiness shining from her face, the green gown perfectly setting off her bright eyes, her hair tumbling over her shoulders from the ribbons that caught it high at the back. She was a perfect young bride, and admiration lit Illann's eyes as the two of them joined hands before Conor, promising to love, trust and be truthful to each other until death sundered them forever. Deirdre's happiness made me happy. But I could not stop thinking of going to bed tonight all by myself in our chamber, without my twin to say good night to. My mind was full of the long months stretching ahead with not a word from the sister who had been closer to me than anyone else in the world.

All too quickly the hand-fasting was over, the celebratory mead and cakes were consumed, and we were bidding Deirdre and her party farewell, for they were to ride to Illann's home at Dun na Ri straightaway. Most of our guests were also leaving. The way through Sevenwaters forest was not easy, especially for folk who were unfamiliar with it, and Father had arranged for the visitors to travel out together with an escort of his men-at-arms. In view of Mother's delicate state of health he was keen to return the household quickly to its former peace, though he had not said so publicly. So I hugged Deirdre and said goodbye, and neither of us shed tears, but as the riders headed down the path and under the trees I felt a little part of me being torn away.

"You know, Sean," said Conor, who was standing close to me, "I'd enjoy sitting awhile over some of that very fine mead, the stuff you didn't get out while our guests were here. Johnny, perhaps your young bardic fellow might be prevailed upon to play for us, something soothing, and we can reflect a little on the passing of time and the changes that lie ahead for us all. Ciarán, will you stay?"

"Thank you, but I will not." Ciarán had his cape on and his staff in his hand, ready to depart. His awkwardness in family gatherings was easy to understand, for he was the son of Lord Colum of Sevenwaters by his second wife, a sorceress descended from a twisted branch of the Fair Folk. Until a few years ago my sisters and I had not known he existed. Then suddenly he had been there among the druids, a member of the family we'd never been told about. It seemed he had overcome his dark legacy, for he was now expected to be chief druid after Conor.

Ciarán inclined his head courteously to my father. "Farewell, Sean. We have shared some momentous times, both painful and joyous. I hope your daughter will be happy with her new husband. Farewell, Aisling; the gods walk with you and your child." With that, he was gone.

"Uncle Conor's right, Father," said my eldest sister, Muirrin, who had reached Sevenwaters just in time for the ritual. "What better occasion could there be for that special mead?"

"I haven't seen Eilis for a while," Mother observed. She was leaning on Father's arm; coming outside for the ritual had tired her. "And where's Coll?"

"I'll find them," I said. I'd seen the children disappearing in the direction of the stables as soon as the ceremony was over, and I feared for their best clothing.

Eilis and Coll were not in the stables. They were not in the yard outside.

"Down yonder, my lady," said one of the grooms, gesturing

toward the lake, which could be glimpsed through the open gates. "They'll be safe; they had one of Johnny's men with them."

A fresh breeze had got up and I was cold in the light wool gown I had worn for the wedding. I hesitated, wondering whether to run inside for a shawl. Best not; Eilis and Coll couldn't have gone far, and the sooner I brought them back the less opportunity there would be for Mother to start worrying.

I headed along the lakeside path, expecting to spot the children at any moment. It was only when I reached a place where the track split into two, with one branch heading uphill into the forest, that I began to feel uneasy. This was surely too far. I couldn't see any trace of them along the shore ahead. Could they have gone up under the trees? The two of them knew quite well that they were expected to be in the hall for the rest of the afternoon. Something was wrong. Something didn't add up.

I stood at the fork in the track, unwelcome memories of yesterday's strange experience crowding my mind. If someone could get close enough to the house to follow me between the hawthorn and home, what was to stop that same someone from abducting my sister and cousin from right under the noses of the family? What about the shadowy figure I'd half glimpsed last night when Cathal had pulled me out of the dance? I shivered. What now? Run back home and fetch a guard? Or go on in the hope that I was not too far behind the children to catch up? If I wasted precious time getting help we might lose them altogether. Besides, what if they were just around the next corner and nothing untoward had happened? I'd be worrying my parents for no good reason. With a sigh, I set off up the track into the forest.

I climbed for some time, long enough to get quite warm. As I went I called out, "Eilis! Where are you? Coll!" but my voice lost itself under the encroaching trees. The only answer was the shrill cry of a bird high above. I hauled myself up a steep rise. My best shoes were coated with mud and the hem of my embroidered gown was seriously the worse for wear. My heart was thumping, partly from effort, partly from a growing fear. My little sister was only nine. She trusted people.

Footsteps behind me, down at the foot of the rise. "Clodagh?" The voice was Aidan's.

Relief washed through me. "Up here," I called back. "I'm looking for Coll and Eilis—I think they went this way."

"Wait for me, then."

He was up in a flash and beside me, and I was blurting out a half-explanation of my fears. ". . . and the groom said one of Johnny's men was with them, but I don't know which—"

"Cathal, I think. One of the maidservants saw him heading off with the children. Johnny suggested I come after you and make myself useful. It may not be very safe for you to be out here on your own."

"We do it all the time," I said, for that was true, though I was beginning to think Aidan's caution might be justified. "This is our home, after all. And the forest has . . . well, it has uncanny methods of keeping out enemies. Outsiders simply lose their way, even if they think they've memorized the paths. Come on, we'd best keep walking." Cathal, I thought. What was that man up to? There was definitely something wrong about him. If I found Eilis and Coll—*when* I found them—I would make it clear they must have nothing at all to do with Cathal from now on. How could Eilis have been so foolish as to go off into the forest with him?

"Eilis!" I shouted again as we came out into a small clearing, and this time there was a reply.

"Over here!" My sister's voice was shaky.

She was in a grove of massive oaks. From the foot of each mossy bole a tangle of heavy roots clawed out. The network of thickly leaved boughs high above cast a mysterious dimness over the place. Beneath one forest giant sat Eilis, blowing her nose on a linen handkerchief. Her eyes were red and she had scratches on her hands and face.

"What happened?" I asked, keeping my tone calm as I put my arms around her. "Has someone hurt you, Eilis? Where's Coll?"

"I climbed down by myself," Eilis announced, the assurance of her words undermined by a noisy sniff. "All the way. But Coll's still up there." She glanced upward; above her, the trunk of the oak towered into the sky. "He's stuck. When I was safely down, Cathal went back up to get him."

I followed Eilis's gaze. If my cousin was in this monstrous tree, he was beyond the place where the canopy blocked my view. My heart bunched up tight; my palms went clammy. The thought that my little sister had been up there made me want to be sick.

"Misguided fool!" Aidan was frowning as he came up beside me. "How dare he cause you such distress? Still, there's no cause for alarm. Cathal is an excellent climber. He will bring the boy down safely."

"But it's so high!" I made myself take a deep breath. "Eilis, you and Coll must have known this was too dangerous. How on earth did you get up the first bit? That bough is a grown man's height from the ground. You may be a good climber, but I know you can't reach so high."

"Cathal helped me."

There was a brief, intense silence, punctuated by the sound of something moving about in the tree high above us.

"Cathal helped you," I said flatly. "So whose idea was this?"

"We wanted to climb trees. Cathal said he'd take us. He said he knew a good place. He was being nice, Clodagh. Don't look so angry."

"I'm not angry," I said through gritted teeth. High above me I could see two human forms now, each no larger than a joint of my little finger. Cathal came first, long legs moving with the confidence of a spider's from one branch to the next. Just above him was Coll, and I could see how Cathal was showing him where to put his feet, where to grip.

"Cathal found these big trees," Eilis said. "He's a really good climber. We couldn't have got up without him helping. Coll said if we went right to the top we'd be able to see the whole forest of Sevenwaters, and maybe even the sea. But I didn't get to the top. Cathal said we'd gone high enough, and he made me climb down."

A shower of twigs and other debris rained on us; up there, someone had slipped. Now I could make out Coll's face, jaw set grimly, skin pasty white, and I could hear Cathal's voice, low and steady, but not the words.

"Then he did one sensible thing, at least," I told my sister. "But you made a big mistake. It's much too high for you. If you'd fallen, you would have—" *You would have been killed.* "You would have broken your arm or your leg. As it is, you're all over scratches. What will Mother say when she sees you?"

There was a cracking, sliding sound overhead and I winced, grabbing Eilis and pulling her aside. A smallish branch crashed to the ground where she had been standing, cutting off her protest half spoken. The three of us looked up. Coll and Cathal were both standing on the same bough, perhaps thirty feet above us.

"Of course," Cathal was saying, "the oaks where I come from are far taller than these—we cut our teeth on them as children. I could climb this in my sleep. But the top's too high for Eilis. She *is* a girl, after all, and younger than you, or so I hear. You're not to do this on your own, understand?"

The fact that Coll did not answer proved how frightened he was. I watched the two of them make a cautious descent toward the lowest branch. For all my anger, I was forced to admit to myself that Cathal was handling things well. At every stage he positioned his own body to provide the greatest support and safety for the younger climber, and his tone was calculated to calm the frightened boy. They reached the lowest branch. As I pondered what I would say to each of them, Cathal spoke briefly to Coll, then suddenly launched himself off the bough as if entirely heedless of the distance to the ground. My heart had time to lurch in fright before he landed with a flourish right beside me, then turned and reached up his arms.

"I'll catch you," he called with complete confidence. "Come on, you can do it!"

Whey-faced and visibly shaking, Coll jumped. Cathal and Aidan caught him, cushioning the worst of the impact.

"No harm done," said Cathal lightly.

"Are you hurt, Coll?" I inquired, ignoring Cathal completely. "Show me your hands."

They were badly abraded on the palms and would need salving. His trousers and shirt were both torn.

"We won't mention this to Mother," I said to the two children. "No point in worrying her now you're safely down. The two of you are to come straight back with me and get into clean clothing, and no arguments about it. You know perfectly well that we're all supposed to gather in the hall this afternoon." I glanced at Aidan. "Johnny did say something about your playing for us. This episode put that right out of my mind." I could feel Cathal's gaze on me. "As for you," I said, not looking at him, "your role in this escapade has been less than responsible. Don't try anything like this again." I held back further words, furious, undisciplined words.

Aidan spoke before his friend could respond. "We'll be on our best behavior, Clodagh, you can be sure of that. I hope you'll help me with the music."

"I might," I said with a diffidence that was mostly feigned.

Cathal spoke up at last. "Gods preserve us," he said, "*two* harps!"

"Back to the house, Eilis," I snapped. "Right now. You too, Coll. Everyone's waiting for us."

"Race you," Cathal said, and was off like a hare. After a moment's startled pause the two children set off in hot pursuit.

"I see no need for us to run," Aidan said. "If we go more slowly, we can discuss what to play. Do you know *Mac Dara's Lament*?"

"What's wrong with that man?" I muttered as the others vanished into the trees on the other side of the clearing.

"Mac Dara?" Aidan's brows went up.

"Not him. Cathal. I know he's your friend, but there's something about him that's . . . peculiar." I could hardly tell him what Cathal had said to me last night, since it had amounted to a warning about Aidan himself. I was not sure if Aidan was supposed to be too good for me or whether it was the other way around. That was irrelevant, anyway, since I planned to take no notice of Cathal's warnings. I doubted very much that Aidan would appreciate his friend's efforts to select which girls he might or might not dance with.

"Did he say something to upset you last night?" Aidan asked, suddenly serious.

"No," I said hastily. "A minor misunderstanding, that was all."

"Cathal doesn't want to be here," Aidan said. "He's ill at ease in chieftains' halls. Edgy. He means no harm by it."

I found that hard to believe. Eilis's explanation for the tree-climbing episode had been plausible from her point of view. But surely no responsible young man would have taken the two children out into the forest alone, when they were clearly meant to be somewhere else, and encouraged them to do something so risky.

What if Coll had been meant to fall, and my arrival with Aidan had spoiled the plan? What if someone else, an accomplice, a gray-cloaked stranger, had been waiting to spirit my little sister away?

"We should walk as quickly as we can," I said, glancing from side to side under the trees and picking up my pace. I shouldn't have let the children run after Cathal. I should have insisted on keeping them in sight all the way back.

"The children will be quite safe, Clodagh." Aidan's expression was quizzical. "There's no need to worry."

"How is it the two of you are friends?" I asked him. "You're so different."

"We were raised together. We've become used to each other."

"You are foster brothers?" I could not recall Aidan making any mention of Cathal during his last visit here.

"Not exactly. He grew up in my father's household; we were born within days of each other. His mother was a local woman of humble origins. Father took Cathal in. We became friends and shared an education. When I decided to try my luck at Inis Eala Cathal came with me, thus ensuring I would not shine in feats of arms. On the island he's considered second only to Johnny. He was supposed to come to Sevenwaters with us last year, but somehow he argued his way out of it."

"Well, he can certainly climb," I conceded.

"He can do many things, including beat me in a fight, but that doesn't trouble me. I'm happy enough that I earned a place as one of Johnny's personal guards. I won't stay at Inis Eala permanently. I plan to return home in a couple of years, settle down, make a different sort of life for myself. My older brother will inherit Whiteshore. But it's a big holding; there's a place there for me."

He wouldn't have bothered to tell me all this, surely, if he were not seriously interested in me. "Is Whiteshore right on the coast?" I asked, feeling both pleased and awkward.

"It's on a hilltop looking out over the western ocean. It can be bleak in the wintertime; the wind is like a whiplash. You'd enjoy the summers, Clodagh. Walking on the sand, collecting shells, exploring the rock pools. Seals come in to lie on the shore there, and it's a resting place for many birds. I wish you could see it. Of course, your home has its own kind of beauty."

"Yours sounds lovely. So I suppose you know lots of sea songs?"

He smiled. "A few. Most of them are too colorful for Lord Sean's family gathering. What about some reels to follow our lament? Which ones do you know?"

By the time we emerged from the forest I was in a far better frame of mind. We found Eilis and Coll balancing along the top of the dry-stone wall, led by Cathal. Eilis had her skirt tucked up into her belt. I shepherded the children up to the house, leaving the two men to their own devices.

I sent Coll off to tidy himself up and took Eilis to her chamber so I could make sure she looked presentable before Mother saw her. Sibeal was there changing her shoes, and I left her in charge while I went to my own chamber next door. The embroidered gown I had worn for the hand-fasting was no longer fit for company, so I found myself a plainer one of a color somewhere between blue and gray, with discreet flower motifs on the undersleeves. I brushed out my hair and replaited it. I put on clean slippers. Then I fetched my harp and went downstairs.

After the bustle of recent days, the hall seemed quiet this afternoon. Low sunlight slanted in through the narrow glazed windows, bringing out notes of vivid color on the wall hangings. These tapestries held much of our family history. There was one Mother had made in the early days of her marriage, showing the tower on a green ground that was her own family symbol, and beside it the blue torcs of Sevenwaters on white. Deirdre and I had spent a whole winter making a piece of our own, which now took pride of place opposite the hearth. We had fashioned the image of a girl walking beside a lake, with six swans in the distance. My grandfather had been especially fond of this one, since the girl pictured had been his much-loved wife. My own favorite was a little tapestry made by my father's older sister, who had died before I was born. This was filled from corner to corner with exuberant images of birds and butterflies, and I could not look at it without my spirits lifting. When she was young, Aunt Niamh must have been a happy person.

Now that our guests had departed, the hall was a place of family once more. Mother was sitting with Muirrin, the two of them busy catching up on their news. After letting Mother know the children were back and would be down soon, I went to join the men, who were deep in discussion before the hearth. Father was still in the black and silver he had worn for the ritual. He looked quite imposing; every bit a chieftain. With him were Conor, Johnny and Gareth, while others stood close by—my cousin's men counted as family insiders while they were at Sevenwaters. I recognized lanky, fair-haired Mikka and a man called Sigurd, both of them from far northern lands. Johnny's band included all sorts, as had indeed the more unusual company his father had led, the mercenary troop that had originally inspired the venture at Inis Eala.

Johnny and Gareth made room for me between them. "We were discussing the nonappearance of the northern chieftains for the hand-fasting, Clodagh," Johnny said. "And what to do about Eoin of Lough Gall."

So much for quiet reflection over a cup of mead. I knew Eoin was the most influential of the northern Uí Néill and the most likely to interpret Deirdre's marriage to a southerner as an insult to his own faction. Father had long remained neutral in the Uí Néill disputes, a wise position since Sevenwaters was situated right in the middle of their territories.

"It's unfortunate," Father said, "that I was unable to send a personal emissary to break the news to Eoin. Ideally he'd have been told of the marriage well in advance, in private, with appropriate reassurances of amity between us and the northern Uí Néill. Eoin's a touchy man at the best of times. He'll be mightily displeased to find this news waiting for him on his return from his lengthy journey. And in his absence, it seems the usually more amenable Naithi and Colman have made a statement for him by staying away."

"You sent word to Eoin's wife, I take it?" Conor asked.

"A brief message, yes. It's awkward; it would have been best to let Eoin know before any of the other northern chieftains, since he's central to their alliance, but he's been gone some months now on his trading venture, and things developed rather more rapidly than anyone expected. I sent the same message to all of them."

"When is Eoin due back?" asked Gareth.

"Within a month or two, I've heard," Father said.

Gareth and Johnny exchanged a glance. "We need a man up there," Johnny said, "ready to get word to us as soon as Eoin's boat makes landfall. The last time another chieftain slighted Eoin, he was on the doorstep soon after with several of his kinsmen and fifty men-at-arms, demanding an apology. Such a dispute can soon flare into war, and we all know the northern Uí Néill don't go out of their way to avoid conflict. Whatever position Eoin takes on this, the others are sure to follow his lead."

"You should be ready to call a council, Sean," said Conor. "Sooner rather than later, I believe. Get all parties together, spell out your position, make it clear Sevenwaters wants only peace and cooperation with both branches of the Uí Néill. Ideally you'd put an invitation in Eoin's hand as he steps ashore, so to speak. Johnny's quite right; this could become serious."

There was a silence, in which the issue of the impending birth of Mother's baby loomed large.

"You're both right, of course," said Father. "In fact I already have an informant at Lough Gall, ready to send me immediate word of Eoin's return. But I'm not prepared to hold a council until Midsummer at the earliest." He did not need to elaborate. The wedding had been too much for Mother; a major council at Sevenwaters, with another influx of guests, was unthinkable until well after her confinement. And Father would not travel away from home with her health so fragile.

"We should set aside such weighty matters for another time," Conor said as my younger sisters came into the hall with Coll close behind. "Clodagh, I see you've brought your harp—will you give us a tune or two?"

"By all means let's have some music," Johnny said. "If Aidan plays too, perhaps we'll succeed in coaxing the Fair Folk out for a visit." Both Aidan and Cathal had entered the hall while we were talking, but neither had joined the discussion.

"The Fair Folk wouldn't come out just to hear someone play the harp, Johnny," said Eilis. "Their music is so beautiful it makes people forget everything about their human lives and wander away into the forest. It's lovely enough to charm birds down from the trees and make rainbows appear in the sky. Folk like that would hardly come out of the forest to hear *Clodagh* play." She rolled her eyes at me and got a penetrating look from Mother.

"Just as well," I said, thinking Eilis had a cheek to make jokes about me after her recent escapade. I found a low seat, set the harp on my knee and began to check the tuning. "The current audience is quite big enough for me. I'm out of practice."

Aidan had fetched his harp and now settled beside me. "Let's start with something slow and work up gradually," he suggested.

"All right. As long as I don't have to sing and play at the same time."

I soon became so involved in the music that I stopped thinking about the audience. The two harps together made a rich sound, filling the hall with a bright embroidery of ringing notes. Aidan nodded encouragement as his fingers flew over the strings. We got better and better at picking up each other's cues, and it was only when we stopped for a rest after an exhilarating set of reels that I realized how much I was enjoying myself.

"Fine entertainment," said Father, who had come over to sit beside Mother and was looking more relaxed than he had for some time. "Your skills are less rusty than you imagine, Clodagh. As for Aidan here, I'm surprised he finds time to keep his hand in. I know how hard you work your men, Johnny."

"What about a song?" suggested Muirrin. "You boys know a few; I've heard them at firsthand." Her smile was mischievous.

"That repertory's hardly suitable for a fine hall such as this," said Gareth. "And the execution's—well, rough is a flattering way to put it."

"Go on," Muirrin said. "Our two musicians need some rest and refreshment. You must have one or two ditties that are suitable for family performance."

The young men formed a line; Aidan got up to join them. With glances at one another, they began to stamp a steady beat and clap a complex rhythm over it. Once this was vibrating around the hall, Mikka began to sing, his light tenor carrying each line of verse, the lower, less polished voices of the others roaring out a refrain. It was a rambling and silly tale of a man who lost a prize ram and got into progressively stickier situations trying to get it back. I imagined there was a more scurrilous version, but in this company the young warriors kept it clean. They could all hold a tune, some more skillfully than others. Even Johnny, whose singing voice was not his most outstanding talent, was contributing to the chorus. But not Cathal. He remained detached from the group and completely silent. None of them had suggested he join in.

I got up to pour myself some mead from the jug on the table. Cathal was leaning against the wall not far away, regarding the singers with his customary expression of boredom. Wretched man! It was obvious he cared nothing at all about the peril he'd put Eilis and Coll in earlier. I would speak to him about it right now.

"I want you to account for your behavior out in the forest," I said under the masking sound of the young men's voices. "You put my sister's life at risk. And Coll's. That was very stupid, Cathal."

He did not look at me, and for a moment I thought he was going to ignore me completely. Then he said, "Would the children have learned a better lesson if they'd been forbidden to climb? They had a fright, yes. But they're here, safe and well. Coll, at least, is not likely to attempt such a feat on his own in future. I'm not sure I can say the same for your sister, but with luck she has learned a little caution. As I said at the time, no harm done."

I began an angry response, then checked myself. I was forced to acknowledge that there was some sense in what Cathal said. Should I ever have children of my own, I would want them to have adventures, to test themselves, to experience what freedoms they could, within reasonable limits. Reasonable limits: that was the key. "It was too high," I said. "They could so easily have fallen."

Cathal looked at me. "You sound as if you suspect me of something, Clodagh."

"After last night's episode, the very least I suspect you of is persistently trying to scare me," I said.

"You seem easily scared," said Cathal, his dark eyes unreadable. "I suppose your upbringing has not equipped you to cope with challenges. You might take a leaf from your little sister's book. *She* appears to be entirely fearless."

I had tried to be courteous. Under the circumstances, I thought I'd done quite well. But this was too much. My hand itched to slap his supercilious cheek, but I suspected he would only laugh at me if I did. I took a deep breath. "If you imagine my upbringing has been a pampered one with a bevy of servants rushing to fulfill my every whim, you're wrong," I said.

"Oh, don't bother justifying yourself to me, please." The tone was one of unutterable weariness. "Your little display before, with Aidan, illustrated quite clearly that you're deaf to any good counsel I try to give you. As for your life history, I couldn't be less interested. I'm certain it's as much of a bore as your harp playing."

"I may not be an expert musician," I said in a furious whisper, for the song had reached its end and the applause that had greeted it was dying down, "but other people seemed to enjoy listening."

"Hardly the most critical audience," observed Cathal. The men were beginning another song, this one with actions suggesting a range of animals: bear, deer, fish, hare. "Half of them are your family."

I felt my cheeks flush with annoyance. "And half of them aren't," I retorted.

"Ah, yes, but that half consists of virile young men, Clodagh." Cathal had not lowered his voice, and I was glad the rousing chorus from the warriors masked his speech from everyone else. "They don't give a toss whether you play well or abominably. They're simply enjoying looking at you in your nice gray gown and imagining taking the pins out of your hair, one by one, and then starting on those laces—"

"That's enough!" Cathal's eyes had traveled to the front fastening of my gown, and my cheeks were burning. "I've never heard such complete rubbish!" I turned my back on him, intending to walk away, but Muirrin was watching us, so I stayed where I was, trembling with fury. "And anyway," I said without turning, "what did you mean last night with those dire warnings about Aidan?"

"You're actually prepared to listen to an explanation?"

I wasn't sure how the conversation had got here. I'd intended never to discuss the topic with him again, since I knew I would not take any advice such a dubious character might have to offer. "An explanation is long overdue," I said, trying for a chilly tone. "I've got bruises from where you grabbed me. It was a strange way to try to make a point."

"I don't think you'll want to hear it," Cathal said, surprising me.

"Then you shouldn't have tried so hard to tell me. Go on, say it, whatever it is. They'll be finished singing soon."

"Since you ask so nicely, I will. My advice to you is to stay out of Aidan's way. Tell your father not to put him on your list of eligible suitors."

"There is no list. Why would you say this? Isn't Aidan your childhood friend?"

"Oh, he's been telling you stories, has he? I bet he didn't mention that he's betrothed to a girl back home. Two years at Inis Eala, then it's back to Whiteshore, a nice wedding to the daughter of the neighboring chieftain, and a life of domesticity. Let him pursue his obvious interest in you and you'll be breaking that young woman's heart. Or your own."

I stared at him, dumbfounded. Aidan with his honest eyes and open smile; Aidan, who had not so long ago told me all about his future plans in a manner that suggested he would like me to become part of them, betrothed to someone else? He'd never spoken a word about any girl back home, either last year or this year. But then, he hadn't mentioned Cathal either. "You're lying," I said, but there was a lack of conviction in my tone.

"Ask him if you want," said Cathal, offhand. "They're just about finished. Go on, ask him now. I dare you."

The singing drew to a riotous close. I applauded along with everyone else, just to give myself a moment. I watched as the young men bowed, smiling. I should have been pouring cups of mead and handing them around. Aidan looked about, spotted me next to Cathal and headed in our direction.

"Not my finest performance ever," he said as he came up. Was I imagining things or was his smile somewhat strained? "We should play again, Clodagh. I might be able to compensate for my limited vocal talents. What were the two of you talking about?"

I'd been right. There was a note in his voice that reminded me of the way he'd looked last night: jealous. "Cathal was telling me about Whiteshore," I said. "I understand you have a young lady waiting for you back home. Your betrothed." I saw him flinch, and made myself go on. "It makes sense of your wish to stay with

Johnny only a year or two—I wondered about that, since most men who win a place amongst his chosen few would not trade it for anything in the world. If they marry, their wives are expected to go to Inis Eala and join the community there, as Muirrin did when she wed Evan. You must be very fond of this girl." I worked hard to keep my tone light.

Aidan's cheeks flushed. He looked straight at Cathal, and now the expression in his nice brown eyes was one of undisguised fury.

"Don't look at me," said Cathal. "I was just making conversation."

"What's her name?" I asked, unable to stop myself.

"Rathnait," said Aidan tightly. "And the situation is not quite as Cathal has painted it to you. If you would allow me to explain—"

"There's no need for that," I said, wishing profoundly that I was somewhere else. "Your home situation is none of my business."

"But I must—"

"Didn't you hear the lady?" As Cathal spoke, Aidan clenched his fists.

"Cathal! Aidan!" The voice was Johnny's; the tone made this a command. "Gareth has suggested we counteract the effects of mead, good food and a day's inactivity with a display of single combat. Knockout bouts, the six of us, with weapons of choice. Since you didn't favor us with your singing, Cathal, I'll expect a particularly fine effort from you."

Cathal straightened from his leaning posture. "Of course," he said, then added in an undertone that only Aidan and I could hear, "What very fortunate timing. This gives my friend here time to work out what possible excuse he can offer, while you, Clodagh, are spared having to listen to it in a hall full of people. Meanwhile, both of you can hope I suffer an unfortunate accident on the field of combat. Come on, Aidan, he did say all six of us."

Aidan turned his back and walked away. His shoulders were set tight.

"Coming out to watch?" Cathal inquired, brows raised. His narrow features were not without a certain charm when he allowed himself to relax.

"Maybe I should be there just to make sure he doesn't kill you," I said. "It's hard to believe the two of you are childhood friends."

"Ah, well," said Cathal, "there are some things only a friend will do."

"Like making someone tell the truth when he doesn't want to, you mean?" Aidan's embarrassment and shame had been written all over him. There had been no formal promise made between Aidan and me; no official mention of a marriage or an alliance. Still, there had been an unspoken understanding, and I was hurt. I had thought Aidan liked me. It seemed I had misjudged the man. It galled me to realize that Cathal had done me a favor.

"Better go," he said. "Wish me luck." With that, he was off.

Mother and Muirrin stayed inside, but the rest of us trooped out to the yard. Coll and Eilis stationed themselves at the front of the crowd—cooks, grooms, men-at-arms and maidservants had all come out to watch. Johnny had a habit of springing sudden displays of this kind on his men when they were at Sevenwaters, to keep their skills sharp.

In the first round they used bare fists. Each warrior had his own style. Mikka was nimble, but no match for Johnny, who had superb technical skill. Gareth and Aidan were more evenly matched, though Aidan's concentration seemed erratic. I expected Gareth's dogged strength to overwhelm him, but it was Aidan who won, a well-timed blow catching his opponent off guard and sending him sprawling. Aidan helped him up, looking at Cathal as he did so. The message in his eyes was quite plain: *You next.*

Sigurd was unfortunate in his adversary. It was quickly plain to me that Cathal had something none of the rest did—an ability to anticipate moves, almost as if he knew what was in his opponent's head, combined with a knack for springing surprises and the physical skills to use that knack to devastating effect. He fought like quicksilver, impossible to pin down, never where his adversary expected, evasive and fluid, yet strong when it mattered. I began to understand why Johnny had kept him. The bout was soon over, with Sigurd laughing as he offered congratulations.

"Another round," Johnny said. "I fight Gareth, Sigurd fights Mikka, Aidan takes on Cathal. If anyone has two wins, a third round determines the overall victor. Gareth, what's your weapon of choice?"

Bouts between these two were always entertaining to watch. They had been inseparable friends for as long as I could remember. We treated Gareth almost as one of the family. On the field of combat they moved with a perfect understanding, almost like a single entity in two parts. The fight came to a close with a dazzling display in which staves flew through the air to be caught, whirled and tossed again, with both combatants executing a somersault or two in between. Finally Johnny swung his staff low and caught Gareth across the calves, sending him toppling to the ground, from where the taller man sprang to his feet to clap his opponent on the shoulder and declare him the victor. Both warriors were grinning.

Mikka and Sigurd fought with swords. Neither managed to fell the other or to relieve him of his weapon, and eventually Johnny declared the bout a draw and congratulated the combatants, then pointed out a couple of things each could have done to gain the advantage. Next, he told Cathal and Aidan to step up. "Weapon of choice?" he asked.

"Knives," said Cathal, quick as a heartbeat.

"All right with you?" Johnny looked at Aidan.

"Fine." Aidan wasn't looking at anyone in particular. He took the knife Gareth offered, examining the blade minutely. I went cold for a moment, then told myself not to be silly. This was a disagreement between friends, that was all. People didn't kill each other over such trifles.

This fight was not like the last two. From the start it was intense and brutal, the pair moving from one tight lock to another, their knives a hairbreadth from wrist or groin or neck. Nobody shouted instructions. The crowd watched in a tense hush as Aidan backed Cathal all the way across the circle, up to the stone wall of the house, only to have Cathal slip sideways almost faster than eye could follow to pop up behind the other man and place a knife across his neck. I held my breath longer than was quite comfortable; I realized my teeth were clenched. Aidan struck backward with his elbow, expertly, and when a winded Cathal let his weapon slide away from his opponent's throat, Aidan hooked a leg around Cathal's and attempted to unbalance him. They staggered, locked together, each seeking an opportunity to wield his knife effectively. I could hardly bear to watch, for there seemed to me to be a violent purpose in both men that put this on a different plane from the other bouts we had seen today. Surely Johnny should call a halt before one of the combatants plunged his weapon into the other's heart.

I glanced in my cousin's direction, but he was watching with every appearance of calm. The look in his gray eyes suggested he was assessing the two fighters' technique, nothing more. He made a quiet comment to Gareth, who stood behind him, and Gareth smiled as he murmured a reply. Mikka and Sigurd, across the circle, looked engrossed but not troubled. Perhaps I was over-reacting. Perhaps this was not as bad as it seemed.

Cathal slipped and fell to one knee. The crowd sucked in its breath. Aidan grabbed Cathal's arms, twisted them behind his back and applied a fearsome grip to his opponent's right wrist, trying to force his knife hand open. Cathal said something under his breath, and Aidan's features were suddenly suffused with rage. For a moment he looked like a different person. He hissed a response, jerking at Cathal's arms, but Cathal writhed like an eel and was out of Aidan's grasp and on his feet again, his knife still in his grip, his expression showing nothing but detached amusement. This time I heard his comment.

"You'll have to do better than that, papa's boy!"

Aidan launched himself at Cathal like a battering ram, heedless of his own safety or that of the circle of onlookers. Cathal dodged out of the way, lightning swift, and Aidan came close to crashing headfirst into a pair of white-faced serving women. He managed to stop in time, spinning to face his opponent, knife at the ready.

"At least I know who my father is," he said in a voice that had gone ominously quiet.

For a moment Cathal froze. Then, in a whirl of movement, the two men met again, and an instant later Aidan was on the ground on his back, with his adversary on top of him and both wrists pinned over his head. I looked for Cathal's knife and saw, to my astonishment, that at some point he had slipped it back in his belt. Cathal's grip tightened. Aidan's right hand opened and his weapon fell to the ground.

"Enough," said Johnny calmly, stepping forward. "Technically very good, Cathal, but you came close to letting your guard down. You must learn to block out your opponent's taunts. Aidan, get up." He reached out a hand to help Aidan to his feet. "If you have not already learned that anger is a hindrance when you fight, now is the time to do so. We are professionals, whether in an exercise such as this or on the field of war. A cool head, impeccable technique and perfect focus are the keys to success. The two of you will settle your differences before nightfall, and there will be no more dispute between you."

Cathal and Aidan looked at each other. Cathal put out a hand, but his expression was stony. After a long moment, Aidan grasped his friend's hand briefly, then turned his back.

"Very well," Johnny said. "Last bout, Cathal. What's it to be? After that fright, I think our audience might prefer that we avoid anything sharp."

Aidan was watching me. He had gone to stand with Sigurd and Mikka, but I could feel his gaze and it troubled me. What was it between him and Cathal? Had this really been all about Aidan leaving out one critical detail in his account of his personal circumstances? That might matter to me, but it seemed unlikely that it would have ignited such a dispute between the two friends. Not only had this revealed a darker side to the placid musician I had been so drawn to, but even the impenetrable Cathal had seemed disturbed by it. Not by the fight itself; he'd handled that as coolly as Johnny would have done. It was that comment about fathers that had rattled him. The two of them knew exactly how to upset each other.

Aidan still had his eyes on me, even though Cathal and Johnny, having settled on wrestling, were squaring off in the combat area. I decided I had had enough. I had nothing to say to Aidan, and it was a foregone conclusion that Johnny would win this bout. He always won. Cathal would be good, but not good enough. I would go back indoors and forget about men, the ones who lied by omission and the ones who had no idea how to deal with women. I would busy myself with overseeing preparations for the evening meal. And if Aidan wanted to entertain the household with music afterward, he'd be doing it with no help from me.

* * *

I couldn't sleep. It was too quiet. I lay on my back in the darkness, missing the gentle sound of my sister's breathing. If only Deirdre hadn't severed the link between us. I could have told her about Aidan, about how he'd concealed the existence of that girl back home even as he set out his credentials as a suitor. I could have discussed the peculiar behavior of both Aidan and Cathal, how they were supposed to be best friends and yet had fought as if they hated each other. I could have asked her what she thought of someone who could be gentle and smiling one moment and full of explosive rage the next. Or of someone with appalling manners and a woeful lack of judgment who demonstrated perfect control when under attack. It wouldn't have mattered that Deirdre knew as little about men as I did. I just wanted to talk to her. We'd always talked about everything.

I didn't like being alone at night. Here in the dark, on my own, I could not keep unwelcome thoughts at bay with constant activity. Here there were no meals to plan, no provisions to order, no supplies to check. There was no pickling or preserving, no washing or mending or record-keeping with which to ward off my troubles. Instead there was the thought of Mother, weary today despite her happiness at seeing Deirdre settled so well; there was the looming nightmare of the birth. There was the strange sensation I'd had yesterday in the forest, of being watched as I walked; there was the shadowy figure I thought I'd seen last night in the courtyard, when Cathal had bundled me around a corner and made his ill-advised attempt to be helpful. There was the troubled look on Father's face as he spoke of Eoin of Lough Gall.

I worried about Johnny, too. How did he feel about the impending birth, and the fact that if Mother had a healthy boy, that child might supplant him as heir to Sevenwaters? While any male of the blood could make a claim to the chieftaincy, a son of direct descent would likely be favored over a cousin, especially a cousin of the female line. Johnny's outstanding qualities as a leader did not outweigh the fact that his father was Bran of Harrowfield.

I stared into the darkness and tried to distract myself by humming a ballad about a woman who fell in love with a toad. It didn't help; I kept seeing Aidan playing the tune on his harp, brown eyes full of smiles. I tried lying on my right side and then on my left. I turned my pillow over, gave it a hard thump and willed my mind to stop churning around. It did not comply. Eventually I got up, put on a cloak over my nightrobe and went down to the hall.

Lamps still burned there, and the fire glowed on the big hearth, though the house was hushed; it must be close to midnight. Before the flames sat Father and Muirrin, he in his big chair with the dogs drowsing at his feet, she on a stool close by. In the flickering light the similarity between them was striking—like Sibeal, Muirrin had inherited Father's dark hair and pale skin, along with his air of grave self-containment. They were looking even more solemn than usual, and I could guess what had kept them up so late. I went over to sit on the rug beside my sister.

"Can't sleep?" Muirrin asked.

"It feels strange without Deirdre."

"It's a time of many changes." There was a note in Father's voice that I had never heard before. "Clodagh, Muirrin and I have been talking about your mother."

I wanted to ask and I didn't want to. I made myself speak. "She seems so tired all the time. Muirrin, what do you think will happen?"

My sister hesitated.

"Be honest, please," I said, clutching my hands together under the concealment of the cloak. "I know there's grave risk involved." I glanced at Father.

"Muirrin," he said, "tell Clodagh what you just told me. She needs to know." His brave attempt at a smile made me want to cry.

"If you're sure," Muirrin said, and I heard how she was making her voice calm, using the same manner she would if she had to tell a peerless warrior that he would never be able to fight again, or a young wife that her new husband had died from his wounds. Healers carried a terrible burden. "Clodagh, you already know how dangerous it is for a woman of Mother's age to bear a child. She's done remarkably well to carry the infant to this stage. But . . . I've told Father I believe there's a high chance we may lose both her and the baby. The rigors of labor and birth take a toll even on a young, strong woman. Then there's the risk of childbed fever. And if Mother survives but loses the child, Father and I both fear very much for her state of mind. She is so full of faith that all will be well."

After a silence, I said, "Thank you for being honest. I knew already, really. But I suppose I hoped you might know something we didn't, something that would make this less frightening. Eilis has no idea what may be about to happen. I don't know what to tell her." Despite my best efforts, my voice shook.

"It is possible," Father said quietly, "that your mother is right. Perhaps the gods do intend this child to be born safely. Your mother cares nothing for herself. That is hard for me to accept."

I got up and put my arm around him, but the gesture of comfort was as much for myself as for my father. It terrified me to hear him sounding less than confident; less than the capable, calm person the world saw day by day, a leader fully in control of himself and his domain. Tonight he sounded like a wounded boy.

"Maybe all will be well," I said, not believing it for an instant. "Perhaps we should trust Mother's instincts."

"I've told Father I'll stay until the child is born, Clodagh," Muirrin said. "It's a pity Aunt Liadan can't be here, since her skills in midwifery far exceed mine, but I will be able to oversee the labor and birth, and perhaps stay on a little after that, depending on what happens. I do need to be back at Inis Eala as soon as I can. It's too much for Evan to handle all the work there on his own."

"I'm grateful, Daughter," Father said. "We must all be strong. Your mother needs hopeful faces around her, not gloomy ones. I've spoken to Sibeal about this and she seems to understand, but Eilis . . . it would be too much of a burden for her."

The look on his face troubled me deeply. I wondered if he had looked like this long ago, when the newborn twin boys had breathed their last. If so, I had been too young, too wrapped up in my own grief to understand it.

"We must pray, I suppose," Father sighed, and I heard in his voice a hope as fragile as a single thread.

CHAPTER 3

I kept myself busy. Our serving people had never been so well supervised, our house never cleaner, our meals never more promptly served or more carefully prepared. Sibeal and Eilis completed twice as much sewing as usual and made dramatic progress with their reading and writing. Accompanied by a maidservant, I walked to the hawthorn early each morning to say a prayer and make an offering before commencing the day's domestic activities. In the evenings I said I was too tired to play the harp, and it was more or less true.

Aidan kept trying to catch me alone in order to offer some kind of explanation. I could hardly be discourteous to him, since to do so would suggest I had had some expectations that the existence of this girl Rathnait had quashed. I would not let him see how much his dishonesty had hurt me.

"Clodagh!"

I was walking from kitchen to grain store, my hair bundled up in a kerchief and my feet in sturdy outdoor boots. Aidan fell into step beside me, shortening his long stride accordingly.

"I want to talk to you. Please."

"I'm busy, Aidan."

"Let me explain to you. About home and the betrothal. It's not the way it sounds, Clodagh, I promise you—"

"I told you," I said, "there's no need for any kind of explanation. It means nothing to me. There's no point in making this into more than it is. Now I must go."

"It means something to me," he said to my retreating back, and I almost stopped and let him tell me whatever it was, for he sounded genuinely upset. I ordered myself not to look back, lest those melting brown eyes make me act against my better judgment.

Time passed; the moon went from dark to full. Mother was persuaded by Muirrin that bed rest was in order and ceased to come down for meals. Several times a day I went in to see her. It helped her to know that the household continued to be run according to her rules. No mouse would poke its head into the food stores, no sheet would be inadequately laundered, no spider would dare build a web in a cupboard while I was in charge. Mother's ankles were swollen and puffy; her face had the same unhealthy look, but her eyes were full of confidence. She praised me for my efforts and expressed a certain pleased surprise that I had apparently managed to absorb all she had tried to teach me over the last few years. I had sometimes thought her too dedicated to perfection in the house; I had wished she would adopt a more relaxed approach. Now I began to realize just how like her I was. Did she, too, maintain the rituals of a perfect household principally to keep her fears at bay?

Two days after full moon the weather turned especially benign. The sun shone, flowers bloomed and the forest came alive with the music of birds and insects about their spring business. Over breakfast in the hall, Father said, "Clodagh, it's time you had a day off. Aidan has asked me if he can take you and your sisters out riding."

Before I could think what to say, a huge smile lit up Eilis's face. "Oh, please can we go, Clodagh? Please, please? We could take a picnic up to the Pudding Bowl and go fishing." The Pudding Bowl was our family name for a little round lake up in the hills, half a morning's ride from the keep.

Coll was beaming too. Even Sibeal looked enthusiastic in her quiet way. I glanced across to the table where Johnny's guards were seated. Aidan was avoiding my eye. It was Cathal's sardonic gaze I met, and he lifted his brows at me quizzically before I looked away.

"I don't know," I said. I'd planned to oversee a clean-out of the root cellar. I realized even as I thought of this how much I would love to get out for a day. I imagined it would mean I'd finally have to listen to Aidan's explanation, whatever it was, but that would surely be less awkward in the setting of a picnic with the children present. If the conversation strayed into areas I did not want to visit, I could always busy myself with fishing. "We'd need an escort."

"I can spare both Aidan and Cathal to go with you," Johnny put in.

This was beginning to look like a conspiracy. I eyed my cousin closely, but he was eating his porridge and appeared not to notice my suspicion.

"I think we'd be better with three guards." I would not be happy with an escort comprising only Aidan and Cathal. As far as I'd been able to observe they were friends again now, but they'd surprised me before and I didn't want an argument developing when we were miles from anywhere.

"I'll instruct Doran to go with you," Father said. "Make sure you tell us what time to expect you back."

Doran was one of my father's most capable guards. He had lived at Sevenwaters since I was a small girl and had children of his own. His wife, Nuala, worked in our kitchen. "Thank you, Father," I said, finding myself warming to the whole idea.

I went to the kitchen after breakfast to organize some supplies, since Eilis wanted to make this an all-day outing. When I got there it was to find Nuala and two helpers busy with the day's baking, and a strange old woman sitting in the chair from which our last cook, Janis, had surveyed her domain with an eagle eye over year after year of plucking, basting, peeling and chopping. We had lost Janis two winters ago, but such had been her influence in our household that her special chair had remained empty since the day of her death. The stranger occupied it as if she had every right to be there. She was a pale little thing, like a skeleton bird, all bright eyes and beaky nose. The shadow-gray garment that swathed her might have been gown, cloak or robe. The moment I walked in her gaze darted to me, piercing and shrewd.

"She wandered in first thing this morning," Nuala whispered in my ear. "Says she wants a few nights' shelter, but she'll only speak to the lady of the house."

I approached the chair. "Good morning," I said. "I am Clodagh, one of Lord Sean's daughters. I'm told you are seeking shelter."

She nodded. "I'm kin to Dan Walker," she said. Dan was leader of the traveling folk. Janis had been his aunt.

"May I ask what the connection is?" I could see the old woman was not lacking in wits: a keen intelligence shone in those assessing eyes.

"I'm his mother's sister." Her voice was too deep and powerful for such a frail creature. It was as resonant and strong as oak wood.

"Are you traveling alone?" It was the wrong time of year for Dan's folk to pass by Sevenwaters, their pattern being to come north in autumn for the horse fairs, not in springtime.

She smiled. It was not the smile of a sweet old lady, but instead knowing and subtle. I felt she could see right through me. "I always travel alone, Clodagh, daughter of Sean," she said. "If you'll shelter me, I'll pay."

"Oh, there's no need for that." I was shocked that she did not realize a great house such as ours provided food and lodgings for wayfarers as a matter of course.

"I'll pay, Clodagh. I'll give you three tales, and they'll be worth every scrap of food I eat while I enjoy the hospitality of your father's hall."

"Thank you," I said after a moment. The old woman's stories would probably be well worth hearing. She'd obviously led a long life and, if she was a traveler, it would have been full of adventures of one kind or another. "What is your name?"

"Which one do you want?"

I might have told her it made no difference to me what her name was. Instead I said, "I'd like your storytelling name."

The crone chuckled. "A good answer, young woman. My name's Willow. I've had a few over the years, but that will serve."

"Just Willow?"

"A tree is never *just* a tree," she said. "It's bigger and deeper and wiser than a girl like you will ever be. Now I'd like to rest; this forest of yours makes journeys longer than they should be. Any corner will do for me, providing it's quiet. Tonight I'll give you a story after supper. You like tales?"

Perhaps she had seen something in my eye. "I love them," I said. "Especially the more magical ones. But of course, you must tell whatever story you choose."

"That's one good thing about getting old, young woman. Folk expect you to break rules, lose your temper, do exactly what you want. Don't worry, I'll behave myself while I'm under your father's roof. He's a strong man, Sean of Sevenwaters; strong in wisdom and goodness. He'll need all his strength for the season to come. But you know that already."

Her words chilled me. She had only just arrived at Sevenwaters; how could she know about my mother and the specter of the impending birth? But then, Dan Walker's folk were no ordinary breed; the gift of Sight was common among them. I did not ask her what she meant. I feared the possible answer.

Willow didn't want to be in the main part of the keep, where the family quarters were located, and she didn't want to share the communal sleeping area of our maidservants. In the end I housed her in the little room adjoining the stables. There was a comfortable smell of clean leather and horses. A quick brushing of the floor and the provision of a blanket or two were all the accommodations our guest seemed to think necessary.

"I've slept in places far rougher than this, Clodagh," the old woman said, setting down her tiny bag at the foot of the makeshift pallet and waiting for me to leave. "A muddy hollow here, the fork of a tree there—give me a soft feather bed and I'll be tossing and turning all night long. Go on now. You seem a busy sort of person, so off and do whatever it is you're supposed to be doing. No need to hover so anxiously. I won't lie down and fail to rise again; there's sap in my old branches yet."

Walking past the stable door on my way back to the kitchen, I heard the voices of two men from within. It took only a moment for me to realize that their conversation was private, but I could not move away now without drawing the speakers' attention. They must be preparing their horses for this morning's ride.

". . . won't even look at me," Aidan was saying. His voice was choked up, not with anger but with distress.

"Why is this so important to you?" That was Cathal, and his voice, too, was different. There was no trace of mockery in it. He sounded genuinely concerned.

"Isn't it obvious?"

"True love, you mean?" Cathal said in something more like his usual tone. "Aidan, if I've made your whole life a misery, I'm sorry. I mean that. I thought only to extricate you before you plunged deeper into a morass of your own making. Perhaps I misinterpreted the depth of your feelings for her. It did all seem rather sudden."

"You weren't here last year," Aidan said. "She likes me. Liked me. If I'd spoken up then it would have been too soon. During that first visit we were friends, we had fun together, that was all it amounted to. It's different this time. I knew it the moment she came running out of the forest and straight into my arms. I should have told her right at the start; she would have listened to me then. But now . . ."

There was a pause, during which I wondered whether to risk bolting for the house, and decided I could not do so without being heard. I could never, ever reveal to Aidan that I'd been listening to this.

"You did lie to her," Cathal pointed out. "Clodagh doesn't seem the kind of person who tolerates lies. Well, you wanted an opportunity to talk to her, and today's ride is that opportunity. Be sure you make good use of it. And calm down or the lady will see you've been having a fit of the vapors. Here."

The sound of someone blowing his nose. "Thanks," Aidan said. "And thanks for speaking to Johnny for me. Getting the whole day off to do this was more than I expected."

"Any time," Cathal said lightly. "Be honest, that's my advice. This isn't a woman you can sweet-talk into forgiveness. If you want her to change her mind, do what you should have done right at the beginning. Tell her the truth."

The sound of horses moving, then, and from around the corner of the stables new voices, Doran's, Eilis's. I seized the opportunity to head off for the house, deeply embarrassed and much surprised. Aidan really was serious about me. And Cathal, it seemed, was not entirely the unpleasant character he appeared to be, at least not where his friend was concerned. Today's picnic had indeed come about through a conspiracy, but it was of Cathal's making. It had been set up solely to give Aidan the opportunity to explain himself to me. I would not have believed Cathal capable of such a generous act of friendship—I did not imagine he himself relished the prospect of such an outing. As I packed up food for our mid-day meal, I was forced to acknowledge that I might possibly have misjudged him.

It was a crisp, bright morning. The sky was cloudless, the forest alive with creatures chirping and buzzing their responses to the spring sunshine. As we rode along the light-dappled tracks, further and further from the keep of Sevenwaters, the magic of the day settled over me. For a little, I thought, I would set aside worries about my mother's health or my father's political problems or indeed about Aidan and the awkward conversation that was looming. I would simply enjoy the day and deal with things as they arose.

"We can go all the way to the Pudding Bowl, can't we, Clodagh?" asked Eilis. I was riding alongside her. Doran was in front with Coll, and the others were spread out behind—Aidan, Sibeal, Cathal. The path rose slowly through the reaches of Sevenwaters forest, winding around the hillside and crossing several streamlets on its way up toward the lake. In some places it was wide enough to accommodate three riders abreast, but there were narrow, steep sections where it must be traversed in single file.

"I told Johnny that's where we'd go," I said. "It means you children can stretch your ponies."

"I wish you wouldn't keep calling us children, Clodagh," said Coll over his shoulder. "I'm nearly eleven, you know. Cormack wasn't much older than that when he fought in his first battle." Cormack was the next brother, and a warrior of some note.

"He was at least fourteen," I said. "And there's a lot of difference in those four years. But if you hate it so much, I won't call you a child. Eilis, now, she's a different matter." I glanced at my little sister. "When she learns to do her share of household duties without a fuss, I might start referring to her as a young lady."

"Race you, Coll!" As Eilis spoke, her pony edged past Doran's mare and cantered ahead down the track. My youngest sister was an expert horsewoman, far more capable than I was. Coll kicked his animal's flanks and was off after Eilis. In the blink of an eye they were out of sight.

"She does know the way," I said grimly. "But one of you had better follow them."

"I will, my lady," Doran offered.

"I'll go." Cathal was already guiding his mount past us, eyes on the path ahead. "It won't take long to overtake them provided they stay on the track." He didn't wait for approval. In response to some invisible signal, his horse picked up its pace and in a flash both animal and rider were gone under the trees.

We rode on with what speed we could. I wasn't particularly worried, though I would have preferred that Doran be the one to go after the children. Eilis and Coll were both good riders and the way to the Pudding Bowl was perfectly straightforward. All the same, I'd be happier when we were all together at our destination.

The path widened slightly. Aidan maneuvered his mount forward so he was beside me; Doran fell back to ride with Sibeal.

"Clodagh?"

I glanced across at Aidan. Was he going to launch into his explanation already? For a moment I wondered if the disappearance of the children, followed by Cathal, had all been part of a grand plan leading to this moment.

"Yes?" I asked coolly, though all of a sudden my heart was racing.

"I know you don't want to listen to this," Aidan said awkwardly. "You've put me off time after time. It saddens me that you won't even play music with me anymore. I don't believe I deserve that. I'm not a liar, Clodagh. Please let me explain to you."

"Very well," I said, hoping Sibeal and Doran were not close

enough to overhear. I would not turn my head to look; that would be too obvious.

Aidan cleared his throat. "I've practiced this in my head every day since Cathal told you about Rathnait, the girl at Whiteshore," he said. "But it's not going to come out right, I know it. Clodagh, Rathnait is only twelve years old. My father and her father made an arrangement years ago that she and I would eventually wed and so strengthen the tie between their adjoining holdings. Rathnait is a shy child, years away from being ready to marry. I've never been able to view her as a prospective bride. She's the little girl next door, playing with her dolls, running about the garden with her terrier, hiding behind her mother whenever the family visited Whiteshore. I'm a grown man, Clodagh. In autumn I'll be one-and-twenty. I'm a warrior. I've killed men, I've weathered battles, I've traveled far from home and witnessed strange and terrible events. When I sing love songs, I put a grown man's passion into them, not the dreams of a child."

"But you're still betrothed to her," I said as we rounded a bend in the track and came in sight of a gushing waterfall between young oaks. In truth I felt considerable sympathy for him, especially in the light of how upset he had been earlier, in the stables. "Your father and her father expect you to marry. Maybe she's only twelve, but little girls do grow up. In four years or so she'll be ready for a husband and children and her own household." Even as I said this, I recognized that most men would prefer to be married well before the age of five-and-twenty. Such were the risks to a young warrior in battle that men like Aidan generally preferred to sire children early. The single status of Johnny, who was two-and-twenty, a leader of men and a chieftain's heir, was considered unusual.

"It's true, that is the arrangement our fathers planned," Aidan said. "But nothing's signed and sealed. The fact is, my father could extricate me from the agreement easily. Especially if the bride I suggested had better prospects than Rathnait's."

I turned a questioning gaze on him and he blushed scarlet. "Prospects?" I queried.

"Gods aid me," said Aidan, "this is like wading through a bog with lead boots on. All my skills with words seem to have deserted me. If I could put it into a song, Clodagh, I would express myself a great deal less awkwardly."

I suppressed a smile. "No songs are necessary," I said. "Just explain clearly what you mean. And hurry. I can't see any sign of Cathal or the children and I'm getting worried."

"My father would require me to marry a girl whose birth was equal to, or higher than, my own—the daughter of a chieftain at least," he said. "He plays no part in the territorial struggles of this region: Whiteshore is too far west for that. But he would make an excellent ally for a chieftain of Ulaid, whether it be Lord Sean or another. He has considerable influence in Connacht, and the leaders there play their parts in the councils of the High King. In his turn, Father would welcome an ally in the east, someone in the mainstream of political affairs. Were I to present Father with the daughter of such a man as a prospective wife, he would at the very least be interested."

"I see." Now I was blushing too. "And what about poor Rathnait? Cathal said her heart might be broken if arrangements changed. Does he know her well?"

Aidan's lips tightened; his eyes darkened. "Cathal likes to meddle," he said. "His talk of broken hearts is nonsense. He's well aware that there's nothing between Rathnait and me but a vague agreement our fathers made years ago. As I said, she's a child. In a few years' time she'll get plenty of offers."

Something was not quite right about this explanation. "If Cathal knew that," I said, "why did he warn me off?"

"What did he say to you, exactly?"

"That if you showed interest in me, I should discourage you." This was getting uncomfortably direct.

Aidan was quiet for a while as we rode on, crossing two of the small streams. As yet there was no sign of the children. Perhaps they were riding on to the Pudding Bowl with Cathal. I had expected them to stop and wait for us. But then, with Cathal one could not know what to expect.

"Perhaps he's jealous," said Aidan eventually.

"Jealous?" I considered this. Did Cathal value his bond with Aidan, a bond that had existed more or less since birth, so much that he would get in the way of Aidan's prospects with a woman?

Could Cathal possibly be jealous of me? Before I had time to weigh this idea, Aidan spoke again.

"He wants you for himself," he said flatly.

"What?"

"He's jealous," Aidan said. "He wants you for himself."

"No, no. That can't be it. Cathal doesn't even like me. He considers me a complete bore. If he's jealous, it's over his friendship with you. Besides, he's of humble birth, isn't he? He must know he'd never meet my father's requirements for a suitor. If that's what we're talking about."

Aidan smiled. "That is what we're talking about, Clodagh. Cathal doesn't think the way other folk do. He doesn't play by other people's rules."

"But he's an Inis Eala warrior. He must be prepared to follow Johnny's orders, at least."

"That's different," said Aidan. "Cathal lives for combat. You've seen how he excels at it. He's only here at Sevenwaters because Johnny ordered him to come. Cathal tried to get out of it. He hates the need to make conversation, to display his best manners, to comply with the codes of a great household like your father's. He chafes at the restrictions. At Inis Eala his eccentricities don't stand out the way they do here, or indeed the way they did at Whiteshore. As a warrior, he never sets a foot wrong."

I was about to ask for an explanation of the taunts the two men had exchanged during that fierce encounter with knives, when there was a sound of approaching hoof beats and around a corner ahead of us came Eilis on her gray pony, looking perfectly calm. Behind her was Coll on his bay.

"We thought we shouldn't go too far ahead," Eilis said, "or you'd be cross, Clodagh. We turned back at the third stream."

"Where's Cathal?" I asked.

Eilis looked at me blankly. "Here, isn't he?" she said, glancing at the others and back at me.

"He went after you. Didn't you see him? Did you and Coll ride off the track?"

"Of course not." Coll spoke up now. "Maybe Cathal's the one who went off another way. If he came along this path he couldn't have missed us."

I swore under my breath. Curse Cathal! How could he have disappeared? The man had a rare talent for complications.

"We'd best ride on," said Aidan, glancing at Doran, who had come up beside us with Sibeal close behind him.

"Agreed," said Doran. "There's only the one track; he can't have gone far. I don't suppose anything untoward has happened, but it's wisest that the rest of us stay together. We should reach the lake soon. Perhaps he's there waiting."

"I'm sorry, Clodagh." Eilis sounded unusually chastened. "We shouldn't have ridden off; I know that."

"All right," I said. "We'll say no more about it now. But don't do it again, please. The same goes for you, Coll."

As we rode on, something inside me was sounding a warning. The Inis Eala men were highly trained, not only in fighting, but also in such skills as tracking and path finding, not to speak of their peerless horsemanship. How could Cathal have lost his way on a perfectly simple track? What exactly was the man playing at?

We reached the lake in good time. It was a lovely spot, nestled in a hollow high on the flanks of a wooded hill. There was a quiet over it that set the mind at peace, for there seemed nothing between the pale water and the arch of sky above but dreams and birdsong. When we came here, I liked to lie on my back on the sward and breathe deeply, letting my troubles go.

That was not possible today. There was no sign of Cathal. While Sibeal and I set out the food and drink that Doran had carried in his saddlebags and the men went down to the water with the children to see if there was any good fishing to be had, I was still working my way through the possibilities and not liking any of them much. The paths through Sevenwaters forest were known to be deceptive. If the Fair Folk wanted a man to lose his way, he would lose it. In the past, certain travelers had ridden into the woods and never come out again. But this particular path was straightforward. That was one of the reasons I'd agreed with Eilis's choice of destination. And if Cathal was with the Sevenwaters family, the Fair Folk should treat him as they would us. *We* never got lost, and nor did the trusted members of our household.

I put no credence in the silly rumors that were circulating beyond the borders of our own territory, about the Tuatha De starting to turn against humankind. Certainly, such folk had great power and were prepared to use it. But not against us. Anyone familiar with the history of our family would know that could not be the explanation for Cathal's disappearance.

Had he ridden off on some mission of his own? That conversation in the stables had suggested Cathal was behind today's outing. Perhaps he hadn't organized it to help his friend, but for a more devious purpose. I thought of spies, abduction and assassination, and began to feel very uneasy. Deirdre's marriage to Illann had offended the northern chieftains. Perhaps Naithi or Colman had decided that kidnapping one of us to gain leverage against my father would impress the influential Eoin of Lough Gall. Perhaps Cathal was out there right now, telling someone exactly where we were.

We had started to eat when he appeared from under the trees on his black gelding. He dismounted, leaving his horse to graze beside ours, and walked over to sit down next to me. As the rest of us stared, mute, he helped himself calmly to a mutton bone. "You could have waited for me," he said.

"Where were you?" I held my annoyance in check, knowing it was only fair to allow him an explanation.

"You know I was looking for Coll and Eilis, Clodagh. But I see they're here and unharmed, unless the Fair Folk have transformed them into ghostly simulacra of themselves—let's see—" He reached out and pinched Eilis lightly on the arm, making her squeal. "No, it's the real thing all right. At least you saved me some food."

"Where did you go, Cathal?" Aidan sounded calm. Of course, he was more used to his friend's oddity than I was. "That was a straight path, and the children turned and came back after quite a short ride. But we saw no sign of you."

Cathal's dark eyes were guarded as he glanced at his friend. "Nor I of you," he said. "I rode after them until I was certain I should have overtaken them. I turned back, thinking they might have ventured along a side path; investigated several of those, discovered nothing and returned to the place where I had left you, but found you gone. I deduced you had ridden on without me. So here I am. Shadow has had good exercise today." He glanced at the gelding.

"I see." I could not keep the note of deep suspicion out of my voice. "How very odd that you missed us."

"The paths through this forest have a habit of changing," said Sibeal gravely, her eyes fixed on Cathal's face. "It's not wise to ride off the track unless you know the place and it knows you."

I saw something alter in his expression, as if a cold breeze had passed over him. It was an odd look. I would almost have said Cathal was afraid. But he answered lightly. "It's not all swordplay and feats of strength at Inis Eala. We are trained in other skills, you know. Coll, pass me those bannocks, will you?"

Sibeal was still staring at him. Folk who did not know our family sometimes found her scrutiny disconcerting, for she had a seer's eyes, such a light blue as to be almost no color, and an uncanny power of concentration. "Being an Inis Eala man doesn't protect you from the Fair Folk," she said now. "If they want to draw you off course, tracking skills won't help you. How can you find your way by signs and sounds if the path moves?"

"That's nothing but superstitious nonsense," Cathal said.

Doran cleared his throat.

"Believe what you like," I said, not wanting our man-at-arms drawn into an awkward argument. "This is your first visit here. If you stay with us long enough you'll discover that it's true. It's one reason Sevenwaters is such a desirable holding. The place is more or less impregnable. Of course, although the presence of the Fair Folk helps protect us, it's a responsibility as well."

"Uh-huh," said Cathal in tones of complete disbelief.

"It's an unusual place," Aidan said. "To grow up surrounded by this great forest, with its strange tales, and then to have to go away and live somewhere quite ordinary . . . I think your sister Deirdre would have found that difficult."

I remembered Deirdre vowing that if our mother died giving birth to a boy she would put Sevenwaters behind her and never come back. "It depends," I said, steering the conversation onto a more comfortable path. "If the alternative is good enough people leave happily. Muirrin, for instance. She loves her new life. My Aunt

Liadan, Johnny's mother, went all the way to Britain. Of course, she—" I broke off, not wanting to discuss my aunt's ability to communicate over distance with the disbelieving Cathal present.

"She what?" Eilis asked idly, cutting herself a slice of cheese.

"She can speak to Father from far away," said Sibeal. "Silently, mind to mind. It's an ability common to twins in our family. It means Aunt Liadan can share her news with Father, and hear ours, without waiting for letters to travel all the way between Harrowfield and Sevenwaters." She was eyeing Cathal closely again. "Deirdre and Clodagh can do it, too," she added.

I rose to my feet, scattering crumbs. "I'm going for a walk around the lake," I said.

"Don't wander off the path or the Fair Folk might get you." Cathal was irrepressible. I must have been wrong, earlier, when I thought Sibeal's words had troubled him.

"It's no joking matter," I said. "Don't get up, Doran. Sibeal will come with me and we'll stay in sight all the way."

On the far side of the Pudding Bowl, my sister and I sat on the rocks by the water. We could see the others across the lake, Coll and Eilis fishing, Aidan helping them with hooks and bait, Doran stationed at a slight distance keeping watch. Cathal was sitting on the grass up near the horses, arms around his knees. It was not a relaxed pose. I thought his dark eyes were on Sibeal and me. But perhaps he was simply staring into space, brooding. For all the biting remarks, the quick retorts, the mischief and mockery, there seemed something sad about the man. I thought about his kindness to Aidan earlier. Then I thought about his peculiar disappearance and what it might mean. Cathal was a mystery. He was a puzzle.

Sibeal was gazing into the water, which was remarkably clear. Small spotted fish darted here and there over a green-brown patchwork of smooth stones, seeking the shelter of underwater ferns. My sister was not in a trance; I had come to recognize that state over the years, and her eyes had not lost their focus, nor was her body so preternaturally still as to suggest she had slipped into a different state of consciousness.

"I could scry here," Sibeal said. "This water holds many visions. But I'm sure you asked me to come with you so we could talk."

"Well, yes," I said. This was awkward, even though she and I understood each other pretty well. As a seer, Sibeal had a window on the future that the rest of us could not open. She did not talk about her visions. Indeed, she usually kept her thoughts very much to herself. "We should talk about Mother and the baby, and what might happen."

"I know she might die." My sister's voice was small and precise. "And the baby, too. Father told me. Or the baby might be a girl. Another disappointment, like me and Eilis. Like all of us, I suppose, except Muirrin, because the first one must be special." She sounded eerily calm.

My heart bled for her. "She loves us all, Sibeal," I said. "Don't ever doubt that." I hesitated. "Have you seen anything about this when you were scrying? Have your visions shown what's going to happen?"

There was a silence. Over the lake, Eilis gave a shout of delight as a fish took her bait. Aidan helped her pull it in. Cathal had not stirred.

"You know I can't talk about these things." Sibeal's voice had a tight sound to it, as if what was in her mind hurt her. "When I see the future, I can't tell if it's what will be, or only what might be. And visions are never clear anyway. They're full of symbols and suggestions and clues—it's up to the seer to interpret all that. Ciarán says when I'm older and better practiced I'll be able to pass on some of what I see so people can use it to help them make decisions. But I'm not going to do it now, Clodagh."

I felt cold. "You mean you *have* seen something about Mother and the baby? You've seen it and you won't tell me?" It came to me suddenly how truly frightening it must be to have the Sight. Sibeal's talent was as much curse as gift.

My sister gave a little nod. "If I can't interpret it, then you probably can't either," she said quietly. "It wasn't straightforward, Clodagh. I don't know what will happen. But if you're concerned that I may not realize how serious this is, don't be. I do understand. The one to worry about is Eilis."

In silence we looked across as, on the far side of the Pudding Bowl, Eilis landed her fish and Aidan helped her deal with it. It looked quite big; Eilis would be triumphant. I hoped she had remembered to say a prayer, expressing thanks for the sacrifice the creature had made so that human folk could be fed.

"Maybe Mother and the baby will both survive and Eilis need never know how close it was," I said. "But then, if we don't warn her and the worst happens, she won't be properly prepared for it. That would be even crueller."

"Clodagh," said Sibeal.

I looked at her and she gazed solemnly back.

"You're very scared, aren't you?" she asked. "Frightened and upset and worrying about everything, not just the big life-and-death things, but the smaller things too, like keeping the household running while Mother's so unwell and Father's so distracted, and making sure all of us do our mending and eat our breakfast . . . You can't do everything, Clodagh. Sometimes we simply have to wait and see what happens."

"You're far too wise for a twelve year old," I told her. "Tell me, what do you think of Cathal?"

Sibeal gave me a penetrating look. "I thought Aidan was the one you liked."

"I'm not asking because I *like* the man," I retorted. "I just wondered if you think he's . . . I don't quite know how to say this. You saw what happened earlier, Sibeal. Cathal acts very oddly. There's being eccentric, and there's being downright suspicious. He did manage to get lost rather quickly. He had no good explanation for going off the path. And . . . well, he's behaved strangely toward me a few times already. I don't trust him."

Sibeal looked owlish now as she gazed out across the lake, her eyes on the small group opposite. Doran and Aidan were making a fire; it seemed Eilis couldn't wait to eat her fish. "Clodagh," my sister said, "you just explained to Cathal about the paths, how they move about to trick unwary travelers. You can't turn around now and say he's suspicious because he lost his way."

"But he was with us, and we're the family."

"He isn't with us," said Sibeal. "He isn't with anyone." And before I could ask her for an explanation, Eilis hailed us from the other side of the water, beckoning us back.

* * *

Since Aidan had been honest with me on the matter of Rathnait, I let him ride home alongside me. He seized the opportunity to tell me about his home in Connacht and his family. I learned that Aidan had first gone to Inis Eala seeking to acquire superior skills in war craft which he could bring home in order to help his father in a territorial dispute. But the problem had resolved itself by more peaceful means. Meanwhile, Aidan had liked what Inis Eala had to offer and had decided to stay on. He made sure I understood that he had put a length of two more years on this; after that time, his place with Johnny would be filled by someone else.

We said nothing more of Rathnait or of the betrothal. With the others riding so close by, such a sensitive topic could not be aired further. Besides, although I found myself happy that we were friends again, I knew I could not make plans for the future until my mother's child was born. What occurred then would inevitably shape the path for us thereafter. I wanted to ask Aidan for more of his friend's story, for I wondered how Cathal had become the difficult, odd man he was, and I thought the clue might be in his origins. A humble birth, the friendship of a chieftain's son, an excess of pride . . . But now was not the time to ask.

We got home late in the day to find a party of men getting ready to ride out through the forest, Gareth, Mikka and Sigurd among them. With dusk approaching, this must mean urgent business. While Aidan and Cathal went over to speak to their fellow warriors, I headed inside to find Father, leaving Doran to help the girls down and deal with the horses.

Father and Johnny were in the small council chamber. The door was open, and I heard Johnny say, "Are you quite sure you don't want me to go in person?"

"I'm sorry to interrupt," I said, feeling I had done more than enough eavesdropping for one day. "Can you tell me what's going on?"

"We've received word that Eoin of Lough Gall is back," said Father. "I want a message to go to him without delay. Gareth's taking it. And no, Johnny, I don't want you to go." He glanced at me, then back at my cousin. "We're facing a challenging time; I'll need you here at Sevenwaters. Gareth knows how to present this to Eoin tactfully. All your other men need to do is stand next to him as a reminder that I do have the forces of Inis Eala backing me, should anyone decide to make this grounds for conflict."

"Are you inviting Eoin to a council?" I asked him.

"Gareth will extend that invitation to him, yes. When he's seen Eoin, he'll ride on to do the same for the other northern chieftains. I won't commit to the exact timing while matters are so uncertain here. With Gareth's party likely to be away for some time, we'd best send for some men-at-arms from Glencarnagh to bolster our numbers here, Johnny. You could see to that in the morning." Glencarnagh was our other holding, to the southwest. It had belonged to my mother's family.

"Is there anything I can do to help, Father?" I asked. "Do the men have adequate provisions for the journey?"

Father smiled, but I could see the anxiety in his eyes. "You might check on that in the kitchen," he said. "There's still time; we have to give Gareth some final instructions. Thank you, Clodagh."

A restless unease lingered over Sevenwaters after the riders' departure. When I went up to see Mother I found that she had been bleeding. I sat with her awhile, trying not to look worried, though her pallor shocked me. I explained what was happening downstairs, emphasizing how reliable Gareth was and telling her Eoin would surely be mollified by an invitation to a council. But my mother was not really listening. Her gaze was turned inward. It seemed to me that every bit of her energy was centered on the tiny life within her. Every scrap of her will was focused on helping that little heart to go on beating until it was strong enough to manage without her. After I left her chamber I had to stand alone outside the door until I was calm enough to go downstairs and face the rest of my family.

Father was unusually quiet at supper. With the question of Eoin hanging over him, not to speak of Mother's doubtful health, I was sure he would want to dispense with any entertainment tonight and send the household off to bed early. But when Willow stood up after supper and walked over, leaning on her staff, to stand before the family table, I saw that she was expecting to tell the first of her stories now. She turned her shrewdly assessing gaze on each of our family in turn, and I wondered what she was seeing as she considered us. Could she tell that Sibeal was a mystic in whose small head tumbled visions of the strange and uncanny? Could she see Johnny's inner goodness, Father's stoical strength, or the irrepressible, joyous energy that was so much a part of Eilis's being? Did she read the uncertainty beneath what I hoped was my air of calm competence? Perhaps it was all too clear to her that each of us walked under a cloud of dark possibilities.

"Lord Sean," the crone said, "I thank you for the hospitality of this great house. I bring you the goodwill of the traveling folk and the respectful greetings of Dan Walker himself."

Father nodded gravely. "Dan's kin are always welcome here," he said. "My daughter tells me you are a storyteller. We would welcome a tale to divert us tonight."

"I will provide good entertainment, my lord. Afterward, perhaps the young musicians of the household will play for us. I like the harp." She glanced in my direction, then allowed Aidan to place a stool for her and sat down a little stiffly, laying the staff on the floor beside her. The assembled household hushed. I saw Cathal standing near the main doorway, looking bored and supercilious. He met my eye and looked away again without the least flicker of acknowledgment.

"These are difficult times," the old woman said, glancing around the circle of attentive faces. "Testing and taxing times. For tonight, I seek to lighten your spirits with a tale, not of the grand folk of the Tuatha De, nor of the follies and aspirations of human lords and ladies, but of smaller people altogether. This is a tale of warring clans that carried out their skirmishes and raids, their maneuvers and retaliations under the lakeside reeds, amongst the roots of oaks, within the tangles of thorn that hide the crumbling stones of ancient walls."

"Clurichauns!" exclaimed Eilis, then clapped a hand over her mouth.

Willow smiled. "Yes indeed, young woman. There were two clans of them, and for want of better names they called themselves the Reds and the Greens. These names allowed the rival bands to distinguish themselves with bold little uniforms in one color or the other. The Reds made their jackets from robins' breast feathers or the leaves of autumn oaks or bright threads filched from a lady's sewing basket. The Greens made helmets from the discarded carapaces of beetles, cloaks of moss and boots of woven grasses. Both clans had weapons—sharpened slivers of elder, chestnuts to hurl, clubs spiked with the thorns of a wild rose. The clurichauns' diminutive size did nothing to dampen their warlike spirit. Each band had its chief, its bard, its champion. Each tribe had its hideout, the Reds among rocks blanketed by a russet-leaved creeper, the Greens in a hollow down by the pond with a bullfrog for a sentinel. I have to tell you that their hatred for each other extended to the colors they wore. If you were a Green you couldn't abide anything red in your life, and the same went the other way. Reds ate meat and rosy apples; Greens ate watercress and sour berries. Woe betide any Green baby born with a head of hair the color of Clodagh's here—his mother would immediately be accused of lying with the enemy.

"And what was it these two rival clans were warring over? It was all to do with a small hill situated between their territories. By your standards and mine, this would be the merest bump on the ground, a protrusion a long-legged man might step over scarcely noticing it. To the clurichauns it was a sacred mountain, the birthplace of a great leader of their kind, Mochaomhóg the Ancestor. Whether Mochaomhóg had been a Red or a Green lay at the heart of the long dispute between these factions, for each clan claimed him as its own."

Willow went on to tell of the long years of strife, the grief of the clurichaun women over their fallen fathers, husbands, brothers and sons, and the attempts of these women to protect their menfolk in battle. "For they used the same little tricks as we do ourselves—the sewing of a rowan cross into the garments of a warrior before he leaves home, the weaving of a triple plait into a man's hair, the packets of protective herbs in the boot or pouch. And if fewer men fell because these charms were employed, so much the better.

"Now there was a certain time when the Greens were dominant. They had established a camp right on Mochaomhóg's hill, in defiance of all the Reds thought proper, and they even made a wee fire there and sat around it, bold as brass. The Reds devised a cunning plan. Not usually known for their skills on water, they would surprise their enemy and approach by boat, slipping silently into a tiny cove below the hill, then making a covert way up through the nest of a water rat to attack from the rear. It was a good enough plan, though I expect our fine war leaders here would find flaws in it." The old woman glanced at Johnny as she said this, and he gave her a smile.

"The Reds dressed in their full battle array. Every one had his cloak wrapped around him, for it was cold out on the water. With some difficulty they launched their barge and poled it across the pond toward Mochaomhóg's hill, where the smoke from the Greens' fire was rising in a plume, conveniently blocking the view. The sound of carousing masked the splash, splash of the little boat's passage. They landed. Two warriors paused to secure the barge; the others advanced through the rat's tunnel, the nest full of ratlings, the upper passages of the creature's den. They went in single file, which was all the cramped space allowed. The two who had tied up the boat hastened to catch up with their fellows, but before they reached the exit a small form came falling back down, a dagger in his heart. A second fell on top, his red uniform stained redder still. A third . . . a fourth . . . One by one, every warrior who had gone up in that first advance was thrust back down the tunnel dead or dying. 'Retreat,' whispered one of the two survivors to the other. They fled down the tunnel, threw themselves onto the barge and poled it frantically away. It came to one of them, at least, that someone must have told the enemy they were coming. Someone had prepared a welcome for them: a welcome in blood.

"Once the sorry tale was heard by the Red clan, folk began to eye one another with suspicion. Who was the traitor? One man accused another because his grandmother had once eaten a pod of beans. A third said a fourth must be the guilty man, since he had once admired the emerald eyes of a certain young lady. It was plain the matter would continue to cause bitter division until it was settled.

"The wise woman of the clan called everyone together. 'Take off your cloaks,' she said. 'Lay them on the ground.'

"Nobody had any idea why the crone would ask such a thing, but they obeyed her as they always did, since she had never been proven wrong in many, many years of sorting out their disputes. Not only the two survivors of the rout but every other man there present laid his cloak down, till there was a blanket of many reds on the forest floor. The old woman paced, examining each cloak minutely. Most of the men had rowan crosses sewn inside their garments, for this is a potent charm against death in battle. It was these the crone seemed to be looking at. As she went through the cloaks, one of the two battle survivors began to look very uneasy. Once or twice he tried to pick up his cloak, pleading that he was cold after that passage over the pond, and the old woman stopped him. 'I am not done yet,' she said."

Willow turned her head and looked straight at me, fixing me with her beady eyes. Startled, I sat bolt upright. Was she trying to tell me something? Was there a message in her tale that was not obvious, an inner meaning I was supposed to make sense of? If so, I had failed to grasp it. I smiled, feeling awkward, and she looked away, resuming the story.

"The crone stooped; she looked. She looked again. She straightened and turned to the elders. 'This man is the traitor,' she said. 'He betrayed you to the enemy. He is . . . a Green.'

"Everyone gasped in horror. The man in question denied it vehemently. He was no traitor. Hadn't he just rushed into the encounter along with the rest of the raiding party? That he was still alive was a matter of luck, not treachery. He'd just happened to be last in line.

"Then the crone showed the elders the man's cloak. It had a rowan cross, just like all the others. But where the thread used by the other warriors' wives or mothers to sew the rowan twigs to the cloth was, as you would expect, red, this warrior's womenfolk had used thread of deepest forest green.

"There was no need for further proof, for everyone knew a Red woman would not set so much as the tip of her little finger on anything green. The man must be an enemy spy. Clurichaun justice being what it is, the punishment was dire; so dire, in fact, that perhaps it shouldn't be spoken of before these young folk." Willow looked over at Coll and Eilis, half smiling.

"You can't not tell us!" Coll protested, outraged.

"Very well," said Willow. "The traitor was taken to the biggest pond in the forest, and they made him walk out on a stone shelf above the deepest part of it, then they pushed him in."

Coll looked mightily disappointed. "Is that all?" he asked.

"There was a very old and very large fish living in that pond," Willow said. "She chased him around and around until he grew so tired he was half drowned. Then she ate him. And that is the end of my story, save to add that, to this day, the clurichauns pursue their war over Mochaomhóg's hill."

It had been a good story, expertly told. As for Willow putting some special meaning in it just for me, I must have been mistaken about that. If she'd chosen tonight's tale for anyone in particular, it was surely Eilis and Coll.

"Thank you," Father said. "We all love tales here. One tends to forget the power they have to make sense of things. Aidan, perhaps we might have a little music before we retire. Clodagh, will you play too? We haven't heard you for a while."

"Maybe tomorrow," I said. I had forgiven Aidan for his lie, but it was far too soon to be playing music with him again. I hadn't forgotten how good that felt before; perilously good. Feeling that way might have me thinking of a future that probably wasn't going to happen, a future in which my mother's child was safely born, and she recovered well enough to resume all her old duties, and Rathnait's father agreed happily to her not marrying Aidan after all, and . . . There were too many *ifs* in this picture, and I knew I could not entertain it, not yet. "I'm too tired tonight. I would only make a mess of it."

"I'll play," Aidan said, and fetched his harp from an alcove nearby. "Such a fine tale deserves a musical end piece. I'm afraid I don't know any songs about clurichauns, so it will have to be something else."

Cathal was looking particularly stony. Perhaps he didn't approve of stories, especially ones with magic in them. He was all too ready to dismiss talk of the Fair Folk as sheer fantasy. If he stayed here long enough, he'd find out how wrong he was.

Aidan sang a ballad, the melody ringing out sweetly in his soft, deep voice, the harp providing mellow accompaniment. It was a love song, and while he did not embarrass me by looking me in the eye as he sang it, I could hardly miss the fact that the lady in the piece had hair like a flaming cloud and eyes like green jewels, or that the swineherd who was trying to win her admired her not only for those qualities but for her forthright nature and her devotion to her family. It was a pretty piece that I was certain he had composed himself. In the end the lady left her family and went off into the forest with the pigs and their keeper, which I liked—I had been expecting a predictable tale in which the swineherd turned out to be a prince in disguise, and the surprise added to the charm of the song.

When it was done, folk seemed in no particular rush to retire to bed, though Father excused himself and left the hall. He had little enough opportunity to spend time with Mother, and if Gareth failed to placate Eoin of Lough Gall and the other northerners, those chances would become even fewer. Despite the presence of Muirrin and a bevy of attendants, I knew how much Mother needed him. He had always been able to calm and reassure her in times of crisis. I worried about Father more than I told anyone. What would happen to him if we lost her? It seemed to me he would not weep and rage, but would retreat inside himself, no longer able to smile at a story or laugh at Eilis's silly jokes.

"I see Aidan's talked himself back into your favor."

I started. I had wandered over to a corner with my cup of mead, so deep in thought that I hadn't even seen Cathal there. "He was honest with me," I said, looking over my shoulder to see if anyone was within earshot. Aidan had gone to put his harp away; Sibeal, Eilis and Coll were all sitting at Willow's feet, asking questions. The men were engaged in conversation around the hearth. "It's true, isn't it, that Rathnait is a child of twelve?"

Cathal nodded, saying nothing.

"And it's true that the betrothal agreement is only a verbal one, made casually years ago between the two fathers?"

"I know nothing of that," Cathal said. He wasn't exactly putting himself out to support his friend's cause. After that conversation in the stables, this surprised me. "You're quick to forgive, Clodagh," he added. "Only today he offers his explanation, such as it is, and already you're letting him make up songs about you."

I felt my cheeks flush. "I didn't ask him to make up the song. And I could hardly storm out just because there was a red-haired woman in it. What's your objection, anyway? Am I so very unsuitable for him?" Curse it, why had I said that? Posing such a question was asking for a catalogue of my faults, with being boring right at the top. "Forget I said that," I muttered, staring at my feet.

"No," Cathal said. "He's unsuitable for you."

"What?" He really had my attention now. "A chieftain's son, a skilled warrior, young, nice-looking and a musician to boot?"

Cathal looked uncomfortable. The supercilious air had disappeared. "On the face of it," he said, "my friend would be a good match for any woman. All the same, you shouldn't rush into this."

"Not that it's any business of yours," I said, astonished that he would take it into his head to give me such advice, "but he did convince me today that the agreement between his father and Rathnait's could be undone with no hurt to anyone. But it doesn't matter anyway. It would be inappropriate for me to encourage any suitor. My mother's about to have a child. She's not well. I'll be needed at home." I had not intended to speak so openly of this, but perhaps, if he heard it, Cathal would stop trying to interfere in my personal life.

"You're doing a pretty poor job of being discouraging," Cathal said flatly. "Of course, you can't see the way you look at him. Just don't blame me if it all goes wrong."

"I won't," I said after a moment. His tone had been neither flippant nor arrogant, but as serious as if he were warning me of some real and imminent danger. "Cathal?"

"What?"

"Today, on the way up to the Pudding Bowl, what really happened? Where did you disappear to?"

Cathal's features closed up, becoming impenetrable. "I've no idea what you mean," he said.

"You do, Cathal." I was not sure how hard to push this. "I don't believe you lost your way; that wouldn't happen to any of Johnny's men. You must have gone somewhere. You couldn't have missed us on that track."

"You seem so certain, Clodagh. And yet with every second breath, it seems, you or another of your family warns me of uncanny folk out in the forest, paths that have minds of their own and any number of oddities to be wary of. I suppose you and your sisters credited every word of the old woman's silly tale tonight. And you speak to me about truth."

It had been a mistake to think it was worth trying to talk to him. "Forget I mentioned it," I said. "I'd best go back to the others."

"Before Aidan gets jealous?" Then, at my look, he added, "The soft-voiced musician has a nasty temper on occasion. But you've seen that. And I don't think you're quite as lacking in imagination as I first believed."

"From you, I suppose that remark could be construed as a compliment. I don't anticipate a broken heart, Cathal. I'm made of stronger stuff than that."

CHAPTER 4

Now there were only three Inis Eala men left at Sevenwaters: Johnny, Aidan and Cathal. The atmosphere was tense as they waited for word from Gareth. He was to send a message as soon as he had spoken with Eoin. Two mornings after our ride to the Pudding Bowl, Father called me to join him and Johnny in the small council chamber. I sat opposite the two of them at the table; Aidan was stationed by the door, acting as a guard.

"We're wrestling with a decision, Clodagh." Father came straight to the point. "It relates to Gareth's mission and the question of a council. Perhaps Gareth can placate Eoin, perhaps not. He must at least persuade him that there was no ulterior motive in my decision to grant Deirdre's hand to a southerner. Still, Eoin being the kind of man he is, the need to call a council is pressing. There have been simmering tensions between north and south since you and Deirdre were little children, and this is likely to inflame them. It could drag Sevenwaters into a full-scale conflict. What we need is a regional treaty."

I remembered the words people generally used when referring to Eoin of Lough Gall: testy, difficult, volatile, influential. "Will Gareth raise that idea with Eoin?" I asked.

"He'll offer him my personal invitation to a council, the timing to be agreed in due course. At this stage, no more than that. We're concerned now that it may not be enough. Without a place, a time, it may seem only a vague promise, offered only to appease. If only I could know what will happen here . . ." Father's frown indicated an internal struggle.

"Far better, in my opinion, if we call the council now," put in Johnny quietly. "Invite both north and south. Be bold. Establish a position of control before somebody else does."

"You have neither wife or child," Father said. "Wait until those you love are at risk, then see if you would provide the same advice." Then, after a moment, "I'm sorry. Believe me, I understand the difficulty, and if all were well here, I would be in full agreement with you. But to proceed with plans for the council straightaway seems . . ." He hesitated, chin on hand, gray eyes troubled. "I will be honest with you. It feels a little like defying the gods, and I will not do that, not with the lives of my wife and unborn child in the balance. Perhaps I'm foolish to hear a voice whispering, *Would you sacrifice those you love best to achieve peace?* I have no reason to heed that; it is not the voice of logic. But I must heed it. I believe the council must wait."

"You're wise to trust your instincts, Father," I said. "They've generally been reliable in the past."

"You're wrong about one thing, Sean." Johnny was managing a smile. "I may have no wife or child, but that does not mean I am without hostages to fortune."

"Indeed," Father said, though I was not sure what my cousin meant. His parents and brothers, Coll excepted, were far away. Certainly, Gareth was his closest friend and the other men who had gone with him his loyal comrades, but it was hardly the same.

"Maybe I should have gone myself," Johnny said.

"We can trust Gareth; he has all the skills required for this mission. He's well-informed, diplomatic and courteously spoken. If not quite a family member, he is close to it. Besides, your own welcome in such households might not be one of undiluted enthusiasm. Clodagh, I seem to have made the decision. Perhaps it's your quiet presence that enables me to see more clearly. Thank you, my dear."

* * *

On the third evening after Willow had told us the tale of warring clurichauns, Aidan persuaded me to bring my harp down to the hall and we played jigs and reels together. Perhaps such exuberant music was not altogether apt, for Mother had been vomiting and purging, and Muirrin's brisk manner and capable expression did not fool me into believing all was well. Still, the household seemed to appreciate the music. Our performance lured a group of maidservants and men-at-arms out to dance. As we worked our way through the final jig the pace got quicker and quicker and we almost came unstuck several times. We survived, I flushed and breathless, Aidan laughing and examining his fingers as if to ascertain that they were all still there. The audience applauded heartily. Father, however, was quiet.

"I have another tale for you tonight." It was Willow's voice, deep and strong, and as I watched the old woman came forward from her corner, her bony hand clutching her staff. "If Lord Sean permits. It is the second of three I owe, and the right one for this day and time."

"Of course," Father said, but it was clear to me his thoughts were elsewhere. I knew he would rather be upstairs with Mother, but he would stay in the hall until the evening's entertainment was over. Folk liked routine; they liked things to conform to a pattern. That made them feel safe. A chieftain could never put his personal concerns first.

As was her habit, Willow had a good look around the hall before she began her tale. Sibeal was here with Eilis and Coll, sitting on the floor in the front. The departure of Gareth's party meant Aidan and Cathal were spending a good deal of their time on duty. Tonight, Aidan had the job of keeping close to Johnny, though he had been allowed time off to play for us. Cathal stood further away, near the entry.

"Would you ever believe," Willow said, fixing Coll and Eilis with her penetrating gaze, "that a mother would abandon her baby in a deep, dark wood at night? Only the most troubled of women would do such a thing. Only a mother too frightened and desperate to offer her child the love that was his birthright would leave him thus to the will of the gods. It happened, and the infant was on the edge of death when the wolf came." The children stared at her, caught up in the tale already.

"Now that wolf," said Willow, "was far more of a mother than the frail, confused girl. She had cubs in a hollow deep in the woods and plenty of milk to feed them with. So she took up the wee one, carefully, with the back of his garments in her sharp teeth, and carried him off home with her. She loved him in keeping with her nature, practically, wisely, and she nurtured him long after her little ones were grown and had gone their own ways. She cleaned him with her rough tongue, learning the patterns of his strange, hairless body; she discovered how weak he truly was. She hunted for him, since he could not seem to master it. She kept him warm at night; she made beds of bracken and leaves to shelter him when his garments wore away to shreds. And in time Wolf-child learned to crawl and to scamper and to run, mostly on all fours like his brothers and sisters, but sometimes up on two legs, awkwardly. He learned the smells and sounds of the forest; he learned ways to protect himself. He learned the growls and barks and whimpers of the wolf pack's language. The others tolerated him because of his mother, for she was high in their order, having whelped many strong litters. The pack leader did not consider Wolf-child a threat, since the hairless one was such a weakling. Among the others, the boy's singular nature earned him a wary respect.

"Years passed, and Wolf-child was a boy the size of this young fellow"—Willow nodded in Coll's direction—"with the skill to make his own shelter and to snare a bird when he wanted meat. His mother still watched over him, but she had reared many cubs since the day she took the waif in, and her human son was learning to do without her. Only when the winter bit hardest, in time of storm and sleet, would she let him sleep next to her, curled up against the warmth of her body. It was their misfortune that men came to that part of the forest early in the morning on such a day, men who saw with disbelief the aging wolf rising from sleep and the half-grown boy, naked in the cold, jumping up and spreading his arms to protect her from their hunting spears. They did not kill the wolf mother—their astonishment made them too slow for that—and she fled away soft-footed under the trees. It was the boy they pursued, and it was the boy they finally caught, hardly knowing what they would do with the snarling, thrashing creature they had in their hands.

"Wolf-child was dragged back to the local settlement. He was like any wild creature suddenly captive: bewildered, afraid, furious. He lashed out at anyone who came near. They confined him in a cellar with a bolt on the door. In time, as he grew hungry, tired and dispirited, the boy became quieter, but he growled a warning each time someone came to leave him food. He could not drink from the cup they provided, spilling the water as he tried to lap at it. The cooked meat was alien to him but he devoured it, crouched down over the platter, not using his hands.

"You might ask, why did his wolf mother not defend him out there in the forest? Why did she run, leaving her child to be taken? But to her he was not a child. It was a long time since this strange cub had first come her way. Her tolerance of his closeness had worn thin as she grew older and more weary. She sensed that her time as first female in the pack was drawing to an end. She would have defended a brood of small cubs to the death, but this one must fend for himself.

"For a while Wolf-child was a wonder to be peered at through a chink in the cellar door, a marvel to be entertained by. But the novelty wore thin soon enough. One or two of the villagers tried to talk to the boy, to gesture in a way he might understand, but he responded only with growls or whining, and they soon lost interest in such an unrewarding creature. As for Wolf-child, he was cold, lonely and confused. They had given him clothing to wear, a rough shirt and trousers, and after a little he did keep them on, feeling their warmth. But in the confines of the cellar he could not clean himself as he would in the forest. The stink of the place became so rank that nobody wanted to come near it.

"The villagers saw that they had made a mistake in thinking there might be a place for the boy among them. He was a human being, sure enough. But he didn't know it, and it was beyond them to teach him. Not wanting simply to let him go, for that seemed no more right than keeping him locked up, they asked the local druid for help.

"Now druids, as we all know, see deeper than the surfaces of things. That's one of their strengths, and another is the ability to be still and quiet; the gift of great patience. They can sit in one spot all day and never get bored. If a man's head is crammed full of lore he's never short of the means to entertain himself. The druid asked the villagers to lend him a cottage with a well-fenced patch of land, and he took Wolf-child there with him and shut the gate after them.

"It took him a long time, but eventually the druid earned the trust of his young companion and was able to teach him certain things. Wolf-child learned to keep himself clean, not in the way a wolf does, by licking or rolling or swimming, but by the use of a cloth and a bucket. The boy learned to drink from a cup and eat from a platter, though he was awkward with a knife or spoon. He learned to sit on a bench, but preferred the floor. The druid encouraged him to stand more upright, to walk on two legs not four, and was partly successful. As for human speech, that was far harder. The druid sensed the boy could understand quite well, but Wolf-child found shaping words with his mouth difficult. One word he learned easily. He would stand by the gate, a gate fastened by an iron chain which his wolfish fingers could not manipulate open, and point toward the forest. '*Out*,' he would say, his tone somewhere between speech and barking. '*Out*.' "

It seemed to me this story was not going to have a happy ending. I was not sure I wanted to hear the rest of it, but I was not in the best position to slip out of the hall unnoticed without offending Willow. There was no fault in her storytelling. I just wasn't in the right mood to hear something sad. With Mother lying upstairs so desperate to hold onto her unborn child, and Father looking so weary and grim, I could do without a tale of a boy who was unlikely to do well in either world, that of well-meaning, ignorant humankind or of animals governed by their instincts. I glanced toward the main door as Aidan brought Willow a cup of ale. Maybe I could take advantage of this pause to vanish outside until the story was finished. As my gaze fell on Cathal my heart missed a beat. Stark and plain on that narrow, guarded face I saw the wretched aloneness of the wolf boy. I saw his recognition that he would always be outside, other, never quite a part of the community on whose fringes he dwelt. I saw that it hurt beyond any pain.

A moment later, Cathal realized I was looking at him. With what must have been a formidable effort of will, he relaxed his features, the thin lips forming their usual derisory smile, the expression conveying nothing more than a general desire to be somewhere else. The dark brows rose as if to question my apparent interest in him. I imagined him saying, *Haven't you got anything better to look at?*

Willow had taken a mouthful of her ale and set the cup down. "Of course, the druid had tried to find out whose son this wild boy was, but his enquiries bore no fruit," she said. "The girl who had left her child out for the wolves was long forgotten. Wolf-child was nobody; a conundrum; a puzzle. The druid, patient man as he was, had a longing to return to his cave out in the forest, his own place where he could sleep under the oaks and make his prayers beneath a canopy of bright stars, unbounded by wall or enclosure. Given years, he might teach the feral child skills sufficient to allow him a place on the very edge of human society. Whether that was right or not was a question one might be a lifetime answering. The boy would grow up neither wolf nor man. His mother had done him no favors that chilly night when she decided to abandon him to fate.

"Now," said Willow, "there are many possible endings to this tale, and the one that suits you best may not be the one I like. There might be one for a warrior and one for a lady and one for a boy of Wolf-child's age. So we'll have three tonight, and you will help me tell them. Let us begin with the warrior, for we have a good supply of those here. What about you, young man?" The storyteller was looking at Johnny.

My cousin smiled. "Aidan is both warrior and bard," he said. "I delegate the task to him."

"Very well," Willow said. "And how would Aidan finish this tale?"

Aidan cleared his throat. He'd been taken off-guard. "I would like to see this boy make something of himself," he ventured. "In my story, the druid persisted in his patient training of his young charge, and in addition he sought the help of the local nobleman"—he nodded courteously in my father's direction—"who should perhaps have been the first person consulted by the villagers. When the nobleman came down to see the lad he brought his own son, a warrior in training. They came on horseback, and while the nobleman discussed matters with the druid, the young warrior took his first steps toward befriending Wolf-child, for they were close in age, if not in understanding. Wolf-child growled at the horse, which laid back its ears and twitched its tail. All the same, that day the wild boy learned something he had not quite realized before. In this fine young man he saw a vision of himself as he might be. From that day things began to change more quickly for Wolf-child, for now he wanted to learn, to grow, to become a man. I would leave the story at that point, where this boy so cruelly abandoned found that he had a real future ahead of him."

Willow nodded. There was no telling what she thought of this ending for her tale. "And you, young man?" she asked, looking at Coll.

"One day the druid left the gate open," Coll said, instantly taking up the challenge. "Maybe by mistake, maybe not. When he remembered and went outside to chain it up again, Wolf-child was gone. And whether the wolf pack took him back as one of their own, or whether they turned him away because he'd been among humankind for too long, nobody ever found out. But sometimes, at dead of night, when the wolves howl at the moon, folk in those parts say they hear another sound mingling with the wolfish voices—the cry of a man whose heart craves what he can never have."

A stunned silence fell over us. I eyed my young cousin with new respect. I knew he loved stories, but I had never heard him tell one before. This had been a strong ending. I looked over at Cathal, wondering what he had thought of it, but he wasn't there. At some point after Willow had cut off her narration so abruptly he had left the hall.

"And you, Clodagh?"

I started in surprise as the old woman addressed me. *One for a lady.* She expected me to provide the third version. The ending that sprang to my mind was even darker than Coll's, and I would not tell it. "The others were very good," I said, playing for time. "I cannot better them."

"Better?" Willow queried with a smile. "There is no better or worse with stories, only different. What would you make of this? How would you resolve it? With sorrow, with gladness, with learning?" That look was in her eyes again, the same I had seen when she told the clurichaun story. It was a look that challenged me to understand, to take from the story some kind of learning that was not obvious. I was unable to grasp what she meant by it. My mind went back to Cathal's stricken face, his haunted, lonely eyes. He'd been upset beyond anything the tale might have conjured. Why?

"The druid, of course, would learn from the situation, however it ended," I said. "It is in a druid's nature to do so." A shadow moved by the doorway; Cathal was still there listening, but hovering on the threshold as if he was not quite sure whether he wanted to hear or not. Suddenly I was determined to do this well and not to end the wretched tale in the misery and failure that seemed to me inevitable. But I would not make it unrealistic, as Aidan's version had been. The damage done to Wolf-child could not be so easily undone. "The druid knew he could not continue the way things were," I said. "It was too late for the boy to go back to his wolf clan. After those seasons away, the pack would no longer accept him as one of their kind. He would look wrong, smell wrong. The boy would miss them, of course. They were the only family he had known. What was the alternative? Perhaps, eventually, the druid might teach Wolf-child to be a man. Was that such a great thing that it merited the erasing of the wisdom this boy had learned among the wolves? His adoptive kin had given him much, and the druid saw that here in this locked enclosure whose high walls shut out the forest, those strengths, those instincts, that bright knowledge would continue to ebb away. Was it right to replace those gifts with skills from a culture of which the boy might never completely become a part? How could such a wild one learn to love, to work, to provide for his own? But Wolf-child could not go back. It was a problem to vex the best-trained mind.

"The druid taught his charge one more skill. He managed to convey that the desperately desired *out* might be attained if Wolf-child was prepared to tolerate a kind of leash, a strong cord to tie his wrist to that of the druid. He trained the boy to this as if he were a dog, hating what he was doing but seeing no other way to keep Wolf-child by him long enough for the boy to understand his intentions. If he simply opened the gate, Wolf-child would flee. That must end in disaster, one way or another.

"The morning after Wolf-child had learned to accept the leash, the druid arose early, packed up his small bundle of belongings and went out to the gate. Wolf-child was already there, staring out into the forest. The druid fastened the leash around the boy's wrist and around his own. He opened the gate.

"They went out together, Wolf-child pulling hard, almost toppling the older man. He could have got away, for he was strong, but the druid had his measure by now and spoke calmly, reassuring the boy by his tone. They walked a long way, far enough so that Wolf-child began to sense they were not going back. The druid saw a change on the features of his companion, an awakening, a brightening, as if the gray veil of despair that had lain over the lad since the time of his capture were slowly peeling away. They climbed to the higher reaches of the great forest, where frothing streams gushed down from rocky fells above the tree line and a stand of guardian pines threw the hillside beneath into deep shadow. Up and up they climbed until they reached the cave where the druid had his solitary dwelling. Beside the entry a rivulet flowed into a round rocky basin whose rim was softened by ferns. Rowans grew close; holly formed a protective barrier.

"The druid set down his bundle. With his free hand he reached into a pouch at his belt and brought out two bannocks and a slab of cheese in a cloth. He set these items on a flat stone. 'My home,' the druid said, pointing to himself, then to the cave entry, sweeping his hand around to encompass the little clearing, the pool, the rocky chamber. 'Go free,' he added, slipping his knife out of his belt and cutting the leash that bound Wolf-child to him. 'I will be here. Home; food; shelter.' He tried to show, with gestures, what he meant. Who knew how much the boy could understand?

"Wolf-child had stood very still while the leash was severed. The druid had felt the tension in the boy, every part of him strained for flight. As the length of leather cord fell, broken, to the ground, Wolf-child remained where he was for a long moment, and in that moment a look passed between him and the druid, a look that was as animal as it was human. That look was too complicated for me to explain to you. An instant later Wolf-child was off into the woods, a blur of movement gone almost before the druid had had time to take in what had happened.

"Now I might end the story there," I said, adopting something of Willow's own style, "but that would leave my listeners dissatisfied. So I will tell you what came next. The druid was right about the wolves—they would not take this lost son back into their clan. The boy hung about on the fringes for days, trying to edge in, to slip himself back among them unobtrusively, but the clan leader kept him off. The wolves would not attack the boy. They knew he was not of ordinary humankind. But they could not receive him as one of them. It was too late for that. Perhaps, even if he had remained among them, this would have occurred anyway when he began to grow into a man. They sensed the danger innate in his kind. Wolves have no sentiment. That he was raised by one of their own meant nothing at all.

"After some time, the druid noticed that he was no longer quite alone in his secluded corner of the forest. Wolf-child would slip in from time to time, hesitating on the edge of the clearing, wary and pale. The druid began to divide his rations into two and set one half out on the flat stones by the rowans. At first Wolf-child would snatch his food and bolt. But as he regained the ability to trust, he would come to squat near the round pool and eat while the druid ate. The druid began to talk to him. A long, long time later, Wolf-child began to answer, not in growls and whining, but in words. And that was the start of a whole new story."

I was done. Willow bowed her head courteously in my direction, giving me the recognition due from one storyteller to another. I felt my face grow warm with pleasure.

"Very good, Clodagh," Aidan said. "I like this ending far better than mine."

"You have something of Conor's storytelling gift, Clodagh," put in Father with a smile. "This tale, in all its versions, has a great deal to teach us."

As a discussion of the story began, I got up quietly and left the hall. I had heard enough about the boy raised by wolves. It was a sad tale whichever way it worked out. If such a thing occurred in real life, the lad would probably be dead before he ever reached the age of manhood. Indeed, the she-wolf would likely have seen the newborn child not as a cub to be nurtured but as an easy supper. I had enough to worry about without dwelling on such things. Besides, there was something else I felt compelled to do.

Cathal was sitting at the top of the steps outside the harness room. He had his arms folded, his head tipped back against the door, his eyes half closed. He'd as likely bite my head off when I spoke as decide to confide in me. But someone had to talk to him; he was obviously feeling quite wretched. I had spent enough nights recently lying awake with my worries and missing Deirdre to understand what it felt like being alone and miserable.

"Tell me what's wrong," I said, seating myself on the middle step. It was cold out here; I wished I had put on my shawl. "What could there possibly be in a story like that to upset you so much?"

"And good evening to you, too," Cathal said in a murmur.

I tried again. "For a man all too ready to scoff at the uncanny, you seemed remarkably disturbed. You left the hall before the ending. Before my version, anyway."

"You know how tedious I find these little entertainments."

I said nothing. Whatever that look on his face had conveyed, it hadn't been boredom.

"In fact," Cathal said after a little, "I did hear your version of the ending. I thought it reflected your preference for your world to be tidy and controlled. Aidan made the tale end as a warrior would, with the wolf boy recognizing his manhood. Coll gave it the form of an ancient myth. Your version was a good compromise. But in its way as unrealistic as the others. This child was not wolf; he was not man. He was condemned to be forever outside."

My neck prickled. I opened my mouth to speak, but his voice, whip-quick, cut across my half-formed words.

"Don't! Don't meddle!"

I swallowed a question about his upbringing. It really was none of my business. But I did think talking might be good for him, and right now I was the only one available to listen. Something had put that terrible look on Cathal's face tonight; something had made him the volatile, touchy creature he was.

"In case the possibility had crossed your mind, I was not raised by wolves," Cathal said into the silence. His tone was calmer now, but when I turned sideways on the steps to look at him, he was dashing a furious hand across his cheek. The flickering light from the torch set nearby cast odd patterns across his face. I saw tears glinting in his eyes, and turned my gaze away lest I embarrass him.

"There is more than one variety of wolf," I said.

"You imagine a past for me that is far more complex and mysterious than the real one, Clodagh. Women are like that, or so I've been told—they're happier creating a fascinating tale than accepting the mundane truth about a person."

"If you think I spend my spare time dreaming up exciting stories about your misspent youth, Cathal, your capacity for self-delusion is more impressive than I realized. Besides, how can I accept the truth if I don't know what it is?"

"Why should you want to know? Have I ever asked you about your childhood?"

"If you did, I'd have no reason not to tell you." As soon as I had said this, I realized how wrong it was—any tale about Sevenwaters had to include the uncanny influence of the Fair Folk. I could imagine how Cathal would respond if I told him, for instance, that Conor and his brothers had once spent three years in the form of swans. "But you wouldn't ask," I added. "In your book, my story would be unutterably boring."

There was a silence, and then he surprised me by saying, "I'm sorry I called you that, Clodagh. These remarks come out sometimes, and once they're spoken it's too late to withdraw them. I did not know you then."

"You scarcely do now, Cathal. Nor I you."

"There's nothing to tell. It's my story that is the boring one. My mother was Aidan's wet-nurse. He and I were born within days of each other and were suckled together. Aidan's father is a good man. He saw that my mother would have difficulty in providing for me as I grew up, so he took me into his household as a friend and companion for his son. Thus I gained an education beyond what might be considered my natural entitlement in the scheme of things. I received a training in arms that allowed me to accompany Aidan when he went to Inis Eala. That's the end of the story.

I told you it was tedious." His elbows were on his knees now, his dark head bowed. He was making his fingers into a knot.

There was an obvious element missing from his story. *At least I know who my father is,* Aidan had said, taunting his friend. It was not something I could ask Cathal about.

"Clodagh." Cathal's tone had changed again.

"What?"

"There's something I need to tell you. You may not like it much. Will you hear me out?"

I was intrigued. "That depends on what it is," I said. "I can't stay out here long."

"I want you to consider a hypothetical situation. It concerns a strategic matter."

This was the last thing I had expected. "You're talking to the wrong person," I told him. "Speak to Johnny. Or to my father."

"Wait till I'm finished, Clodagh, will you? You remember what Sibeal said about twins in your family and the special ability they are supposed to have?"

"Yes," I said cautiously. "I thought that where such phenomena were concerned you were a complete cynic."

"Forget that. Tell me, how would you respond if your twin sister contacted you in this way now, perhaps speaking of strategic matters, the deployment of warriors or plans for councils? Would you speak to her? What would you tell her?"

I twisted around to stare at him. "Why on earth would you want to know that?" I asked him. "Anyway, Deirdre and I don't communicate that way anymore. She made a decision that we wouldn't after she left home, and she's kept to it. What can this possibly have to do with you, Cathal?"

"Your father is particularly concerned about Eoin of Lough Gall just now; he fears an escalation of unrest in the north. I wonder if there could be another possibility, one that perhaps Lord Sean has not considered. Your twin sister has just married a southern neighbor, a powerful one. What if your father were looking in the wrong direction? What if the real threat were not Eoin but your sister's new husband, Illann?"

"What?" I was on my feet, bristling with outrage. "Illann? How can you suggest such a thing?" It was ridiculous. Why would

Illann wed a daughter of our family only to turn almost immediately against her father?

"You said you'd hear me out."

"This is silly, Cathal. It couldn't be true. Even if it were, why would you tell *me*?" He sat there saying nothing, his dark eyes on me, and after a moment I added, "Why the questions about Deirdre? What are you implying?"

He unfolded himself from the steps and came to stand beside me. "Why would I tell you?" he echoed, and there was none of the old mocking tone in his voice. "This is not something I can take to Johnny or to your father, Clodagh. I've no evidence, only a hunch. My instincts tell me you may be personally at risk. It is only fair to warn you. As Illann's wife, your twin is perfectly placed to spy for him. She need only exchange news with you by this special link the two of you possess, she need only ask an innocent question or two about what Lord Sean is doing, where he's sending his men, which territorial disputes he's involved with or which councils he's attending. Why wouldn't you answer her? She's your sister; you trust her."

I was quivering with anger. "Your instincts are quite wrong," I said. "Deirdre wouldn't dream of spying. We're all loyal to our father. We love him. We love Sevenwaters. It's a sacred trust to the whole family—"

"Clodagh." Cathal put his hands on my shoulders. "Listen to me. Please."

His touch set my whole body on edge. "Don't!" I snapped, wrenching myself from his grip. Then, hearing the shrill sound of my own voice, I added more calmly, "All right, I'll listen. But no more baseless accusations. Where did this notion come from? And why can't we take it straight to Johnny?"

"No!" Cathal's hands came up as if to touch me again, then he lowered them to his sides. "This is between you and me, Clodagh. At this point it is nothing more than surmise. An informed guess. There should be no need for action unless . . ."

"Unless Deirdre gets in contact with me and asks the kinds of questions a rival chieftain would ask?"

Cathal sighed. "If she does, you should tell your father immediately. Imagine how it could be if you passed on information to your sister and Illann then used it as the basis for an attack on Sevenwaters. That would look ill for you."

"This makes no sense," I said flatly. "An attack, what attack? Why would Illann take any such action? He and Father are allies."

"It's only a theory." He was pacing now, arms wrapped around himself. "But possible nonetheless. How can I convince you to give it some credence?"

"You can't," I said. "I had thought we were edging toward being friends, Cathal. But these accusations against Deirdre are deeply offensive. And they're rubbish. How can you possibly know something like that? How could you know what Illann might be planning if Johnny doesn't?"

Cathal sighed. "Let me paint a picture for you, Clodagh. We're in the west somewhere, right on the borders of your father's land. At dusk a raiding party surrounds a substantial house owned by Lord Sean. The place is fortified, but it's less well defended than it might be. The raiding party is large, thirty men at least, and they're not led by Illann, but he's behind the enterprise. Why, I cannot tell you, but perhaps it has to do with his links among the kinsmen of the High King. The place they're attacking has elms and oaks close to the house. There's a stream, a pond, a beech hedge. Two men have been sent in advance to disable the forward sentry post. As a result, the raiders get close enough to set fire to the main dwelling house before their presence is noticed. In the ensuing panic they kill most of the opposing fighters, and the custodian of the house is forced to flee into the woods with his family. The place burns down. The raiders report to the man who sent them: Illann. And Illann thanks his wife for passing on the information that she gleaned for him: that the place was not well defended, since their marriage had allayed any fears of attack in this quarter."

Most of this long speech passed me in a blur; I had no wish to listen to such utter nonsense. Either the man was completely mad or this was an elaborate joke of some kind. In a moment he'd probably burst into derisive laughter and make some comment like, *You actually believed me!*

"The question remains, why would Illann attack my father?" I asked coolly.

"Such acts are generally carried out in order to seize some strategic advantage. At the very least, the news of such a coup would pass a message to all that Lord Sean's authority is easier to shake than previously believed. With the imminent birth of a child who could replace Johnny as your father's heir, folk will be anticipating a period of unrest at Sevenwaters. Perhaps northern and southern Uí Néill are in cooperation and plan to challenge your father from either side. Clodagh, don't look at me like that. I'm serious."

"If you are serious, tell my father."

"Would he credit such a tale without a skerrick of proof? Would Johnny? All I want to do is warn you. If you know, you can avoid becoming involved. You can perhaps prevent this from occurring at all by refusing to give your sister any knowledge her husband could use to help him in such an endeavor."

Any sympathy I'd been feeling for him after the Wolf-child tale had faded completely. My first impression of Cathal had been right after all: he was an arrant troublemaker. More than that, there was something seriously askew in his mind. "You're one of Johnny's men," I reminded him. "Isn't your first priority to do the right thing by him? I thought all his warriors were flawlessly loyal."

"I am neither more nor less loyal than the others. Johnny believes Illann is an ally; so does Lord Sean. I have doubts. But I will not go to either of them with information I cannot support with evidence."

"Then why bring it to me? Have you assessed me as completely gullible?"

His mouth formed a self-mocking twist. "Why indeed, since it is plain you will not listen?"

"I'm going inside," I said. "I won't promise not to speak of this to Father. He should know that you are questioning the motives of his close kin. Good night, Cathal. Please don't come to me with any more wild theories. I've enough to worry about already." I turned and walked away.

His voice came softly from behind me. "I didn't come to you," he said. "You came to me."

I entered the hall fully intending to report the whole conversation to my father. He'd recognize instantly how ridiculous Cathal's suggestions were. Deirdre a traitor to the family? It was so silly it wasn't worth thinking about. Not only was my twin devoted to our parents, she had never had the slightest interest in matters strategic or political. In the unlikely event that someone wanted her to obtain useful information, Deirdre wouldn't even know what questions to ask.

I was two steps inside the door when Sibeal came rushing down the main stairs, calling my name. The look on her face made something clench tight inside me.

"Where were you, Clodagh?" My sister's voice wobbled; she was making a heroic effort to sound calm. "I've been looking for you everywhere. Muirrin needs you upstairs right now." As we went up together, Sibeal told me what I had guessed the moment I saw her. "The baby's coming early. It shouldn't be born for ages yet. Clodagh, I'm scared."

I did not think Muirrin would need me for midwifery duties, and I was right. She was dealing capably with everything and had plenty of serving women to help her. Mother was sitting on the bed with Eithne supporting her. Her features formed a grotesque mask of pain. Aromatic herbs were burning on the hearth; their scent did not quite disguise the smell of blood. I waited until the spasm was over, then said something reassuring, I hardly knew what. Quite certain my terror must show on my face, I was deeply relieved when Muirrin drew me back toward the door.

"Clodagh, I'm assuming you'll keep things calm downstairs," my sister said in an undertone. "I'm afraid you won't be getting much sleep. Johnny says he'll sit up with Father. Please keep the younger ones away from here until this is over."

A hush fell over the household. Whatever occurred, this would be a night of change for all of us. Our serving people were discreet, making regular appearances with jugs of ale or platters of food, vanishing from the hall when not required. From time to time one of the women would come down with a request from Muirrin—fresh linen, hot water, provisions for the childbed attendants. I went in and out of the kitchen making sure these supplies were provided promptly. Nobody went to bed. People who did not know her well might think that our mother, with her brisk manner and her insistence on everything being just so, would not be well loved by her serving folk. This was quite wrong. She had married Father when she was only sixteen, and the people of Sevenwaters had been witness to every joy and sorrow of her life since then. The sturdiest washerwoman and the dourest man-at-arms had tears in their eyes tonight. I reminded myself that I was the lady of the house, if only temporarily, and that I must be strong.

Sibeal and Eilis had both refused to go to bed. They had settled themselves by the fire with a blanket apiece, and now Aidan was cross-legged on the flagstones beside them, teaching them tricks with dice. Father kept getting up and sitting down again, lifting his cup of ale and putting it back on the tray untasted. Johnny was trying to engage him in conversation, but he might as well have been talking to a storm-tossed oak.

I didn't give a thought to Cathal until I sat down much later, on Johnny's orders, to have some food and drink. I looked over toward the main door, now closed against the cold, and realized I had not seen Cathal since our conversation in the yard. Watching Father as he paced, observing the furrow on his brow and the tight set of his jaw, I knew now was no time to pass on the crazy theory about Illann. "Is Cathal on duty tonight, Johnny?" I asked my cousin.

"I gave him the rest of the night off. If he's got any sense he'll be asleep. Why do you ask?"

"No reason," I said, thinking that if this was true, Cathal must be the only person in the whole household who was not spending the night in edgy vigil. I was about to frame a question to Aidan about his childhood when a serving woman came running down the stairs and into the hall. Her words tumbled out. "My lord, the child's born! You have a son!"

Father turned white. "Aisling," he whispered. Before the woman could speak again, Muirrin appeared behind her with a tiny bundle in her arms, a little blanket wrapped around something no bigger than a doll.

"Mother's doing quite well, considering." My sister's voice was less steady than usual. "You'll be able to see her soon, Father."

When Father did not move forward to take his new son in his arms, Muirrin offered the baby to me.

He was very light, like a young rabbit or a hen. I folded the swathing blanket back and saw a neat face, the delicate lids closed over eyes whose color I could only guess at, the nose forthright, the fragile skull thatched with a good crop of dark hair, plastered flat by the debris of birth. His complexion was a mottled red. Sibeal came up on one side of me and Eilis on the other, and I showed them. A sweet smile played on Eilis's face, but Sibeal reached out, expression grave, and touched the infant's brow with one finger.

"What name will you give him, Father?" she asked.

"I hadn't really thought . . ." Father sounded far away, as if he had been deeply shocked. I realized, to my wonder, that he had not until this moment ever considered it possible that both Mother and the child would survive. He sat down suddenly, his face in his hands.

Instinct told me what I must do. I moved to crouch by him, lifting the child alongside his knee. "Hold him, Father," I murmured. "He's Mother's gift to you. Take him."

He gathered the baby up, laying him on his lap. With a gentle hand he smoothed back the hair from the little brow. "He's so small," Father said. His fingers traced the faint brows, the strong nose, the tiny bud of the mouth. The child made a tentative sucking motion, and one hand appeared from the swathing cloth, miniature fingers clutching.

"He has the Sevenwaters look, Sean," Johnny said quietly. "Perhaps he should be Colum, for your grandfather."

The infant gave a snuffling sigh and closed his fingers around one of Father's.

"No," said Father shakily. "He'll be called Finbar."

CHAPTER 5

There were no celebrations. The birth of a son to the Sevenwaters family was a momentous event, but for now it was overshadowed by Mother's precarious health. Although her labor had not been long, it had taxed her hard and the risk of childbed fever was high. Every time Muirrin came down to the hall the rest of us fell silent, anticipating bad news.

Because Mother was so frail, the baby did not stay in her chamber but was housed in the one next door, under the care of a nursemaid. Sibeal and I took turns watching him when the girl was eating or having her time off. It was not exactly hard work, as Finbar slept most of the time. It was hard to believe this was the same child who had kicked so vigorously against the confines of his mother's belly. I liked sitting with him in the quiet of the nursery chamber. I liked his shadowy eyelids and his fine little fingers. When he did wake, I saw that his eyes would be the same as Sibeal's, such a light gray-blue as to be almost colorless, and I thought the name Father had given him might be all too apt. "I don't think it's a very happy life, being a seer," I whispered to my baby brother. "I wonder if it's too late to change your mind?"

The drama of Finbar's arrival, followed by the continuing unease of Mother's illness, had crowded everything else out of my thoughts. Suppers were conducted in a somber hush; nobody wanted entertainment. When Finbar was five days old, the haunted look in Muirrin's eyes began to fade and I heard her say, cautiously, that Mother was doing better than expected.

That evening Willow stepped forward after supper and addressed herself to my father. "Lord Sean, I offer the congratulations of the traveling people on the birth of your son," the old woman said. "May he grow as strong in wisdom and as clear in vision as his namesake." Finbar had been named after a beloved kinsman, one of Conor's brothers, who had lived much of his life in lonely exile and had died in an act of noble self-sacrifice. Someone in our household must have told Willow this story. No doubt it would be grist to her mill, the stuff of future tales. "I must move on in the morning," Willow added, "and I have yet one tale to tell. I would not walk away from this hospitable home in debt."

"By all means tell us your tale tonight," Father said. "We will welcome it."

The old woman glanced around the hall, as if taking in exactly who was present and what might suit their need for learning. "I will not dwell on the problems of humankind," said Willow. "I will tell a tale that belongs principally to the realm of the Fair Folk. You know of Mac Dara, the powerful prince of the Tuatha De Danann. I hope it will not shock the young folk here if I tell you that individuals like Mac Dara father children in the human world from time to time. And it's not just the princes who get up to such antics. The fair ladies of the Tuatha De oft-times have their dalliance with human men and bear the fruits of it. Sometimes they act thus to gain a lever by which they can make mortals such as your fine selves dance to their tunes. Sometimes it's for love, but such a passion fades all too quickly. What woman wants a lover who'll be wrinkled and gray and bent while she is still in the fragrant blush of youth? Sometimes it's for the simplest of reasons. The Fair Folk don't breed easily among their own kind. The surest way to conceive a child is to couple with a young and healthy mortal.

"This tale deals with such goings-on. It tells of the particular curse that lies over those whose ancestry is both fairy and mortal.

Of course, the family of Sevenwaters has some knowledge of that already."

She must be talking about Ciarán, whose father had been Lord Colum of Sevenwaters, my great-grandfather, and whose mother had been a sorceress descended through a dark line of the Fair Folk. The old woman seemed to know a lot about us.

"We won't speak of Mac Dara himself," Willow went on. "He's too shadowy and troublesome a character by far. Let's start with a lovely lady, we'll call her Albha, who had long hankered for a child of her own, a baby to love and nurture and dress up in cobweb and gossamer and swansdown, the sort of garments favored by the folk of the Tuatha De. Now the Fair Folk, as you must well know, are not renowned for their finer feelings. They've little capacity for love or forgiveness, loyalty or compassion. They do know desire, jealousy, anger and pride. Should they conceive a will to possess a thing, they pursue it with all their considerable power. Should they lose a prize, they exercise the same single-mindedness. The Tuatha De don't like to be thwarted. They can't abide coming out second best.

"That understood, you won't be surprised to hear that Albha went about achieving her goal quite coldly. She had no desire to couple with a mortal, but she knew this was her best chance to have her own baby. So she selected a suitable man, choosing him not for his high birth or wisdom or power in the mortal world, but for his strong body and pleasing features. It was an easy job to persuade him to perform the duty she required of him—like all her kind, Albha had a beauty far beyond that of the most comely of mortal women. She stayed with the fellow as long as she needed to. When she felt her belly beginning to swell, she left her lover and returned to the realm of the Tuatha De. She had what she wanted."

A brief silence. "What about the man?" I asked. "What happened to him?"

Willow smiled, lifting her brows. "He plays no further part in this story, Clodagh. Albha cared nothing for him beyond his capacity to give her a child. Perhaps he became wiser as a result of his experience and was careful to stay away from fairy women after that. Perhaps, like so many men in the tales, he wore himself to death searching for his Otherworld lover. Maybe he killed himself from grief." She sounded as if this was of no matter.

"But—" I said, then fell silent. It was only a story, after all. If it seemed unjust, perhaps that was a reflection of real life, especially where dealings with the Fair Folk were concerned.

"In due course the wee girl was born, and she was every bit as lovely and fey as her mother, for all she was half human. Her mother called her Saorla, and loved her as well as the Tuatha De have it in them to love. Time passed. Saorla grew into a beautiful young woman. Up till her fifteenth birthday, she had never asked who her father might be. Indeed, she had always assumed it was Mac Dara, who made no secret of his virility and laid claim to parentage of more children than any man could have had the time or energy to sire, be he human or Tuatha De. But we know Mac Dara's capacity for mischief. One day he took it into his head to meddle. He told Saorla who her real father was and how Albha had used a mortal man the way a stud bull might be used, solely to engender a healthy child."

"I thought you said Mac Dara wouldn't be in this story," said Coll.

"Don't interrupt," Johnny told his little brother. "Mac Dara makes his way into stories whether people want him there or not. I'm sure that's what Willow would tell you."

"That's indeed so, my lord," Willow said. "Be glad your own parentage is beyond question. And yours, young man." She gave Coll a penetrating look and my irrepressible young cousin wilted under it. "Whether or not we can say the same of every man and woman in this hall remains a mystery. So, back to Saorla. In the moment that Mac Dara told her the uncomfortable truth, the girl determined to return to the mortal world and to find the father who had been so wronged. Saorla was disgusted by what Albha had done. It explained everything, she thought—the way she had always felt out of place; her fascination with the idea of a world beyond her own; her distaste for the machinations of folk such as the all-powerful Mac Dara. Saorla decided she would turn her back on the Fair Folk. She would walk away and never return to the Otherworld.

"It was not so easy, of course. Albha got wind of what her

daughter intended and pursued her through that realm, using all her considerable power to stop her. But Saorla had not wasted the fifteen years she'd spent growing up amongst the Fair Folk. She'd learned a few tricks of her own. Out through a little wee portal she slipped and away into the human world, and there was no holding her back."

The tale expanded into a long and dangerous duel between mother and daughter, as time and again Albha tricked Saorla onto the margins of the Otherworld only to be bested at the last moment when Saorla sensed she was in danger and maneuvered her way out again. I could not guess how it would end.

"I'm sorry to interrupt," said Sibeal politely at a certain point. "But the Fair Folk in your stories seem rather different from the ones we know of. This family has had wise advice over the years from the Tuatha De Danann, especially the one we call the Lady of the Forest. They have guided our decisions and helped us with difficult choices. These folk you speak of, Mac Dara and Albha, sound like lesser beings, caught up in their own deceit and selfishness. Is it only at Sevenwaters that the Fair Folk can be wise and good?"

"An interesting question, which I might debate with you at length, Sibeal, had we the time for it." There was respect in Willow's eyes as they rested on my sister. "Of course, it is only a tale. But Mac Dara is in many tales. They say he's a creature of Connacht, in the west. Of course, the realm of the Tuatha De stretches across the length and breadth of Erin, and it's laid out much as our own land is, so there's no reason why Mac Dara should not turn up at Sevenwaters if he chooses, nor any bar on your Lady of the Forest paying him a visit in his home territory. It's said that the Tuatha De are fading before a great tide of change. Sevenwaters is old. It's housed such folk long after their havens in other parts have disappeared. But the grand ones, the noble ones, are passing away, perhaps to the isles of the west, perhaps into memory, child. And when the wise ones depart, what's left is Mac Dara and his like. The realm of the Fair Folk is a darker place than it once was. A little seer might go out to seek wisdom in the clear water of a forest pool, and instead of the lovely lady who used to appear to give her guidance, all she might get is a selfish creature like Albha. You should take care. We should all take care."

Sibeal said nothing, but she looked stricken. Perhaps there was truth in those odd rumors after all.

Willow told of a time when the fey woman and her half-human daughter came almost face-to-face, so close that as Saorla fled away toward the nearest settlement of men, she could hear her mother's voice behind her, sharp as glass, as Albha cast a spell:

"Cross the river left then right
Mortal world fades out of sight
Step into the field of time
Fall so far you cannot climb
Sorrow's pathway tread in tears
Paved with sadness, doubts and fears
At the gate of thorn entwined
Say farewell to humankind
Set your foot inside the door
You'll be mine forever more . . ."

The tale was not yet finished, but I saw Muirrin at the back of the hall beckoning to me, and I excused myself.

Mother had asked to see me. When I reached her chamber she was feeding the baby. Finbar was beating time to an inaudible tune against the pearly flesh of her breast, all the time sucking busily. I drew up a stool beside the bed, and with an effort Mother took her eyes off the child and turned them on me.

"I wanted to thank you, Clodagh. This is the first day I've felt strong enough to do much more than lie here and let Muirrin look after me, I'm afraid. It feels so wrong. When you girls were born I was up and about again within a day or two. Maybe boys are different. And I'm older, of course, as everyone keeps reminding me."

"Thank me? For what?" I was heartened, for her manner had something of its old spirit, and the waxy, wan look was almost gone from her face. Maybe, finally, I could allow the possibility of happy endings into my mind.

"For handling the household arrangements so capably while I've been indisposed. Everyone tells me how much energy you've put into keeping everything the way I like it to be. I know how much work it is. With Deirdre gone there is really nobody to share the load. Your father is deeply concerned over this trouble with the northern chieftains, although he's good at hiding how much these things worry him. It helps very much, my dear, that you have been able to spare him the need to think about domestic issues during this time. You'll make someone a fine wife when your turn comes."

"Thank you, Mother." Her words warmed me even as I thought how sad it would be if this was the best anyone would ever be able to say about me. "It's no trouble."

"Despite what you may have believed, I had noticed how tired and anxious you were becoming. You're doing a wonderful job, Clodagh. Your father and I are both proud of you."

Tears flooded my eyes. My mother did not often praise me. Her standards were high; she assumed other folk's were the same. "I'll keep trying my best," I said shakily. "He's a lovely baby, Mother. You should have seen the look in Father's eyes when he first held him. He didn't expect—I mean—"

"The gods have been kind," Mother said quietly, stroking Finbar's thatch of dark hair with her free hand as he continued to suckle. "It's more than I deserve."

"You deserve every bit of happiness, Mother," I told her. "It's going to be interesting having a little boy growing up at Sevenwaters after all of us girls. I wonder if he'll be like Coll?"

Mother's eyes went distant. "I shouldn't think so," she said, and I remembered that she had never entirely approved of Bran of Harrowfield, father of both Coll and Johnny. The question of inheritance was like a dim shadow in my mind, something that would remain there until the issue was resolved one way or the other. Maybe Finbar was only a tiny scrap right now, but nobody would be able to put aside what he might one day become.

"That's probably just as well," I said briskly. "Coll's a bright boy, but he seems to take up far more than his share of space. Now I'd best leave you to rest."

"No doubt Muirrin will be back in a moment to ply me with herbal potions. Clodagh, before you go, I've a favor to ask."

"Of course, Mother."

"Your father may have forgotten to send word to Deirdre and

Illann about Finbar's arrival. Between worrying about me and concern over the northerners, I suspect it was the last thing in his mind. I know you can convey the good news to your sister in a much quicker way. I would be pleased if you could do so. Deirdre would want to know."

The request caught me by surprise. Suggestions of treachery and betrayal came sharply back to me, as unwelcome as they'd been when first spoken, and for a moment I could not answer. I knew that, whatever the circumstances, I would no longer be able to speak with Deirdre mind to mind without feeling constant suspicion. Wretched Cathal, for planting the seed of distrust in my thoughts!

"I don't know if I can, Mother," I said. "Deirdre told me she wouldn't speak to me that way anymore, not now she's married and away from home."

"Deirdre would want to know she has a little brother, Clodagh." There was a note of reproach in Mother's voice now.

"Of course." No doubt she would, now that it seemed the gods had not required our mother's life as the price of the longed-for son. "I'll try, of course. And I'll make sure a messenger goes as well. I should have thought of it."

Mother smiled. She was looking tired now. The baby had fallen asleep at the breast. "You can't think of everything, Clodagh. Thank you for all you've done. You are a good daughter."

I lay awake that night planning what I would say, how much I would tell Deirdre and what I would hold back. I would try in the morning while I was taking my turn to sit with the baby. The quiet and solitude of the nursery should allow me to focus my thoughts on my twin and perhaps reestablish the link she had broken. If Deirdre was prepared to let me in, I would ask her how it felt to be running her own household and whether she might pay a visit to Sevenwaters now it seemed her worst fear would not be realized. If I did not offer any news save that of Finbar's birth and Mother's improving health, Cathal's stupid theory need not even be put to the test.

* * *

Finbar was asleep. He had recently been fed and now lay rolled tightly in a shawl, tucked into his basket of willow. The chamber was warm; a little fire burned on the hearth. I had scattered dried berries of rowan and juniper on the flames, for these herbs had a power to clarify the mind. It was the first time I had felt the need for such aids.

Deirdre?

She did not answer. I sat very still, concentrating all my thoughts on her. She would hear me; I had no doubt of that. When we were younger, we had been so closely in tune with each other that the least whisper in the mind had been enough to alert us to a query, a feeling, a plan to be shared. As we had grown older, each of us had learned the skill of closing that portal between our minds, slipping a shutter over it to conceal our own thoughts. One did not always want to share what was in one's mind, even with a beloved twin. I wished I had spoken to Father more about this bond, since he still used the same link with his own twin, Liadan. No doubt his sister had already heard about the birth of a son and had passed the news on to the household at Harrowfield, including my sister Maeve. Mother was right. It wasn't fair that Deirdre be kept in ignorance.

Deirdre? I have some news for you.

I could feel nothing of her; nothing at all.

Good news. Let me in, Deirdre. It's a message from Mother.

And then, abruptly, she was with me. *I told you, Clodagh! I told you I wouldn't do this—*

We have a baby brother, Deirdre. And Mother is well.

Nothing for a little, though I could sense that she was bursting with feelings, a swirl of emotions in which relief and pleasure formed only part of the picture.

This is true? I thought she hardly dared believe it.

Of course it's true! The baby came early. Everything seems to be all right. His name's Finbar. Mother asked me to tell you. I wouldn't have broken our agreement otherwise.

Another silence, then I felt her say, *Are you sure, Clodagh? This is . . . It's hard to take in. I don't know what to say.*

There were tears in my eyes. It was so good to talk to her again. *Muirrin says the baby is strong and well even though he came early.*

And Mother seems to be recovering, though she's tired. I can't predict the future, Deirdre. Even a seer can't do that accurately. But this is cause for happiness. You can forget all those terrible things you were saying before you left, about never coming back to Sevenwaters. You'll want to see baby Finbar. He's lovely. You must come and visit us. I glanced across at the basket, where all that was visible of my brother was a roll of woollen blanket with a tuft of dark hair sticking out the end.

Please tell Mother I'm very happy for her.

She seemed rather cool. Perhaps she was finding it hard to absorb the unexpected good news. *I miss you, Deirdre.*

A silence, then, *I miss you too, Clodagh. More than I ever expected.* Was she perhaps crying?

Oh, Deirdre. Is everything all right?

For a moment her presence wavered, as if she were about to withdraw beyond my reach, then she said, *Of course it's all right. Why wouldn't it be? Only it's . . . different. There's so much to do, and . . . I didn't realize how used I was to having you always there. You should come and visit me. There are lots of eligible men here. You might find a sweetheart, someone better than Aidan. He is only a younger son, after all.*

It was just as well she couldn't see my expression. *I might visit some time, but you can forget about the sweetheart. Besides, there's no shortage of young men at Sevenwaters while Johnny's here.*

He's still with you, then?

For now, anyway.

He doesn't mind about the baby being a boy? Won't that cut him out of his inheritance?

Perhaps, I told her. *But Finbar's only a baby. Johnny doesn't seem at all upset. Besides, he has other things on his mind.*

Don't tell me our cousin has finally become interested in a girl.

It's nothing to do with women. Just an issue with one of the local chieftains, you know the kind of thing. Johnny's a little edgy and so is Father. It's nothing important.

One of the chieftains? Which one?

The hair stood up on the back of my neck. I could almost hear Cathal whispering in my ear, *I told you.*

I'm not sure, I lied. *You know Father expected this. That the northern leaders might see your marriage to Illann as an affront, I mean.*

You must be able to remember which chieftain it is.

I can't, Deirdre. I really have no idea.

But you're always so interested in these things, Clodagh.

And you're not, I thought. Or weren't before. *I've been too busy to take much notice,* I told her. *Finbar's arrival has set the household upside down. I don't think it's anything to be concerned about.* I did not mention Father's furrowed brow, or the serious conversations the men seemed to be having all the time now, talk that often included the name Eoin of Lough Gall.

Really? I hate to think of Father riding out to battle with a new baby at home.

He's not riding out to battle, Deirdre. It's nothing like that, only Gareth and some other men going north with a message, that's all. My heart was thumping now. Either Cathal was right and I'd already said more than I should, or he was wrong and I would upset my sister for no good reason by refusing to answer perfectly reasonable questions. Suddenly, talking to Deirdre was like balancing along a very thin line indeed. *I have to go,* I said. *I'm supposed to be looking after Finbar and I can hear him crying.* As if to prevent me from lying, the baby stirred, making a small sleepy sound, then fell silent once more.

Oh. So he's right there with you? Where are you? Who else is there?

Deirdre, I have to go.

A little silence, then she said, *Can we do this again, Clodagh? I know what I said before, but I didn't realize how much I was going to miss you. It would make such a difference, just being able to talk to you sometimes, exchange our news, find out how everyone is . . . Can we?*

Of course, I told her, but there was a cold, tight feeling in my chest. If news was what she wanted, why hadn't she asked after a single one of our sisters? She'd questioned me over the northern chieftains, but she hadn't so much as mentioned Muirrin or Sibeal or Eilis. This was Deirdre; Deirdre who to the best of my recollection had never in her life discussed strategic matters with me. *Goodbye for now, Deirdre. I'll tell the others you sent your love.*

The moment she was gone from my head a wave of exhaustion hit me. I sank down onto the bench beside the little hearth, glad that the baby seemed to have fallen asleep again, for I did not think I could find the strength so much as to pick him up, let alone change his wrappings or carry him to my mother's chamber to be fed. A tear dribbled down my cheek. What was wrong with me? I did not feel at all like a young woman whose mother had not so long ago thanked her for being competent. I fished for a handkerchief and wiped my eyes.

Someone tapped on the door. I cursed under my breath. Company was the last thing I needed right now. Still, it was probably only Sibeal come early for her turn with Finbar. She wouldn't ask awkward questions if she found me in tears.

I opened the door and found myself face-to-face with the person I least wanted to see.

"You're crying," observed Cathal, brows up.

"Go away." I began to close the door, but he stuck out his foot and stopped me.

"Clodagh. Tell me what's wrong."

"None of your business. What are you doing up here? I'm supposed to be looking after the baby."

"You can look after him and talk to me. There's no rule against that. It would be more civilized if you invited me in so we could sit down and talk in more comfort. These doorway trysts are so awkward."

"Get your foot out of the door, Cathal."

"Tell me what's wrong and I will."

"I told you, it's none of your concern. What do you want, anyway?"

"Come out here and talk to me and then I'll go away. I promise."

"I doubt if your promises are worth much, Cathal." How could I get rid of him without attracting attention? This hallway was a thoroughfare for serving people and family alike. "All right, I'll talk, but only for a moment. I can't leave Finbar."

Cathal took a step back. I could have slammed the door in his face, but that did seem rather childish. I stepped out of the chamber to stand with one hand holding the door ajar, so I could still see the willow cradle with its small occupant drowsing in the firelight. "Why are you here?" I asked. Cathal was wearing his big cloak and his riding boots. I saw now that, despite his flippant manner, he looked pale and drawn. "What's wrong?" I added despite myself. "You seem upset."

He didn't answer. He was leaning against the wall by the door now, shoulders hunched, eyes not on me but on a patch of flagstoned floor.

"Cathal?"

"I might not see you for a while," he said. "I don't think it's wise for me to be here."

I had not expected this. "Is Johnny sending you north? Has there been news from Gareth?" The awkward conversation with Deirdre came sharply back, but I knew I was not going to discuss it with him. If it hadn't been for his disturbing theory, I would have given my twin the family's happy news and felt nothing but pleasure that Deirdre was prepared to talk to me again. It was entirely his fault that I was filled with wretched confusion. As for his leaving, I was not at all sure how I felt about that.

"Not exactly. But I don't expect to be here much longer. I know you find my presence irksome and disruptive, Clodagh. All the same, I didn't want to go without saying goodbye."

His tone chilled me. I hated the lost look in those dark eyes, which held none of their usual mischief today. "What is this?" I asked him. "You sound like you're going away forever. Isn't Johnny staying here over the summer? Is Aidan leaving too?"

He attempted a smile; it was a sad wraith of a thing. "Not him, just me. I suppose you will be glad to see the back of me."

I did not dismiss this as a bid for sympathy as I might once have done. "I have mixed views on the matter," I said, wondering why I couldn't put together the pieces of this and make sense of it. "Besides, you'll come back, won't you? Johnny's here almost every year. I will see you again some time."

The forlorn smile appeared once more. Willow's Wolf-child story came sharply back to me and my heart twisted. What was this? I didn't even like the man. Why did I feel the urge to give him a reassuring hug and tell him everything would be all right?

"Doubtful," Cathal said. "Now you'd best get back to that baby. Good practice for when you have one or two of your own. Goodbye, Clodagh," and he leaned across and kissed me. For a moment I was too taken aback to move, and for another I allowed myself to enjoy the pressure of his lips on mine, a sweet, intense feeling that made my whole body spring to life in an utterly surprising way. When his hand came up to touch my neck I had to force myself not to nestle closer and slip my arms around him. Instead I pushed him away, shocked at my response and appalled that I had allowed such familiarity here in the family quarters of the house. I shouldn't even have let Cathal linger outside the door.

"Stop it!" I hissed. "This is madness! Just go, will you?"

Cathal's eyes met mine, and there was not the least trace of mockery in them. He turned on his heel, his cloak swirling around him, and I saw a curious sight: across the lining of his garment were scattered many small items, sewn there in the manner of charms placed for protection, as with the rowan cross of the clurichaun story. There was a cross in Cathal's cloak, certainly. There was also a feather, a snippet of bright silken cloth and something made of green glass. There were more tiny trinkets, but I had no time to identify them, for in a heartbeat he was gone, shadow swift and completely silent. I caught a movement further along the hallway. My mother's maid, Eithne, was standing there staring at us, a pile of folded cloths in her arms. She met my gaze, then scurried into Mother's chamber. I was in no doubt that she had seen the whole interchange, kiss and all.

Now I was really crying, with no good reason for it. I retreated into the nursery chamber and shut the door, then sat down on the floor by the hearth with my arms around my knees. There was some comfort in the small glow of the fire. By the time Sibeal came I would be calm again if I worked at it. Chances were I would go downstairs later and find that Cathal had simply been playing games again. I should put him right out of my mind; I should not let him upset me so. Why on earth had he come up to see me? And what had that kiss been all about, that tender, frightening, completely inappropriate kiss? How dare Cathal sneak under my defenses at the same time as saying, more or less, goodbye forever? The thought that he was going away gave me a strange hollow feeling inside, and that was completely wrong. I should, as he had pointed out, be glad to see the back of him.

I sat there staring into the flames, breathing the faint scent of the herbs I had strewn earlier and trying to make sense of the utterly inscrutable. Cathal, Deirdre, Johnny, Father . . . There was too much to think about, and it was all too easy to give in to feeling sorry for myself. I should be happy Cathal was going. I should be pleased Aidan was staying. I must get a grip on myself.

Finbar stirred, making his basket creak, and I realized I had been lost in my thoughts for some while. It must be well past time for the baby's next feed. I must take him in to Mother and hope she did not notice my red eyes. What if Eithne was there and had already mentioned she'd seen me behaving as if I didn't know what decorum was?

Finbar made a little sound. My whole body stiffened in alarm. His voice was different; wrong. It was not the cry of a healthy, hungry baby but a curious, painful rasp. No normal child made a sound like that. Finbar must be sick. He was choking, he couldn't breathe . . . I sprang up and hastened to the basket, my heart racing. I looked down, an image of my baby brother still fresh in my mind—the delicate fingers, the soft eyelids, the peachy skin and rosebud mouth. My heart gave a single wild thump and was still. Now I was cold all over. Finbar was gone. All that lay in his little bed was a curious jumble of sticks and stones, leaves and moss.

The baby couldn't be far away. *Breathe,* I ordered myself, forcing down panic. He couldn't even be out of the room, because he'd been in the basket, I'd seen him with my own eyes, and I'd never gone further than the doorway. I'd had Finbar in sight the whole time, even when I stepped outside the door. I'd made sure of it. Except . . . except for a moment or two, when my attention was on Cathal. Except for when he kissed me. Even then, nobody could have walked past me unseen—I'd been right by the doorway. My brother must be here. He must be.

I began a frantic hunt, knowing all the time that there was nowhere in the chamber that a baby could be successfully hidden for more than a moment. Under the pile of towels. Behind the bench. In the alcove. Nothing. My heart was pounding. My skin was clammy with terror. How could this be? How could he be gone? I'd hardly taken my eyes off him. *This must be a bad dream. Let me wake up now, please, please.* It was only after I had spent what seemed an age scrabbling about looking in every corner that I remembered the sound I had heard from the basket. Sticks and stones do not cry out. Maybe the whole thing had been a delusion. Perhaps the Fair Folk had sent me a malign vision of some kind. I made myself take two deep breaths, then approached the basket again.

The little pile of sticks and stones still lay there on the pale linen of the under-blanket. No vision, then. My heart dropped down, leaden again. Finbar was gone. I must call for help, I must tell them . . .

The sound began once more, a plaintive, scratchy crying like a mockery of a baby's voice. And the sticks and stones were . . . They were . . . My gorge rose. I made myself go on looking, and saw mossy lids opening over pebble eyes, a little mouth shaped from twigs stretching to reveal brown, barky gums, a pair of hands with skinny sticks for fingers reaching up toward me as if begging for the comfort of my embrace. The thing was crying; it was hungry. It kicked the blankets away—my baby brother's soft blankets—to show its form as that of a newborn infant, but bizarrely made of the debris of the forest, here a stick of rowan, there a brown leaf, here a crust of moss, there a polished stone in mottled black and white. Its head was covered, not with thick fine hair like Finbar's, but with a random patching of what looked like the breast feathers of a crow. Its voice was crowlike, too, rasping a louder and louder demand for attention. I pinched myself on the arm, hard, but all that happened was an escalation of the squawking cries. I was awake, and it was true. Someone had taken my brother, the long-desired son of Sevenwaters, my mother's gift from the gods, and in his place had left us the ugliest changeling in the world.

CHAPTER 6

I locked the little chamber behind me and ran downstairs. Father was in the hall with Johnny and Aidan. The moment they caught sight of me the three of them fell silent.

"Father, something terrible has happened. It's Finbar. He's . . . he's been taken." I saw him flinch as if struck. He got up, his face ashen. I made myself go on. "Switched. I don't know how it happened, I was there the whole time, but—"

He was already racing up the stairs. I picked up my skirts and ran after him. "Father, wait! I need to tell you . . . Father, there's a . . . a sort of changeling in the cradle . . ."

He wasn't listening. We passed the closed doorway to Mother's chamber. When we reached the nursery, my hands were shaking so hard that Father grabbed the keys from me and unlocked the door himself.

The signs of my futile, frantic search were everywhere, cloths strewn over the floor, stools upturned, vessels on their sides. Father strode to the cradle, lifted away the blanket, took one look at what lay there and turned to seize me by the shoulders, so hard it hurt. "What happened? Tell me quickly!"

By now Johnny was in the doorway with Aidan behind him. The scratchy sobs of the sticks-and-stones baby filled the chamber.

"I only took my eyes off him for a moment, Father, only a moment. I never went further than the doorway. But when I next looked at him, he was gone and the changeling was there in his place. I don't know how it could have happened."

"How long ago?" Father had clamped a mask of control over his features, but his voice was only marginally steadier than mine. His hands bit into my shoulders.

"Just now, Father, only a few moments ago. I looked everywhere in this chamber and then I came straight to fetch you."

"Start a search," Father said, letting me go abruptly and turning to Johnny. "One group inside, upstairs first, then through the whole house. A second group outside, fanning out toward the forest in all directions. Gods, why didn't I consider the possibility of abduction?"

Johnny and Aidan were gone almost before he finished speaking. I heard my cousin issuing crisp orders as he descended the stairs. There was a sound of people running.

"Are you telling me someone removed the baby while you were here?" Father asked. "How could that be?"

"Father, I don't think this is an abduction—I mean, not a political one. No ordinary person could have got in without my seeing them. I was only outside the door for a moment. It must be the work of uncanny folk. I mean, what about the—the little creature, the changeling—" The willow basket was creaking as its occupant thrashed about, screaming for attention. I could hardly hear my own voice above the din. My father stepped over to the cradle again, looking down at the thing that had taken his son's place.

"A cruel travesty," he said. "A superficial likeness of a child, but it's no more than a bundle of sticks and stones, Clodagh."

"But . . ." I stared at him, not understanding. The changeling was shrieking. It was waving its arms frantically, desperate for a response to its cries of woe. Surely I wasn't the only one who could hear it?

"You stepped outside the door," Father said flatly. "You left Finbar alone. Why?"

I wanted to curl up small and hide. I wanted to shrink down

into a little ball and roll away into a corner where nobody could find me. My insides had turned into a quivering jelly. "I was just there, in the doorway," I croaked. "Right there. Talking to Cathal. I came straight back in. Father, nobody could have walked past me. They'd have had to be invisible. Father, can't you hear the child crying?"

"You can hear him? Finbar?" A sudden hope dawned on his face.

"No," I said, confused and wretched, "the changeling, the sticks-and-stones baby—Father, I can see it moving, I can hear it screaming. Father, this must be the work of the Fair Folk, you remember what Willow said about them becoming different—"

He turned a certain gaze on me. It was the kind of look he might have used on a rival chieftain daring to challenge his authority. My father had never, ever looked at me that way before.

"You're overwrought," he said. "I hear nothing. That is no changeling. It is nothing but a cruel trick."

"But—" The cries were ear-piercing. Why couldn't he hear?

"I won't hear any more of this, Clodagh. Take a few deep breaths and compose yourself." Father's tone was sufficient to silence further protests. "This chamber is to remain locked. You'll keep the key on your person. Nobody's to come in or out. I'll call the household together later, when Johnny reports back. Are you sure"—his voice cracked—"are you quite sure you saw nobody else up here? No serving folk, no man-at-arms, nobody?"

"Eithne came out of Mother's chamber while I was in the doorway, and Cathal was up here for a few moments, but there was nobody else."

"Your mother must be told." His voice was almost detached now, as if he were putting his own grief and shock away inside somewhere in order to act as a chieftain must. "I don't suppose there's any point in delaying it. Come, Clodagh."

The changeling's throaty cries lanced through me as I followed my father into the hallway. The sound made my chest hurt. Father waited while I locked the door on the creature. Then we went to break my mother's heart.

* * *

Some time later, I stood before my father in the small council chamber, my stomach tying itself into knots of grief and anxiety. Finbar had not been found in the house, or in the courtyard or outbuildings, or anywhere nearby in the forest. There were no marks of feet or hooves or wheels; whoever had taken the baby had left no trail to follow. Johnny was organizing a wide search, using every man-at-arms who could be spared.

I should have been out there calming the children and making sure the ordinary business of the household continued despite the crisis. But my usual duties seemed to have been taken out of my hands as if, now that I had allowed my brother to be kidnapped, I could no longer be trusted with anything at all. To make matters worse, Father had Aidan in the chamber with us, presumably as a guard. What did he imagine, that his own daughter was somehow a danger to him now? His eyes, fixed on me, were bleak and distant. In his head, I thought, there must be endlessly playing the same sound that filled my own thoughts: my mother's wrenching wail when we told her. Afterward, her face had seemed little and shrunken, like that of a dead creature.

I had told Father everything again, step by step: I had been in the chamber, Cathal had come to the door, I had spoken to him briefly but had kept an eye on the cradle. I had gone back in, sat down for a while, then when I had checked on Finbar, he was gone. I tried once more to explain why this could not be a political abduction, but my father, a tolerant, reasonable man, was completely deaf on this particular point. Worse than that, he seemed to construe my attempts to explain as meaning either that I had temporarily lost my wits, or that I was using the Fair Folk as an excuse for my own negligence. What possible reason could the Tuatha De have to abduct a newborn son of Sevenwaters, he asked. Our family had been custodians and protectors of the forest since ancient times; it was a refuge for the Fair Folk. Why would they wish us ill? Besides, it was clear the changeling existed only in my mind—neither Father himself, nor Johnny, nor Aidan had perceived it as more than a crude wooden manikin. When I protested again, he cut me off short, for I was wasting precious time. With every moment that passed, one of his political rivals was taking Finbar further from home.

The interrogation continued. "Why would Cathal come to see you?" Father asked.

"He came to tell me he was going away somewhere. To say goodbye."

"Going where?"

"I don't know, Father. He didn't say."

"Aidan?" Father asked, glancing over his shoulder.

"I know nothing about this, Lord Sean. Johnny had given us no orders to ride out." Aidan was pointedly not looking at me. His expression was grim.

"He seemed to think he would be leaving soon and not returning to Sevenwaters," I said. "I don't imagine he would have come upstairs unless he thought it was important."

"Why you especially?" Father asked, suspicion evident in his tone.

"I don't know, Father." I stared at the floor.

"Has it not occurred to you, Clodagh," Father said, "that the timing is a strange coincidence? Cathal decides to come upstairs, right into the family quarters, apparently to speak specifically to you when you are watching over my son. At that precise moment the baby is taken."

His tone was perfectly steady. I knew how much that must be costing him. I wanted to tell him, *Let go, weep, rage, throw things. Being a chieftain does not require you to be more than human*. But I did not say it. My mother was barely holding onto her sanity. Finbar was out there somewhere, a tiny infant in the vastness of the forest. If my father could be strong, so must I be.

"Why wouldn't I believe that the distraction offered by Cathal provided someone with a perfect opportunity to snatch my son?" Father demanded. "If this isn't a conspiracy devised by one of the northern chieftains, what in the name of the gods is it?"

"My lord!" Aidan protested. "What are you suggesting?"

"I'm suggesting nothing," Father said. "My son's been taken. I must look at all the possibilities, however distressing they may be to you or to anyone else. You think it's easy for me to interrogate my own daughter?" He checked himself, clearly regretting that he had spoken so freely, and arranged his features in an expression that simulated calm.

I hated this; I hated every cruel moment of it. "Ask Cathal," I said. "He will tell you he simply came to say goodbye. Father, I'm not lying to you."

"Then explain this." Father rose to his feet, his hands on the table. His skin had a grayish tinge and his eyes were those of an old man. "Eithne saw you and Cathal in the upper hallway at the time you mention. Not merely passing the time of day, not engaged in casual conversation, not making a courteous farewell. The two of you were locked in an embrace. A passionate embrace, that was the way she put it. If this is true, and your blush indicates it must be, then how can you possibly maintain you were watching your brother?"

I said nothing. Aidan gazed at the opposite wall. He, too, was working hard to remain calm, but I could see the fury he was suppressing, the same fury that had blazed in his eyes when he held his knife to Cathal's throat.

"Answer me, Clodagh," said Father. "We have no time to waste."

"Yes, Cathal kissed me. No, I didn't invite him to do so—I was so taken aback I took a few moments to extricate myself. But it wasn't a passionate embrace, Father; there is nothing like that between Cathal and me. Eithne is mistaken. It was a . . . a friendly goodbye kiss, that was all. And it was only a moment. I told you before, nobody could have got past without my seeing them."

"But someone did," Father said. "Aidan, fetch Cathal here now. Johnny would be shocked at the notion that one of his trusted men might be somehow implicated in this, but we must hear what Cathal has to say, if only to rule out that possibility. Let us get to the bottom of this."

Cathal could not be brought to account, for he was nowhere to be found. An investigation of his quarters revealed not only that he was missing, but that he had taken his pack and belongings with him. His horse was still in the stables. Apart from his cryptic conversation with me, he had not left word with anyone. Despite the presence of guards all around the keep, nobody had seen him go.

Meanwhile, I found that decisions were being made without

my being consulted at all. Muirrin had asked that Coll and Eilis move to the part of the keep that housed those men-at-arms who had wives and children, to be watched over by Doran and Nuala while Mother was dealing with the initial shock of the baby's disappearance. Having seen Mother earlier, I recognized that this was a sensible idea, but I should have been the one to arrange it, and they should have waited until I could talk to the children, reassure them, let them ask their questions. As it was, when Father finally let me go back upstairs, it was to find that Sibeal had already taken the younger ones over to Doran's quarters and would stay there to help them settle in tonight. Muirrin came out of Mother's room to tell me this, and to say, not unkindly, that Mother did not want to see me or indeed anyone other than Father, Eithne, and Muirrin herself. There would be hard times ahead if Finbar was not found soon.

"Don't look like that, Clodagh," Muirrin said. She'd been crying; her eyes were puffy and red.

"I can't help it," I whispered, close to tears again myself. "They think it's my fault, Father, Mother, everyone. Nobody trusts me anymore. I was watching him the whole time, apart from just an instant." I did not put my worst fear into words. Father had suggested I was losing my wits. Maybe it was true.

"They don't really blame you," Muirrin said. "They're too shocked to think clearly. Later on they'll realize it couldn't have been your fault, but right now they're too hurt to be rational about it. You must let this wash over you, Clodagh. Just keep up your normal routine and take one day at a time. That's all we can do."

"I can't even do that," I said. "Nobody seems to want me for anything anymore."

"I expect the household can function reasonably well without you. You're just used to doing things Mother's way, which means supervising absolutely everything."

"But Eilis and Coll—I didn't even see them before they were whisked away—"

"Father thinks you're too disturbed by what's happened to perform your usual duties," Muirrin said. "It's actually better to let Sibeal cope with the younger ones, under the circumstances."

"He thinks I'm imagining things," I muttered. "But I'm not. I'm not going mad, I can't be. What's in there is no bundle of sticks and stones, it's a little person with arms and legs and a voice. Maybe some people can't see it, but that doesn't mean it isn't there." I met my sister's gaze. "Will you come and look at it, Muirrin?" I asked. "Father won't believe it's a changeling, and if he can't see that, he won't search in the right places, and he'll never find Finbar."

Muirrin's lips tightened. "Father said the nursery was to be kept locked up," she said. "Mother wanted to go and look. He told her he'd ordered the place closed until he decides what to do."

"I have the keys," I said quietly. "Please, Muirrin. It will only take a moment."

In silence, she followed me along the passageway and waited while I unlocked the nursery door. There was no sound from inside. I took a deep breath. Perhaps the sticks-and-stones baby really had been conjured from my imagination and my shock at Finbar's sudden disappearance. The cradle was not creaking and jerking now, but completely still. We walked over and looked in.

The blanket had been kicked aside again, but the changeling was not thrashing about. It was sleeping, curled up with a twiggy thumb in its mouth. Its mossy cheeks seemed more hollow than before, its eye sockets more shadowed. I was seized with an urge to bend down, wrap the blanket around the little creature and scoop it up in my arms. I made myself stand still as Muirrin bent over, looking carefully.

"I . . ." She hesitated.

"What?" I said, knowing from her tone what was coming.

"It's a clever copy of a child's form," Muirrin said, "but not real, Clodagh. Not even real in an uncanny, eldritch way. If you tried to pick it up, it would fall apart into twigs and leaves. What a cruel trick! Why on earth would someone go to such lengths? Imagine if Mother had seen this! You must make sure the door stays locked. We can't risk her coming in here, and she will if she gets a chance; she can't really believe that Finbar's gone. I've had to put Orlagh on door duty so she can't go out on her own." She looked at me sharply. "You still think it's real, don't you? Clodagh, you're deluding yourself. Look, this is just a bundle of bits and pieces." She reached down and took a sliver from the changeling's leg, a slip of birch bark the length of my little finger. "See?" she asked, and moved to throw the fragment onto the dying fire.

"No!" I shouted, snatching it from her hand. Whether in response to my cry or to the wound it had suffered, the changeling's pebble eyes snapped open, its limbs twitched, and it began a harsh wailing. "You're hurting it!" I put the slip of bark back as close as I could to the place it had come from. The cries were escalating. I rolled the blanket around the tiny creature so it was swathed tight; its whole body was vibrating, making the cradle shiver. I patted its back rhythmically, longing to pick the child up and comfort it but not prepared to take that step while my sister was watching me.

"Leave it, Clodagh!" Muirrin's sharp order was like a blow. For her to speak to me in that tone was a first; one of many for today. I took my hand off the child and backed away from the little bed. "Come out now, and lock the door behind you," my sister added.

As I retreated to the door the tone of the crying changed, becoming so woeful it made my heart ache. The compulsion to take the infant from its cradle and hold it was so strong I had to force myself to walk out of the chamber. How could I let something so small and helpless be abandoned to the dark and chill and loneliness of that room at night? And what about food? How long could a newborn infant survive without nourishment? Perversely, it seemed to me that those who had taken Finbar would at the very least be making sure he got milk. When the Fair Folk abducted human children it was not generally to harm them, but to raise them as their own. They would steal human women to use as wet nurses. If they had left one of their own infants in my brother's place, wasn't it important for us to provide for that child if we wanted Finbar to be well treated?

"You don't believe me," I said as I turned the key in the lock. Once the door was closed I could not hear the forlorn sobbing. But in my head it still went on. *Touch me! Feed me! Love me!*

"I don't know what to believe," said Muirrin slowly. "I know you believe in what you're seeing, Clodagh. I know you wouldn't make it up, not even if it was to cover something improper. Yes, I heard about Cathal. Eithne made sure of that by announcing to all and sundry that she'd seen the two of you behaving like lovers. But I can't view that bundle of rubbish as a child. Father's going to send for Conor. He could be here in a day or so. As a druid, surely he will be able to tell us what the sticks and stones really mean and what we should do with them."

Not if the Fair Folk have decided I'm the only one who'll be allowed to see the changeling properly, I thought. "Yes, I suppose that is sensible," I murmured. As Muirrin returned to Mother's quarters, I went off to my own chamber, where I sat on my bed and cried.

The day of Finbar's disappearance there was no formal supper at Sevenwaters. The search continued until the light faded and made hunting in the forest impossible. Men rode in and out at various odd hours. The kitchen people fed them with little need for my intervention. Muirrin's blunt assessment had been right. I, who had thought myself such an indispensable part of this household, was not really needed at all.

It didn't matter about supper, since I had no appetite. Nonetheless, I did go down to the kitchen, just to make sure the folk who had remained on duty took a little time for their own rest and refreshment. While I was there I filled a small jug with today's fresh milk and took it back to my chamber under a cloth.

I sat there waiting for a long time, long enough to be fairly sure our serving folk would all be abed. Father would be awake somewhere, just as I was, worrying, planning, asking himself whether there was anything he could have done to prevent this disaster from overtaking his household. Perhaps Johnny would be with him. Muirrin would have given Mother a sleeping draft. I was unlikely to encounter anyone on the short walk from my chamber to the nursery and back again. I prepared an excuse, just in case—that I had lost a favorite shawl and thought I might have left it in that chamber.

Candle and key in one hand, jug in the other, I crept along the hallway, where a single lamp burned to illuminate the darkness. The key turned soundlessly in the lock thanks to the oil I had applied earlier. The sound assaulted my ears the moment I opened the door: gulping, gasping, more desperate than before, but also weaker. The changeling was fading. If I did not act now, it might be dead by morning.

My grandfather, my father's father, had known all about looking after plants and creatures. He'd saved many a newborn calf or lamb that another farmer would have abandoned as too weak to be worth the bother. I'd learned a lot at Grandfather's knee, and it seemed to me that what would work for a lamb would work for a baby just as well. I set the jug on a little table. Finbar's things were scattered around the floor after my frantic search earlier. I retrieved a square of fine muslin and set it by the jug, with one corner dipped into the milk. I went to the cradle and picked up the changeling.

He was very light, far lighter than the warm, solid form of my baby brother. His little twiggy mouth was wide open, the cries pitifully scratchy. As I held him against me he began a frantic scrabbling, his hand gripping a fold of my nightrobe, his head turning against my body, his strange mouth open as if to seek his mother's breast. The tone of his cries changed as I moved to sit by the table, murmuring to him all the while, "There, there. It's all right, I'll look after you."

I held him against me with one arm while I moved the milk-soaked corner of the cloth to his mouth. It was awkward; holding him was not at all like holding Finbar, who had generally been a warm, relaxed bundle with no apparent wish to fight me. The changeling was almost frenzied. I squeezed a few drops of milk between his lips, praying that he would drink.

He sucked; he swallowed. A blissful silence spread across the chamber, and I allowed myself to breathe. I dipped the cloth again, my mind racing ahead to work out ways of escaping the notice of my family, Muirrin in particular. If I could get in here a few times a day, I could keep him alive until I managed to convince someone he was real.

A hideous choking sound came from the changeling's lips. His back arched violently and I nearly dropped him. "Hush, hush, what's the matter?" His eyes were squeezed tightly shut, his mouth was gaping, his body was possessed by shuddering spasms. "Oh, gods, what's wrong? What did I do?"

Acting on instinct, I put the baby up against my shoulder. A moment later he was sick, the small amount of milk he had taken spewed out violently onto my nightrobe and the floor beneath my chair. The changeling gasped and hiccupped, then, after a brief silence, began to cry again, a feverish, starving cry: *Feed me!*

I would not try the milk again. Human babies thrived on it, but it seemed that uncanny ones did not. Holding the child in my arms, pacing up and down the short length of the nursery chamber, I whispered my thoughts to him, hoping my voice would help calm him. "I wish Deirdre was here. It wouldn't matter if she didn't believe me; I just want her to listen. We always listen to each other. I want to tell her everything, but I can't mind-call, not now. There's what Cathal said about her, and the odd questions she asked when I talked to her yesterday. Everything's changed. Everything's turned upside down and I hate it. I hate that look of judgment on Father's face. I hate not being able to feed you, you poor little thing. What is it you need? What can I give you?"

The changeling's cries eventually dwindled to an exhausted whimpering. I sat down again and let the infant suck the end of my little finger—I had seen Nuala using this trick to pacify one of her babes and thought it worth trying. The changeling's lips were not soft and damp like those of a human infant, but dry and brittle. My finger hurt. I let the baby suck on, since he seemed to derive some comfort from it.

"You need a name," I told him. "You should have a handsome, fine one, a name that shows you deserve the love any baby gets, even if you look a little . . . unusual." I considered the patchy black hair, the greenish hue to the cheeks and brow, the barky, leafy, twiggy body. I wondered if I should try to dress the little creature—did changelings get cold? The fire was out now, and the chamber was far too chilly for a human child to thrive in. It would feel wrong to put him in Finbar's clothes.

The candle I had carried here illuminated the ashes on the hearth, the hangings stirring in the draft. To stay in the nursery all night would be to take an unacceptable risk of discovery, though there was a pallet in the corner where Finbar's nursemaid had slept. If I did not want the baby to freeze to death, I was going to have to take him to my own chamber. My heart sank. How long could I keep him hidden there, even supposing I worked out how to feed him? This was crazy; it could only end in sorrow.

The baby released my finger and turned his head toward my breast. I felt his awkward form, all hard lines and angles, relax against me with a shuddering sigh. "I'm going to call you Becan," I murmured. "That has a strong sound to it. It's a survivor's name." It was not possible to tell if the changeling was a boy or a girl, but as he had been substituted for my brother, I assumed he was male. "Sleep now, little one. Sweet dreams." I hummed an old lullaby I half remembered, and saw the shadowy lids gradually drop down over the pebble eyes. Safe in my arms, Becan slept.

When I judged that he was deep enough in slumber not to wake awhile, I slipped out of the nursery and carried him along the hallway to my bedchamber. I had to leave him there, nestled between two cushions, while I returned to the nursery to fetch my candle, jug and cloth, and to make sure the door was securely locked. Back in my own room, I set up a makeshift hiding place behind my storage chest, lining the area with a blanket and setting the cushions at either end. It would not serve for long. A maidservant would come in, or one of my sisters, and the secret would be out straightaway. Besides, if I could not feed Becan he would not survive long. By the time he woke again I must have something else ready to try.

I lay on my bed, wide awake, my mind full of the shocks, confusions and sorrows of the day's events: my baby brother, so tiny and new, out there in the forest somewhere with none of his own people to comfort him; Mother with that dead look on her face, her joy wiped away in an instant; Father cold and severe, as if I'd suddenly turned into a different person, one he neither liked nor trusted. And Cathal. He was the most puzzling element in all of this. Earlier it had seemed as if Father was accusing him of being party to my brother's abduction in some way. I hadn't been mistaken in that; Aidan had heard it too, but Father had cut off his protest. Could it be true? Could Johnny, whose ability to assess a man's true quality was almost legendary, have been harboring a traitor in his band?

It was easy enough to believe that Cathal's kiss had nothing to do with a sudden surge of feeling for me, but was part of some kind of plot. He had made his dislike of me quite clear since our first encounter. He had been marginally friendlier lately, but nothing beyond that. I recalled Aidan's words after that fight: *He wants you for himself*. But that was nonsense. If Cathal liked me, he wouldn't keep reminding me of my faults. A man like him would not be too shy to declare himself. Perhaps that kiss, which I had enjoyed more than I should have, had indeed been contrived as a distraction. But even then, I knew nobody could have slipped past in the time it had taken. No human, anyway.

Where was Cathal now? Why had he disappeared in precisely the circumstances that would indicate guilt? He was too subtle a man, surely, to draw attention to himself in such a way. Perhaps he would be back in the morning, having been on some perfectly legitimate business, and it would turn out he had nothing to do with all this. I found myself hoping he would return and provide a good account of himself. I didn't like the man, I didn't trust him, but I didn't want him to be a spy or a kidnapper either. I tried to banish from my mind the shadowy figure that might or might not have been there that night in the courtyard, the odd disappearance on the way up to the Pudding Bowl, the inscrutable warnings he had given me. It was too hard; I could not put it together in any sensible way.

Becan was very quiet. Was he still breathing? Once, twice, a dozen times I got up from the bed and crouched down to check on him, reassured only when I heard the slight snuffling of his breath and saw the little chest rise and fall under the shawl I had put around him. Poor thing; he'd been as cruelly wrenched from his true home as Finbar had. I loved my brother. I wanted him to be safely back at Sevenwaters and for my world to be at rights. But this sorry course of events had not one, but two babies in it. Why had I been singled out as the only person to see that?

Before dawn I slept a little and dreamed I was out in the forest, pursued by monsters that looked like trees. Baby Finbar lay all alone in a deep cave, with shadowy figures keeping a vigil around him. I had to reach him before he died of cold, but the trees stuck out their roots and tripped me, they tangled my hair in their branches; a strange wind howled through their leaves, like the cry of a starving infant . . . I woke in a cold sweat, my pillow soaked with tears. Outside my narrow window the sky was washed with the first light of dawn, and from the courtyard below came the sound of hooves on the flagstones. A rider, so early. A messenger arriving with news? Perhaps Finbar had been found safe and well. Perhaps he had been found lying in a cave, cold and dead because nobody had got there in time. Shivering, I rose and splashed my face in the bowl of chill water that stood in the alcove. Water, I thought suddenly. Trees, plants . . . Perhaps a baby made of all manner of forest materials did not need milk at all, but something far simpler.

Folk were accustomed to seeing me in the kitchen early, since I was the one who generally saw to it that the baking was underway and the clearing and setting of fires being attended to. I observed that without my supervision the day's domestic activities were unfolding precisely as they should. All I did this morning was refill my water jug and help myself, surreptitiously, to a small crock of honey. I glanced into the hall, saw no sign of activity, and fled back upstairs. Perhaps that rider had not been a messenger after all.

The sound hit me as soon as I opened my chamber door. The changeling had flung off the swathing shawl. His limbs were flailing, his eyes were screwed shut and he was crying in jerky sobs interspersed with gasping breaths. Setting down my jug and jar I hastened to gather him up, to wrap the shawl around his twiggy form, to reassure him. "There, there . . . Hush, sweetheart, I'm here now . . ." His small body was rigid with distress; he seemed beyond comforting. I had not been gone long, but he had woken alone and starving. I could feel his terror in my own body.

I put him against my shoulder and managed to get the stopper off the honey jar. I tipped a few drops into the water jug. I found a cloth. The baby raged and sobbed against me. Right now, it was just as well I was the only one who could hear him. "Hush, little one," I murmured. "I need you to help me. Be calm now."

I sat on the bed, cradling him in one arm, and dipped the cloth into the bowl. I squeezed a drop or two into his gaping mouth. "Just a bit," I murmured. "Slowly does it." *Please don't be sick,* I begged. *Please, please be able to drink this.*

He drank, choked, drank again. He was sobbing so violently he could not really swallow. I lifted him, held him against my shoulder once more, sang a verse of the lullaby. *"Oo-roo, little dove, stars are twinkling high above, owls are gliding, shadow-gray, time to bid farewell to day."*

The sobs were dying down. He nuzzled my shoulder, turning

his head from side to side. When I tried the honey water again, he drank more thirstily and did not choke. He sucked hard at the soaked cloth; he was swallowing the mixture as quickly as I could gather it up. When I paused to add more honey he squalled in protest. "Hush, hush," I murmured. "Just wait a little." As I began to feed him again his eyes softened, then closed in contentment. I was hard put not to burst into exhausted tears. After all, I would not have to watch him starve.

The jug was empty; Becan had drunk it dry. I sat on the edge of my bed with him cradled in my arms. His little scratchy hand emerged from the shawl to scrabble at, then claw into, the fabric of my gown. He turned his strange head against my breast. I hummed quietly, watching as he fell gradually asleep.

"You're safe, little one," I murmured. "Now what in the name of the gods am I going to do with you?"

When Becan was settled on the cushions once more, I made my way back downstairs. I wanted to stay with him, to watch over him, and to spend time working out a plan of action. The baby couldn't stay in my chamber undetected for long. Since everyone thought he was only some kind of manikin, it was all too easy to guess what might happen to him if he were found there, or if Father went back into the nursery and discovered him gone. He'd be sure to do that when Conor arrived, and he'd suspect me immediately. That gave me a day, at best, to find a solution.

Sticking to my normal routine, as far as I could, seemed a good idea. I'd have to go upstairs to feed the baby quite often, but in between I would be least obtrusive if I went through my usual daily tasks.

By the time I reached the hall an early breakfast of sorts had been set out for those who needed it. Father was in there, fully dressed and looking as if he hadn't slept at all. He gave me a sharp nod, saying nothing. His jaw was set tight. I did not feel I could offer an embrace or words of reassurance. After yesterday, I did not think I could be a proper daughter to him ever again.

Johnny came in with Aidan behind him. "A man's arrived from the north," he said. "He has a message from Gareth." He glanced from Father to me. "We need his news straightaway."

"Of course," Father said, not even looking at me. "Clodagh, ask the serving people to stay out until we've heard this messenger." His tone was curt, clipped; I heard in it that he had been hoping beyond hope for good tidings of Finbar.

Then, at last, there was some positive news. Gareth had met with Eoin of Lough Gall. Although the northern chieftain had not been well pleased about Deirdre's marriage to Illann, he had said he would give serious consideration to the matter of a council, and had offered Gareth's party the hospitality of his house for two nights. They were to ride from there to Eoin's nearest neighbor, and then continue their round of diplomatic visits.

Father thanked the messenger, and Johnny took him off for some rest and refreshment, leaving Father, Aidan and me standing in awkward silence in the middle of the big chamber. I could not bring myself to state the obvious: that if Eoin of Lough Gall had responded in such a civil fashion to Gareth's message, he surely couldn't be responsible for the abduction of Finbar. There were other northern chieftains, of course. But shouldn't the news make Father give fresh consideration to my theory? He was looking so forbidding that all I asked was, "How is Mother this morning?"

"Not herself." His voice was flat. "Muirrin's sleeping drafts have not been effective. We must widen the search today. If we don't find him soon, I fear . . ." The words trailed off.

I understood him perfectly. I had seen that wretched face peering at me from the pillow yesterday, not my mother's sweet features but those of a death's-head. If Finbar was not found safe and well, and soon, she would indeed slip away from us. There had to be some way of putting this right. But I couldn't say anything. To do so was to risk Becan's life. It was not just that he was little and frail and in need of nurture. Somewhere deep inside me I felt a growing conviction that his survival was tied up with Finbar's; that if we let the changeling die, my parents would never again see their only son.

"Lord Sean," Aidan said, "you spoke yesterday of Cathal and of a conspiracy. I feel I must speak up. I know Cathal would not do anything such as you suspect. He may be abrasive at times, but he is faultlessly loyal. He admires Johnny above any man. To be one of the Inis Eala warriors was a dream come true for him, especially as his origins are quite humble. Whatever it may look like, I am absolutely certain he had nothing to do with . . ."

"With my son's abduction?" Father's eyes were chill. "You cannot know this, Aidan. Your bond of loyalty with Cathal is strong, and no wonder, since you were childhood friends. But children grow into men, and men have causes for dispute that children do not. Matters of birth and blood." He glanced in my direction. "Rivalries over women."

"There's no real evidence for any accusations against Cathal, and I don't wish to hear them made without it." Johnny had come back into the hall. His tone was level, but I heard in its iron strength the quality that made men worship him as a leader. "He is gone without explanation, that is true, but this is not the first time that has occurred. There's always a good reason, some of them surprising, all of them providing a sound basis for independent action. If I see a need to discipline Cathal I will do so when he returns. It would be a mistake to leap to conclusions about this. I know the man. So does Aidan."

"My son is missing," said Father simply. "Cathal diverted Clodagh's attention at the precise moment when someone snatched him. That, coupled with his abrupt departure without explanation, seems sufficient evidence for suspicion. You expect me to sit back if any path toward finding Finbar is unexplored?"

It was the closest I had ever seen the two of them to an argument, and it made me deeply uneasy. It seemed to me that Finbar's abduction had sent a widening circle of wrongness through our whole household. What was this? Were the Fair Folk playing a particularly dark game with us, or had their plot somehow got mixed up with the plans of one of Father's worldly enemies? I thought of Willow's tales, and the way she'd looked at me when she told them, as if I should be able to get some particular wisdom from them. Were the tales and the changeling parts of the same mystery? Why couldn't I make sense of this?

"I'm sorry, Sean," Johnny said. "Of course I don't, and I will help you all I can to find your son. But my men are my responsibility, and I don't like to hear their integrity questioned without solid evidence. It's very likely Cathal's presence outside the nursery at that particular time was coincidental. Until I have good reason to doubt that, I will not hear him accused. Let him return and account for himself, and then we can judge his actions."

We moved to sit at the table. While I crumbled my bread onto my platter, the men made plans for today's search.

"I'll lead the group that's headed west on the Glencarnagh track," Johnny said. "Aidan will stay with you. I'm happier if at least one of my men is here in such a time of uncertainty, though I recognize that you have good guards of your own. In fact, the Sevenwaters men have an advantage in such a search, since they know the forest so well. We covered a wide area yesterday, Sean. We must consider the possibility that whoever took Finbar has by now conveyed him beyond your borders."

"Only if they rode all night," Father said.

Or if they went somewhere beyond the human world, I thought.

"You know we could not continue the search in the darkness," Johnny said quietly. "Believe me, I will give all my energy to this until we find him."

Father nodded wearily. "Whoever has done this is highly skilled. We should have overtaken them."

"Father?" It felt terrible to be afraid to ask a simple question.

He looked at me but did not speak.

"Have you considered asking Sibeal to scry? I know she doesn't like sharing what she sees, but when it's so important . . ."

"Sibeal is only twelve years old. I recognize her gift, but I think it best that we wait for Conor. He should be here by tomorrow. I would not place so great a burden on one so young. You hope, I suppose, that she will come up with an answer supporting your own theory, that that heap of debris up there is in fact a living, breathing being."

"No, Father," I lied, my heart cold. "I am beginning to think maybe I was wrong about that. I was shocked and upset. And guilty, even though I can't understand how someone could get in and out so quickly and invisibly. I'm sorry if my behavior has only made things worse." Whether it was convincing or not, I could not tell. Aidan and Johnny were both looking at me, Johnny quizzically, Aidan with narrowed eyes. And although I had told a lie to avert attention from what I had concealed upstairs, I realized as I sat miserable under their scrutiny that I was beginning to doubt the evidence of my own eyes and ears. While my heart still knew I was right about Becan, it was becoming harder to ignore the possibility that my mind was playing tricks. These were good, sensible men, men who usually treated me with respect and kindness. How could all of them be wrong? Why would the Fair Folk show me the truth and not Muirrin? It made no sense.

"You can assist us today by arranging provisions for the searchers," Father said, and I took it as a slight thawing of his attitude. "They'll be riding out as soon as they've had breakfast. Aidan, you look as if you need sleep. If you're to act as a family guard in Johnny's absence, take some time now to rest, and come to find me later in the morning."

"Yes, my lord." Aidan got up and left the hall promptly. A little later, I did the same, heading for the kitchen where I gave the necessary instructions about provisions and acquired a fresh supply of water and honey. It was still early. Muirrin had not come down, but Eithne was there filling a tray with breakfast items.

"How is Mother?" I asked her, grimly setting aside the matter of an ill-timed kiss she might better have kept to herself.

"Not so well, my lady." She had the grace to blush. "This is for Muirrin and me and Orlagh, who's watching the door. Lady Aisling won't eat. It's been hard to get her to take even water. She's just sitting on the bed staring at nothing. I don't think she really understands what's happened."

"I see. Well, I'm sure you're doing your best." What more could I say? I wanted to go in there and put my arms around my mother. I wanted to tell her that if this really was my fault I was sorrier than anyone could ever imagine, and that I wished above anything in the world that I had the power to make things right for her. But what was the point of that? I couldn't fix it. Nobody would listen to me. If anyone had asked me yesterday whether I would ever lie to my father, I would have been affronted that they considered such a thing possible. Today I had done it. And in my bedchamber, tucked up in Finbar's soft shawl, lay the thing that had been left in place of my mother's darling son.

When I came out of the kitchen into the downstairs hallway Aidan was there waiting for me. He hadn't rushed off to snatch well-deserved sleep after all.

"Aidan," I said, jug and pot clutched awkwardly to my chest.

"May I speak to you for a moment?" He sounded constrained, formal. It was another mark of how much things had changed since yesterday.

"Of course. Thank you for helping my father."

"This may seem discourteous, Clodagh, but I have to ask it. What happened yesterday with Cathal? What did he say to you? I know you've told it already, but . . ."

At least he hadn't asked, *Did you encourage him to kiss you?* "Something about going away," I said, setting my load down in an alcove. "He implied that it might be better if he wasn't here. He didn't explain it properly. He said I'd probably be glad he was gone, and I said I had mixed feelings about it. I asked him where he was going, but he didn't say. But it was plain to me he wasn't expecting to come back. Not ever."

"And he kissed you."

"If he hadn't, Aidan, be sure I wouldn't have said he did. It wasn't the way Eithne told it. It was quick and not in the least passionate. A farewell kiss, that was all." Not quite true: a chaste farewell kiss would not have caused me to respond in the way I had. It had been a lovely kiss, a kiss that I could never have imagined a man like Cathal had it in him to give. "He took me by surprise. It was an odd thing for him to do, since we weren't even friends. Then he left without another word."

Aidan looked at the floor. "He didn't say anything to me," he said. "He left without even telling me."

"Maybe Johnny's right. Didn't he say Cathal has done something like this before? He'll probably be back by nightfall with some good explanation." I could see that Aidan believed this no more than I did. "I'm sorry," I said. "He's upset you. The two of you seem to have a knack for doing that."

He grimaced. "We know each other too well. We've had all our lives to learn each other's weak spots. And Cathal's never stopped trying to prove he's as good as me, or better, whether it's in feats of daring or skill in arms or just making a spectacle of himself. Thanks to his prickly nature, I had few other friends as a child. My father has a genuine affection for him. The rest of my family tolerates him. For all the opportunities my father provided, Cathal has never learned to behave in a way folk think quite fitting. The rivalry's been irksome sometimes. Worse than that recently. His behavior here at Sevenwaters has tried me hard."

I remembered the conversation I'd overheard at the stables, and the unexpected kindness in Cathal's voice as he comforted his friend. I recalled that it was Aidan who had lied to me. I thought of the stricken look on Cathal's face the night he heard the Wolfchild story. "Do you know who Cathal's father was?" I asked. "I know your father took him in because his mother couldn't cope, but . . ."

"She was a woman from the village. Poor, unmarried, expecting a child. She never said who the father was. Cathal won't speak of it. I don't know if she ever told him, or even if she knew herself."

I did not much like the implication of that last remark. "Is she still living?"

Aidan shook his head. "She died when he was seven or eight. Cathal and I may have our disagreements, but we're like brothers, Clodagh. I'm closer to him than I am to my real brothers. That's what makes his behavior so galling. A brother doesn't kiss his brother's sweetheart." He suddenly blushed scarlet.

"And a brother doesn't go away without telling his brother where and why," I said, deciding I would pretend I hadn't heard the last part of his speech. "He sounded upset. Sad. I wish he had explained a little more."

"So you do care about him." An edge in his voice now; if I'd thought the jealous anger of that earlier time was absent, I'd been wrong.

"Only as I would care about any person who was a guest in my house and was unhappy," I said. "Aidan, I have to go. And you're supposed to be resting."

"Clodagh?"

"Yes?"

"I spoke out of turn then; said more than I should have. I didn't mean to offend you. I have the highest regard for you." He took my hand and lifted it to his lips. "I know it is the wrong time to speak of such matters. Your baby brother . . . you must be so worried."

"I wasn't offended," I said, withdrawing my hand from his and turning away before he could see how close I was to bursting into tears. Those few gently spoken words had almost undone my best efforts to keep control of myself. I ached for him to put his arms around me and tell me everything was going to be all right. That was foolish. Nobody could make this better, not so easily. "Now you should go to rest, and I'm needed upstairs. Goodbye, Aidan." I made myself walk away and not look back.

As I passed the door to Mother's chamber it opened and Muirrin came out, looking wretched.

"Are you all right?" I asked her. Silly question; one look at her had told me the answer must be no.

"I'll cope," my eldest sister said in a brittle tone that sounded so like Mother's it jolted me. "Clodagh, you know Father didn't want her to go into the nursery. I'm wondering if he was wrong."

"Why?" I croaked, my nerves jangling in alarm.

There was a strained silence. "I've tried everything," Muirrin said eventually. There were dark circles under her eyes. "I don't seem to be able to help her. We must do something to snap her out of this trance. She won't listen to reason, Clodagh. With Finbar gone, milk fever is almost inevitable. She won't let me touch her; insists that if we try to relieve the pressure in her breasts there won't be anything for the baby to drink when he comes home. She won't even listen to Father, not properly."

"This is all wrong," I said, my pent-up feelings getting the better of me. To see capable Muirrin shaking and defeated was deeply disturbing. "I wish she'd let us go in and visit her. She needs people to hug her, cry with her, share her grief . . ." *And so do I,* I thought, remembering how close I had come to throwing myself into Aidan's arms not long ago just because he'd spoken kindly to me.

After a moment Muirrin said, "I've been doing my best."

Now I'd hurt her. "Of course. But there's only one of you, and you're a healer, you're busy with other things."

"Clodagh, I do think we should let Mother go into the nursery chamber as she asked to. That might help her accept that Finbar is actually gone."

"Isn't it rather soon for that?" I asked quickly. "It might be too much of a shock. Maybe you should wait a bit. You could consult Conor when he arrives."

Muirrin looked a little surprised, but she said, "I don't suppose another day will make much difference. It may be better not to trouble Father with this right now. I expect Conor will be here in the morning."

CHAPTER 7

One day. One day was all I had to save Becan and find a solution to the nightmare that had fallen over everyone I loved. As a druid, Conor would be open to the other-worldly. But he and my father had a long-established trust. They tended to agree about things. He'd probably see Becan the way Father and Muirrin and Johnny did, as a crude simulacrum of a child. I was sure Father would take Conor into the nursery. They would ask me where the manikin was. That meant I had to get Becan safely out of the house before Conor arrived. And that was only the immediate problem. My family was doing the wrong thing; I was becoming more and more certain of it. I wasn't losing my mind. I refused to accept that. I was exactly the same person I'd been before this happened, whatever anyone else might think. My instincts told me Johnny's party might search the forest forever and not find my baby brother. He had been taken beyond the world of men.

I sat in my bedchamber with my mind darting from one impossible plan to the next, while Becan slept soundly in his improvised cradle. At some point in the morning he woke and I fed him again and changed his wrappings, which were damp. I made replacements by tearing up an old shift. I had just settled him once more when I heard a commotion from downstairs. My father did not often raise his voice, but he was doing so now: "What? I cannot believe this!" I heard Johnny, who was supposed to be out searching for Finbar, replying in more measured tones.

They'd found Finbar. Something terrible had happened to him. What else would make Father shout like that? My stomach churning, I left my chamber, shutting the door firmly behind me, and hurried down to the hall.

A man stood before my father, his chest heaving, his clothing in disarray. His hair looked as if it had been singed and there was a red mark across his cheek. Johnny stood close by, in his riding clothes. There were two of Father's men-at-arms by the door. I went quietly over to the hearth, waiting to hear the worst.

"Glencarnagh," the man gasped. "An attack—a terrible fire—" He bent double, fighting for breath.

"Take your time, Cronan," Father said, though alarm was written all over his face. "Johnny, where did you come upon him?"

"On the main track westward," Johnny said. "We rode straight back here. The assault on Glencarnagh happened yesterday, at dusk. It seems many men have been killed."

"My lord," Cronan said, his breath still rasping, "it was utter carnage. The fire took hold so quickly . . . As we fled the house, they attacked."

"What of Lughan and his family?" Father asked. Lughan was the steward who looked after Glencarnagh for us; I knew his wife and daughter well.

"We got them out safely, my lord. We kept watch over them in the forest until the raiders were gone. At first light Lughan sent me to give you the news." The man took a gasping breath. "So many lost, my lord. To use fire in that way, heedless of the women and children . . . Of Lughan's household guard, I am one of only three survivors. And the house is gone. Gone up in flames . . ." Cronan swayed where he stood.

"This man has suffered burns," Johnny said. "He should be attended to before he tells us more."

Father looked grim as death. "Cronan, who were these attackers?" he asked in a voice whose very quietness was frightening. If he had seemed on the verge of losing control not long ago, now he was a different man. "Can you hazard a guess? Who would dare make such a mockery of my authority?"

"I don't know who they were, my lord. They had masks on and plain clothing. No insignia; nothing. And it was growing dark. It was a party of perhaps thirty men. We had no warning at all. They must have disabled the forward sentry posts."

A deep chill was creeping through me. This tale was in my head already. Glencarnagh: a gracious house surrounded by oaks and elms. A hedge of beech, a pond, a garden. Thirty men. The sentry posts. I had known about this. Cathal had told me about it and I'd hardly listened to him because the whole thing sounded so impossible. I hadn't even realized what place he was speaking of. And now the details were all coming back to me, and they were the same, just the same . . . As the men-at-arms ushered the injured Cronan out I stood frozen before the hearth, my head swimming. The mysterious figure in the night; the peculiar disappearance on the day of the picnic. The odd statements: *My instincts tell me you may be personally at risk,* and, *I don't think it's wise for me to be here.*

"Father," I made myself say, "I have something to tell you. Aidan should be here when I say it. And I think we need to be somewhere more private."

We went into the small council chamber, where the table was spread with the various maps, charts and notes by which Father was maintaining meticulous control of the search for Finbar. A lamp burned and a small fire glowed on the hearth. Johnny fetched a yawning Aidan, then shut the door. Standing before the men, I stammered out an account of the hints and clues and warnings I had been given since the day Aidan and Cathal had first come to Sevenwaters; signs I had dismissed as either my own imaginings or Cathal's mischief. Despite the fire it felt cold in the chamber. Father's expression was wintry; Johnny's was fierce. Aidan tried to interrupt several times and was silenced by Johnny.

I explained how Cathal's description of a possible raid on Father's holdings matched exactly what that poor man, Cronan, had just told us. "I never thought of Glencarnagh, Father. I'm sorry. I didn't entertain for a moment that this might be something that would really happen. I mean, Cathal is—was—always saying outrageous things. I thought he was just playing games. He does that a lot. But in Cronan's account, all the details were the same: men going ahead to disable the forward sentries, the estimate of numbers, the fire, the family fleeing into the woods . . . And his description of the house was like Glencarnagh, only I never thought . . ."

"How could Cathal know?" asked Aidan. "He's never been to Glencarnagh. Couldn't this be sheer coincidence?"

"Why would Cathal describe this to you, Clodagh?" That was Johnny, his tone very grim indeed.

Now for the hardest part. "He thought Illann might be behind it," I said miserably. "And because he knew I could communicate with Deirdre, he wanted to warn me not to let slip anything important. I told him that was ridiculous, that Illann is family and an ally, and that Deirdre wouldn't be involved in anything underhand anyway. Cathal suggested I might get myself in trouble by giving her information that Illann could use to strategic advantage. I did tell him he should bring it to you, Johnny, or to Father. He said you wouldn't believe him if there was no evidence."

"In the name of the gods, Clodagh, why didn't you tell me about this at the time?" Father was holding back his fury, but it trembled in his voice.

"There was Mother, and the baby, and the trouble in the north," I whispered. "This sounded like nonsense. I didn't want to bother you with it, Father."

"Tell us again about the night of the wedding feast." Johnny spoke sharply. "What exactly was it you saw?"

"A figure down by the far end of the barn. Someone in a gray cloak."

"And Cathal was out there as well."

"He was, yes. But the figure—I couldn't even be completely sure I'd seen it. I thought I did, but when I looked again it was gone. None of this was enough to justify troubling you with my fears and imaginings."

"And in the woods, when you were riding?" Father's eyes were on me, judging. My stomach was churning with tension.

"Eilis and Coll rode ahead; Cathal went after them. They came back, he did not. You know that's a simple path. He turned up later at the lake and said he'd gone a short way down a couple of side tracks, but nothing more. It was a plausible explanation, Father."

"But Cathal was gone long enough to have met up with someone in the forest. He could have exchanged information. Both times."

"Lord Sean!" Aidan protested. "Cathal is no spy! He's a loyal—"

"Enough," Father said. "Men died at Glencarnagh last night. My son has been cruelly snatched. We will get to the bottom of this, and if Cathal is in any way responsible he will pay the ultimate price for his treachery."

"Sean." Johnny's face was white under his raven tattoo. "There is no proof that Cathal was involved either in the attack on Glencarnagh or the abduction of Finbar. Clodagh's first assessment could be correct; the odd accuracy of Cathal's account may be coincidental. I find it almost impossible to believe he would be involved in this. My men are faultlessly loyal. The tests of skill and character they must pass to be admitted to my band are thorough and taxing."

"Cathal never says much about his feelings," Aidan said quietly. "But Johnny knows, and I know, what it meant to him to be accepted into the community of Inis Eala. Becoming one of Johnny's trusted men wasn't only being received into a brotherhood of peerless warriors, it was . . . it was like coming home for him. Finding a home he'd never had before. He could not have done this, Lord Sean."

"He has been adept, perhaps," Father said, "in deceiving even those who most trusted him." He looked at Johnny. "You are quick enough to plead his innocence. If what Aidan says is true, Cathal owes you a particular debt for accepting him into the small number of your personal protectors—an elite within an elite. We know Cathal admires you. Like all your men, he strives to please you. We know also that his behavior is unconventional. Might not such a man decide to act unilaterally to remove someone he saw as a future threat to you?"

There was a pause. I clutched my hands together behind my back and tried not to see the way Johnny's jaw tightened, or the anguish on Aidan's features, or my father's cold look of judgment. I knew what he meant and it made my heart shrink.

Johnny was the one who put it into words. "Sean, are you suggesting a plot to remove your son because he will in time be my rival for the chieftaincy of Sevenwaters? You believe Finbar has not been taken for ransom, but . . ." He did not finish the sentence; the alternative was too terrible.

"It's not true!" Aidan burst out, speaking the words I was forcing back. "That's wild speculation! I will not hear this—"

"Sit down." Johnny sounded terrible; weary to the point of tears, though men like him do not weep. "Sean's right. We must consider all the possibilities. In fact, Cathal cannot have been responsible for Finbar's abduction, since Clodagh would have seen him carry it out."

"The two events are not necessarily linked," I ventured. "This attack on Glencarnagh and the baby's removal, I mean."

"Coincidence again? I think not," said Father. "Someone seeks to undermine me on two fronts. To weaken my authority in any way he can. As for Cathal's inability to seize the baby, there's an accomplice, or so it seems—the shadowy figure Clodagh saw on at least one occasion. More than one accomplice, perhaps. Cathal may not have removed Finbar himself, but he provided the distraction that made it possible." His eyes turned to me. "I would not like to think, Clodagh, that you were in any way trying to shield this young man. It seems the two of you were closer than anyone ever imagined. If there is anything that you have not told us, now is the time to disclose it. Your motives for holding back this information for so long must be suspect."

This felt like being whipped. "Why would I protect someone who meant harm to my brother?" I choked. "How can you think that of me, Father?"

"It occurs to me," he said, "that your wild story of changelings might have been concocted to allow your friend to make good his escape."

"That's crazy—" Aidan began, but Johnny silenced him with a sharp gesture.

"It was not a wild story, Father," I managed. My heart was hammering and my skin felt clammy. "I did believe it. I still believe it was not worldly forces that snatched Finbar, but uncanny ones. I'm convinced that unless you search in a different way you will not find him. As for Cathal, there's no reason why I would lie to protect him."

"He gives you a very particular warning, with information included that could, if passed on, incriminate him. He enters an area of the house where he has no business in order to bid you farewell. He embraces you passionately. You prove to be the only member of the entire household whom he told of his impending departure. And you expect me to believe there is nothing between you."

"I can't tell you what to believe, Father." It was becoming harder and harder to get the words out. He was looking at me as if he despised me. "I understand that you must find out who is responsible for the attack on Glencarnagh. Cathal's actions do seem incriminating, though why he would be involved in that I can't imagine. I have to tell you that I did speak to Deirdre not long before Finbar was taken. It was at Mother's request, to tell her the good news of the baby's safe arrival." My throat was tight. "I mentioned that Gareth had been sent away on a mission, and Deirdre questioned me about it. I stopped answering after a bit, but I did let slip that it involved the northern chieftains. It is possible she might have thought that your sending a party north could leave Glencarnagh undermanned. But you know Deirdre. She's never been interested in these things."

Father sat frozen. Into the silence, Johnny said, "Anything you told her, Clodagh, would have come far too late to influence what happened at Glencarnagh."

His kindness was almost my undoing. I met Aidan's gaze for a moment, then looked hurriedly away before my tears spilled.

"That may be true," said Father. "It doesn't alter the fact that if you had come to me as soon as Cathal gave you that first description of a hypothetical raid, we'd have been in time to stop it and lives would have been saved. Illann. Can that possibly be true? Why in the name of the gods would he do such a thing? Glencarnagh's right on his border."

"Father," I said, "I don't believe Finbar's abduction has anything to do with the raid and the fire. The way it was carried out, the figure in the cradle, the impossible timing—it must be the work of the Fair Folk. Nobody else could have got him out so quickly or so invisibly."

Another charged silence. "Clodagh," said my father in that quiet tone that sent shivers down my spine, "I hope you were being honest with me earlier today when you admitted to being mistaken on this particular matter. I hope you are not about to tell me again that someone has left a living, breathing creature in my son's place. You've already shocked and disappointed me today with your wayward disregard for common sense. Your negligence in the matter of Cathal has proven costly indeed."

"I'm sorry, Father." I held myself rigidly straight, clenching my jaw tight, but my lips trembled and my voice shook. "I'm truly sorry if those men died at Glencarnagh because of me. I've tried to do the right thing. That's all I've ever tried to do."

Father did not respond by so much as a nod. It seemed to me he was having as much difficulty holding himself together as I was. The old Clodagh, the girl I had been yesterday, would have put her arms around him and offered words of comfort. I stood very still, blinking back my tears. I would never be that girl again.

"I think we might allow Clodagh to leave us, Sean," Johnny said. "We can call her back if we need her. We have some decisions to make quickly." He took my arm and walked me to the door, which he opened for me. He said nothing more, but as I stepped out he put his hand on my shoulder for a moment, and when I glanced at him, he gave a little smile. I turned away abruptly, the tears starting to stream down my face, and heard the door shut behind me.

I waited in the hall, unwilling to retreat to my bedchamber in case Father called for me. If he sent someone to find me they'd almost certainly stumble on Becan. I paced nervously as serving people and men-at-arms came in and out on their various duties, their glances touching me, then sliding away. I made pleats in my skirt; I poked the fire and set on more wood; I fiddled with the empty ale cups on the little table. My whole body was on edge. Who could hate Father so much that they would burn the lovely house of Glencarnagh and kill so many men? Why would Cathal be involved in such an undertaking? Why would he warn me about the attack when to do so must suggest he was in some way implicated? For it seemed to me he could not have known the precise details without a link to the perpetrators. If he wasn't spying for Johnny, then he must have been allied with the other side, whether they were Illann's folk or someone else's. Why? Why throw away his position with Johnny, the home and profession he had apparently longed for? It didn't make any sense at all. My mind raced from one unlikely explanation to the next. All the while, my heart was sick with the memory of Father's stern face, his cold voice as he interrogated me.

I could hear raised voices in the council room, but not the words. A moment later the door slammed open and Aidan strode out, followed by Johnny.

"I'm not going!" Aidan shouted. "He's my friend! You can't ask me to do this!"

They had not seen me. Four paces into the hall, Johnny put a restraining hand on Aidan's shoulder and the other man whipped around to face him, fists clenched. I shrank back into the shadows.

"Are you refusing an order?" Johnny asked, his voice deadly quiet.

"I can't do it!"

"Take a breath," Johnny said. "Calm yourself. We are professionals; we do not allow personal loyalties to interfere with the missions we undertake. If you cannot respect that, you have no place among my men, Aidan."

"Maybe I don't want one," Aidan snarled, wrenching away from Johnny's touch. "Not if it means hunting down my best friend and dragging him back to face an inquisition."

"Aidan." I heard in Johnny's voice that he was fighting for calm. "Believe me, if there were anyone else to whom I could entrust this, I would ask him in your stead. You are the only man I have left right now."

"Since you're so ready to believe Cathal guilty," Aidan growled, "go after him yourself. Have you no sense of loyalty, that you would ask me to do this?"

Momentarily, Johnny closed his eyes, and I saw my father's face in his, the face of a leader who must bear burden upon burden and remain strong. I was about to alert them to my presence, for this was certainly not for my ears, but Johnny spoke first. "I cannot go," he said. "I must head straight to Glencarnagh and find out what party was responsible for that act of violence. We must be ready to retaliate without delay. And the search for Finbar must be maintained; Sean will continue to coordinate it from here, but his own men must undertake it without my assistance for now. We need Cathal found and apprehended. If there is a link between the two events, the abduction and the attack, he is the key to it. Select two or three of the Sevenwaters men and track him down with all the skill you have. Take the dogs. And don't speak to me of loyalty, Aidan. When Cathal is brought in I'll give him the opportunity to explain himself. I have not made an arbitrary decision as to his guilt or otherwise. The question remains: if he's innocent of any involvement in this, why isn't he here?"

"You are ready to point to Cathal," Aidan said grimly. "Have you considered that others may point to you?" He was keeping his voice down now, though the anger vibrated through every word.

For a moment Johnny did not answer. When he spoke, it was with remarkable restraint. "I have considered it. Perhaps the perpetrator of these ills has acted with the sole purpose of casting suspicion on me, of setting a wedge between me and my uncle. Someone believes me capable of harming my infant cousin and of destabilizing Sean's rule by destroying one of the jewels of his holding. They imagine I view Finbar as a threat. Or at least, they believe others will think that credible. My father was not well loved in these parts. There are folk who fear my influence on my uncle." There was something new in his face; something deeply unsettling.

I saw Aidan's gaze flick toward the doorway of the council chamber and back to Johnny. A moment later, the door was quietly closed from the inside.

"Surely *he* does not doubt you," Aidan said, and the anger was gone from his voice.

"I don't know," said Johnny. I had never before heard such a note of uncertainty in his tone, and it shocked me. "I wish Gareth was back. I wish I did not need to ask this of you, Aidan. But I must. The sooner Cathal is found, the sooner he can account for himself. If your faith in him is justified there's nothing to fear. But we may have a major undertaking on our hands very soon and I need to be prepared for it."

I cleared my throat, and both men spun around to face me where I stood to one side of the hearth. "I'm sorry," I said. "There was no good moment to interrupt. I was waiting in case Father needed me."

Johnny gave me a nod of acknowledgment. "Well?" he asked Aidan.

"You want this hunting party to set off immediately, I take it?"

"The longer you leave it, the colder the trail will be. Before you assemble your group, talk to Clodagh. Clodagh, tell him everything about that last conversation with Cathal, will you? Every detail you can remember. Something you believe insignificant could be a vital clue. Aidan, you haven't answered me."

"It seems I have no choice."

"Your choice is to obey me or to take yourself off home to Whiteshore. If that sounds blunt, circumstances demand it. Give me your answer. I, too, must make a swift departure."

"I'll do it. You may say that's a choice, but we both know I won't go home and turn my back on him." Aidan hesitated. "Johnny?"

"If you have questions, be quick with them."

"I want to take part in the counterattack. I don't want to be left here as a household guard. Lord Sean's men can do that capably."

"You know I don't make bargains," Johnny said. "Do what you've been asked to do and we'll discuss it afterward. Believe me, I understand your difficulty. Dealing with these things is part of the discipline of being a warrior, Aidan. It is an opportunity to show what you are made of."

Aidan stood in stony silence as my cousin left the hall. Then the two of us looked at each other.

"You're a loyal friend," I said, and my voice came out sounding choked.

"I don't know how I can bring myself to do it," said Aidan. "Self-discipline is supposed to be the key element of our training. At times like this, I have grave doubts as to my ability to summon it. Perhaps he's right. Perhaps I don't belong at Inis Eala."

I reached to take his hand. "Better if you're the one to do this," I told him, not quite sure if I believed it. "You can explain to Cathal. You can make sure he understands that Johnny is prepared to hear what he has to say." I thought Cathal might be no more prepared to explain himself to Johnny than he had been to me. After all, he'd left without a word to anyone else. Even his best friend hadn't been warned. Looking at Aidan's white face, his stricken eyes, I saw how cruel that had been.

Aidan put both his hands around mine. "Since Johnny has laid this on me, I must do it," he said. "And I must go quickly. What he said . . . about Cathal and his conversation with you . . ."

"There's nothing more to tell. I went through it all before." As I spoke I remembered reprimanding Cathal after that kiss, and the way he had turned, his cloak swirling out behind him. Another memory stirred, oddly: Willow and her clurichauns. The red and the green; the telltale color. "His cloak," I said, an odd feeling coming over me. "Have you noticed all the little things he has sewn into the lining? I saw that for the first time and . . . well, it seemed strange." Something made of green glass. Green: the mark of a traitor. I shivered.

"A source of ongoing amusement at Inis Eala," Aidan said. "Another of my friend's eccentricities. Most of the men do have a rowan cross sewn into their clothing, but Cathal carries a lifetime of memories in that well-worn garment. There's a white pebble there from a time when the two of us were four or five and spent a memorable morning learning how to skip stones across a pond. A feather found on the shore one summer; a strip of leather from a dog's collar. A length of wool from a garment Cathal wore as an infant. A trinket his mother gave him."

This sounded harmless, if eccentric. Indeed, it cast a whole new light on Cathal. He had gathered up remnants of good times, of friendship, love, recognition. He had wrapped them around him to strengthen him in the times of loneliness, which had perhaps filled far more of his life than those rare moments of warmth or joy. I'd be foolish to leap to conclusions on the basis of a lighthearted story. On the other hand, Father did have good reason for suspicion; there was no getting past the fact that Cathal had outlined the attack on Glencarnagh to me in altogether too much detail for the thing to be coincidence.

"Clodagh, I must go," Aidan said, still holding my hands. "I don't like seeing you so sad and worried. I'm sorry this has caused trouble between you and your father. I wish things were different."

"Me, too," I said, thinking of Becan hidden upstairs and the decisions that lay before me. "You're a good man, Aidan. This is very hard for you. Johnny's right, you know. If Cathal is innocent, nothing bad will happen to him. My father may be distressed and angry right now, but he is a just man."

Aidan said nothing more. I wanted to offer him a farewell embrace, a kiss on the cheek, something that would let him know I recognized the whirl of emotions he was feeling. But it seemed to me that he was fighting to keep control of himself, and that if I made such a gesture he might lose that control in a way he would find shaming. "Ride safely, Aidan," I said, and withdrew my hands from his. I watched as he made his way out.

Beyond the door of the council chamber, all was silent. As the swan tapestry stirred in the draft, I thought of Deirdre. Would Father ask me to contact her? Would he want me to ask probing questions that might lead to a revelation that Illann was indeed involved in this? If he did, I would feel just as Aidan must be feeling right now. It didn't bear thinking of. Someone must hate us powerfully. These terrible tricks were destroying our family from the inside out.

Somehow the rest of the day passed. I went back upstairs and when Becan awoke I fed him again. Now that his requirements were being met he made less noise, seeming content to snuggle into his makeshift bed between meals and drowse as a healthy baby should. I studied his grotesque little face, whose component pieces of bark, wood, moss and stone were held together in a manner that defied all logic. I touched his twiggy hand and felt the sharp fingers clutch onto one of mine, as if even in this deep sleep he sensed how very close he was to the peril of being left all alone. I thought of the Wolf-child story, and of Cathal's wretched face as he'd listened to it. There had been obvious lessons in each of the tales. Truth will out. Be understanding of difference. Hold onto what matters to you. But maybe there was more than that. The clurichaun and the green thread; the three different endings for Wolf-child. Maybe, if I considered the tales more deeply, they would provide answers to the problem that faced me. For here in my arms was the changeling I had told Father was a mere figment of my imagination. Here, wrapped in a soft blanket, was the pile of debris I had agreed was inanimate, a mere manikin. And before me were many tomorrows to be faced, and a secret that could not be contained within this chamber, nor indeed within the stone walls of this keep. My heart quailed at the enormity of what I had done and what I must do.

With so many demands—the mission to the northern chieftains, the search for Finbar, the hunt for Cathal—most of our menfolk were away from home. The need for men-at-arms to accompany Johnny to Glencarnagh and for others to ride out with Aidan's party meant grooms and serving people had set their duties aside to join those looking for the baby, and at suppertime the hall was almost empty. We ate in silence. Muirrin did not come down. Eithne took a tray upstairs; she looked as if she hadn't slept for days.

Eilis and Coll did not appear for supper, and nor did Sibeal. I sat there in silence, unable to eat more than a mouthful or two. I felt like a stranger in my own home, and an unwelcome one at that.

In keeping with custom, the household waited for Father to rise before leaving the table. As soon as I could I fled upstairs, unwilling to be engaged in talk by anyone. Outside Mother's door I hesitated, for there was a powerful need in me to see her, to tell her that I loved her and that I was sorry if what had happened was my fault. But I could not bring myself to knock. She wouldn't want to see me. She wouldn't want to confront the daughter who, through sheer negligence, had brought down this darkness on the household. Or so everyone seemed to believe.

I walked into my bedchamber and stopped short. Sibeal was seated on Deirdre's bed, cross-legged, gazing down at the sleeping form of Becan where he lay rolled in his blanket behind the storage chest. She looked pensive.

I shut the door behind me, my heart thumping. The secret was a secret no longer. "How did you get up here?" I asked. In fact the answer was obvious; there were narrow steps at the other end of the passageway, leading up from a back entry used mostly by serving people. These made it possible to come upstairs unseen by folk in the hall.

"What do you see when you look at this?" Sibeal asked, ignoring my question as she continued to scrutinize Becan. "Muirrin said you were so upset that your mind was confused."

"What do *you* see?" I responded, hoping beyond hope that this sister, known since she was tiny for her exceptional powers as a visionary, might share my conviction that Becan was more than a bundle of sticks and stones.

"You speak first, Clodagh. Then I'll tell you."

I did not argue. If she wanted to, Sibeal could run to Father right now with the news that I had rescued what he wanted locked away. She could tell him I'd been willfully disobedient. "I see a newborn baby made of all the stuff of the forest," I told her. "He's sleeping now, but I can see his chest going in and out and hear his breathing. When he's hungry he cries. When he's frightened he screams. He drinks honey water; he clutches onto my finger. He's alive, Sibeal. He's a changeling."

There was a long, long pause while my sister studied the tiny, wrapped-up figure. Eventually I said, "You can't see him. Even you think I'm imagining this."

"It's not as simple as that," said Sibeal. "It's true, I do see a bundle of sticks there, with a couple of pebbles where the eyes would be. It's a figure of a baby, that much is plain, though how it holds together I can't work out. But, Clodagh, that's not all I've seen."

"What?" I whispered, reminding myself to breathe. "What do you mean?"

"In visions," she said, "I've seen this creature as a child, moving about, making noise, acting like any human baby. Always with you, Clodagh. Always in your arms, with you patting and singing and carrying him about. Not here in the house. In other places: hiding in the forest, crossing a river, going down a sort of underground passage. Sometimes alone, sometimes with someone else, but I couldn't tell who it was. When I look at it—him—I see both at once. I see what Father and the others see, and I see the child of the visions: a changeling. Clodagh, you're crying."

"Sorry," I said, sitting down suddenly on my bed and wiping my eyes. "You're the only person who's even half believed me. Father's been so cold about it, cold and angry, not like himself at all. And I feel guilty. Father thinks it's my fault that someone took Finbar, because . . ."

"Because you were kissing Cathal, yes, everyone knows that story now," Sibeal said gravely. "That doesn't matter, Clodagh. What matters is what you're going to do about this."

"I thought maybe you could help me. If you've seen visions that explain what Becan is, can't you speak to Father or to Johnny? If they keep looking for Finbar in places where a human abductor might take him, they'll never find him." The baby was stirring; I got up and began to prepare a new batch of honey water. My sister regarded me solemnly.

"You can't risk that," she said. "I might tell them and they might dismiss it. Then your Becan—that's a good name, by the way—could be taken from you and disposed of. Clodagh, I did once hear a story about someone getting a little girl back when she was taken by the Fair Folk."

"Tell me," I said.

"They went to fetch her," said Sibeal, making my jaw drop. "They found the one who had taken her and negotiated an exchange."

"Where?" I asked, as hope and dread fought a battle inside me. "You mean someone found a portal to the Otherworld? How?"

"I can't remember that part. I do know that when the child came back she was . . . different."

My imagination conjured up an infant who had sprouted wings like an owl, or whose legs had been transformed into a salmon's tail. "Different in what way?" I asked as Becan came fully awake and began to squall. It was plain that Sibeal could not hear his cries.

"Just different. She looked the same. But I think if a person stays in the realm of the Fair Folk for any length of time, he or she becomes a little like them. That might be good or bad."

My throat felt constricted. I made myself sit down again, the baby in my arms now, and forced my breathing to steady as I dipped the cloth, ready to feed him. "Do you know the way in?"

I asked her. "I mean, the Lady of the Forest comes to talk to you sometimes, doesn't she?"

Sibeal looked down at her hands, interlinked on her lap. "The Lady hasn't come for a long time," she said. "That old woman, Willow, was right. Something's changed in the world of the Tuatha De. As for a way in . . . I don't know. In the tales, people usually stumble on them by accident."

Becan's twiggy mouth stretched open. His lips fastened around the soaked cloth and he began to suck. I hummed under my breath. "*Oo-roo, little dove . . .*"

Sibeal was looking at me strangely. After a bit, she said, "Ciarán might know."

"Ciarán? Why?"

"Because his mother was one of *them*. He doesn't like to talk about it."

"We can't ask him," I said, dipping the cloth again. "The forest is full of men searching for Finbar or hunting for Cathal. There would be no way to get to the nemetons unseen. Conor's coming, but he'll probably share Father's view."

"Hunting for Cathal? Where's he supposed to have gone?"

I explained what had happened.

My sister turned her big, clear eyes on me. "It does look as if you'll have to do this, Clodagh," she said. "You'll have to take Becan back and try to swap him for Finbar. I don't see any other way out of this. Maybe when you're in the forest a doorway to the Otherworld will reveal itself to you. That's if you're the one who is meant to bring Finbar home."

My heart did a flip in my chest. My mind shied away from a notion that seemed foolish, ridiculous, misguided in the extreme. And yet I knew she was right. My instincts had been telling me this since last night, when I had held Becan in my arms and felt his desperate need for love. But I was afraid.

"I suppose it must be possible," I said shakily. "If it's in the tales it must have been done once, at least."

"I think so, Clodagh." My sister squared her narrow shoulders. "I'll cover for you for as long as I can. Once you're safely away I can tell Father what you're doing. Otherwise he's going to think you've run off to warn Cathal, or that you've been abducted yourself. You'll have to go first thing in the morning. That's the only time you're likely to get out unseen. I've already told Doran and Nuala that I'll be sleeping up here tonight to keep you company."

"You've—you mean you knew this already, Sibeal? You anticipated it?"

"I am a seer, Clodagh," Sibeal reminded me. She was watching Becan now; the level in the water jug was rapidly going down. "You'll need to take swaddling cloths," she observed. "If he drinks as much as that, he's going to keep wetting himself. And I think it may be quite a long way."

Next morning, we stood together under the solitary hawthorn. Above the dark trees a faint wash of gold spread across the sky; it would soon be sunrise. Neither of us had slept more than a snatch or two, but I was strung too tight to feel my weariness. Sibeal had walked the first part of my journey with me, carrying strips of cloth to tie on the branches so we had a flimsy excuse for being out in the forest so early. It wouldn't have helped much if we'd encountered anyone from the household, since I was carrying Becan against my chest, held by a rudimentary sling.

I set down my bag for a moment and put my arm around my sister. "Thank you, Sibeal," I said. "I don't know when I'll be home again." I did not shed tears, but the immensity of what I was doing chilled me to the bone. Perhaps I would never come back. If those tales were true, the ones about human folk straying into the realm of the Tuatha De and being trapped there to emerge and find a hundred years had passed, this might be the last time I would see Sibeal. I might never see any of my family again. I had lain awake with this fear knotting my belly as I considered how unlikely it was that the Fair Folk would take any interest in my arguments as to why Finbar should be returned, supposing I ever succeeded in finding them.

While the household was asleep I had crept downstairs to obtain essential items for the journey—a water-skin, more honey in a little crock, a supply of hard bread, cloth-wrapped cheese, a flint and a knife. Sibeal had raided the stillroom and brought back healing herbs which we'd sewn into packets and stored at the bottom of the bag. I hadn't much clothing with me—a spare shawl for Becan, a change of small-clothes, a roll of swaddling, that was about it. The scale of this journey was impossible to encompass. I might be home tomorrow. I might be a lifetime wandering.

"Goodbye, Clodagh." Sibeal was composed, as usual. In a few years' time she would make a fine druid. "If there's an entry to be found, it might be in a place where earth and water meet—a cave by a stream, or a spring near oaks, or a rocky cleft close to the lake shore. I can't give you any other advice, except that if the Fair Folk want you to make this journey, you'll find the way."

"Why would they want me to? They've got Finbar, haven't they? They've got what they want."

Sibeal regarded me, eyes solemn. "I don't know, Clodagh. I've been asking myself that question since I realized you had rescued Becan. There's something extremely odd about the way all this has happened. When I first heard that you thought he was a changeling I wondered if there was a charm over you to make you see differently from the rest of us. But maybe you're the only one whose vision remains true—maybe the spell lies over everyone else, including me. Maybe you were meant to do this."

It was hardly reassuring. "I can't think of any reason why that should be, Sibeal."

"Nor me," my sister said, "but that doesn't mean none exists. You'd better go now, Clodagh. I hope you bring him home safely. With luck, everyone will be too busy to notice you're gone until much later in the day. I'll do as we agreed—I'll tell Uncle Conor first, and on his own. We'll light a candle for you."

"Thank you," I said, and turned away. The tears came now, a river of them, blinding my eyes. As I walked off across the clearing, heading for the shadows beneath the oaks, I knew without needing to look that Sibeal was tying her offering onto the mossy branch of the ancient hawthorn and sending up a silent prayer for me.

CHAPTER 8

I walked for most of the day without seeing anyone. I stayed off the paths, making myself wander into corners of the forest I usually thought best avoided: places where the trees grew densely, cutting off the sunlight, setting a deep shade on the forest floor beneath. Ferns were thick underfoot. Mosses made a spongy carpet and toadstools sprouted in grotesque clumps like miniature turreted villages. Where the ground rose, threads of water made their various ways over the rocks, trickling, pooling, leaping from tiny cliffs to cast droplets over the clinging greenery. I thought of warring clurichauns and started at each rustle in the leaves, each sudden cry of birds overhead. Despite what Sibeal had said about water, I stayed away from the lake, for on the shore I would be all too visible. If someone spotted me it wouldn't take long for word to get back to Father. Once Sibeal told him I'd gone off on my own he would send men to find me. Likely he'd believe I had finally gone right out of my wits. I hoped Conor would listen to what Sibeal had to say. I thought he might. He knew she was wise beyond her years. Maybe they'd send for Ciarán. Maybe he'd counsel Father to trust me and to wait.

From time to time, as I walked, Becan would wake and demand food and I would stop and tend to him. He seemed to like the sling. Each time I returned him to it he would curl up with his face against my breast and slip back into a contented slumber, soothed by the steady movement of my walking. He held on, one hand clamped around a fold of my clothing, even when fast asleep. Sometimes his arm or leg dug into me, for his body was all sharp corners, but I liked the feeling of holding him. I felt his trust in the way he relaxed against me; I thought I could see understanding in his pebble eyes. "At least you believe in me," I murmured. "Of course, that could be misguided, since I don't know the way."

By late afternoon I was so weary I knew I could not go much further. It would be cold out here overnight and I had only a cloak to protect the two of us from the chill. I could not risk making fire until I had set more distance between myself and the keep. My plan had been to head for a place I remembered where a rock wall rose behind a stand of closely spaced birches. Once, when we were younger, Deirdre and I had camped there overnight. It was well fringed by ferns and bracken and would be as good a spot as any to sleep. I sighed, hitching Becan up and tightening the sling. I'd been stupid to hope I might stumble on an opening to the Otherworld before nightfall on the very first day of this journey. Sibeal had implied that by rushing off to find Finbar myself, I might be fulfilling the intentions of the Fair Folk. But if that were so, wouldn't I have found a portal by now? Anyway, why would I be the one chosen to see Becan as he really was? Why would it be my mission to fetch my baby brother home? I was nobody: the boring sister. There was no reason at all for me to be singled out.

If I kept up the pace I should be able to reach the rock wall before dusk. I emerged from under the trees to find myself on the edge of a broad grassy slope. On its other side the forest began again, tall oaks above sharp-leaved hollies, dark and dense. Somewhere in there was the place I sought. To reach it I must cross this open ground. The only alternative was to climb much higher and traverse a stony area at the top of the rise, almost impossible while carrying Becan and my bag. On the other hand, for the time it would take to run across the slope to that deeper cover I would be in full view of anyone who happened to be close by. I'd been cautious all day, keeping off the paths, staying under the trees when I could, dodging from one place of concealment to the next. I glanced up and down the hill and across to the oaks on the other side of the open area. Nothing was moving save the hovering shape of a bird of prey, perhaps a kestrel, waiting its moment to swoop and seize.

As I gathered myself for a sprint, a clamor came from down the hill behind me: the deep, arresting voices of Father's wolfhounds. I froze. Gods, they sounded close. Now came the voices of men. "This way! Up under those oaks!" Then someone cursing, and a slipping, sliding sound further down the steep path.

I ran. Pure instinct drove me; my mind held only a will for flight. I jarred my right ankle halfway across the hillside, slipping on the wet grass, but I went on running. Ahead of me, in the shadow of the oaks on the far side, something moved. Behind me someone yelled, "Over there!" It sounded like Aidan. Becan was whimpering with distress as he was bounced up and down in the sling. I kept on going. Ten paces more, five, three . . .

I was under the trees, gasping for breath, knowing I must lose myself in the forest before dogs or men could find me. I snatched a glance over my shoulder and saw them standing over on the other side, at the point where I had started to run. A tall, brown-haired man: Aidan. With him were two others from our own household. The dogs were leashed. Nobody seemed to be coming after me. Instead the men stood conferring, and one of them pointed further uphill as if to say, *That way. She'll have gone that way.* Perhaps, against the odds, they had not actually seen me. I made myself melt into shadow, treading warily. A sudden move might catch a man's eye; a slow one might be taken as a mere shifting of light on leaves, a stirring of the late afternoon breeze. I threaded a way between the closely growing trees. The hollies left their marks on my skin. Thornbushes reached out to claw at my cloak and rip my stockings. I ducked beneath archways of tangled foliage and came up with my hair all cobwebs. It grew darker. I could hear the dogs somewhere higher up. It grew darker still. Becan started to cry.

"Hush, little one, hush now. Soon we'll be somewhere safe." Perhaps nowhere was safe. If they found me I would be taken home in shame. The changeling would be committed to the fire, and the last chance of getting Finbar back would be gone. Perhaps I had been utterly foolish ever to believe I could make things right again.

I heard them as I went: the barking, the rustling movement, sometimes the voices, though I could not catch their words. After a time the voices ceased, but I did not imagine the searchers had given up. The hounds were following a scent. They would keep going until they found the quarry.

I came to the bank of a coursing stream swollen by spring rains. There was no bridge; I would have to wade across. If I remembered correctly, the rock wall was not much further along this hillside, though the trees grew so densely here I could not see it. The light was fading; here in the depths of the wood it was like dusk already. It seemed men and dogs had anticipated where I would go and traversed the stony area further up the hill while I toiled through the forest. Might they now have circled around, ready to confront me when I reached the rock wall? What if I emerged from cover to be apprehended and conveyed home like a runaway child? Aidan . . . For Aidan to be faced with that task would be beyond mortification for the two of us.

Close by the stream was a weathered boulder over which a tangle of bramble bushes formed a thorny net. Under it was a space that looked adequate for a smallish person to hide in. I slipped the bag from my back, getting down on all fours to thrust it in ahead of me. Then, cradling Becan's head with one hand, I wriggled my body in. The hollow was a lucky find, bigger than it had seemed from the outside, with a dry earthen floor. My heart was pounding; my palms were clammy. I made myself breathe slowly.

Something flashed past the opening, jolting my heart. A man running, long legs, a swirling cloak, passing so close I felt the air stir against my face. I heard his breathing, hard but controlled, and his feet light on the forest floor, then splashing as he crossed the stream. And now, from up the hill, the dogs again, their clamor more insistent, moving fast—the pursuers had indeed gone higher, then circled back. It sounded as if the hounds had been unleashed and were pelting fast toward their quarry: the man whose clothing had provided their scent. The man who had just run in their direction. I hadn't been thinking straight before. It wasn't me Aidan had been sent out to find. It was Cathal.

They were coming. They were coming down the hill, and Aidan would have to apprehend his childhood friend. I clenched my teeth, forcing myself to keep still. Going out there would achieve nothing. It would only mean I, too, would be dragged off home. Why, then, did every instinct tell me to do it, to rush out and interpose myself between the two of them, to stop something truly terrible from happening? I had seen the way they fought, as if they were not dear friends but bitterest enemies. I did not think this could end well.

Becan's crying became an ear-splitting wail of panic. *No,* I mouthed. *No, hush!* But the noise only grew louder. I uncurled myself to sit upright, surprised again at how big the hollow was. I took the baby from the sling, held him against my shoulder and patted his back. I did not dare speak words of reassurance. For the first time I prayed that nobody else would be able to hear him.

Splashing again; someone was crossing the stream the other way. The dim light from the opening was suddenly gone. I shrank back in fright, anticipating a hunting dog, but it was a man who rolled through, swift as a sword stroke, and came up hard against me with an oath. In the near-darkness our eyes met, his wide with shock, mine no doubt exactly the same. His gaze dropped to the child in my arms and his eyes widened still further. He pointed to Becan, then put his finger to his lips. The message was quite plain, even in such poor light. *Make him be quiet.* He motioned to the opening of the little cave, then tried to indicate that men were following; that Becan's noise would lead Aidan's party to us. He could hear the crying. Cathal could hear it.

If I hadn't been so scared I might have wept for sheer relief. I stuck the tip of my little finger into the baby's mouth and felt his hard gums clamp around it as he sucked. The wailing ceased. Cathal took off his cloak and bunched it up to block the gap, plunging us into darkness. I heard Aidan's men go straight past. As far as I could tell, even the dogs didn't pause outside our hiding place. We waited a long time after the last of the sounds had died away. When Cathal removed the cloak, it was almost as dark outside as it was in our bolthole.

"What in the name of the gods are you doing out here?" he whispered.

"You can hear his voice," I breathed, still hardly believing it.

"Clodagh, answer my question," Cathal hissed. "Why were you hiding from them?"

"The same reason as you, I suppose," I murmured, shivering. "I didn't want to be taken back to the house. You must have some idea of why." Gods, it was cold. I wished I'd had room for a blanket in my pack.

After a moment Cathal said, "I must? When I left, you seemed to be quite content busying yourself with household affairs and helping with your new brother. And you and Aidan were enjoying each other's company. Now here we are. Forgive me for asking the obvious, but won't your mother be wanting her baby back?"

I stared at him, but it was too dark to read his features. Perhaps it had been too dark for him to see Becan properly before. Perhaps he actually didn't know what had happened. "You're joking, I presume," I said, and this time my voice was not quite steady.

"Still determined to think the worst of me, I see." Cathal spoke quietly, as if there might still be men out there to overhear him. "Clodagh, you need better shelter, for the child especially. I can't take you home, but I can walk with you to wherever you're going and make sure you don't come to harm in the dark. I have the wherewithal to make a fire."

"So do I. But I wasn't planning to light a fire tonight. They might see it."

"Who, our little hunting party out there? Why would you be afraid of Aidan? The fellow's besotted with you. And I don't imagine it's my safety you're concerned about. How much further were you planning to go?"

There seemed no point in holding back this information. Becan would certainly be safer if I had someone with me for the last part of the walk, over the stream and up through the forest in the dark. I told Cathal where I thought the rock wall was. "There will be moonlight soon," I said. "We should wait until then. And this is not Finbar. It's something that was left in his place."

"Something?" I felt him lean closer and reach out to touch

the shawl I had wrapped around the child. "What do you mean, Clodagh?"

"I'll show you when we get up there. He's a . . . I think he's a changeling. But when I told them, nobody would believe me. They would have thrown him away."

The darkness grew deeper; shadows wrapped our hiding place, sealing us off from the outer world. The silence drew out. I could not even hear Cathal's breathing. After some time I asked, "Are you all right, Cathal? You're not injured, are you?"

"A changeling," he said flatly.

"A baby made out of sticks, stones and leaves," I said, waiting for him to tell me how implausible that was. "Left in Finbar's place while you and I were . . . saying goodbye outside the door. Father suspects you were involved. He thinks you deliberately distracted me at a critical moment. Everyone believes it was a political abduction, even Johnny."

"If this changeling is visible, why don't they believe your story?" His tone was calm. Beyond the opening in the rock, a faint silvery light spread across the ground. The moon was rising over the forest. An owl hooted somewhere up in the oaks, and another replied.

"To them he looks like a roughly made manikin, not a living child. And I'm the only one who can hear his voice, apart from you. Even Sibeal couldn't, though she believed me when I told her what he was." Another long silence. The moonlight brightened. "Cathal, there might be enough light out there for us to find our way," I said. "We should go; it's not getting any warmer."

"You're prepared to have me come with you?" His voice was hesitant; not at all its usual mocking self.

"Crossing open ground by night with a baby in my arms is not something I do often," I said, wondering if he might be about to lead me into a trap. "If you intend me no ill, I'll gladly accept your help."

"Ill?" he echoed. "Well, I suppose your opinion of me was never so very high. I do owe you something for keeping quiet. I can't say the same for your changeling, but it seems Aidan's hunters couldn't hear him squalling and nor could their dogs. Have you thought how odd *that* is? I'll carry the two of you over the stream. My boots are wet already, no need for you to suffer the same inconvenience. Where's your bag? I'll get out first, then you can pass me the child."

"I'll carry him." There was no way I was handing Becan over to anyone.

The rock wall was where I had remembered, not so very far away. When we got there Cathal insisted on making a fire. "It's too cold for you. I know how to shield it, Clodagh. And I have good ears. In the unlikely event that they keep on searching overnight, I can get you away before they reach us."

"Really?" I was unfastening the sling again, getting out the second shawl to wrap the baby in against the piercing cold. "That's a little hard to believe. Didn't you almost run right into them before?"

"They didn't find us, did they? Lugh's bollocks, that's the ugliest infant I've ever seen."

"It's not his fault," I said, wondering how it was that Cathal accepted the unlikely truth so readily. Of all the people I knew, he was the last one I would have expected to share my ability to see and hear the child as he really was. I watched in silence now as he made a makeshift hearth of stones, stacked fallen wood, then took knife and flint from his pack to strike a spark and kindle the fire. He was efficient, as one would expect of an Inis Eala man. "Are you sure this won't bring them straight to us?" I asked eventually, as the fire began to burn. Amid the cool blue of the moonlit stones, the silvery fronds of the ferns, the pale gleam of the birch trunks, its glow was like a small, warm heart. I moved closer.

"No, I'm not sure," Cathal said. "But I'll know if they're coming. And you seem to be good at finding hiding places."

It was less than reassuring. "Can I do anything to help?" I asked. It felt uncomfortable to be idle while he was so busy. Now he had a small pan on the fire and was heating water. Becan was asleep in my arms, snug in his double shawl.

"This is the bit I can do," Cathal said. "You look after him; that's the bit I can't do. Got any food?"

"Some bread. It's in my bag." Another convulsive shiver ran through me. I held the baby close against my chest. Even with the fire, I was chill to the bone.

"Here."

Before I could protest, Cathal had unclasped his cloak and dropped it around my shoulders, over my own cloak. Instantly I was warm. The feeling was blissful. "But what about you?" I protested.

"Unlike you, I do some preparation before I set off on these expeditions. I have a blanket in my pack. Clodagh, what in the name of the gods were you doing, coming out here on your own?" He'd found the bread and was crumbling some of it into his pot of water.

"Why would I tell you?"

He sat back on his heels, dark eyes regarding me warily. "Why wouldn't you?" he asked.

"Because of what just happened. The attack on Glencarnagh. The fact that you described it to me almost exactly, days beforehand. How could you know about it unless—"

"Wait a moment." He held up a hand, arresting the flow of words. "Glencarnagh?"

I could have sworn he was genuinely confused. "My father's holding in the southwest; the place you spoke of when you were trying to tell me Deirdre and Illann might turn against him. It was attacked and burned. Most of the guards were killed. Once I heard about it I . . . I had to tell him, Cathal. It matched so exactly, the description of the house, the way they did it, everything."

"I see," he said after a moment. "When did this attack happen?"

"The night before last. Johnny met a survivor on the track and brought him home. I was there. I had no choice but to tell them what you'd said. Johnny sent Aidan out to bring you back."

Cathal turned his attention to his pot, stirring its contents with a stick. I was sure he did not want me to see what was in his eyes. "I feared as much," he said. "So they all believe me guilty. Even Johnny."

"You didn't exactly help by disappearing when you did. And I don't see how you could know so much about the attack before it happened unless you . . ."

"Unless what?" His tone was bitter. "Unless I plotted with your father's enemies to make the raid easier in some way? What possible cause would I have to do so, Clodagh? Why would I sacrifice my place with Johnny?"

"I don't know," I said. "I was as shocked as anyone. There seems no reason why anyone would attack Glencarnagh. It was my mother's ancestral home: the loveliest part of our holding. I don't know why you would have anything to do with it, but if you were somehow involved I wish you would confess to it and help Father find the perpetrator. This is tearing my family apart, Cathal. Finbar's abduction has almost destroyed my mother. And now this attack . . . Father's losing his good judgment, and that never happens. It's caused a rift between him and Johnny. It made Johnny and Aidan argue. Father blames me; he thinks he can't trust me anymore. And it hurts."

"He distrusts you? Why?"

"Because of what you and I were doing when Finbar was taken," I said with some reluctance. "Father was angry that I waited until the attack happened to tell him what you'd said. He thought I had personal reasons for protecting you."

"Hah!" Not a laugh, more an explosion of disbelief. "You disabused him of that notion, no doubt. It sounds as if your name is on the list of those who believe me some kind of traitor. Here. It's not of the standard to which you're accustomed, but it's hot." He offered me a metal cup full of the steaming bread and water brew. I settled the sleeping Becan on the ground in his shawls, wedged between my pack and Cathal's, and took the cup. It was warm between my hands.

"The evidence is not exactly in your favor," I said. "I've kept an open mind. So has Aidan. He argued very strongly in your defense. He didn't want to go after you. Johnny threatened to expel him from Inis Eala if he didn't obey. As I said, this has turned everything awry. It's as if someone is playing with us all; someone intent on stirring up as much trouble as possible."

Cathal moved to lean his back against the rock wall. As there was only one cup, he scooped his share from the pot. There was a lengthy silence.

"So," I said eventually, "are you going to tell me the truth?"

"About what?"

"About how you knew that attack might happen if you aren't

allied with whoever carried it out. And about why you left Sevenwaters so abruptly the moment this all began, without even telling Aidan what you were doing. Where were you going, anyway, and why are you still here?"

"You could at least express a little gratitude that I appeared just when you needed someone to make a fire and cook supper," he said lightly. "Forget those things. They're in the past; talking about them can't change anything. Clodagh, where are you running to? You must know your father will send men out to bring you back. You can't keep ahead of them on foot."

I didn't answer. He'd given me no reason to trust him.

Cathal sighed. "All right, I'll put my theory to you, and you can tell me if I'm right. You think to return the changeling to the place where it came from and bargain to get your brother back. You're going on your own because nobody believed you when you told them what this child was. Since changelings are supposed to originate from the Otherworld, that's where you're intending to go. Only you don't know the way, so you're wandering around at random hoping to stumble on it before you and the child die of cold or hunger or are apprehended by Lord Sean's search parties. An accurate summary? Don't look at me like that, Clodagh, it suggests you think I lack the wits to make a few simple deductions."

"You make me sound foolish, Cathal. I'm doing the best I can."

After a moment he said, "I know that. But this won't be the same as smoothing sheets and preparing the perfect supper, you realize."

I blinked at him. "This?" I asked. "What, exactly?"

"What comes next," said Cathal, using a finger to scoop the last scraps of sodden bread from the bottom of the little pot. "It's going to be difficult. Dangerous. As long as you understand that."

"That really isn't your concern," I told him, wishing he could have waited until the sun was up before putting this into words. "Of course I know it's dangerous. All the stories of the Otherworld make that quite clear. And I don't want to go. But I'm going anyway. I don't see any other choice."

"No, I suppose you wouldn't," Cathal said quietly, and when I glanced over, he was almost smiling.

"That's right, mock my attempt to make things better," I said. "You need put up with me only until dawn, Cathal. Then we can go our separate ways. Indeed, perhaps you shouldn't wait so long; you're perilously close to the keep still. The longer you stay with me and Becan, the greater your chances of being captured. I can't help you; I can only hinder you."

"That's true enough; you can't help me," Cathal said flatly, his eyes turned away now to stare into the darkness under the oaks. "But I think I can help you."

"You?" I could not keep the incredulity from my voice. "A fugitive? A man known to scoff at the least mention of the strange and uncanny? I don't see how, even if I could trust you enough to accept your assistance." This was perhaps a little unfair. He had heard Becan's voice; he had accepted my explanation of the infant's nature and origins. But maybe this was all part of some piece of trickery.

"You accepted the cloak," he pointed out.

"Here, take the wretched thing." I got up, fumbling with the clasp, and something within the garment's folds caught the firelight, flashing green. My hands stilled. I peered closer. A ring, glass by the look of it, plain and unadorned, sewn securely into the lining. Close to it, an owl feather, a white pebble, a fragment of bright silk. Precious things. A man's past, carried on his back for want of a real home to keep it in. Green, the sign of a traitor. There was much wisdom to be learned from stories. But their interpretations were many and it could be hard to choose which one was right.

"Wear it, Clodagh. You won't get a good night's sleep if you're cold. Maybe we should talk about this in the morning."

"No, now," I said, hugging the cloak back around me and sitting down again. I decided not to ask him about the ring. "In the morning there will be folk out looking for both of us. I need to find a portal to the Otherworld. I know such doorways exist in the Sevenwaters forest. If I'm meant to do this, I should be shown one before anyone catches up with me. I thought it would be today, but . . . Cathal, what is it?" His expression had changed abruptly. His thin features wore a look I had seen there before. I had found it as unsettling then as I did now. It was both grim and amused, as if he saw some irony in the situation that was quite lost on me. "What's wrong?"

"You read me too well," he said. "Why not today, one might ask; why tomorrow? So that you would not make the journey alone, perhaps. Clodagh, I can find your portal for you."

"You? What utter rubbish. How can you find something if you don't believe it exists? Don't play games with me, Cathal."

"I'm an Inis Eala man. We're well trained. I know how to find all sorts of things."

"I'll wager the training on the island does not include dealing with the powers of the Otherworld," I said. "True, Johnny was once the subject of a prophecy. He's long been destined by the Fair Folk to become Lord of Sevenwaters one day. But I've never heard that he or his men had abilities beyond the natural."

"But you were trying to find this doorway on your own, Clodagh. You can't be telling me that *you* possess such abilities." His gaze reflected me back to myself, a young woman whose best talent lay in running a perfect household.

"You know I don't, Cathal. But I think I'm meant to try. I think it's a task that's been laid on me."

He regarded me quizzically, dark eyes intense in a face whose pallor was warmed by the firelight. He was sitting on a fallen branch with his long legs stretched out toward the flames. His hands were restless, the fingers twining together. "You don't have a lot of time," he said quietly. "I can find it for you. It's up to you to let me do it or not. If you prefer, I'll go off at first light and leave you to your own devices. My prediction is that your father will track you down before midday. If you're serious about this quest of yours, you'll trust me, at least until I've found what you seek: a way in."

I slept rolled in Cathal's cloak with Becan tucked up next to me. Whether Cathal slept or not, I did not know. My last waking glimpse was of him sitting on the far side of the fire, staring into the flames, his arms around his knees, his blanket thrown over his shoulders. He looked deeply unsettled. I suspected his impulse to help me, perhaps in an attempt to compensate for the wrongs he had done, was warring with the entirely sensible desire to put as many miles between himself and Sevenwaters as he could. In the morning, I thought, I should tell him to go. Then I slept.

Before dawn he woke me with another brew, this time wild onions in hot water, and while I ate, then fed the baby, he covered the remnants of the fire with earth and packed up our things with a warrior's efficiency. I went briefly into the woods to relieve myself. When I returned he was squatting down beside the changeling, examining him closely without touching.

"Becan, did you say?"

"It's as good a name as any. It didn't seem right not to give him one. It was bad enough that everyone dismissed him as just a . . . thing." I was surprised that he had remembered the name; I must have mentioned it once or twice at most.

Cathal gave me his quizzical look. "You don't think this is taking family loyalty to too much of an extreme?" he asked.

"I'm doing what seems the right thing, that's all." I found his scrutiny unnerving, and looked away as I unfastened the cloak. I made myself say what was necessary. "You'd better take this back. I think you should leave us, Cathal. I had hoped you might turn yourself in and offer my father some explanations. Perhaps you don't realize how much trouble you caused by leaving so abruptly. If you won't go back and account for yourself, you could at least offer me some explanation. You dismissed that as unimportant. It's important to me."

Cathal shrugged, saying nothing at all.

"Well then," I said, disappointed even though this was more or less what I had expected, "you'd best get off Father's land as quickly as you can."

"You don't want my help?" he asked, and his dark eyes were still fixed on me, assessing.

I did want it. I didn't believe for a moment that he knew how to get into the Otherworld, but I shrank from the prospect of another day of wandering, another night in the open, this time without fire or the warmth of the cloak or companionship to stave off the myriad troubles that crowded my mind. "I think it's best if you go," I said.

"Best for whom?"

I could have lied, but I didn't. "For you," I told him. "Maybe you think you can find a portal, but in the stories people don't do it easily. Usually these ways only open when the Fair Folk have reasons for wanting someone to go in. Sometimes people need a charm or token to let them pass one way or the other. Or they have to chance on something, a mushroom circle for instance."

"There isn't time to argue the point," Cathal said. "I know Aidan and he knows me. He almost caught me yesterday. He and his men will have camped up here somewhere overnight. They'll be out again as soon as they've had a hasty bite to eat. In other words, they'll be in the forest when we are. Aidan may not want to be the one who apprehends me, but he's Johnny's man. If Johnny's given him an order he'll execute it efficiently even if it breaks his heart. For all sorts of reasons, I don't want him to do it. That means we have to move quickly."

"Didn't you hear me?" I was startled that it was not the fear of being captured that troubled him, but the fact that his friend would have to take him in. "I said go. On your own, now, while you still have time to get away." I thought perhaps I could hear dogs in the distance. So early. By midday I could be back at the keep and facing my father's excoriating questions. I could be seeing the sorrow and disappointment in his eyes; I could be looking at the pathetic, sunken remnant of a woman that was all that was left of my mother.

"I know you don't think much of me," Cathal said, flinging the cloak on. He hitched his pack onto his back and picked up mine. "Believe me, when you're being as pig-headed as this the feeling is mutual. Listen, now, and don't interrupt. Here are three reasons to trust me. One, I told you about the attack on Glencarnagh in a genuine attempt to warn you. That it was ineffective is not my fault. Two, I recognized that unprepossessing infant for what it was and I heard its wretched voice. I believed you when nobody else would. Three, I'm here, I'm willing to help, I have certain physical skills that could come in handy for protecting you and the child while you get to where you're going. And I do know how to find a portal."

"That's more like six," I said, wondering what it was that was making him put himself out to help me. Not altruism, that was certain; not a misguided desire to win my affections, despite that kiss. There was nothing soft in his expression. All I could see in it was impatience to be off. "Are you saying that you'll not only find this portal, but actually come with me when I go through it?" How could I accept such a mad offer? It would be risky enough to walk across that perilous margin myself. It would be beyond all sense to take someone else with me, someone who had no part at all in this particular mission. And yet, a profound relief had washed through me as he spoke of protection. If I ever got to the Otherworld all manner of dangers would face me. A warrior who could fight as Cathal had that day in the courtyard might be the best companion I could have.

"That's what I'm saying, Clodagh. Make up your mind quickly."

"Why? Why would you do such a thing?"

Cathal sighed, rolling his eyes. "I imagine even Johnny would find me hard to track down in the Otherworld," he said dryly. "Is that a good enough reason for you?"

"I don't know," I said, wanting to say yes, sure I should say no.

"Can we start walking, at least? Or do you plan to stand here arguing the point until Aidan's hounds come running up and sink their teeth into us?"

"All right. Take me to wherever you think the portal is. Let's put that to the test and worry about the other part later." I had fastened Becan into the sling. I reached out for my bag, but Cathal put it under his arm.

"I'll carry this; you've got him to manage. Ready?"

"No. But I'm going anyway."

He gave a lopsided smile. "Come on, then. I have a feeling it won't be far."

I followed Cathal in a direction I judged to be roughly northwest. We did not go by visible tracks, but took a dodging, swerving, zigzagging course between the rocks and trees. Cathal moved as if he knew where he was going. I suspected his apparent confidence had more to do with maintaining a semblance of control than anything else. No outsider knew the way through the Sevenwaters forest. They couldn't. For them, the way never stayed the same.

Silently, I prayed that the Fair Folk would reveal a portal to us sooner rather than later.

From time to time I heard the dogs somewhere behind us, not getting much closer, but not moving away either, and I wondered if Aidan was using the same techniques as Cathal for finding a path across the difficult terrain in this part of the woods. There were deceptive slopes that proved far steeper than they looked; rocks that jutted out in just the wrong places to provide secure purchase for hand or foot; sudden patches of sucking bog hidden beneath dark mats of last autumn's decaying leaf litter. We crossed a stream on a narrow log, Cathal taking the two packs over then returning with sure-footed confidence to grasp my hand and guide me across. I remembered him balancing along a dry-stone wall with Eilis and Coll. Eilis . . . I had not seen my little sister since Finbar was taken.

"What?" asked Cathal, scrutinizing my face as I stepped down to safety on the far bank.

"Nothing. Are we getting any closer?"

"I'm heading for the river. It can't be far from here."

My heart sank. "What river? There is no river, only the seven streams. The outflow from the lake is at the eastward end, far from here." I remembered what Sibeal had said about the meeting of earth and water, and how doors to the Otherworld would likely be found where this occurred. A moment later I recalled something else she had said: that I would not be undertaking my quest alone.

"No river," said Cathal flatly. "I was certain . . . Never mind. I think it's this way."

My memory of Sibeal's words stopped me from questioning his judgment, and we moved off again, down a hill through a grove of young birches, our feet sliding on the muddy incline. It began to rain. The narrow trunks of the trees were useful for slowing our dangerous progress, but their delicate foliage provided little cover from the weather. My hood refused to stay up over my head. The sling protected Becan for now, but it would soon be wet through. I could hear the dogs, and they sounded closer.

Near the foot of the slope I lost my balance and came down heavily on my hip. Becan squalled in fright. Tears sprang to my eyes.

"Quick, Clodagh!" Cathal spoke with a new note of urgency. He seized my hand and hauled me to my feet. "Can you hear it?"

Up the hill behind us someone shouted. I glanced back, but said nothing.

"Not them, the river. We're nearly there. Run!"

I could hear no river. There was no river, not on Sevenwaters land. But I ran, my body protesting at every step. The shouting came again, Aidan's voice urging the others on and the dogs clamoring. My hand was still in Cathal's. Rather than fall headlong I forced myself to keep up with him. Becan maintained a screaming protest, making my belly clench tight in sympathy. We raced along a narrow way under an arch of bigger trees, their pale trunks flashing by, the rain drizzling and dripping from every leaf to drench our clothing and our hair. Cathal swept his dark locks back from his face with an impatient hand. The pace never slackened.

We pelted out from the birch wood and into a curtain of rain. Suddenly there was no seeing the way. Water before, behind, on either side, a silver-gray veil obscuring rock, tree, path, everything but the little patch of ground at our feet. We slowed; to run on was to invite disaster. Cathal's grip tightened on my hand.

"Cathal!" Aidan's voice, somewhere within the downpour. "Don't make me set the dogs on you, you fool! Give yourself up, I know you're down there!"

"Good sign," murmured Cathal, moving forward into the rain and pulling me after him. "He hasn't let the dogs off yet. What are you doing, Clodagh, move!"

I moved, the alternative being to relinquish his hand and wait until the dogs arrived. The ground sloped down again, sharply. We could have been walking into anything at all. Three times, as we descended, Cathal had to brace himself and grab me by the arms to stop me from falling. I could feel Becan's cries vibrating through his small body. And then, above his wailing, above the drumming of the rain, I heard something else: a surging, rolling, washing music, the sound of a great body of flowing water. The veils of rain parted oddly and there before me, in as many shades of gray as there are stars in the sky, was the river.

This was not one of the seven streams. Even when swollen by

the rains of an unusually wet winter, the largest of those waterways would have been dwarfed by this. Its channel was as wide as a substantial grazing field, its surface eerily smooth, its flow quick; scraps of leaf or bark, borne crazily down, turned and twisted and passed like small eccentric racers. It looked deep. It looked cold. On its other side was a landscape unlike anything I had ever seen in the forest of Sevenwaters. The trees were massive, their trunks and branches knotted and gnarled and old. They were of no kind I recognized. A profound shade lay over them, and within that cloak of darkness it seemed to me no bird would have the courage to sing, no creature the heart to venture forth in search of nourishment. I saw no bridge, and was glad of it, for my heart quailed at the thought of setting foot on that far shore. Such a river did not exist on my father's territory. And yet, here it was.

"Cathal!"

I started in fright; Aidan's voice came from close behind me. I made to turn and look back, and under his breath Cathal said, "Down there. The boat. Quick, Clodagh."

A boat. Danu preserve us. As Cathal helped me down the last sharp drop I saw it: a raft, its wooden decking dark with age, its edges crumbling, its surface just big enough for two people if they sat close together and kept very still. It floated in the shallows, rocking ominously, tethered by a short rope. Another rope, thicker, much longer, stretched all the considerable way from this bank to the far side, dipping in the middle to a mere handspan above the fast-moving surface of the waterway. The poles that held it at either end looked far from substantial. A coil of the lighter rope lay on the raft. Perhaps there was some way of fastening it to the unlikely-looking line and pulling or pushing the thing across. The thought of it turned me cold.

We were at the river's edge. Cathal took my arm, tugging me toward the bobbing craft. I trembled with terror. My cowardice appalled me, but I could not make myself be brave about this. In my mind I saw the ramshackle conveyance tipping midstream and sending us into the swift-flowing water. Becan would be borne away in a heartbeat. And I could not swim.

"No," I whispered even as we reached the raft. "There has to be another way."

"In the name of the gods, Clodagh," Cathal snapped, "do you have a mission or don't you? This is it. There is no other way."

"Stop!" The voice was loud and commanding. I looked over my shoulder and my heart froze. Aidan was standing ten strides up the bank, visible between the oddly separated sheets of rain, his brown hair plastered flat to his head, his jaw set grimly, the arrow in his hunting bow aimed squarely in our direction. "Let her go, Cathal. Now." It was a warrior's tone, deathly calm. The moment Cathal obeyed him, he would be ready to shoot. If Cathal would not give himself up, his best friend was going to make an end of him.

"Aidan, don't!" I called. This couldn't be right. Neither my father nor Johnny would have wanted Cathal dead. "Don't do this!"

I might as well not have spoken. "Let her go, Cathal," Aidan said again. "She's not for you. I don't know what you're planning, but Clodagh has no part in it." The bow was perfectly steady.

Cathal let go of my hand. I was between him and Aidan's arrow. Aidan would not release it while there was a risk of hitting me. And now Cathal was giving me the choice. Be safe; go home. Forget him and his rash offer of help. Or . . .

"Get on the raft," I said. "Left foot first. Keep behind me. Take my hand, please. I'd rather not slip and go into the water."

His hand closed around mine again; I heard his indrawn breath. He had actually thought I would walk away. He'd really believed I would leave him facing that arrow. The raft creaked as he stepped on; I felt his grip tighten as the thing rocked and he fought for balance. A moment later I was standing there beside him, wobbling, my gut clenching in fear. Up on the bank, Aidan had lowered his bow. He looked like a man watching something dear to him perish before his eyes. His two companions had appeared behind him now, each with a straining dog on a rope. One gestured, clearly asking if the hounds should be loosed, and Aidan answered with a sharp negative.

I couldn't balance; it was impossible to stay upright. I tried to keep my body between Cathal and the shore while he did something complicated with the coil of rope, whistling through his teeth as he worked. I waited for Aidan to set the dogs on us; while we were moored here, they could reach us easily. I waited for him to come down and try to cut the rope. I waited for the three men to launch a concerted attack on Cathal—even a warrior of his talents could surely not prevail in such an uneven contest. But all Aidan did was put the arrow back in his quiver. As the shorter rope was fastened to the longer by means of an elaborately carved bone hook and Cathal began to pull us out onto the river hand over hand, his childhood friend stood utterly still, eyes dark in an ashen face, and simply watched us go.

CHAPTER 9

The river was swift. Its flow caught the raft a short distance out from the bank, sweeping us under the long rope and pulling the short tether so taut I was sure it would snap. Cathal was breathing hard; the muscles in his arms were bunched as he struggled to move us across the current. I crouched beside him, sheltering Becan. It was raining upstream and downstream, but not here. The downpour stopped a little short of our rope on either side, as if whoever had chosen to play with us had decided rain might be one challenge too many right now. Nonetheless, my cloak was sodden and Becan's sling was damp; he must be cold. I held him close, making myself keep my eyes open, though every instinct told me to curl up and shut out reality until this passage was over. There was nothing to hold onto. Each time the raft dipped one way or the other, freezing river water washed across its surface, drenching my skirt anew. My stomach was tight with fear. My back ached with the effort of keeping my balance.

Cathal's hand slipped on the rope. Cursing, he snatched and held. His narrow face wore an expression of fierce concentration. I dared not utter a word. What had I been thinking of, to let him risk his own safety coming with me? If he fell off, not only would he likely drown, but I would be stuck out in the middle of the river, lacking the strength to pull the raft to one side or the other. I should never, ever have allowed this to happen.

I risked a glance back. For a moment, just a moment, I saw the diminishing figure of Aidan on the shore behind us, and it seemed to me he half raised one hand in a tentative salute of farewell. Before I could respond, the rain descended over him. There was nothing to be seen but a sheet of gray. Ahead, the shadowy expanse of the unknown forest loomed ever closer as Cathal inched us forward, hand by straining hand, breath by labored breath.

"All right?" I asked, ashamed that my terror held me cringing on the raft, unable to help him.

"Mm. You?" was all he could manage.

I opened my mouth to tell him I was fine. Before I could utter this blatant lie, something flashed past a handspan from my eyes, whirring, creaking, crying out in sharp derision. I flinched back. Cathal swore as another of the creatures dived close, then rose, flapping, toward the trees on the far side. The raft jerked and began to rock crazily in the current. I clutched Becan; he screamed in fright. When I looked up again I saw that Cathal had lost his hold on the guide rope. We were still linked to it by the shorter tie, but the river was doing a powerful job of straining that tether to snapping point.

"All I can say is, I very much hope there's another way back." Grim-faced, Cathal took hold of the shorter rope with both hands and worked his way up it, leaning out over the water, until he could grasp the guide rope again. His palms were red raw; they would be all blisters.

"You're doing well," I said, eyeing the far bank. It still looked rather a long way away. And what if those creatures came back, bats, birds, something in between? "I'm sorry I'm not helping."

"You are helping," said Cathal. "Someone has to hold the child. Keep down, they're coming back."

Out of the corner of my eye I saw them approaching. They were feathered and beaked like crows, but their bodies resembled those of bats, with clawlike hands and feet. Pale eyes gleamed amid the coal-dark plumage. At a certain point in their flapping progress they simply folded up their bodies and plummeted straight toward us. This time I felt a sharp, raking blow across my cheek and I cried out in fright, pressing Becan's head against my chest. Cathal took one hand off the rope, reaching for the dagger in his belt. His eyes narrowed as he watched the creatures circling in preparation for a third assault.

"Leave it, just get us across," I gasped. I could feel blood trickling down my face. "I'm all right."

"A pox on it!" Cathal hissed, his jaw tight. He drew the dagger, weighing it in his hand as if preparing to throw. The raft swung this way, that way; water washed over my legs.

"Please, Cathal! Forget them, just get us to the other side. Ahh!" A swoop, a dive. Something sharp drew a line across my brow. Blood filled my eyes, blinding me. I hunched myself over Becan and muttered an incoherent prayer. The raft seemed to be moving more quickly now; Cathal had seen the wisdom in my words and was concentrating on hauling us over.

"Off, vermin!" he shouted. I felt sharp pain on the back of my neck, then across my arm, through the fabric of cloak and shirt. "Off!" And then, "Clodagh, here!" He was offering me the knife. The raft was dancing about on the water; I grabbed the weapon with difficulty. Cathal put his hand back on the rope and we steadied. "Try to fend them off," he said, his tone calm, his eyes far less so.

"It's not far now," I whispered, wondering if I might faint and knowing I could not possibly afford to do so. Cathal was only in this mess because of me. As for Becan, I was all he had. "I'm fine. Really." Brighid help me, the way the raft was rocking I'd as likely stick the knife into Cathal himself as land a blow on one of the attackers.

The things came again, three in formation, swooping low. They were aiming for me and me alone. With my left arm around the baby, I held the knife in my right hand, waving it more or less at random, for my head was muzzy now, my vision blurring. "Get off!" I yelled. As battle cries went, it was hardly impressive, but this time the creatures passed without making a mark on me.

"Good girl," I heard Cathal say. "Firm grip; keep your arm relaxed. Be ready for them."

I was, next time. The three dived toward me. I slashed with purpose and felt the weapon connect. There was an eldritch shriek as the wounded creature veered away from the raft, its companions creaking heavily after it. Their dark shapes merged into the gray obscurity of the rain. My hand relaxed on the dagger, then tightened again. I must not drop it. If one thing was sure, it was that we'd need a weapon on the other side. Cathal's tall form wavered before my eyes. The bank was closer now, but I could see it only as a shadowy blur. I thought maybe I was crying, or perhaps it was the blood.

"Clodagh!" Cathal's voice was sharp. "Don't faint, stay with me! I can't help you now, but we're nearly there. Hold onto the child; do your job."

Becan. I wiped my eyes again, noting with some detachment that my hand came away red, and looked down at the baby. He was hiccupping weakly; he had gone beyond fright. "Nearly there," I murmured to him. "Nearly there, sweetheart. *Oo-roo, little dove . . .*" My voice was rough as a toad's, but Becan didn't seem to mind. While Cathal wrestled with the rope, heaving us across the water, I continued the lullaby. The infant quieted, his sobs subsiding, his little twiggy hand curling trustfully into the sodden fabric of my shirt, his lips forming what looked oddly like a smile. Did babies smile so early? *"Time to bid farewell to day,"* I sang, and we reached the other side.

Cathal hooked our craft to a weathered pole set among rocks. He held out his hand to help me up. My legs were not keen to support me.

"Left or right this time?" he asked, standing on the edge of the raft. He sounded admirably calm.

"Left going in," I said. "Right coming back. I heard a tale about it once."

"What happens if you make a mistake?" He stepped off with his left foot, guiding me after him. The shore was covered with tiny white stones as smooth and regular as eggs. They crunched as we walked forward.

"I don't know. I think you might end up somewhere different, not where you wanted to go. Or you might not be able to cross the margin at all. These things matter. I wish I could remember properly." I reached up to wipe my face again.

"Here," Cathal said. He had put the two bags on the ground. Now he began to unfasten his, perhaps seeking a cloth with which to stem the flow of blood.

"Don't worry about that, I'm fine." I heard my own voice as if down a tunnel, its tone distant and hollow. "Shelter. We must get dry . . ." A moment later trees, rocks and pebbles spun before me and everything went dark.

I woke to the crackling of a fire and the sound of Cathal muttering, "All right, all right, I'm doing the best I can." Becan was crying. I had Cathal's cloak around me, and when I opened my eyes I could see the sky. It was a shadowy purple-gray with neither sun nor moon in evidence. I could not tell whether it was day or night. Dusk? Had I lain in a dead faint most of the day? I lifted a cautious hand to my face, feeling for damage, and winced as I touched swollen, abraded skin. My hair was sticky with blood.

I sat up. A wave of dizziness went through me, making my stomach churn. I swallowed, breathed, sat a moment waiting for the nausea to subside. I could not afford any more weakness.

"You're awake," Cathal said. "Good. My efforts to feed our friend here haven't gone well, and he's loud. I'm concerned his cries will bring company we don't want. Judging by the reception we received on the way across, I'd say we can't expect an easy trip. Can you take him?"

He was sitting cross-legged not far away with Becan in his arms. The infant's arms and legs had come free of his shawls. His cries held a tone of outrage.

"Pass him over here." I held out my arms and realized belatedly that underneath the cloak I wasn't wearing much at all. "Where are my clothes?"

"Drying out," Cathal said. "See, over there." My gown, cloak, shift and stockings were hanging over a makeshift frame of branches and bracken on the far side of the fire, steaming gently in company with various garments of Cathal's. "No need to blush," he added. "You're still covered, just. It's cold here. The things you were wearing were sodden, and the spares in your bag weren't much better. I didn't really have a choice."

I couldn't think of a thing to say, so I gathered the cloak around me as best I could and took the infant on my lap to feed him. A little later, with Becan relaxed and sucking steadily, Cathal and I regarded each other in the firelight, and if his gaze was wary, I imagine mine was more so. We were in the forest, that strange forest we had glimpsed across the river. The trees were big enough to dwarf the most massive oak at Sevenwaters, and the spaces under them were full of an intense and disturbing darkness like that of a vast subterranean chamber. There was an eerie stillness about the place, a sense of anticipation that was not allayed by the little crackle of our fire. From the area of level ground where we were camped the terrain fell in a gentle slope to the east. I thought I could hear the murmuring voice of the river some distance away.

"How did you get me up here?" I asked, and even though there was nobody to be seen but the three of us I kept my voice down.

"You were easy enough to carry," Cathal said. "The difficult part was leaving you and the child here while I went back for the bags. I half expected that some mysterious entity would snatch you away the instant my back was turned, just to remind me that this place is . . . different."

I didn't really want to owe him still more of a debt, but it seemed I did. He had not only carried me to safety, he had undressed me, cleaned me up, then left me to sleep while he made a fire, dried out my clothing and tried to look after Becan as well. In view of our situation, the fact that Cathal had seen me at close quarters in my small-clothes seemed far less shocking than it would have done a day ago.

"How's your face?" he asked. "Does it hurt?"

"Not much. I feel sick, but it will pass. How bad are the cuts?"

"Not so bad. I'll tend to them again tomorrow." He was matter-of-fact about this.

"Cathal, how long was I unconscious? Is it really dusk already?"

"Believe me, if that were so I would have been trying to rouse you long before this. As it was, Becan took a great deal of my attention. He has a powerful voice. How very fortunate that he doesn't need milk. Imagine bringing a goat across on that raft. So, what now?"

"We go on, I suppose. But maybe not right away. How soon will our things be dry enough to wear?"

"Your clothing won't be ready before morning. I'm sure you don't want to walk on dressed like that, so we'd best stay here overnight and keep the fire going. I did hesitate over lighting it. The smoke will draw attention if there's anyone about. Which way are we headed next?"

I looked at him. He appeared remarkably sanguine, considering everything. Another part of the training, I supposed. And he hadn't uttered a single word of reproach. It was almost annoying. It made me feel deeply inadequate, and I didn't like that. "I thought you were the one who knew the way," I said.

"I promised to find a portal. I've done that."

True enough. Wherever we were, we were no longer in the forest of Sevenwaters. "I hate to say this," I said, "but I think we just keep on walking, and sooner or later we'll find what we're looking for. That is, someone who can tell us where my baby brother is. Then we go there and I ask these people to give him back."

"And you hand over Becan in exchange." There was something slightly odd in his tone, as if there were an unspoken question beneath this statement.

"What's wrong with that?" I asked.

"Nothing at all, Clodagh. It makes perfect sense, if the rules of our world are applied to the problem."

"I don't have any other rules to apply," I said quietly. "Cathal, how did you know we had to cross the river? How did you know there *was* a river? There's no such place on any map of Sevenwaters, and I know we didn't go beyond Father's borders."

He shrugged. "A hunch," he said.

"Like the one that told you Glencarnagh was going to be attacked."

"Mm-hm. Does it matter? You wanted to be here and you're here. Cold and wet, underdressed, with a few scars you'd probably rather not have, but in the land of the Tuatha De Danann. At least, one supposes that is where we are." For a moment I saw a look of deep disquiet on his face. He masked it quickly, his features assuming a bland expression.

"Why is that so easy for you to believe now, when you scorned the very existence of such folk back at the keep?" I asked him.

Another shrug.

"Stop *doing* that!" I snapped, making Becan wail in fright. "Shh, shh," I whispered, lifting the baby up against my shoulder while trying to keep the cloak modestly around me.

"Stop doing what?"

"Refusing to answer me properly. Acting as if nothing in the past matters. Pretending it wasn't completely mad for you to come here with me. Not explaining why you're doing anything at all. What about you and Aidan? Didn't you see his expression when we set off from the shore? He looked as if we were breaking his heart. How can you be so . . . so detached about it all?"

He had unpacked his little cook pot and set it on the flames. It already held water, and now he produced a small harvest of mushrooms, which he proceeded to break into the pot. The silence drew out between us as the brew came to the boil and a savory smell arose, making me realize how hungry I was. Cathal added a handful of greenery to the mixture and stirred it. Eventually he looked up, meeting my eye across the fire. "The shirt I was wearing is almost dry," he said. "Here." The garment was hanging from a bush; he took it down and tossed it in my general direction. "Bear in mind," he added, "that I've already seen you with a lot less on than that, and don't let it trouble you too much. I'm bone weary after that river crossing and I haven't the least inclination to take advantage of you."

I looked at him a moment, then said, "Thank you."

"It's not altruism," Cathal said. "If we're attacked again, it's going to help if you have both hands free to defend yourself. The requirement to keep your modesty shielded with a cloak would make that difficult. I want you to keep one of my knives, Clodagh. We can't know what's coming, but after that episode with the bats, or whatever they were, I think we can assume we're not entirely welcome here. What are you going to do if these people won't give your brother back?"

Since I had no answer to this, I gave him a little of his own treatment, responding with a shrug. Becan had fallen asleep against my shoulder. His shawls were damp, and so were his swaddling cloths. "Curse it," I said. "I'm going to have to wash these."

"Eat first," Cathal said.

"Where did you pick the mushrooms?" I asked. "We shouldn't eat anything from here, that's one of the rules."

"Or?"

"Or we have to stay in the Otherworld forever." Gods, it smelled good.

"I had them in my pack before we crossed over," Cathal said. "Savor every mouthful; if you're right about the food here, we'll be on limited rations until we get back across. How long do you think this will take? And what about *him*?" He nodded toward the sleeping child. I had placed Becan on the ground while I took off the cloak and donned the shirt over my damp small-clothes. Under the circumstances, the best I could do for modesty was to turn my back and hope Cathal wasn't looking.

"He seems to thrive on the honey water," I said. "I can fill my water-skin from the streams on this side. I can't see any reason why Becan shouldn't partake of Otherworld food. I don't know how long the journey will take. Not too long, I hope. My mother is fading fast; she needs Finbar back."

"It suits you," Cathal observed as I finished fastening the cords on his shirt and turned to face him. The garment was of good quality wool, warm and light. It came down to my knees.

I tried to imagine how I looked. My hand went to my face, touching the welts gingerly. "I'm going to have scars, aren't I?" I asked.

"Think of it as adding character."

I grimaced. "To my boring face? Oh well, I suppose that's the least of my worries right now. Cathal, I should go back to the river to wash these shawls."

"Does it really matter if he's wet or smells a bit? It's not as if he's a flesh and blood child, after all. He seems more plant than baby to me. It's natural for plants to be wet."

I looked down at the sleeping child, curled in his damp shawls on the forest floor. Leaf-lids covered the pebble eyes, and the bark slivers that formed his lips moved gently in and out as if he dreamed of sucking. His hands were open, trusting. "He's a real child with real needs and feelings, despite his odd appearance," I said. "He deserves to be cared for just as Finbar does, just as any human baby does. It wouldn't be right to neglect him. Clean clothing is only part of it. There are stories and singing; food and shelter and love. Every child needs those things. Becan shouldn't be denied them just because he's . . . different." Perhaps, when I got home and looked in my mirror, I would be different too. Perhaps I would be so scarred that my chances of attracting a good husband, someone like Aidan, would have all vanished away. I thought of my sister Maeve, far off in Harrowfield, with the cruel marks of her burns disfiguring her face.

"Very well," said Cathal. "When we've eaten, I'll show you a place I spotted where there's a small stream and a pool. We can wrap him in the cloak; I'll give you my tunic to wear in the meantime." He was removing it even as he spoke. "Now let's try these mushrooms."

Approaching the pool later, we disturbed a badger drinking. I held my breath, watching it turn its head to peer in our direction then retreat into the shelter of the ferns that fringed the waterway. An ordinary badger, with no sign of eldritch qualities at all. Somewhere high in the canopy above us birds were exchanging mournful cries, confirming that there was indeed life on this side of the river. In the undergrowth something scurried away, fearful of our cautious footsteps.

I settled the sleeping baby between the massive roots of a tree. Cathal stationed himself on a flat rock and I knelt by the pool's edge to wash out the two shawls and the swaddling. The water was preternaturally chill; it was like plunging my hands into liquid ice. As I pounded the cloth on the stones, I tried to concentrate on a plan for tomorrow. How far could we reasonably expect to walk? Perhaps we should look for high ground so we could assess the lie of the land. If we saw any signs of life, would it be better to hide or to reveal ourselves? Somehow, stepping out and asking to be taken to Finbar's abductors did not seem altogether a wise course of action. Those creatures at the river had been intent on attacking us.

"Are you done?" Cathal asked quietly. "We should return to the fire."

"I suppose these are clean; the light isn't good enough to see properly." Perhaps it really was dusk now. The presence of badgers and owls suggested that. But maybe in this place it was always dusk. The prospect was disturbing. It was so much easier to feel confident by sunlight.

"You look tired," Cathal said when we were settled by our fire once more. "You must sleep. Hold the child close to you and use my cloak. You should be warm enough. I'll stay on watch and keep the fire going."

"All night?" I studied him, taking in the long face, the grave features now quite devoid of their customary look of derision. "I can't let you do that. You must wake me after a few hours. I know I can't defend us against an attack, but I can keep watch and alert you if I see or hear anyone coming."

The thin lips twisted into a smile. "If you insist."

"I do," I told him. "I don't want you staying heroically awake all night, then being too tired to make yourself useful in the morning. If there is a morning." I shivered.

"There will be, Clodagh." As Cathal spoke, a silvery light began to steal across the forest floor, touching the boles of the great trees, where rich layers of moss glowed green, and revealing in the spaces above us a host of tiny flying creatures on iridescent wings, moving so quickly their exact shapes were unclear. Not insects. Not birds. Something else. "Morrigan's britches," murmured Cathal. "What are they?"

"At least they're small," I said, remembering the attack at the river. "Cathal, promise you'll wake me."

"My word on it, Clodagh. You know, you are not quite the girl I took you for when we first met."

"Oh, I'm exactly as I seemed then," I said with some bitterness. "My chief strength is in household management. I'm the kind of girl who'll make a nice little wife for someone one day. I have none of the skills required for an expedition like this. I can't swim. I can't fight. I'm not brave. I'm not persuasive when it counts. I wish I had the capacity to surprise you, Cathal, but I am no more than I appear to be." Becan's pebble eyes were open now and fixed on me as I rewrapped him, using lengths torn from a spare shirt Cathal had produced. The infant made little cooing sounds. His voice had softened; I wondered that I had at first thought it harsh as a crow's.

"I regret what I said to you when we first met," Cathal said, putting his arms around his knees. "As Aidan has no doubt told you, I've always lacked the ability to summon the kind of conversation deemed acceptable in the halls of the nobly born. I am unable to play that game without sabotaging my own efforts; I cannot take it seriously. Clodagh, it seems to me you expend all your energy trying to make those around you happy. Do you care nothing for your own welfare? It is hard for me to understand that."

Abruptly, I was on the verge of tears. I must indeed be tired. I blinked them back, picking up the swaddled Becan and cradling him in my arms. "It's hard not to worry about my family," I said. "Mother especially. She's waited all these years for a boy. She and Father had twin sons, a long time ago. The boys lived less than a day. I can remember Muirrin taking us up to the hawthorn—Deirdre, Maeve and me—when the boys were born, so we could say prayers for their good health." Perhaps that was when I had started to lose my faith in the benign influence of the Otherworld. It had been a hard test for a little child. "Cathal, if we don't get this right, if we don't manage to bring Finbar back, I'm sure my mother won't survive. She'll just let herself . . . fade away. I wish I could know what's happening at home." The tears dripped down my cheeks. "A pox on it. I don't want to cry," I said, wiping my nose on the sleeve of the borrowed shirt. "They'll know where I've gone, at least. I told Sibeal what I'm trying to do. She said she'd tell them."

Cathal took his time about answering. It was odd; a day or two ago I would never have spoken thus in his company. If I had, I would have expected him to respond with a cutting remark about my great capacity to feel sorry for myself. I was profoundly aware that on this side of the river everything was different, even him. "I know little of such matters," he said eventually. "It does seem to me that this might be reasonable cause for tears. Does it embarrass you to shed them before me?"

I looked at him curiously. "Wouldn't it embarrass you to weep with me watching you?" I asked.

"I don't know," Cathal said. "If I ever have reason to do so, I'll be sure to tell you how it feels. Clodagh, did you say you can't swim?"

I nodded. "Somehow I could never learn."

"And you still got on the raft?"

"At the time there wasn't much choice."

Cathal made no comment. He had taken some strips of dried meat from his pack and added them to the pot. I was hungry enough to find the smell quite appealing. I rocked Becan again, singing him to sleep.

When the child was tucked back into the cloak, Cathal passed me the cup, full of the meat and water brew. "We'll run out of drinking water soon," he said. "Does this rule about not eating Otherworld food really extend to the streams and ponds as well?"

I tried to remember stories I had heard on the subject. "I don't know. I do believe the Fair Folk intend me to do this. It must be possible for me to find Finbar and bring him back. Perhaps drinking the water will be safe. I mean, there's no reason why the Fair Folk would want to trap me in the Otherworld."

After a silence that seemed slightly too long, Cathal said, "True. Well, if our journey lasts more than another day or two, we'll have no choice but to put that to the test."

"Cathal?"

"Yes?"

"This cloak. It intrigues me."

"Uh-huh." His tone was less than encouraging.

"Aidan said the tokens sewn into it are from your past; that they're memories. I'm wondering . . ."

"What, Clodagh?" In his voice I heard the old Cathal, the one who would more likely snap at me for being a busybody than offer any kind of explanation. "You seek a confidence in exchange for the ones you have provided?"

I waited a little, watching his expression. The unease was there again, the shadow of a deep-seated fear. I was certain of it. "I just thought you might be prepared to talk about it," I said. "Especially now, when there's nobody but me to hear you."

"There's nothing to tell." Cathal shifted uneasily, prodding the fire with a stick. "You mentioned that you were exactly the person I saw when I first met you: a paragon of the domestic arts with not much to her beneath the surface. I am precisely the man I was when you clapped eyes on me: a selfish, arrogant outsider even shorter on manners than he is on common sense. What more could you need to know?" He tossed the stick onto the fire.

I sat silent. True, I'd said not long ago that my only potential was as a nice wife for someone. That didn't mean I liked hearing Cathal confirm the fact.

"I was wrong, of course," he said. "You're not that woman at all. But I, unfortunately, am that man. Peel away my layers and all you'll find is more of the same. All dazzle and no substance."

"I don't believe you." I kept my voice level, holding his gaze. "If that were true you'd be happy to answer questions about your past, because you wouldn't care about it. A man who doesn't care doesn't carry his memories around with him everywhere like charms of protection."

"Charms," he said flatly. "The way other men carry rowan crosses, you mean. You know I don't believe in such things."

"And you don't believe in the Otherworld, isn't that right?" I gazed at him across the fire. "You'll have to do better than that, Cathal. I'm happy that you no longer think me a shallow, domesticated creature. If it's of any interest to you, I've had cause to revise my opinion of you too. If that weren't so, I wouldn't dream of asking you about this. Actually, I thought mine was a fairly safe question. There are others that would be far more challenging."

"Such as?" His expression dared me to speak and face his scorn.

I drew a deep breath. "I could ask who your father was," I said. I recalled the way Aidan had tried to convince my father that Cathal was no traitor, as if it were desperately important to him. I remembered how kind Cathal had been to Aidan that morning in the stables, when I'd overheard their private conversation. I thought of the taunts they'd exchanged as they battled it out on the practice ground. I had a theory about Cathal's parentage, one that I could not tell him. Two boys raised together, as close as brothers; the exceptional generosity shown by a chieftain to a low-born local lad; a mother who would not reveal the name of the man who had fathered her son . . .

"But you won't," he said. Whether it was a statement or a warning I could not tell.

"It wouldn't be appropriate," I said. "Though I have wondered if that is the key to your unhappiness, Cathal. I suppose if you decide to trust me as a friend, some day perhaps you'll tell me of your own free will."

"As far as you're concerned, I have no father," Cathal said shortly. "You were unhappy that Lord Sean didn't believe your story about the changeling, that he seemed to have stopped trusting you. That will pass. I predict with complete confidence that when you arrive back home your father will throw his arms around you and thank the gods for your safe return, whether or not you succeed in finding your brother. And then he will apologize and admit that he misjudged you. Be glad that you have such a father, Clodagh. He may seem hard to you at times, but he is the best of men."

"I know that," I said, my throat tight. "This isn't fair, Cathal. We weren't talking about me."

"Ah, yes, the cloak. Well, it amuses me to collect bits and pieces, and it seems appropriate to carry them with me. Each has its own story, that is true. You might think of it as part of a carefully cultivated image: that of an eccentric man without a fixed abode. Hence my need to carry reminders of who I am and where I came from."

This was a most unsatisfactory answer. "When we were hiding under that rock, when Aidan nearly caught us with the dogs, you stuffed the cloak into the gap," I said. "And the dogs ran straight past us. I know those dogs. They're highly trained. They wouldn't have missed us."

Cathal said nothing.

"The cloak stayed dry when we crossed the river. Most of our other clothing ended up soaked," I said. "When I've got it on I feel warm right through, not just because it's made of thick felt but . . . something else as well. I feel safer, somehow. This will sound strange, Cathal, but I've wondered if those charms have some power beyond themselves. Don't shrug like that, I'm serious. Uncle Conor told me once that hearth magic, like putting white stones under the doorstep to keep a house safe or weaving withies in a special way to protect stock in a pen, can be quite effective if it's carried out with sincere belief. I am wondering if . . . if tokens of good times, symbols of love and friendship, for instance, may have a protective power in a garment such as this cloak. See,

I'm not asking a difficult personal question now, merely posing a theoretical one for you."

"You're setting a trap," Cathal said.

"I don't set traps for friends."

A silence. Then he said, "Perhaps you misunderstand my reasons for being here."

"Perhaps you should tell me what they really are." Suddenly the air between us was thick with something unspoken and dangerous. My skin prickled strangely.

"I can't talk about it," he said. "I can't give an explanation. Clodagh, I had a friend back on the other shore. Look what happened there. The last sight I got of him, he was trying to kill me."

I didn't like the way this was going at all. We were deep in the forest, in this strange unknown country, and the only companion I had was pushing me away. Meanwhile, those small sparkling entities that had been swirling and twirling overhead were gone, and all of a sudden the forest felt very big and empty. "You didn't have to come with me," I said, trying not to sound as upset as I felt.

Cathal sighed. "Go to sleep, Clodagh." I heard in his words a curt dismissal. He didn't want to talk to me. He didn't want to listen. I'd been a fool to try to get any closer.

I set aside my empty cup and lay down beside Becan, drawing the cloak around both of us. Something cool and smooth slid across my abraded cheek, and I put up a hand to touch it. The ring; green glass, plain and small. A woman's size. It would fit me, I thought.

"My mother's," said Cathal, who surely couldn't see from where he sat. "The only thing of hers that I have. I don't want to talk about it, and I don't want to talk about her. Or him. Not now, not ever. It's better if you and I keep our distance. Anything else is . . . it's just too dangerous. I'm not here because of a burning desire to be your friend and tell you all my secrets. I'm here because I think this whole sorry mess, every last bit of it, has happened because of me. I told Johnny I didn't want to come to Sevenwaters. When he brought me, he brought disaster to his family. Now go to sleep. I suspect tomorrow will be a long day."

CHAPTER 10

It was not Cathal who woke me before dawn, but Becan, shrilly requesting nourishment. I fed him, yawning. Cathal reported that he had seen nothing untoward, and agreed with some reluctance to sleep for a little while I kept watch. He refused to put on his cloak, insisting that I would be too cold without it. I waited until he had fallen asleep, then laid it over him, settling by the fire with Becan in my arms. The forest was quiet. Nothing stirred in the bracken; nothing cried out in the trees above me. The moonlight was gone, and the color of the sky suggested sunrise might not be far off, if the sun ever showed its face in this uncanny realm. Although the air was cool and fresh, there was something about the place that made me feel as if I were underground, a weight pressing down on me. I longed for my little bedchamber, the familiar halls and stairways of Sevenwaters, the comfort of my daily routines. I longed for clarity of mind. What had Cathal meant, that all of this was his doing? Was it, in fact, a confession of treachery? I found myself reluctant to believe that. Cathal had fled Sevenwaters just before the attack was reported. He had distracted me at the moment when Finbar was taken. And then he had hung about in the forest instead of escaping, and come with me all the way to the Otherworld. It made no sense at all.

I regarded the sleeping Cathal, stretched out under the cloak with his head pillowed on one bent arm. In repose his features were pleasing: not handsome like Aidan's or harmonious like Johnny's, but grave and strong. The eyelids were shadowed with weariness; the bold strokes of the fox tattoo emphasized the dark, emphatic brows, the straight nose and prominent cheekbones. The contours of his face were all angular, with nothing soft about them, though his lips looked less severe in slumber. If he was actually Aidan's half-brother, as I suspected, there was little physical evidence of it. *It's better if you and I keep our distance,* he'd said. I wondered, again, why he had kissed me.

"I don't want him to be an enemy," I whispered.

There was a sound like a dry cough from low down in the undergrowth right by me. I started violently, clutching Becan to my chest. "Who's there?" I hissed, telling myself it was probably only a hedgehog and knowing in my bones that it wasn't.

A patter of feet in the bushes. Not claws, not paws; feet in shoes. Crazily, I thought of clurichauns in little green boots.

Cathal stirred, flinging an arm over his eyes, then rolled so his back was to me. I really didn't want to wake him up, not unless I couldn't cope alone. He'd looked so exhausted. In sleep, he seemed almost peaceful. If this thing, whatever it was, popped out armed to the teeth, I wouldn't hesitate to scream. There wasn't much point in having a warrior of Inis Eala by my side if I couldn't make use of him in a crisis.

"Show yourself," I said as boldly as I could, my hand curling around the hilt of the little knife in my belt. "Friend or foe?"

A low chuckle emanated from the ferns, and a moment later out stepped a small figure in a hooded cloak of gray fur. I could not see its face, for it held a mask before its features, a dog mask made of shining silver, wrought with stunning detail down to each tooth in the gaping mouth, each hair on the shining pelt. The ears were pricked like those of a hunting hound on alert. The creature behind this concealment was child-sized. Its hand, holding the silver rod that supported the false face, was human in shape but covered in fur like the cloak. Maybe gloved; maybe not. Through holes in the mask I could see a hint of lustrous eyes. "A challenge!" The being's voice was deep and strong; this was no child. "Friend or foe: I like that. Why are you traveling with *him*?" The creature jerked its head toward Cathal. "He smells wrong. Why did you bring him here? Best lose him as quick as you can."

"What?" I was shocked. The fact that I had just been considering whether my companion was a traitor seemed irrelevant. "Why? And what concern is that of yours?" This small entity did not seem particularly threatening, but I must be careful. Whatever this dog-person was, it surely wasn't one of the Fair Folk.

"Lose him!" the creature hissed. "Bad blood! Shadows and darkness!"

Out of the corner of my eye, I saw Cathal stir again. I did not turn my head. "Why should I listen to you?" I asked as calmly as I could, though the creature's words had chilled me.

"You want a guide, don't you? I can guide you. But I won't take *him* anywhere. Go on with him and you'll be on the sure path to heartbreak. You must lose him tomorrow. Walk one way, let him walk the other. While he stays with you, you'll be beset by difficulties. You'll be attacked, hurt, scarred, damaged. You think your beauty marred by those cuts. Believe me, there'll be far worse to come if you keep him by your side. You don't need him, Clodagh. You don't want him. His kind are scum."

"How do you know my name?" This was deeply unsettling.

"We know. *How* doesn't matter. Get rid of him, quickly."

"I'd never have got across the river without Cathal," I said, keeping my voice quiet though I was becoming angry. "Without him, I'd never even have found it. Whatever he may have done in the human world, he's here because he wants to help me. He said so and I believe him."

The mask turned toward me. "You pity him." The creature's tone was flat. "As you pity the little scrap you have there on your knee."

I laid a protective hand on Becan's curled-up form, swathed in Cathal's tunic. "Pity?" I said. "I don't think so. I try to give folk the benefit of the doubt, that's all. I try not to judge too quickly."

"Ah, well," Dog Mask said airily, "don't say you didn't get your chance of help." Its squat form began to fade away before my eyes.

"Wait!" I cried. The creature halted, wavering in and out of visibility. "What are you? Why would you offer to help me?"

"That's immaterial if you choose to keep *him* with you. Do that and you'll be finding the way yourself."

"He's an Inis Eala man," I said, wondering if I was being extremely foolhardy, but knowing I would not give in to threats. "He'll find it for me."

A peal of derisive laughter, a rustle in the ferns, and the creature was gone. All around the camp there was a shifting and a moving in the shadows, as if there had been not one small being here, but many. I had a sense of their folding back into the landscape, merging with the earth and the tree trunks and the bushes. Then, utter silence. I hugged Becan close. "Don't tell me," I murmured. "I probably imagined the whole thing. A bang on the head can do that."

I tried to remember all the tales I'd heard about the various folk who lived in the Otherworld, the grand and powerful Tuatha De Danann and the other races with whom they shared that realm. These included a tribe commonly referred to as the Old Ones, known for their remarkable ability to blend into the landscape, assuming forms not unlike those of trees or stones or streams. Sometimes they were no more than shadowy voices. Sometimes they took creature shapes. They were no friends of the Fair Folk. Indeed, there was a bitter rivalry between the two peoples, dating back to ancient times when a great war had raged across Erin and the Old Ones had been driven back to their deep caves, their wells and their remote islands. I wished one of my druid uncles were here so I could ask about them. I seemed to remember that one of the original ancestors of Sevenwaters had wed a woman of the Old Ones. That meant there was a little of their blood in my veins.

"Still," I murmured to Becan, "that doesn't mean they're trustworthy. I don't want to do this on my own, little one. I don't want to leave Cathal behind. That would feel wrong. Heartbreak, the creature said. Does that mean I won't get Finbar back unless I go on alone? Or is this all some kind of trap?"

But Becan was asleep again, his odd little face peaceful within the folds of the tunic. I was cold. Cathal had been right, his cloak was the only item we had with the capacity to keep out the chill of this forest at night. Fleetingly, I allowed myself to imagine creeping under it and curling up next to him, our bodies warming each other. I felt my cheeks flush. Silly, really, that one might risk freezing to death rather than act improperly. If it grew any colder I would be sorely tempted. Still, I was supposed to be on watch. Sighing, I got up and checked my own cloak, still hanging by the fire. It was almost dry. I put it on and settled to wait until morning. How long it would take to come, there was no telling. Time passed differently here; the stories made that starkly evident. Our journey might seem to last only a few days, yet devour far more time in the human world. I did not think I would cope at all well if I returned triumphant, with Finbar in my arms, to find my family aged by twenty, thirty, forty years, my parents dead, Sibeal and Eilis middle-aged women, my home changed by the passage of a whole generation. More, perhaps: a hundred years, and everyone gone. I patted Becan's sleeping form for reassurance. In the tales, some folk never came home.

By the time Cathal woke, I had almost persuaded myself not to tell him what had happened. The need to explain why I had refused an offer of help was especially awkward in view of the fact that he had made it clear he felt no friendship toward me, only a bizarre sense of obligation. I knew he wouldn't explain what he had meant about the ills that had befallen my family somehow being his fault. He never explained anything. If I wanted to find out what that was all about, I would have to work much harder at earning his trust. And perhaps my nocturnal visitor had been right after all. Perhaps Cathal was the trickster I had first believed him to be, and I was marching into battle in company with an enemy. Perhaps I was letting my feelings get the better of me. Whatever they were. Not pity; the creature had certainly got that wrong. One couldn't pity a person like Cathal. He intrigued me. I had never met anyone who was so much an outsider. It seemed to me he worked against himself, unable to fit in, therefore making a point of shifting himself still further beyond the rules of us ordinary folk. And yet there was a profound unhappiness in him. If being odd, eccentric and unpredictable was his choice, it wasn't one he made gladly. I would swear that what he wanted above all was to fit in somewhere—to belong. Perhaps, at Inis Eala, he had found a place where that was possible. Johnny had done Cathal no favors by bringing him to Sevenwaters. No doubt the man wished he'd never clapped eyes on me.

In the end, I told him everything as we packed up our camp after a quick breakfast. A strange visitor, a cryptic warning, an offer of help if certain conditions were met.

"So I said no," I told him. "I said I trusted you to find the way for me."

Cathal had been silent for most of my lengthy recounting; he stayed silent now, concentrating on fastening the straps around his pack.

"Maybe that was foolish," I said as I adjusted Becan's position in the sling. It was day. The sun could not be seen, but a hazy light filled the forest around us and beyond the latticed branches of the tall trees the sky was golden. In my dry clothes, with my cloak over the top, I was comfortably warm at last. I could feel my courage coming back.

"You should have woken me," Cathal said. "What if the creature had attacked you? That's the point of my being here, to protect you."

"You looked tired. I wanted you to get some sleep. And it didn't attack me. As things turned out, if you'd been awake it probably wouldn't have spoken to me. It tried to convince me you were a danger. Scum, I think that was the word used."

"Ah, well," Cathal said, "I've been called worse before. As for the way, we'll find it together. Are you ready?" He reached out a hand to me, and I saw a rare expression on his face, a sweet, uncomplicated smile that was gone almost before it appeared.

"I'm ready," I said, and we walked on together.

The forest was quiet, but it was not an empty stillness today. Under every great mossy tree, in every small depression of the land, around each rocky outcrop there was a sense of anticipation. I felt eyes on us from everywhere. They were waiting for us; they were watching us. I walked with my skin in goose bumps, reminding myself to keep my breathing steady. Cathal set the pace; I kept up. My legs began to hurt, but I did not complain.

After what felt like a full morning's walking, the spaces between the trees became gradually wider, the trees themselves more slender, younger, the light brighter. Still that haze was over everything, a golden shimmer that made it hard to see far ahead. We emerged from the forest onto a grassy hillside that sloped away down, the ground vanishing into the brightness. Nothing could be seen of the landscape; there was only the shining uncertainty of the haze.

We paused, side by side, peering ahead into the obscurity.

"I wonder if it will clear, as a mist might," Cathal murmured. "We'd best stop here and see if the conditions change. I'm not happy about heading on into that. Maybe there's another way."

The thought of going back into the forest to search for a different path was daunting. I had been happy to step out of its dim expanses, relieved to lose the weight of those unseen eyes following us as we passed. "All right," I said, since there really was no choice.

We sat in silence a while, passing Cathal's water-skin between us. Our eyes met as the vessel changed hands, acknowledging that by the end of today it would be empty. Eventually I thought that in one area the misty shroud before us was a little less dense. White stones were appearing in the grass, arranged in threes and fives and sevens: a pathway. I could see perhaps twelve paces ahead. "I think we can go on," I said. "It looks as though someone has left markers for us."

We moved down the hillside into the brightness, following the narrow pathway. It was becoming quite clear that if we were to advance further into this realm, it would be done according to someone else's rules. The dazzling veil retreated just far enough for us to keep going, but not to see what lay around us. It had been much the same crossing the river, when the way ahead had been revealed while the bank behind us was curtained. I didn't like it, and I could see Cathal felt the same way. There was a tightness about his jaw that told me he would far rather be finding his own path. Very possibly we were being led straight into some kind of trap. In the sling, Becan slumbered peacefully. His profound trust filled me with unease.

The ground leveled. Around our feet, now, plants grew between the stones, low, green-gray, aromatic. The place smelled like an herb garden. The scent brought a vivid memory of myself as a young girl, in the kitchen at Sevenwaters with Mother, learning the best way to make vegetable broth: Mother's cloud of red hair shining in a ray of sun from the window; well-scoured pots and pans gleaming on their hooks; my eyes watering as I chopped onions. Bunches of dried herbs were hanging overhead, rosemary, lavender, thyme, and a selection of fresh leaves lay on the chopping block before me. *Good, Clodagh,* said my mother, and my heart warmed. *You have a real flair for this.*

I stumbled on a rock, blinking back tears. The haze had dimmed slightly and Cathal had picked up his pace, striding along ahead of me. He forgot how much shorter my legs were than his. I scurried after him, one arm curved around Becan.

The smell grew stronger. It filled my nostrils, my throat, my lungs. My head began to swim. I was falling behind again. My legs felt suddenly weak; my body demanded rest. Every part of me protested: *too far, too fast, too long . . . Sit down . . . Lie down . . . Sleep . . .*

Up ahead, Cathal staggered. He took two more paces, then dropped to one knee, a hand to his brow. His cloak dragged on the ground, brushing the low plants and releasing a still more powerful wave of that soporific aroma. I heard his voice as if in a dream.

"Clodagh? Clodagh, where are you?"

It seemed an immense effort to answer him. "Here," I called, but my voice came out as a murmur, for I could not fill my lungs with air. Something weighed me down. Something pressed on my eyelids; I could not keep them open. Becan was so heavy . . . If I untied the sling I could put him down for a while. I must rest . . .

I crouched to do it, noting idly that here the white stones were set in a little spiral with a tiny plant in the middle, a variety of thyme perhaps, with gray-green leaves and miniature bunches of delicate pink flowerets. It was so warm here . . . Maybe I would take off my cloak, spread it out and lie down awhile . . . In such a lovely place, surely I would have good dreams.

"Clodagh!" A hand on my arm, gripping so hard it made me wince. Cathal was kneeling beside me. I looked up. His cloaked form wavered before my eyes, now that of a man, now that of some other creature, one that was surely more foe than friend.

"Clodagh, get up! Come on!" He gave me a shake. When I did not respond he slapped me across the cheek, hard.

On top of yesterday's cuts, it was cruel. I whimpered, crouching low and trying to shield the baby.

"Clodagh, in the name of the gods, get up, will you? There's some kind of charm over this place. We must move on!"

"No," I moaned, squeezing my eyes shut. My limbs were leaden. Almost within reach were fair dreams, dreams of warmth and love and happiness. It was unfair of him to take it away, so unfair . . . That creature in the woods had been right, Cathal was not a friend at all, he wanted to spoil everything . . .

I found myself grabbed by both arms, hauled to my feet and slung bodily over my companion's shoulder. Caught in the middle of it all, Becan began to scream. "Stop it!" I yelled, suddenly and painfully awake. "You'll crush him! Put me down, I can walk! Cathal, please!"

He ignored me, striding on into the obscurity of the haze at a pace much too fast for safety.

"Cathal, I can walk! What are you doing?"

"Stop fighting me, Clodagh." He didn't even sound out of breath. "Once we're out of this cursed place you can walk all you want." He had adjusted his grip to allow Becan more room, but the baby was terrified now. His shrieks filled my ears and set my stomach churning. There was no way to reassure him; I was upside down, my head dangling, and it was as much as I could do to make sure he did not fall right out of the sling. I shut my eyes and gritted my teeth. My cheek stung. My nose was blocked with tears.

Cathal did not stop walking until the herbal carpet underfoot gave way to stony ground and the path began to climb. The smell receded. My head cleared, though being conveyed like a sack of vegetables had started up a throbbing ache in my temples. When Cathal finally put me down my legs gave way under me and I collapsed in a heap. He squatted beside me, dropping the two bags. I had not thought, until then, how much of a load he had carried.

I burst into tears. It was a woeful performance, entirely unworthy of a girl who was supposed to be performing a quest, but I couldn't help it.

Cathal unfastened his bag and got out a square of clean linen, a little pot of salve and his water-skin. He dampened the cloth. After I had sniffed myself to a sodden, heaving stop, he said, "Take a few deep breaths and then keep still for me." He proceeded to dab at the wounds on my face. The cloth moved along the lines of yesterday's cuts. It touched the corners of my eyes, the welt on my brow. When everything was clean, he salved the injuries, his fingers gentle against my skin. His eyes were deep and solemn, his lips pressed together in concentration. He didn't say a single thing more. I found that I was holding my breath. In the sling, Becan had fallen quiet, though his little chest still heaved with outrage.

"I'm sorry," I said, knowing how inadequate that was. "I kept seeing images of home, home the way it was before, when things were good. And I wanted to sleep, oh, so badly . . ."

"Me, too," Cathal said, sitting back on his heels and examining my face critically.

"I saw you half fall," I told him. "But then everything blurred and I couldn't . . . I really am sorry, Cathal. How did you manage to do that, to keep awake and get us out safely?"

He grimaced, packing away his materials. "Who knows?" he said lightly. "The training, I suppose. We learn how to withstand various assaults, including those aimed at the mind. I think we should move on straightaway, Clodagh. Can you manage?"

"Of course," I said, lifting my chin.

"What about him?" Cathal was packed up now, ready to move on. He nodded toward Becan. "I'm sorry if I hurt him. I did what seemed necessary at the time."

"He's all right, I think." I got to my feet. My knees still felt unreliable. I wanted to be brave and strong; I had thought I could be. It was a matter of profound shame that I seemed all too ready to melt into tears at the slightest reversal.

Cathal was hitching his pack onto his back and picking up mine. "You're not a warrior," he said diffidently. "You're doing your best. Nobody can do more than that."

I said nothing. There was a certain comfort in his words, for I knew he was not the kind of man to speak thus solely out of a wish to make me feel better. All the same, my best was falling far short of what I had expected.

He murmured something else, his back to me.

"What was that?"

"I didn't particularly want to hit you," Cathal said.

"I'll try to stay awake from now on so you won't have to do it again," I told him grimly. "On we go, then."

We climbed, and the light changed. The golden haze faded; with infinite slowness the landscape around us emerged from the veil: bizarre outcrops of rock, narrow pebbly pathways mazing in and out, stunted trees clinging tenaciously between the great stones. In the distance, rugged hills, deep, secret valleys. A cloak of trees over the lower reaches, obscuring details. Bare fells above, their slopes rising to crags resembling grotesque fortresses, from which I expected any moment to see swarms of giant bats or predatory birds wing outward on a mission of attack. The sky was leaden gray. The last of the warm light was gone. There was something oppressive about that sky. I felt again the sensation of weight, as if the whole of this realm existed somehow underground. And yet, last night there had been moonlight.

"What are we looking for?" asked Cathal, shading his eyes against an invisible sun as he stared across the wooded valleys below us. "A settlement? A fortification? Where do these folk live?"

Stories tumbled through my mind. "Under lakes," I said. "In hollow hills. In caverns. In deep forests. I don't think there will be any settlements. The tales usually talk about halls, palaces, that kind of thing. Or folk that just . . . float about in the woods."

"What about hilltops?" Cathal was casting his glance up toward the unusual crag that had caught my attention, the one that resembled a fortification. "There's something moving around up there, and it's not trees in the wind. Perhaps we should take cover, just until we work out what it is. Down here."

We crouched behind the rocks. "What did you see?" I whispered.

"Maybe only young eagles in a nest." It didn't sound convincing.

"Or?"

"Or a sentry post of some kind, though it would be difficult to get up and down. Do these people have wings?"

"I don't think so." It was the smaller ones that flew about, masquerading as birds or insects. The Fair Folk, as far as I knew, resembled human beings, save that they were taller, more beautiful, altogether more remarkable.

"Get lower down, here." There was a sort of shelf, a level space well sheltered between big boulders but partly open to the hillside below. Cathal set the two bags down there. "I'm going to climb higher and see if I can get a better view. Don't put your head up above these rocks unless I say it's safe."

For a little, all was quiet. I spread out my cloak and tended to the child, my mind on last night's odd visitor. In view of the difficulties we'd faced today, I'd been stupid to refuse the creature's offer of guidance. If I'd handled things more cleverly I could probably have persuaded it to take both me and Cathal onward. I hadn't even asked if it knew where Finbar was. My brother . . . His image was fading in my mind, the soft infant features, the fuzz of dark hair becoming no more than a vague memory, a blend of all the human babies I had seen. The child in my arms, with his sharply angular limbs and his fragile body of twisted withies and leaves, was far more real now. When Cathal had heaved me onto his shoulder and Becan had been caught between us for a moment, I had felt a gut-twisting anguish at the thought that he might be crushed. "I won't let anyone hurt you," I murmured. "Nobody. I'll keep you safe. I promise."

I'm not sure which I heard first, Cathal's shout or the deep, rumbling sound of shifting stones. It happened in an eye blink. One moment I was sitting cross-legged with the child in my arms, watching him drink; the next, the boulders that surrounded our small haven were moving inexorably toward me, trundling forward of their own accord as if to roll right onto me. I sprang to my feet, dropping rag and water-skin to clutch Becan against my chest. "Cathal!" I screamed, and backed away as the wall of stones bore down on me. Frantic, I looked for a way around, under, over, but with the child in my arms there was no getting back to the path. The only way I could go was down the hill. The slope was not too steep to negotiate, but it was uneven, studded with smaller rocks and patched with slippery-looking mosses. A moderate distance below me, bushes formed a screen. There was no telling what lay beyond them.

The rocks grumbled, grinding against one another. "Cathal!" I screamed again, then fled down the hill, supplies abandoned. I snatched one look over my shoulder as the boulders reached the edge of the shelf and teetered there, rolling up to the lip then falling back as if to tease me. If they came over I had no chance at all of dodging them. Becan and I would be obliterated.

"Clodagh!"

Somewhere up there beyond the outcrop, Cathal had heard me. I glanced back again but could see nothing of him. I scrambled sideways, trying to keep my purchase on the tricky slope.

A boulder tipped over the edge. With a crunching, splitting noise it toppled down the hillside, not following a logical path, but hurtling straight toward me with apparent intent, as if an invisible giant were playing skittles. I froze, unable to make myself move either way. The missile passed a hairbreadth from me. A warning. Not left. Not right. Straight down.

Heart hammering, I ran down the hillside as Becan began a belated protest over the interrupted meal and the headlong, jostling movement.

"Clodagh!" yelled Cathal, sounding closer this time, but now I could not look, for other stones were coming, to left, to right, leaving me no choice at all but to take a middle path. I pelted directly toward those bushes. Something passed in the air above me, something on wings, dark and heavy. I ducked, shielding the baby as best I could, then ran on. Ahead of me, the stones crashed through the line of greenery and disappeared beyond. The creature circled and returned, swooping low over my head with a cry, driving me on. With the child pressed close, I ran between the bushes and fell headlong into nothingness.

In a heartbeat of time everyone I cared about flashed through my mind: my sisters, my parents, Johnny, Aidan . . . Becan, who would die with me; Cathal, whose story I would never learn now. Finbar, lost forever in the Otherworld . . . Down, down I fell, the air ripping at my hair and snatching at my clothing as I clutched the baby close, trying to curl around him in a futile attempt to cushion his landing. My guts turned to water; my heart was too terrified to beat . . .

We landed, not in a welter of smashed flesh and splintered bones, but with a springy thump that did no more than drive the air temporarily out of my chest. My eyes were squeezed shut. Every muscle in my body was screwed up tight. Now I felt something under me, holding me up, a pliant surface like a net. The voices of birds were all around me. A cool breeze was blowing my hair over my face. Becan was squalling. I opened my eyes.

We were in a tree, perhaps a stunted form of willow. It grew from a tiny pocket of soil lodged in a crack of the cliff face down which we'd plummeted. Its roots must have delved deep to hold it in so tenuous a spot. Its tangle of branches, stretched out over the void, had caught us. Spring's new growth had cushioned our landing. We were safe. We were alive.

A moment's elation; a moment's recognition that this was an amazing gift. Then I looked around me and my heart sank. There was no way out. We were trapped. The roots of the tree had found a purchase on the cliff. For human feet there was no space at all. I could see no shelf or ledge to which I might scramble, even supposing I could traverse the horizontal trunk while holding the baby in my arms. Try that and I would fall, taking Becan with me. Peering downward through the foliage, I saw the canopy of the forest below us, and a silver ribbon that might be quite a large river. A cold hand of terror clawed at my belly. Birds circled down there, pale dots against the deep blue-green of the distant trees. We had fallen perhaps halfway down the cliff. Above us the rock face reared high, its surface steep, sheer and devoid of any chink wide enough to accommodate so much as a clurichaun.

I fought back panic, scrambling for solutions. Cathal, at the top . . . I had heard him shouting before. Perhaps he was lying crushed and broken up there, victim to those sinister rolling boulders. If even the stones had minds of their own in this place, what chance did we have? *Stop it, Clodagh. Make a plan.* I did not think this had been an accident. Someone had set things up so I would fall. Perhaps it was a test. If the Fair Folk intended me to undertake this journey and to rescue my brother, there must be some way I could get out of this situation. Cathal was a good climber;

he'd been nimble as a squirrel the day he'd rescued Coll from that massive oak. I eyed the cliff face again, with its sheer surface and complete lack of useful ledges. The most agile climber in the world could not do it. *Stop shivering, Clodagh. Show some backbone.* It was hard with the baby's frightened screams assaulting my ears and that endless drop below me, only one false move away.

"Make a list," I muttered to myself. Back home that trick had helped me stay calm in a number of panicky situations. I made an inventory of what I had on my side. I was unhurt, apart from the scratches and bumps I had borne before this particular disaster. Becan was distressed but seemed unharmed. I had a small knife in my belt. The list of what I didn't have was longer: no bag, no food, no water. No rope. No Cathal. Even if he was all right, he might not be able to see or hear me from up there. And what could he do anyway?

If this had been an old tale, friendly birds might have come and borne us to the foot of the cliff, or a magical doorway might have opened by the roots of the willow. It wasn't going to happen here. When I had refused the only offer of aid that had come my way in this realm, I'd probably doomed myself to die in this tree. Worse, I'd have to watch Becan die first, the child I had brought all this way in a futile attempt to do the right thing. He would look at me with that expression of utter trust and I wouldn't even be able to give him water. "A pox on it," I muttered. "I won't give up. There must be a way out."

A shout from the cliff top. I craned my neck and made out a tiny figure in a pale shirt, standing between the screening bushes and the sudden sharp edge that I had not seen until I was over it and falling. My heart soared, defying logic. "Here!" I screamed. Perhaps Cathal could fetch help—a guard post, he'd mentioned a guard post—maybe someone would have a rope or something— No, I was being stupid. There was no guard post. There were no helpful folk here. The cliff was too high, too steep, impossible . . .

Cathal jumped. It was a bold, athletic move, controlled in every particular. He used his long limbs to ensure a particular path to his fall. In the few moments it took for him to come down, I saw that he was aiming precisely for the tree in which I sat perched. He landed beside me, his weight making the branches dip and shake with some violence. I clung to a limb with one hand and held onto Becan with the other. Then I drew a shuddering breath, the first I had taken since I saw him leap.

"You utter, utter fool," I whispered.

"You're all right, then," said Cathal, his tone marginally less steady than usual.

"We're not hurt. But there's no way down from here. Why on earth did you do that?"

"Shall I climb back up and head off home? You prefer to be alone?"

I shook my head, trying to smile.

"Clodagh," Cathal said, "you're right, we do have very limited choices here." He glanced down between the branches, then back at me.

I did not have to look to see the river winking up at me, a narrow, bright strand in the green. "Don't tell me," I said as my heart turned to ice. "We have to jump."

"Correct," he said, rising precariously to his feet. "There's only one way out: straight down. And I think we should do it before we have time to think too much. You hold onto the child and I'll hold onto you. If we aim for the water we have a good chance."

Brighid save us. Perhaps he'd forgotten that I couldn't swim. I stood, wobbling. I held Becan tightly with my right arm and put my left hand in Cathal's. His grip was warm and strong.

"I'll look after you," Cathal said. "You'll be fine and so will Becan. Shut your eyes if it helps."

"No, I . . . Oh, gods, Cathal, I don't think I can do this . . ."

"You can do it, Clodagh. Take a few deep breaths. It'll be over before you know it." He was as pale as linen. Perhaps, despite his apparent confidence, his stomach was roiling with terror just as mine was.

"You will keep hold, won't you?" I might land safely, but if he let go of me I would drown and so would Becan.

"I will," he said. "You know, there were a lot of logical reasons for staying up at the top. But logic doesn't seem to be playing much of a part in my decisions any more. And just in case . . ." He bent his head and kissed me. It was like the last time, only not like it. The touch of his lips on mine thrilled through my body as it had then. The fact that we were perilously balanced and about to make a suicidal leap made no difference. But this kiss had a promise in it, and a farewell, and regret, and trust, and all manner of secrets that might be uncovered if only there were more time. We drew apart, and it seemed to me his breathing was as unsteady as mine, but his grip on my hand stayed firm.

"Ready?" he asked.

"Yes," I lied.

"On the count of three, then. One . . . two . . . three . . ."

And away down. Down, down. His hold on me the only anchor to reality. Becan's screams snatched away by the speed of our flight, dissipating in the air as we hurtled through it. The cliff a blur of gray, brown, blue, black. A glimpse of Cathal's face, ashen white, his eyes huge and shadowed, his dark hair flying up from his brow. His cloak, catching the wind, billowing out to reveal the treasury within. The green glass ring glinting, though there was no sun in the sky. My heart drumming in my breast, sounding a litany of regret. *If I die now, I'll never get to know him properly. If I die now, I'll never have children of my own. If I die now, I'll have failed everyone . . .*

I had just time to draw in one good breath before the water took us. We plunged deep, the chill of it shocking, and instantly I lost hold of Cathal's hand. Becan, oh gods, Becan . . . Clutching the baby tightly, I kicked my way up to the surface, a long, long way up, to emerge with lungs bursting. I sucked in a panicky breath before the water closed over my head again. My gown and cloak were leaden, their folds dragging me down. I flailed with one arm, kicking wildly, desperate to stay afloat. There was a sharp pain in my chest. Becan, Becan . . . I couldn't get my own head above the surface, let alone hold his little face clear. The current carried us along, the forested banks moving past swiftly as I struggled in the middle of the river. Get swept too far and I had no chance of finding Cathal again. Water went up my nose and down my throat. I couldn't breathe. *Becan* . . . He was immobile in my arms, probably already drowned.

I slammed into something, painfully, and grabbed hold. A fallen tree lay halfway across the river, a mass of debris lodged in its dead branches. I held on like grim death, inching myself up until I was half in, half out of the water. Becan's pebble eyes were glassy, his mouth sagged open. He looked no more than the lifeless manikin everyone at home had believed him to be. Terror gripped me. He couldn't die, he mustn't die, not so little and so helpless . . . "Cathal!" I shrieked, but my voice was drowned by the rushing of the river. "Cathal, help!" I turned my head one way, the other way, desperate for some sign of him, but there was nothing.

Somehow I managed to drag myself along the log until my feet touched the river bottom. I staggered up to the bank and laid the sodden, motionless Becan down on the sand, then turned aside to retch up the contents of my stomach. I looked along the river under the trees and out into the flow of the water. Empty; all empty. Cathal was gone. I blocked out the thought of him drowned or swept so far downstream he could not reach me. Right now I must save Becan. Dimly, I recalled an old rhyme for children about a dog that stopped breathing and a tiny magical woman who brought it to life by singing into its nostrils. If I could stop gasping and shaking I would try something similar, ridiculous as it sounded. I had nothing else. I bent over the baby's still form. With every scrap of will I could summon, I steadied myself. I put my mouth over Becan's and breathed for him. One, two; one, two. The forest shivered around me; the river passed on its way, the same as yesterday and the day before, oblivious to the small dramas of life and death that played themselves out on its banks. One, two; one, two. There was room in my mind for nothing more than this, the pattern of survival.

I knelt and breathed until my limbs ached with cramp and my eyes stung with tears. He was dead. There was no point in going on. I had lost him. I had stolen him away and now I had let him die before he had the chance to know anything of the world but loneliness, terror and flight . . . All the same, I kept breathing. I couldn't bring myself to stop. And at last, twisting my heart within me, Becan coughed, choked, twitched, breathed. Cried. That woeful sobbing was the loveliest sound I had heard in my life. My hair, saturated from its immersion in the river, dripped cold water down my face to mingle with the warmth of my tears. Nothing to wrap him in. Nothing to feed him with. But he was alive. For a few moments all I felt was sheer joy, and then memory returned. Cathal. Where was Cathal?

"Clodagh!"

My heart leapt at his voice. I turned my head to see him much further downstream, dark hair dripping, cloak swirling around him as he ran along the riverbank toward us. There was a look on his face that stopped my heart: he was sheet white, terrified, his eyes full of ghosts. "Clodagh, oh gods, Clodagh, you're alive!" He sprinted the last hundred paces, stumbling over debris as he came, and flung himself down beside me where I sat with the now screaming Becan hugged against my breast. "I couldn't keep hold, and then I couldn't find you, and I thought . . ." His voice cracked. A moment later his arms came around the two of us, and I turned my face against his chest, closing my eyes.

"I hate you," I said indistinctly, slipping my free arm around him and pressing close. "How dare you make us do that? You're crazy. Becan nearly drowned. I had to breathe for him, to bring him back . . . And then you were gone . . ." My heart was racing; my head was swimming. I held onto him as if he were a lifeline. It was impossible, now, to believe that we had actually done it; we really had performed that leap and lived to tell the tale.

"I'm sorry," Cathal said against my hair. "Sorry I made you do it, sorry I couldn't keep hold, and sorrier still that we have none of our supplies with us. I hope it's not too much further. You'd best have my cloak, Clodagh, and carry the child protected by it. And we'll be putting that water rule to the test today. The rest of our journey will be determined by streams and ponds, since we have no vessel in which to carry a supply."

We disengaged ourselves and got to our feet. Suddenly, sharply, I became aware that I was soaked through and chill to the bone. Cathal was dripping, though his cloak had survived unscathed as usual, and when he draped it around me I felt the familiar sense of well-being the garment seemed to convey. A bruise was darkening on his cheek and his right hand was bleeding. While I fought my battle with the river, my companion had probably faced a similar struggle further down.

"You forgot to bring the bags," I said, only half joking. Now that my elation over Becan's survival was dying down, the reality of our situation began to weigh on me: no flint, no honey for the baby, no dry clothing, no food . . .

"An oversight for which Johnny would reprimand me, no doubt," said Cathal quietly. It sounded as if his teeth were chattering.

"Why did you jump from the cliff top? That was an act of sheer lunacy, Cathal." I was folding the baby in the cloak, rubbing his back, doing what I could to get him warm.

Cathal grimaced. "I assessed the situation and acted as I judged best. It seemed to me you might fall. The bags became unimportant."

"All that in a heartbeat." He had paused on the cliff's edge for no longer than that. "You could have been killed."

"When I couldn't find you, I thought you had already fallen to your death. Then, when I saw you in the tree, I . . . Never mind that. So, now we're in a predicament. I should be able to make fire without a flint. We'd best find a place of shelter first."

We looked toward the forest, dense, dark, forbidding.

"I suppose there will be a path," I said. "I was forced down here, more or less. The rocks started rolling, and all I could do was run. And fall. So I suppose this is the right way. I hope this is almost over, Cathal."

But Cathal had nothing to say. He looked at me, and I looked at him, and we set off together under the trees and into the darkness.

CHAPTER 11

We were in no fit state for a lengthy walk. Becan wept. I felt his misery in my heart and could do little to help him. Without the sling, I had to hold him in my arms, and perhaps my unease transferred itself to his small body. Cathal went ahead along a narrow, barely definable pathway we had found, and I followed, knowing it was entirely reasonable for me to wear his cloak, since I had Becan to think of, but wishing there were some way I could share it with him. He couldn't be warm enough in just shirt, tunic and trousers, all three wet through. He looked wretched, his skin pallid, his features set in a fierce determination that forbade any expression of concern for his welfare. As for me, despite the remarkable fact that all three of us had survived, I was beginning to lose heart. The forest seemed full of menace, a realm of sudden darkness, thorny branches, evil-smelling pools and deceptive slopes. Fungi sprouted among the roots, slickly luminous. Pale, many-legged things crawled in the leaf litter. Becan's cries lost themselves in the empty spaces between the trees. There was nobody here. We might walk on until we died a sad death from exhaustion, hunger and despair.

The little path followed the course of a stream. My boots squelched. I could feel more blisters forming. There would be no hope of getting anything dry in here, even supposing Cathal could really make fire without a flint. I had seen Johnny do that once; Deirdre had been most impressed. Oh, Deirdre . . . How I longed to talk to her, to tell her how I was feeling, to hear her going on about her hair or her gown or how fine Illann looked on horseback, just so I could remember there was another world out there, one where I need not be confused and afraid. How I longed to hug Sibeal and Eilis, and to tell my mother I was getting closer to finding Finbar. I wanted to ask Father to forgive me for everything I had got wrong, and to tell him I loved him even when he was cold to me . . . *I will not cry,* I told myself fiercely. *Cathal's keeping going, and he hasn't even got the cloak.*

"Perhaps we should rest for a little." He stopped walking and turned to wait for me. "You look exhausted. Sit down awhile, Clodagh. There's a spot under that oak." He took a knife from his belt.

"What are you doing?" I obeyed him, for now that I had stopped walking my legs did not want to hold me up a moment longer.

"We'll need a cloth to feed the baby. He won't survive long without water. I suppose we can dip this into the stream for him." Before I could speak, he removed his tunic and used the weapon to rip off a length of linen from the shirt he had on underneath. "Better than nothing."

"Thank you," I said, lost for anything else to say. I watched as he shrugged back into the tunic, stepped over to the stream and wet the cloth, wringing it lightly, then brought it back to me. Becan's cries had increased when we stopped walking; he was anticipating food. At first he sucked hungrily, needing the liquid. Then he realized there was no honey this time and jerked his head away, wailing an outraged protest.

What followed was more battle than meal. Becan was desperately thirsty, but I struggled to get even a small amount of water into him. After what seemed an age, he fell into a restless sleep. I set him down with the cloak around him and rose to my feet, scrubbing the tears from my face. My head was throbbing. A moment later, Cathal put his arm around me, as a brother might, and said,

"It's all right, you know. You don't have to be brave every single moment." I let myself lean on him, my forehead against his chest, but not for long. Something had changed between us when we came down the cliff. The touch of his hands, the warmth of his body against mine, awakened feelings in me that were not at all those of a sister. I had embraced him before, by the river, and even in that extreme had felt it—a glow, a warmth, an awareness in certain parts of my body that was quite new to me, and made sense of certain remarks of Deirdre's about Illann and her wedding night. Tired and despondent as I was, my body was not letting me ignore those feelings. I should have realized, when Cathal kissed me in the hallway, that my response was the first raindrop heralding a storm. This was perilous. I stepped back out of his embrace.

"Clodagh," my companion said quietly, "we must drink before we move on. Shall we try this water together?"

"If we turn into toads, at least we'll be good company for each other." I forced a smile. "All right, let's do it."

Side by side we knelt on the mossy bank of the little stream and scooped up handfuls of the brownish water. Side by side we drank. It tasted fresh, sweet, a little peaty. I noticed a clump of crimson toadstools further upstream, and a patch of cress. It would be possible to eat here, if a person didn't mind risk.

"You look . . . tired," I said as I sat back on the bank. It was an understatement.

"Ah, well," said Cathal, lips twisting in a familiar way, "it's not been the easiest of days. Did you know your hair goes even wilder when it gets wet?"

I put a hand up involuntarily, as if it mattered in the least whether my hair resembled a rat's nest right now. "Cathal?"

"Mm?"

"We can't go on very far like this, can we? I made a stupid mistake when I refused that offer of help." I bowed my head against my drawn-up knees.

After a moment he said, "Most folk would agree with you, I'm sure. Perhaps I should, too. If you'd accepted, I'd have been left behind. I could have been back at Sevenwaters by now, enjoying a hot bath and a solid meal."

Neither of us mentioned Glencarnagh, and my father, and the

fact that Aidan had been hunting his friend to bring him back for an accounting.

"I'd never leave you behind," I said.

There was a long silence, and when I glanced up, wondering why he had not spoken, I saw a strange look on his face. "What?" I asked. "What's wrong?" for he had gone pale again, as if he'd seen something that frightened him more than a vision of death.

Cathal shook his head as if to clear it. He would not meet my eye now. "Nothing," he said. "Clodagh, if the offer of help comes again you must take it. Don't trouble yourself with me. I've seen what a great capacity for sympathy you have. For impossible causes. Like Becan. Like me. If you get a chance of guidance, take it immediately and forget about me."

I stared at him in shock. "But . . . Cathal, I need you with me. To keep me safe; to guard Becan; to—"

"If these folk want you to achieve your quest, they will keep you safe," he said, and his tone set a distance between us. "They will provide all the guards you need. I'm not doing a good job, Clodagh. I mean, look at us." His gaze went around the dark forest, taking in the exhausted baby, our wet clothing, the shadows that seemed to creep in on us from every side. "When we fell into the river I lost hold of you. You can't swim. I thought you had drowned. And before that, when the stones rolled, I thought I would find you crushed underneath or broken at the foot of the cliff. You owe me absolutely nothing. I'm no good to you. I'm no good to anyone. Especially in this cursed place."

"Don't say that!" The words burst out of me, a fierce protest. Before I could think too hard, I leaned toward him and slapped him across the cheek, hard enough to make a red mark. I didn't like doing it, but at least the shock that filled his eyes was better than that forlorn, hopeless look. "Now we're even," I said. "Don't you dare give up on me, Cathal. I need you. I want you here with me. I don't care if you get things wrong and make mistakes; I'm making plenty of my own. I'm tired, I'm cold, I'm terribly afraid. I can't go on without a friend."

For a little he just looked at me, and I could not tell what was in his mind. Then he said, "Are you telling me that if this guide reappears you'll say no again?"

"Under the circumstances that would be foolhardy," I said. "If it comes back I'll negotiate. There must be some way to bargain so these folk will guide both of us on. I'm sorry I struck you, Cathal."

"Any time."

"We should move on," I said. "This place seems to breed sadness." As I spoke, a memory stirred dimly. Something about sorrow and sadness. Something about a pathway. Where had I heard that? Was it possible my state of despondency was less to do with shock, exhaustion and fear, and more to do with exactly where we were? Perhaps Cathal's attack of self-doubt had the same cause.

"That field, with the herbs," I said. "The smell made us sleepy; it made us both want to stop trying. And now we're feeling sad and wretched. Maybe all we need to do is move forward, get out of here." I rose to my feet. "We must keep walking, Cathal. And we must stop fighting each other. I think this spot may have a charm over it, something that makes people feel despondent and hopeless."

Cathal said nothing, but he got up too, and when I had gathered Becan we set off again along the pathway. For a while, a long while, the pervasive gloom oppressed us, the shadows clung deep and grim around us, the forest remained dark and dank as before, though from time to time now I heard a distant, eerie cry. I could not tell if it was made by a bird or an animal or something far stranger. There was a piercing, edgy note in it that filled my heart with sorrow. I tried whistling a tune to keep up my spirits, but it faded into nothing almost before it left my lips. Becan's sleep was fitful. When I glanced down at him, it seemed to me his twiggy cheeks were sunken and his pebble eyes clouded, as if he were starting to slip away from me. Perhaps I had been foolish to think my efforts had saved his life. No, I must stop thinking that way. It was only a charm; a charm of despair. I would not give in to it.

A few paces ahead of me Cathal came to a sudden halt. I almost crashed into him.

"What?" I said.

"It's opening up." He took a step forward. "And look, there, it's almost like a hall, something man-made."

"Man probably isn't the word," I said, looking. Ahead of us the trees were taller, their boles further apart. The spaces between them were carpeted with grass. Light penetrated the canopy here, pale and pure, touching the leaves to a hundred shades of green. There was a curious symmetry about the pattern of foliage that put me in mind of tapestries or banners. The shape of it drew the eye forward as if encouraging a visitor to walk on between the trees, where the path broadened into what seemed a grand ceremonial way. For a moment my eyes showed me a procession traveling along it, lords and ladies clad in shimmering garments, horses caparisoned in silks and satins, a rich cavalcade. I blinked and they were gone. There were only the three of us, a man, a woman, a baby, bedraggled and weary, lost in the vastness of it all. "I think we may be almost there," I said.

As if in response to my words, there stepped out in front of us a small figure in gray, its face concealed by a silver dog mask. Both Cathal and I flinched in shock, and Cathal's hand went to his dagger.

I bit back an impolite comment such as, *You again*. "It's the creature I met before," I murmured. "Let me talk." I stepped around Cathal, placing myself between him and the gray-cloaked being.

"Well, well," the little creature said. "You've come a long way. Changed your mind yet?"

"No," I said firmly. "Please tell us where Finbar is. How much further do we have to go?"

Behind me I could hear Cathal moving. I knew without looking that he had drawn the dagger and stood poised to use it the moment he decided I was at risk.

"Tell her," he said, and his tone frightened even me. "We have no time to waste. If you can help us, do so without delay."

The creature hissed. The eyes behind the mask turned their gaze from me to Cathal, then slowly back to me. "Our kind does not speak to *his* kind," the small being growled. "If you insist on keeping him with you, you bring down sorrow on yourself. Bitter sorrow."

"I'll be the judge of that." What sorrow could be more bitter than the abduction of a child? "If you can tell me, please do so. Is this the right way? When will we reach the place where my brother is being held?"

"This is the way. Close by is a place where you may rest and recover yourself." I sensed the creature was eyeing me up and down, and I saw myself as it might: my hair a filthy tangle, my gown hanging muddy and crushed around me, my boots soaked, my face livid with cuts. Neither Cathal nor I had washed properly since we met in the forest of Sevenwaters. Immersion in the river hardly counted.

"You won't make much of a showing looking like that," Dog Mask said dryly. "Anyway, he won't be there until dusk tomorrow. Use the time wisely. Ready yourself to present a strong case."

"He won't be there? Who?"

"The Lord of the Oak." This imposing name was spoken in a derisive tone. "The one who's taken on authority in these parts since those others departed. He rules all now; all dance to his tune."

"Even you?" I could not help asking.

A gurgle of laughter. "Oh, not us! His kind has never ruled over ours, daughter of Sevenwaters. We go our own way; make our own paths. But he's the one who took your brother, and he's the one with the power to give him back. He won't be impressed by that raggedy hair and that apology for a gown. Best use the time to tidy yourself up."

"Don't speak to her like that." Cathal's voice had an edge like a blade.

"Follow me, daughter," said the creature, ignoring him completely. It turned, walking away down the broadening stretch of sward.

"Wait, Clodagh," whispered Cathal in my ear. "Are you sure—"

"Not really," I said. "But I suppose this may be safe, as long as we stay together."

Dog Mask led us a short distance ahead, then turned down a side pathway paved in white stones and bordered by a miniature hedge of an aromatic plant I did not recognize. This way was clearly not natural but constructed. It curved around under the trees and came up to a hedge of thornbushes in which a curious gate had been formed, the prickly branches twisted and tied into a pattern of lines radiating out from a central point. Here the slender lengths of wood met in a complex knotted tangle, its shape resembling a grotesque, grinning face with worm holes for eyes. A mouthlike slash below these empty sockets gaped suddenly open, making me gasp. "Password?" demanded a creaky voice.

But our guide didn't seem bothered by passwords. It simply held up one furred hand and the gate swung open. When we had walked through, it slammed shut behind us.

The thorn hedge enclosed a grassy space the size of a small field. To one side was a grove of gnarled and ancient trees whose type I could not guess. A tiny stream ran between these and out into the open space, where it trickled into a round pond. Close by, a campfire burned between stones. There was a stack of wood nearby, and beside it was a roll of bedding. Next to this lay our two packs.

"Dagda preserve us," said Cathal mildly.

"All that you need is here." Our guide made a sweeping gesture encompassing the space within the hedge. "Make wise use of it. Be ready at tomorrow's sunset, and remember what I said. He'll be more inclined to listen if you look your best. Pity about those cuts on your face."

I sensed that Cathal was about to speak unwisely, and got in first. "You brought our things," I said, profound relief sweeping through me. "I can feed the baby . . . Thank you. We are most grateful."

"Hmm," said Dog Mask. "If you'd been prepared to listen, you'd have lost *him* long ago. There will be tears before this is over, mark my words. Now I'll be gone. When it's time I'll come for you. Don't stray. Within the hedge of thorn you will be safe. Beyond it, risk is everywhere. Farewell for now." It melted away before our eyes.

Whoever had prepared this spot for us had done so with surprising care. Not only had all our supplies been returned to us, but our spare clothing was clean and dry, our water-skins had been refilled, and the roll of bedding proved to contain three thick blankets. There were garments in the bottom of my pack that had not been there before. I fished out a fine shift, a gown of pale green wool with butterflies embroidered around the hem in stitches so tiny a mouse might have made them, and a gossamer-soft shawl. Someone, it seemed, not only wanted us to complete our quest, but intended us to do it in style.

I asked Cathal to turn his back while I got out of my wet things and put on shift, gown and shawl. He obeyed. This did not prevent me from imagining him watching me undress, and wondering what he might be thinking as he did so. When I was done, I averted my gaze while he changed into his spare outfit. Everything I needed for Becan was there, and when I had fed him he fell into a deep, contented sleep. I hung our wet things over the bushes while Cathal made up a brew of hot water and dried meat. We sat down close to the fire to eat it. It felt so good to be dry. The soft fabric of the green gown was bliss against my bruised skin; the warmth of the fire was balm to my weary body. The watery brew tasted like ambrosia. Across the flames Cathal and I regarded each other warily.

"So," he said, "you have friends here."

"I think that creature is a distant relation," I said.

His brows went up.

"They're called the Old Ones. A long time ago, a man from the Sevenwaters family married one of their women. Perhaps they aid us out of a sense of obligation, because of kinship. That may explain why they are prepared to help me but not you. *His* kind, that creature kept saying. Meaning, I presume, humankind without any streak of the uncanny."

"I see." Cathal was wearing his haunted look. The sudden provision of every comfort we could have hoped for had done little to improve his mood.

"Are you all right?" I asked.

"Don't worry about me, Clodagh." The tone was dismissive.

"I do worry. You keep looking as if you expect to see ghosts. As if something's coming that is worse than I could possibly imagine. I'm concerned for you."

"Don't be. I'm happy that you're so close to the end of your quest. I'm hopeful that you will succeed. You shouldn't trouble yourself over me. As you see, I'm fine."

"If you say so." I didn't believe him for a moment. There was much in his eyes; too much to interpret. It troubled me to hear him talking about *you*, not *we*, as if my mission were really nothing to do with him. "I know something's wrong," I ventured cautiously. "Wouldn't it be better if you told me what it is?"

"Leave it, Clodagh."

It was a snarl this time, and rendered me immediately silent. I concentrated on my soup, warming my hands around the cup. Time passed. The longer we sat there, the heavier grew the weight of what lay unspoken. Out there in the forest, that thing sent out its sorrowful call again. Eventually Cathal cleared away pot and cup, washing them in the stream, and I sat staring into the fire with my lids dropping over my eyes. It was still day, but I could not stay awake.

"Why don't you sleep awhile?" Cathal passed me one of the blankets. "I'll keep watch."

"I think it should be safe for both of us to rest," I said. "That's what the creature seemed to be telling us. No need to worry until dusk tomorrow."

"Nonetheless, I'll stay awake for now. Go on, sleep. You need rest. Have good dreams."

I rolled myself up in the blanket and was asleep almost before I laid my head down, but there was not a good dream to be had. A jumble of images assailed my mind: a group of hard-faced, tattooed warriors riding into the courtyard at Sevenwaters. Sibeal running through the forest all alone, her face white as chalk. Mother lying on her bed with her face turned to the wall, her eyes open but unseeing. Muirrin weeping. Coll and Eilis, sitting together halfway up the stone steps to the tower in total silence, their small faces wearing pinched expressions as they listened to a raging argument from the hall below: Father shouting, Johnny responding in clipped, hurt tones. A creature in a silver dog mask, warning of sorrow to come. Then I was falling, falling, the rocks coming up to meet me . . .

I sat up, my skin drenched in cold sweat, my heart hammering. The glow of the fire made a warm circle, but there was a chill in the air. High in the trees around us, birds were calling restlessly, exchanging warnings. *Be ready!* warned one. *Be ready!* And another challenged: *Now or never!* And still, somewhere beyond the safe enclosure, that wailing rang out in the forest.

I had slept for much longer than I'd expected. Though the light in this place could be deceptive, I judged that it was nearly dusk and past time for me to take my turn on watch. Becan was still fast asleep, wrapped in the cloak, breathing gently. I looked around for Cathal, thinking I might offer to prepare another meal.

For a moment, when I could not see him, I thought the worst: not that he had come to some harm, for I had believed our guide's assurances of safety, but that he had fallen victim to his doubts and had walked away, abandoning the mission now that it was almost over. Then I spotted him seated cross-legged by the pond. I opened my mouth to call him and shut it again with his name unspoken. His pose was familiar to me. He was preternaturally still, his back very straight, and he was gazing into the water with the same air of intense concentration as my sister Sibeal assumed when she was in a visionary trance. I knew that if I spoke to him he would not hear me. Cathal, scrying. Cathal, who until a day or so ago had scoffed at the least hint of the uncanny. Cathal, who was valuable to Johnny because of his infallible instincts; Cathal, who had known about the attack on Glencarnagh before it happened. If that knowledge had come to him because he had a seer's gift, why in the name of the gods hadn't he *said*?

I waited for him to finish, my heart thumping as I tried to put it all together: the things he'd told me; the things he'd left out. The description of the house at Glencarnagh but not the name, because he'd seen it but didn't know what it was called. Illann and Deirdre; had he seen them in a vision plotting against my father, or had that been only the hunch he'd said it was? Visions didn't always reflect reality anyway; that was one reason why Sibeal didn't share hers. They might show only what could be, or what might have been, or they might give a cryptic picture, something that could only be understood by a druid skilled in the interpretation of symbols. Whatever Cathal was, he was no druid. Gods, he had left himself open to accusations of basest treachery, he had fled in the manner most calculated to make him look guilty, when all he had needed to do was tell Johnny the source of his knowledge. He couldn't have imagined that Johnny would doubt the wisdom of such a vision, Johnny whose own mother was a seer of some note. What had Cathal been thinking of? With my mind leaping from question to question, I made up the fire, boiled water and busied myself producing another meal of the dried-meat soup while the baby slept on, exhausted by the day's travails.

By the time I had the brew ready Cathal was stirring, stretching, doing the things a seer needed to do to awaken the clay self and retreat from the strange, compelling world of the vision. That could take a while. I had sat with Sibeal often enough to know it must be allowed to take its own pace or the seer might be left with a severe headache and the loss of all useful memory of the gods' wisdom. I said nothing as Cathal came back to the fire. I held my tongue as he sat down not far from me. I handed him his share of the food and set about eating my own. I hadn't forgotten the mood he'd been in earlier, snapping like a wild creature prodded incessantly by a curious child.

After a long time, he said, "Thank you." His voice was ragged.

"For the soup?" I said lightly. "When we get home to Sevenwaters I'll cook you a proper one. It's something I'm supposed to be good at."

"For the soup, yes. And for . . . for being forbearing."

"Ah. Something I'm not usually good at." I felt nervous and edgy. I wanted him to confide in me but I was afraid he would close up, the way he often did, and leave all my questions unanswered. Suddenly it was more important than anything in the world that he should trust me.

"I don't do it often," Cathal muttered, looking fixedly into the flames. "It's not a skill I'm proud of. But it's a . . . a compulsion. Sometimes. Sometimes I can't help myself. And it's useful. To Johnny. It helps me keep my place with him. If it weren't for this I'd be back at Whiteshore, treading that uneasy line between chieftain's ward and lowborn bastard."

After a little I said, "Your skills as a warrior are exceptional, Cathal. Even I can see that. I'm certain Johnny would keep you in his band whether you had this . . . instinct or not."

"Instinct. I've passed it off as that. I imagine Johnny has some idea of where my hunches come from. He's very astute. But he doesn't comment, and I don't offer explanations."

"Does Aidan know?"

"No." He set down his soup and stared into the flames.

"Cathal."

"Why didn't I tell you I could do this? Why did I give you the account of an attack and not say why I was certain it would happen? In hindsight I regret that bitterly. I didn't know you then. Not as I do now. And . . . I've never told anyone about this, not a living soul. I hate it. I despise it. It's a curse."

"A curse?" He had sounded like a furious, wounded child, and I felt a powerful urge to move around the fire and embrace him. But he was not a child, and I stayed where I was, frightened by the yearning tug of body and heart. "Cathal, in my family visionary ability is viewed as a wonderful gift. I know how hard it is to possess it. Sibeal talks to me, and I understand what a weight such knowledge puts on the seer's shoulders. All the same, it's something to be proud of, not cause for anger or shame."

"It's different for me."

"Why, Cathal?" As I spoke, the answer came to me. I held my breath, waiting.

"Because it's from *him*. It must be. My mother was an ordinary woman, a fisherman's daughter, hardworking, poor, with not a fey bone in her body. Fine looking in her youth; that was her misfortune. Whatever gift I have for seeing the future, it's not because I am her son, Clodagh. It's because I'm his. A man I want to forget ever existed. A man who broke my mother's heart with promises he didn't keep. He took advantage of her trust and made casual use of her body, then walked away as if her gift of herself were nothing. He never returned to see the son he fathered on her. Seven years she waited for him to come back. Then she died. Believe me, I would burn and beat and scourge this uncanny talent from my body if I could. It's supremely ironic that my ability to see what is to come has earned me a home on Inis Eala, the only place where I've ever felt I belonged."

This was like feast after famine. For so long Cathal had refused to tell me a word about his past. These sudden revelations were hard to take in. I summoned my courage and said exactly what was in my heart. "You are truly welcome here, Cathal. Wherever I am, there's a place for you."

He looked up, his eyes black pools in which the firelight made flickering golden points. "Ah," he said, his lips twisting, "you really know how to hit a man when he's down."

What did he mean? Had I caused him to lay his heart open, a

heart already full of sorrow, and then burdened him with something that finally made the weight unbearable? All I had done was speak the truth. In the back of my mind a song began to write itself, a sad one. "May I ask you something?" I ventured.

"Mm."

"I had thought perhaps you and Aidan were half-brothers; that his father, the lord of Whiteshore, was your father too. It seems that isn't right."

Cathal shook his head. "There were folk at Whiteshore who believed that. Still do, I expect. Lord Murtagh is a fine man. He's made in the same mold as your father. Such men do not stray from their wives. He took me in out of sheer goodness of heart. Aidan and I became friends, and that earned me my education and other opportunities. Lord Murtagh provided for my mother as well, but she would never come to live in his household, not after Aidan and I were weaned. She stayed in the village. We used to see her on the bridge, like a wan ghost. She'd spend hours there, staring into the water. Waiting. Waiting until she could wait no more."

I did not ask if his mother had killed herself or had simply faded away out of despair. The dream I had had of my own mother lingered all too close—her haunted face, her eyes on the wall. "Did she tell you anything about your father?" I asked.

He shook his head. "She went out of her way not to talk to me, not to be seen with me, as if I somehow shamed her. I can remember her telling Aidan and me not to come to her house in the settlement." His tone was matter-of-fact now, but I could hear the hurt in it, buried deep. "Living in Lord Murtagh's household, I had a more privileged existence than she could ever have provided. I suppose my mother was happy with that, though I never saw her smile. When that fellow took advantage of her, he sucked all the life out of her. She had nothing left for me. When she finally accepted that he wasn't coming back, she had nothing to live for. I was only seven, Clodagh. I didn't see it coming. A child doesn't understand that kind of despair. Aidan and I found her in the river." His shoulders were hunched. He was seeing things in the fire, memories that hollowed his cheeks and set a hard line on his brow. "After that I nearly let hatred eat me up. Aidan saved me. He was there when I needed him. He put up with me when nobody else would. Because of him I never lost sight of the fact that life went on, no matter how hot the rage, no matter how deep the sorrow of it. Aidan has his faults, and I don't let him get away with them. He keeps me in check in much the same way." He took a breath. "If you and he . . . When you go back, I imagine . . . What I said about his betrothed, Rathnait, and the future . . . Just ignore it, Clodagh. Do what your heart bids you do. There's been too much bitterness. You and Aidan would be happy together. You're strong. You could help him control his anger. If it's what you want, you should open your arms and take it."

I said nothing at all. Two days ago, I would probably have thought this very good counsel. Now, watching him across the fire—the long, sad planes of his face, the wounded mouth, the shadowed eyes—I knew with utter certainty that, whatever happened when we got home to Sevenwaters, I would not be marrying Aidan. I could not say this aloud. Indeed, I should turn my eyes away from Cathal, lest he see something on my face that I was not ready to share.

Becan began to stir and fret.

"Ah, well," observed Cathal in an attempt at his familiar drawl, "life goes on."

"I have another question." I loosened the cloak around the baby so he could kick freely. "You spoke of seeing the future. You said you were certain the attack on Glencarnagh would happen. Sibeal says her visions don't always show what's to come, but all manner of possibilities, which it's easy to misinterpret. But you implied . . ."

"What I've seen has always been true," he said with devastating simplicity. "I wish it were otherwise. It's far more comfortable to know nothing of the future. Not to have roads blocked off, possibilities closed down. I avoid still water. I shun mirrors. I hate my father for destroying my mother and for laying this curse on me. Everything bad in me, every quirk and trick and unpleasantness, I owe to his blood. His legacy means I cannot be part of your world, Clodagh. I'm doomed to tease and goad and hurt, over and over."

"That is not the man you are, Cathal," I said quietly. "You are not your father. You are yourself. Maybe you owe it to her, to the mother you loved so much, to rise above this. To be strong enough to transcend it."

There was a little silence. Then he said, "You didn't ask me what I saw."

"Sibeal has taught me that one should not do so. If you have something useful to tell me, perhaps you will. But I don't expect it."

Cathal sighed. "I hoped to see something that would help us. What I saw was obscure. I could do nothing to interpret it."

"If I were a seer right now," I said, "I would want a vision of Sevenwaters. To know how my family is coping. I had distressing dreams about them."

"I'll try again in the morning, if you want."

"I had a sad sort of dream," I told him. "It seemed to show how things might be at Sevenwaters if we don't achieve this quest. At the end I saw warriors of Inis Eala riding to battle."

"The Painted Men." Cathal smiled. "The fighters of that legendary leader, Bran of Harrowfield. Your uncle is revered on the island. His rare visits are cause for great celebration, with drinking, feasting and extraordinary feats of arms."

I had never been able to think of Aunt Liadan's husband as an uncle. There was too much danger about him; his outlaw past set him beyond all that was ordinary. I wondered what he had made of Cathal when they met.

"I liked those older men when I visited Inis Eala," I said cautiously. "It seems to me that the ones who were part of Bran's mercenary band have something that ordinary people don't. A . . . a tolerance, I suppose it could be called. As if they have seen and endured so much that they can rise above everyday difficulties."

Cathal shot me a look. "You wouldn't be trying to teach me something, would you?" he asked.

"If I were I would be far more subtle about it, Cathal. I think this lesson is one the two of us may take time to learn. We need to get home and weigh it, free of the fears and challenges that await us here."

"How very wise and measured of you, Clodagh." He was mocking me. "What if there is no time?"

"Then I suppose we'll stay as we are," I said, a lump in my

throat. "With important things unsaid. With mysteries unsolved. With treasure still buried, waiting forever to be found. With secrets unshared."

Cathal looked at me, not mocking now. "It might be safer that way," he said.

In the human world spring had been well advanced and the soft evening light had made outdoor activities possible long after suppertime. In this eldritch realm nothing was predictable, not even the passage of sun and moon across the sky. Today the dark came rapidly, as if a great hand had drawn a blanket over all, shutting us in with the shadows. Beyond the circle of light cast by our small blaze there now lay a profound blackness. I took a walk to relieve myself in a secluded corner and could barely find my way back. From twenty paces away the campfire could be discerned only as a faint glow in the gloom.

Becan lay on the cloak waving his twiggy hands, and beside him sat Cathal with legs stretched out. As I approached I heard him addressing the infant in a serious tone. ". . . hope you realize how good she is to you. You're privileged, young man."

As I came closer he glanced up. "It won't be easy for you to relinquish him," he said. "Are you prepared for it?"

I wished I could pretend to him, to myself, that the thought of handing the baby over to the Fair Folk did not fill me with anguish. Becan was so vulnerable. I had only had him in my care a few days, but he trusted me. He knew me. He'd been left at Sevenwaters without a thought. If I had not saved him, he would be dead by now. How could I know his own folk would look after him? How could I be sure they would love him as I did? "I'm not prepared at all," I said. "When it comes to the point, I suppose I'll just do it."

"As long as you know it's going to hurt," Cathal said. "I see how much you care for him and it fills me with wonder. He's such a dried-up little scrap of a thing."

"Even a scrap is worthy of love," I said. "I suppose Becan has a mother and father in this realm, but I'm not looking forward to returning him. I didn't think about it much until we were brought here and it started to look as if the quest might actually succeed. If it does, if we get Finbar back, then there will be another problem to face." The warmth I had felt when I overheard those words of praise was gone. In my mind was the long, dark way through the forest; the river; the cliff, which must this time be scaled; the fields whose sweet scent lulled the mind to sleep; the perilous raft we must rely on to bear us through the portal to our own world. A baby who, this time, could not survive long on honey water.

"The homeward path may be different," Cathal said quietly. "If, as it seems, you were intended all along to achieve your quest, surely these folk will not let you fail for want of a little milk."

"They might," I said, imagining the cruel possibility that I might win Finbar's release and head for home only to see him perish from hunger before I reached Sevenwaters. "You heard that creature confirm what Willow said, that darker forces now hold sway here. That is just such a trick as they might play."

"Clodagh," Cathal said.

"Yes?"

"There's evidently a certain animosity toward me in these parts. That creature made it clear I'm unwelcome. I concur with what it suggested—I believe my presence endangers you. I think my role as protector may be over now. From a certain point on, you will do better without me."

This chilled me utterly. "No, Cathal!" I said, panic making my voice shake. "You must stay with me! If we split up we might never find each other again."

His brows arched. "And you would wish to do so?"

"I can't believe you need to ask that!" I dropped my gaze. Let too much feeling slip into my voice and I might drive him back behind his old barriers: cynicism, cutting wit, silence. I gathered Becan up, cradling him in my arms. I should settle him for the night.

"You underestimate your own courage, Clodagh." The firelight cast a strange red glow on Cathal's features. His hands were restless, the long fingers knotting and twisting. "You started the mission without me. If I hadn't met you in the forest as I fled, you'd have kept going on your own. You'd have found your brother and brought him home, I'm sure of it. No"—he glanced up, sensing a question in my mind—"I'm not speaking from the certainty of a vision. I cannot tell you how this will fall out. But I have faith in you. Such a capacity for love must surely see you triumph. If there is one weight dragging you down, it's my presence. These folk don't want me here. And indeed, if I had not accompanied Johnny to Sevenwaters, I suspect your baby brother would never have been taken."

"You said something like that before. What do you mean? How can the two possibly be connected?"

He sighed. "This is a thing I cannot tell you; not even now, when you have learned some of my best-kept secrets. If this turns out well . . . if the two of us reach the home shore again and Lord Sean's heir is saved, I will answer any question you want to ask. That's a promise, Clodagh."

"I'll hold you to it," I said after a moment. "Lord Sean's heir. Finbar isn't that, not the way things stand. There was a prophecy, believed to represent the will of the Tuatha De. It was always interpreted to mean that Johnny would be chieftain of Sevenwaters some day. My father has promised that and he's a man of his word."

Cathal hesitated before speaking. "A man might change his mind once he had a son of his own," he said. "Not all fathers dismiss such a gift as worthless. And what of Johnny's opinion on the matter? Perhaps becoming chieftain, settling down, producing his own heirs, is not a prospect that he truly welcomes."

"He's always seemed perfectly happy with the idea," I said, surprised. "True, Father made that promise at a time when he believed he'd never have a son. But it would be hard on Johnny if he did change his mind. Bran's holding at Harrowfield is to go to his second son, Fintan, because Johnny is expected to take on Sevenwaters. If what you suggest happened, Johnny could be left with nothing."

"Ah," said Cathal. "But maybe that doesn't trouble him. Maybe he'd rather things stayed as they are right now. He has a home and a calling on Inis Eala."

"But no chieftaincy; no holding beyond the island itself. No wife and children. Inis Eala is not a particularly good place for families."

"That is true, Clodagh." His tone was a little odd, and when

I looked at him I saw an expression on his face that seemed part compassion, part sorrow. "Johnny's adept at maintaining a good face; like his father, he seldom lets others see deep. Clodagh, he loves the island. He loves his work as a leader of men. As for the other, he doesn't want a wife and children. You must know how things stand between him and Gareth."

For a moment I failed to understand what he meant. Then I wondered if he was teasing me in the way that had become all too familiar at Sevenwaters. But he'd looked and sounded entirely serious. Rather than utter the denial that sprang to my lips—for what he suggested was a complete surprise to me—I held my tongue and considered the possibility that it might be true. I recalled my visit to the island and Johnny's trips to Sevenwaters, on most of which Gareth had accompanied him. They were certainly very close, the two of them. But if there was something more than friendship between them, they were expert at concealing it.

"Are you sure?" I asked.

"I am, though perhaps I should not have told you. I thought you would know. On the island it is not a secret."

"I didn't know, Cathal." I thought again about Mother's ambivalent attitude to Johnny as heir to Sevenwaters, which I had always put down to the fact that she had never quite approved of his father. Nobody could dislike Johnny himself. He was the kind of man everyone wanted as a friend. "Maybe my parents do, but it's not the sort of thing they would discuss with me—we aren't quite as open in our conversation as that. Poor Johnny; such expectations of him, and all likely to leave him deeply unhappy for the rest of his life."

"A man can marry and father sons even if he is not that way inclined," Cathal said dryly. "But there would be little love in such a partnership."

"Love?" I echoed. "In our circles, marriages are made for reasons of strategic alliance. I count Deirdre lucky that she actually likes Illann. None of us expects love."

"How fortunate that you met Aidan, then. With him you will have both a strategic alliance and love. I most certainly should not set any obstacles in your way."

"Obstacles? You mean, such as an existing promise? You didn't exactly set that in the way, Cathal. You merely made sure I knew about it. I may not have been grateful at the time, but really you were doing Aidan and me both a favor. A relationship can't be founded on lies. Anyway, this is a ridiculous conversation for us to be having here, now. It's dark, it's cold, we're miles from anywhere. Once Becan's sleeping I'll take my turn on watch. You should get some rest."

"In fact, I was not speaking of Aidan's betrothal to Rathnait." His voice was very quiet. "It is possible I exaggerated the importance of that just a little."

I glanced across at him and immediately he dropped his gaze so I could not see what was in his eyes. "Then what were you speaking of, Cathal?" I asked.

"Nothing. Forget it." His tone forbade further questioning. "As for rest, I doubt very much that I will sleep tonight. This place disturbs me."

He did lie down after I had settled the baby. I thought he would drop off to sleep quickly, disturbed or not, for it had been a long and eventful day. As for me, I had plenty to keep my mind occupied during the hours of my watch. I had learned more about Cathal today than during his entire time at Sevenwaters. His mother's story was a sad one, though not so very unusual. Often enough poor women did fall victim to selfish men. I could hardly imagine how terrible it must have been for those two little boys to find her body; for young Cathal to realize that his mother had not thought her son's existence enough to go on living for. Cathal had grown up in the conviction that every part of his own character that he disliked was inherited from his unknown parent. Privileged by Lord Murtagh's kindness, he had longed for his mother's love. He had both welcomed and resented his place in the chieftain's household. That was exactly echoed in his edgy relationship with Aidan. They were as close as brothers; they knew each other's weak spots. Like Deirdre and me, I thought. Often my twin irritated me beyond measure. That did not stop me from keeping a special corner of my heart especially for her. It didn't matter what Deirdre did, I would always love her. I spared a thought for Aidan, remembering him as he'd watched our departure from the human world. He had stood there with his bow in his hands and his eyes full of tears. Not for me, for Cathal. If my companion thought himself unloved, he was quite wrong.

I glanced across at him again. He was lying quite still, his eyes closed, the blanket covering him to the chin. I wished him better dreams than mine had been.

The birds had fallen silent in the trees as darkness came, and the fire was all I had for companionship. I must stay awake and alert until Cathal had had a proper rest. He'd been more than tired. Something was troubling him, something more than a belief that he should not accompany me right to the end of this journey. Beneath the strength and resourcefulness that made him such a good companion, Cathal was afraid.

At home, when I needed to stay awake, I would keep both mind and hands busy by tackling a complex piece of embroidery or practicing the harp. Neither was possible here, but one task was long overdue. My hair was full of knots. I hunted through my bag and found my comb. Setting my tangled locks to rights was going to be a long and painful job, and I didn't have Deirdre to keep me entertained. But I could sing. Cathal appeared to be sound asleep now, so I shouldn't disturb him as long as I kept it quiet. A ballad had been unfolding in my mind for quite some time, based on a traditional form but with its own words and tune. While I combed, I would work on that.

Where have you wandered, my dear one, my own
Where have you wandered, my handsome young man?
I've been to the river, I've been to the well
I've seen my reflection, I've gazed into hell
But I still cannot find my way home
I still cannot find my way home.

I played with the tune until I had it just right, with an uncertainty to the ending that reflected the words, words that had started to come to me earlier today. I wondered what Aidan would have thought of the piece.

Where have you wandered, my dear one, my own
Where have you wandered, my handsome young man?

I've run through the forest, I've climbed up the hill
I've fought with my dreams and surrendered my will
And I still cannot find my way home
I still cannot find my way home.

I winced as the comb struck another recalcitrant twist. Making myself look even half tidy was going to take all night. Still, I must persevere. It sounded as if this Lord of the Oak would be influenced as much by my appearance as by the heartfelt plea I intended to make to him. I must do whatever I could to get my brother back.

I hummed quietly to myself, working on a new verse. *I've strayed in a wilderness tangled and wild . . .* I hadn't intended the song to be about Cathal, but it undoubtedly was. All the same, the sadness in it went beyond his story. When I thought of him as a boy, finding his mother dead, I thought of my own mother and the way she had looked when we told her Finbar was gone. I considered Father's disappointment in me, and I thought of Johnny and Gareth, and how difficult it must be to love somebody and to have to keep it concealed from most of the world. I looked at Cathal again. He was lying on his back with his head turned away from me, his dark hair spread across the ground, the pale skin of his neck exposed above the fabric of his shirt. He had one arm outstretched, his hand open, the long fingers relaxed.

My heart stood still. Suddenly, urgently, I wanted to touch, to stroke, to lay my hand against his neck or his cheek. His pose was that of a sleeping child, all trust. But the feelings that surged in me were those of a woman for a man, the same I had felt earlier, but a hundred times more powerful. I wanted to lie down there beside him. I wanted to feel his body against mine. I imagined his hands touching me with tenderness and passion, and mine responding in the same way. I had not felt like this when Aidan smiled and spoke sweet words to me. My body had not responded in this way when I danced with him. And although Aidan and I had made excellent music together, I'd never had the slightest inclination to make up a song about him. The yearning that had stirred within me at Cathal's first kiss, when we had thought we were saying goodbye, was growing so strong that there would come a time when it was impossible to conceal. Here by the fire at night, with the forest silent around us, it would be all too easy to surrender to it. I considered Cathal's remark about setting obstacles between me and Aidan, the one he had refused to explain. His attitude to me had softened greatly; I'd have been blind if I hadn't noticed that. Was there something more in it? Perhaps that was wishful thinking on my part. He did keep pushing me away.

I imagined saying *I love you* to Cathal. Or, still more shocking, *I want you.* How would he answer that? With tenderness or with mocking laughter? Once we were back in our own world, very likely he would be the old Cathal again, the one I could never be quite sure of. The trickster.

"Ouch," I muttered as the comb snagged itself again.

A familiar, eldritch cry rang out in the forest. Beyond the barrier of thorn, something moved. My skin rose in goose bumps. I sat very still, peering into the darkness, wondering if it had been only a bird or a fox. Perhaps Dog Mask had come to check up on us. But maybe it was something else. Maybe that thing that cried so forlornly was crouched right next to the hedge. I was supposed to be on watch. I got slowly to my feet, my heart thumping. I couldn't wake Cathal every time the leaves shook in the breeze. On the other hand, if there was a threat I shouldn't just sit here and wait for it to arrive. I bent and took hold of a burning stick from the fire, wincing as a splinter speared the skin of my hand. I walked in the general direction of the gate, the makeshift torch casting a wayward light over my path. It wasn't far; the arch of twisted branches soon came into view. The gate stood closed. I had no intention of venturing outside it without our guide. I stood four paces away and lifted my torch as high as I could.

Beyond the thorn hedge, the forest seemed empty of all life. The wailing had ceased. Nothing stirred; no bird uttered a sleepy call, no hedgehog or mouse made a rustling progress through the leaf litter. I was about to lower the brand and retreat to the fire when I saw them: a procession of gray-cloaked figures moving with slow purpose around the perimeter of our enclosure. Each walked alone. They maintained a distance of about four strides from one another. Their footfalls were silent; they passed like shadows. What were they doing? Patrolling the hedge to keep us safe, to ward off intruders? Or ensuring we stayed confined? One thing was certain: their great height marked these minders out as no kin of Dog Mask. In the tales, the Old Ones were always described as squat and small.

My eyes were becoming accustomed to the odd light, the flickering cast by the fire stick, the shadowy darkness around and beyond the gate. The walkers in the forest were deeply hooded; I could see nothing of their faces. Here and there the burning brand caught a pinpoint of light, as of a bright eye, and here and there a long-fingered white hand showed against the gray of a garment. I thought I could hear a sound of slow breathing. I felt the chill of the uncanny deep inside me and was afraid.

"Come out," someone whispered. "Open the gate. You want your brother, don't you? Come and fetch him."

CHAPTER 12

Finbar. Gods, was he just beyond the hedge, perhaps held in the arms of one of these gray ghosts? It was dark and cold. I must bring him in to the fire . . . I took a step toward the gate and stumbled over a stone, almost dropping my brand. I clutched at the stick. A jab of pain went through my hand, where the splinter was lodged in the skin. What had got into me? It was crazy to consider going out there. *Beyond that barrier, risk is everywhere,* Dog Mask had said.

"Clodagh." Someone spoke across the gate, soft-voiced. A woman. Framed by her gray hood, her face was oval and lovely. Her eyes were the blue of a summer sky, her skin like fresh cream. My mouth dried up; my heart beat faster. Was not this Deirdre of the Forest, the woman of the Tuatha De who had once guided my grandmother when she undertook a fearsome test of endurance? She seemed exactly the way Sibeal had described her. Now she was smiling, though her eyes were sad. She looked like a friend.

"My lady," I said, my voice coming out as a nervous croak, "what do you want from me?"

"We have your brother," the woman said. "Just over there—look." I craned my neck. One of the other figures had moved up closer and was holding a small bundle. In the uneven light I could not see it clearly. "Open the gate, Clodagh, step through. I'm here to help you, daughter of Sevenwaters. Your mission is at an end."

So easy. All I had to do was unlatch the gate and take five or six steps and I could have Finbar in my arms. My mother's hope, my father's joy. He was almost within my grasp. But . . .

"What about the password?" I asked.

She chuckled in amusement. "Don't worry about that. The gate will let you out; the password is only for going in. A trick devised by meddlesome folk. Ignore it. Come, my dear, come and fetch the child. You must be longing to take him home."

Something was wrong here. No mention of Becan. Wasn't this supposed to be an exchange? And if they wanted to help me, why didn't they pass Finbar over the gate or bring him in to me?

"Please hold him up where I can see him," I said, shivering at my own temerity. It was not for a human girl to question the motives of the Tuatha De. They were folk of immense power.

The woman clicked her long white fingers, and the other person stepped up beside the gate, holding the bundle for my scrutiny. I was not tall enough to look over the top of the gate, so I peered between the woven twigs and branches, trying to position the brand without setting fire to anything. Within the folds of gray, a baby slept peacefully. Rosebud lips; a decisive nose; a lock of dark hair. My breath caught in my throat. It really was Finbar. Only a step away. I didn't even need to leave the sanctuary of the clearing. All that was required was to unlatch the gate, put one foot out and take him in my arms.

"You will not have to face the Lord of the Oak," the woman said. "Take your brother now and make your escape before Mac Dara learns of your presence, and you can be back at Sevenwaters by morning. The path home is easier."

Mac Dara? The Lord of the Oak was the same person as the devious prince of the old tales? How could I possibly face up to such a legendary figure, surely one of the most powerful forces in the Otherworld? I should snatch this opportunity and get away as soon as I could. "I thought this would be an exchange," I made myself say. "The . . ." I would not call Becan a changeling. "The other child for my brother."

There was a little silence. "No need for that," the woman said. "Come, step through the gate."

Was she saying that against all expectation I could take both babies home to Sevenwaters with me? That I could spare Becan the uncertainty of a future amongst folk who were prepared to give him away, and save my brother as well? If I did not seize this chance I would regret it forever.

"All right," I said, and reached to unfasten the gate. It was awkward with the fire stick in my hands.

"Clodagh!" A shout, and running footsteps behind me. A hand snatching the burning brand from me, another grabbing my fingers and wrenching them from the latch. "What are you doing?"

"No, Cathal! Let me go! You don't understand, they have Finbar—" I struggled to get my fingers on the gate, but Cathal had dragged me back out of reach. Now he had his arm around my waist from behind, his grip iron strong. "Let me go!" I sobbed. "He's just there, I can reach him! Cathal, please!"

On the far side of the hedge the woman in gray stood silent, eyes fixed on us. She watched awhile as I fought and pleaded, then she spoke again. Her frosty tone turned me still and silent in Cathal's arms.

"As a guardian, you do a poor job," she observed. "You almost let her drown. Now you sleep while she wanders."

"What do you want with us?" It was a challenge, bold and strong, but I could feel a trembling in Cathal's body that belied the confidence in his words.

"All this way, and you do not know?" the woman asked, and I wondered that I had ever thought her friendly, for now her lovely eyes were hostile.

"You lied to her," Cathal said. "Do that again and you'll answer to me." This time I heard something in his voice that frightened me, and to my surprise, the woman of the Fair Folk took a step backward.

"A warning for you," she said with a little cold smile. "Do not leave her alone again. Next time she might go too far for you to follow." She motioned to her companion, and together they turned their backs and walked away without another word, carrying Finbar with them.

"No—wait—!" I cried, but they moved into the shadows and were gone.

"Back to the fire," Cathal said.

I stood frozen, resisting the pull of his arm. Had I got this so wrong? Had I been utterly blind? That *had* been my brother. I was sure of it. "They had Finbar," I said, and my voice came out small and wobbly. My nose and eyes were running and my hand hurt. "They had him, Cathal. He was right there."

"Come, Clodagh. Whether that was Finbar or not, he's gone now and those folk with him. You're cold and shocked. Come back to the fire and you can shout at me all you want."

But when we reached the fire, I sat down and found that my anger was all gone, with only sorrow left in its place. "I was so sure she was Deirdre of the Forest," I said, "the woman who has appeared to Sibeal in the past, as she did to my grandmother long ago. A benign presence. It seemed so easy. She said she wanted to help us. It seemed right, Cathal." I bent over my hand, trying to get my fingernails around the end of the splinter.

"Let me." He sat down beside me, took my hand in his and examined the sliver of wood through narrowed eyes. "It's in deep; I might need to use a knife."

"Just do it, please. I'm sorry, Cathal. The look in her eyes at the end . . . I forgot the warnings. She mocked the Old Ones. She said they were only meddling. And perhaps they are. I don't know whom to believe anymore. I don't know whom to trust."

"Trusting me might be a good first step." He had taken out a long-bladed knife. He held my hand firmly and maneuvered the weapon with skill. I shut my eyes; that seemed to make it hurt less.

"If I didn't trust you, would I be letting you do this?" I said grimly. "Cathal?"

"Mm? Keep still."

"She said the Lord of the Oak was the same person as Mac Dara. You know, the Otherworld prince from the old tales, the one who was always scheming and plotting and trying to get more power for himself. A great battle leader, but quite devoid of any sense of right and wrong."

"Uh-huh. Take a deep breath, Clodagh." A sharp pain. A moment later, shocking in its sweetness, the touch of his lips on the palm of my hand, where the hurt had been. My eyes flew open, but he had already released his hold and was turning away. "Best let me put some salve on that. I'll tend to your cuts at the same time. I should have done it earlier."

"You've hardly had any sleep—"

"When I did fall asleep I nearly lost you."

"I said I was sorry." I felt my shoulders droop. "I should have known this was too easy: the safe place, all our things provided for us, time to think, to reflect . . . But why would those people bring Finbar and then take him away? Weren't they the Tuatha De? They're Mac Dara's folk; if I'm supposed to present a case to him tomorrow, why would they do this? That woman, she was . . ." A shiver ran through me. "I thought she was a friend, but the way she spoke . . . she seemed angry."

"I cannot tell you who they were," said Cathal. "But I believe their sole intention was to lure you outside the hedge on your own. To draw you away from my protection, Clodagh."

"If that's true, I've been stupid. Dog Mask said it was dangerous to go outside the hedge, and still I would have done it."

"Don't blame yourself," Cathal said, sitting down again with a pot of salve. "We've both made mistakes. It's human to do so. Believe me, I have no great certainty that my choices are right. Let me tend to your face, Clodagh. Look at me."

I looked at him, and perhaps there was something in my eyes that I had intended to keep veiled until another time, another place, but right now I had not the strength to guard my expression. Cathal took an unsteady breath and let it out in a sigh. "I swore to myself I wouldn't," he murmured, then put his long hands on either side of my face and kissed me. And although he had done so twice before, this felt like the very first time. It was tender and lovely, deep and thrilling. It was like the pealing of bells, the singing of a lark in the dawn sky, the scent of apple blossom, the colors of a rainbow. I wrapped my arms around his neck, pressing myself close to him. I felt his hands against my back, my waist, then his fingers gentle on the swell of my breast, kindling a fire deep in my body. I made an involuntary sound of pleasure and felt him go suddenly still. A moment later his lips left mine and his hands were withdrawn.

"No," he said shakily. "I can't. I can't do this, not here, not now."

Bitter disappointment flooded through me. My body was aching for him; the feelings in me were beyond what I had believed possible. "Why not?" I burst out.

Cathal put his hands up in front of him, palms toward me, as if he were warding me off. "I can't allow it to happen," he said. "It isn't right. When you get back to Sevenwaters you'll thank me for this, Clodagh."

"Not *allow* this to happen?" My distress made me shrill, but I couldn't help it. "Do you think I have no mind of my own?"

He was avoiding my eye now. "You know what my father did," he said. "My mother offered herself to him, believing his false promises. He took his pleasure then abandoned her without another thought. I'm that man's son. Now tell me you still don't understand why I have to say no."

"That's rubbish," I said, struggling for some measure of calm. "I'm nothing like your mother; I'm a completely different woman. Besides, I don't remember your making any promises, false or otherwise, except to keep me safe on my mission. Anyway, we don't actually have to . . ." I felt my face grow hot.

"Go on," said Cathal, sounding a little more like his old self.

I drew a deep breath. "I wasn't suggesting, necessarily, that we would . . ." I could imagine Deirdre listening to this speech and laughing at me. "I mean, we may be alone out here, far from our own world, but . . ."

"You're tired, shocked and upset," Cathal said. Now he sounded like a father counseling a wayward child. "If you weren't, you'd never dream of considering this, Clodagh. You're Lord Sean's daughter. I'm . . . what I am. If I let this develop any further I'd be taking advantage of you at a time of weakness, whether you choose to call it that or not. Save yourself for Aidan. You'll be grateful to me, believe it."

"Bollocks," I snapped, a tide of humiliation sweeping over me. "Forget the whole idea. Clearly I misjudged the situation." I tried very hard to conceal how close I was to tears. "Pass me that salve, I'll tend to my cuts myself."

"I'll do it," Cathal said. "It'll be an exercise in self-restraint."

And it was, for both of us. Whatever his motives were for rejecting me, I had been wrong to think for a moment that he was indifferent. His fingers were as gentle as the first time he'd done this, but far less sure. They were shaking as they moved along the lines on my face. I saw the desire in his eyes, and in the softening of his tight lips, and I heard it in his breathing, as unsteady as my own. I kept very still. Tears brimmed in my eyes but did not fall. I hadn't misjudged the situation so very much after all. He was making no attempt to disguise the fact that he wanted me. "When we get home," I whispered, "I'm not letting you run away. I just won't have it."

"Ah, well," said Cathal, "if that day comes, I might have some things to say to you that can't be said now." He reached with his thumb to brush the soft skin below my eye, arresting the spill of tears. "This job is done, and now you should try to sleep, Clodagh. Whatever happens tomorrow, you'll need your wits about you. These folk twist our minds with ease. I'm hoping your dog-masked guardian will stay by your side while you finish your quest, and keep you from straying again. I'd rather not have to restrain you by force."

"I can't bear to think of Finbar so close and being taken out of reach again. They didn't seem interested in Becan at all." I glanced over at the sleeping child, a tiny mound under his blanket.

"A trick. Whoever that was at the gate, it was not the person you must deal with here. These are not the kind of folk who grant favors without payment. It must be an exchange, as you expected. I can't say I took to that thing in the dog mask, but the evidence suggests you will be safer trusting it than these others."

"Because of the bond of kinship, you mean?"

Cathal's smile was all self-mockery. There was not a trace of amusement in his eyes. "A bond of kinship is not necessarily a guarantee of trust," he said. "But here we are, with little knowledge of the realm we stray in, facing the need for life or death decisions. If I were you I would consider these Old Ones as benign as anyone can be in such a place. When it comes to the final audience, or whatever it is that awaits you, you'd be best to rely only on yourself. Trust no one."

"Except you, you mean."

"When it comes to the end that may not be relevant, Clodagh. Now wrap yourself up and get some rest. I'll stand watch until morning."

The night seemed long. I slept in fitful bursts, my slumber a tangle of troubling dreams, and woke from time to time to see Cathal on guard, seated before the fire or standing close by, gazing out toward the hedge of thorn, which was invisible in the thick darkness. At one point I was woken abruptly as the silent voice of my twin sister broke into my thoughts: *Clodagh! Answer me!* I slammed down my mental shutters, blocking Deirdre out. Tonight I simply did not have room for her in my mind.

A little later, Becan awoke and I tended to him, then lay down again with him next to me, knowing it would be the last night I would feel his curious, sharp-edged body snuggled close to mine. It was almost time to say goodbye. I hummed to him as he fell asleep, using the tune of my ballad, but not the words. That song was too sad for a little child. Out in the forest, the wailing creature added its sorrowful voice to the music.

There was a dawn of sorts. A faint light filtered down through the trees; birds uttered tentative cries. *Maybe, maybe!* called one, and another answered, *Too soon! Too soon!* It wasn't a particularly encouraging start to the day, but at least it was bright enough to see what we were doing. Cathal walked the perimeter of the hedged area and reported that apart from the birds there was no sign of life outside it, though he had looked over the gate and discerned footprints on the soft earth there. I built up the fire and prepared food. At home my father, an early riser, would be sitting down to his porridge and perhaps devising a strategy to deal with whoever had attacked Glencarnagh. Men would still be out on the search for Finbar. By tomorrow night or the day after, perhaps we would be walking back into the courtyard with the baby safe and sound. *Be strong, Mother,* I willed her. *I'm bringing him home.*

We ate in silence, keeping a distance between us. There was a look on Cathal's face that mirrored the feeling inside me. My stomach was twisting with nervousness. There was a lot to lose if this confrontation with the Fair Folk did not go well. I must get home safely, not only to deliver my brother into the arms of my family, but also to tell my father that Cathal was a good man, that he had never been a traitor, that it was for his own reasons that he had concealed the source of his unusual knowledge. I must get home safely so I could . . . what? Convince Cathal that what he felt for me was more than physical desire, when I was not entirely sure that was true? Persuade him that he should consider spending the rest of his life with me, when it was quite clear that such an outsider would not fit into my world? Explain to Father that Cathal was a better prospect as a future husband than the personable and well-connected Aidan? Perhaps being in the Otherworld had addled my wits.

"You look worried," observed Cathal.

"I am worried. So much depends on this, and I can't be sure of anything. Those folk last night disturbed me. In the old tales, when people undertake quests they find themselves fighting dragons or serpents or giant dogs. Or maybe dark warriors of some kind, folk who are enemies from the start. But it's far more frightening when someone seems friendly and good, as that woman did, and turns out to be different altogether. The odd and uncanny are not terrifying in themselves. The most disturbing thing is the ordinary turned strange. Things familiar and safe becoming suddenly . . . not right." I thought of home, and how my place as loved and trusted daughter of the house had vanished in an instant. I thought of Mother's hollow cheeks and vacant stare.

"That's one reason it's easier to have no attachments," Cathal said. "That way there's nothing to lose."

I stared at him. "That's terrible," I said. "You'd be living your whole life without love. Letting fear rule you."

He shrugged, as if such considerations meant nothing to him.

Anyway, I thought, *it's not true. You may dismiss whatever it is you feel for me, but you can't disregard your bond with Aidan. Or your love for your mother. You can't set aside your loyalty to Johnny.* But I did not say it. He looked troubled enough without having to listen to my opinions. But for me, he wouldn't be in this situation at all.

"In fact," Cathal said, attempting a smile, "I find myself rather glad that we haven't encountered any dragons. Clodagh, I know you're anxious about your family. I'll try to see Sevenwaters for you later. I hope I will be able to tell you what's happening there."

"You can do that? See whatever you seek in the water?" Sibeal did sometimes scry for answers to particular problems, but her visions were just as likely to show her something entirely unrelated.

"I'll either see that or just a jumble, like last time."

"Are you sure you don't mind doing this?"

"I'm going to be precious little help to you from this point on, I suspect. This is relatively easy. If it will reassure you, I'll do it gladly."

"Thank you, Cathal. I'll stay over here, out of your way, and keep a lookout."

"Come and sit with me if you want." The offer was made with diffidence.

"Are you sure that won't distract you?"

"Quite sure, Clodagh. It might even help summon the vision we want. I should salve those cuts again first. They're looking better. Starting to heal."

"If we're going to be sitting by the pond, I can do it myself. I haven't dared look at my reflection yet. I have to face it some time."

Later in the morning, the two of us sat side by side at the water's edge with Becan tucked into blankets and shawls close by. While Cathal settled immediately into a seer's pose and fixed his eyes on the unknown, I confronted my own image in the still surface of the pond.

If my cuts were looking better now, I hated to think how they'd looked yesterday. One was a slash right across my forehead, straight and deep. A second marked me from the outer end of my right eye halfway to my chin. A third complemented it, tracing an untidy shape resembling a bird or a bat on my left cheek. I imagined people looking at me as they had at my sister Maeve after she was burned, seeing only the disfigurement, not the girl underneath. I wondered if Muirrin might have any treatment that would make these marks fade, or whether I would bear the wounds of my self-appointed mission for the rest of my life. I pressed my lips together and began to anoint my face with salve.

I was almost finished when Cathal made a slight sound, then stretched out toward me without taking his eyes from the water. I took his hand; it was trembling. His face had gone ghostly white. My gaze stilled, following the line of his sight, and a jolt of shock went through me. The water that had shown me my own damaged face a moment ago was now full of movement and color, images of a man riding, of trees, of cloaked figures moving in and out of dappled light . . . It seemed that as soon as I had taken Cathal's hand I had been drawn into his vision. His gift must be powerful indeed.

His grip had tightened. I edged closer until I was kneeling right beside him on the bank. His dark eyes were wide, his jaw grim. He was breathing hard. I made myself stare into the water.

A man was riding through the forest, a young man with brown hair and an open, handsome face. Aidan. He was on his own, though the two hunting dogs were running at his horse's feet. He had his bow slung over his shoulder, and he was wearing the same clothing he'd had on when he pursued us to the river's edge. He passed under monumental oaks, their great trunks dark and massive, the spaces between them wide and shadowy. I knew the place. It was within the forest of Sevenwaters, near the nemetons that housed Uncle Conor's community of druids. Aidan kept glancing over his shoulder as if he thought someone was following him, but he also seemed to be searching for something. The dogs were keeping close; they made no forays off the path. The horse looked nervous and so did the rider.

Another path; another avenue of oaks. Aidan picked up the pace and the dogs stayed right by him. The horse cantered down a short slope and halted abruptly, obedient to its rider's signal. Aidan dismounted and took three strides toward one of the big trees, then knelt suddenly. Our field of vision altered slightly, and now we were looking over his shoulder into the blank, open eyes of the man who lay there, an arrow through his neck, his blood congealing in a pool beneath. It was one of the two who had ridden out with Aidan in search of Cathal only two days ago.

I swallowed an exclamation of horror; Cathal inhaled sharply. We saw Aidan reach to close his companion's eyes, say something, perhaps a prayer, then rise slowly to his feet. The dogs waited by the horse, keeping their distance.

Aidan went suddenly still. His hand crept toward the dagger at his belt. And now I could see what he could, a figure emerging from cover twenty paces ahead of him with bow in hand and arrow already on the string. A figure in a gray hooded cloak similar to those all of Johnny's men wore in the field, but subtly different in its style, a cloak with a certain shape and swirl that made it unusual. The wearer was tall, dark-haired, with a pale, intense face and thin lips. I couldn't hold back a little sound of shock. Cathal, there in the vision? Cathal stalking Aidan in the forest of Sevenwaters when he was right here beside me? Could what we were seeing be in the past? No, that man lying dead there under the oaks had been alive and well when we set out across the river and Cathal had been with me ever since. Was this a vision of events yet to come?

The Cathal of the image took a step forward and said something. He appeared quite calm. Perhaps he was inviting Aidan to lay his arms aside and talk the matter through. Aidan had not completed the movement that would have put his knife in his hand. With the other man's weapon trained on him, he had no choice but to capitulate. His face blazing with anger, he raised his hands, showing them open and empty—a gesture of parley. An instant later, sudden and brutal, the arrow took him in the chest and he crumpled to the ground.

Cathal went rigid, as if it were he who had taken the bolt. My head swam; my heart thumped in shock. *It's not true, it can't be, it's only a vision,* babbled a voice inside me, the voice of a panicky child. *Just symbols, that's all it is.* But Cathal had told me what he saw was always true. My hand clutched in his, I forced myself to go on looking, for if he was brave enough to follow this to its end, so must I be.

I had known when I saw Aidan fall that he could not recover from such a wound. He lay sprawled under the trees, close to the body of his dead comrade, and the figure that was almost Cathal but not quite—as he moved closer, I could see many subtle differences—walked over to the fallen man and, after a moment's scrutiny, knelt to relieve him of his weapons. Aidan's bow was trapped half under his inert body. The cloaked man rolled him over casually to retrieve it, then wiped his bloody hands on the grass. He removed a ring from Aidan's finger. He stood, tall and lean in his sweeping cloak, then stalked over to the horse and set a hand on its neck. The hunting hounds had retreated into the ferns, tails down.

The man who looked like Cathal swung himself onto Aidan's horse and rode off without a backward glance. Before they had gone ten paces, horse and rider merged into the shadows between the oaks. The vision blurred and dissipated. The surface of the pond showed our reflections: Cathal's, white and wretched, and mine, contorted by an expression of horrified disbelief. It had been so . . . so casual.

I was used to waiting for Sibeal to take what time she needed when emerging from a trance. Cathal took no time. As soon as the images were gone he sprang to his feet. A wordless shout burst out of him, a sound of fury and anguish. He cupped his open hands before his face then swept them violently downward, and I knew exactly what was in his mind. *I should have been there. If I had been there, perhaps I could have saved him.* Then, before I could say a word, he strode away, hands clutched into his hair, his body plainly possessed by the urge to take action, to make this right again, and the absolute knowledge that it was too late to do anything at all. He reached the fire, seized a log from our wood pile and hurled it into the flames with such violence that embers scattered all around the campsite. A moment later he was at the hedge, gripping the trunk of a thornbush, beating his head against the wood as if to drive the images from it. Since that first cry he had uttered no sound, but now, as if summoned by the pain he was inflicting on himself, words began to spill forth.

"This is my doing, it's my fault, all of it! If I hadn't come to Sevenwaters, if I hadn't let them persuade me . . . To die all alone, no kind hands to gather him up, nobody to speak words of comfort, no friend to bear him home . . . And he thought it was me! He died believing I had killed him! How dare they, how dare they do this?"

There were no right words to say. I could not embrace him; he was slamming his forehead against the tree, his body shaking with rage and grief. Touch him, and I would likely be cast off with violence. I walked over quietly and settled myself on the ground a few paces away from him. My cheeks were wet with tears. Aidan dead, lovely Aidan with his sweet smile and his music . . . He had not deserved such a sudden and brutal end. I could hardly believe that he was gone. If it was true.

I waited, not saying anything, and after a while the flow of furious words ceased and Cathal quieted, subsiding to a crouch at the foot of the hedge. The day had brightened; the deceptive sky gave a hint of sun behind clouds. High above us, a lark burst suddenly into jubilant song.

"Cathal," I said quietly, "I'm sorry. I'm more sorry than I can say. I suppose this must be a true vision, a vision of present times, since you said the water never lies to you. Wherever Aidan is now, he knows you did not do this."

His hands went over his face. "How could he know, when the murderer bore my face?" he whispered.

"He does know, because he knows you are a good man. He knows you better than anyone, didn't you say so yourself?" I moved across to him, cautiously, for I could not be sure what he would do. "Give me your hands, Cathal. Please." Kneeling before him, I took his hands in mine, drawing them gently away from his face. His shoulders were hunched, his knees drawn up, his jaw clenched tight. There was a violent trembling coursing through him. I leaned over and touched my lips to his brow, where the skin was torn and bloody. "You've hurt yourself, dear one," I said. "Whatever you think you've done, he would forgive you. In your heart you know that."

He drew a ragged breath, and then, suddenly, he was kneeling too, his head bowed onto my shoulder, and my arms went around him, and he was weeping, not silently, but with a full-throated and wrenching sorrow that rang across the clearing and vibrated through every part of me. I held him, and he wept, and a little breeze passed through the foliage of the oaks beyond the hedge, sounding a rustling counterpoint. Eventually, like an exhausted child, he sobbed himself into silence, but we stayed there awhile longer, arms around each other, unable to move beyond the unthinkable thing that had happened. It was Becan's hungry wailing that broke the spell.

"Go," said Cathal, releasing me and dashing a hand across his cheeks. "Go and tend to him, go on."

I sat back on my heels, regarding him closely. "He can wait," I said. "Cathal, come over to the fire with me."

He rose to his feet and I did the same. My legs were numb with cramp; I had a good excuse to put my arm around him as we made our way back, gathering Becan up on the way. It helped that there were things to do; it is hard to ignore a screaming baby. Cathal tended to the fire. I fed the child. When he was finished, I took the pot of water Cathal had heated and added some of the precious supply of honey, then divided the brew between Cathal and me.

"Drink it," I told him. "Honey's a restorative. We need this."

He drank in silence, seated cross-legged, staring into the fire. The look on his face frightened me. When he began to speak, I expected a statement of vengeance; perhaps a vow to hunt down whoever had killed his friend in cold blood. But he said, "I'm sorry. I forgot how you must be feeling. You and Aidan . . . You meant so much to him . . . He was always talking about you. And your father liked him. Approved of him. If I hadn't allowed my friend to die, you and he would have . . . I've stolen your future, Clodagh. How can you forgive me?"

I looked at the wound on his brow, raw oozing flesh, a livid bruise coming up. The cup was shaking in his hands. I must choose my words carefully. "You didn't do any of it," I said, "unless you've developed the ability to be in two places at once. Someone else killed Aidan; someone who is able to change his appearance at will so he can resemble you closely, if not exactly. Why anyone would want to do that I can't imagine. But you shouldn't blame yourself for Aidan's death, or for anything that might change because of it. You came to Sevenwaters because you work for Johnny. You're here with me now because, for your own reasons, you decided to help me. If you and Aidan found yourselves on opposite sides of a dispute, that was purely ill luck. Perhaps that man with the bow was connected with whoever attacked Glencarnagh; perhaps what we saw was part of a bigger battle."

"I don't think so. Aidan stood back and let us cross the river, Clodagh, but probably only because you had positioned yourself to shield me. In the vision he was still out on the search for me. He had the hounds with him. He was looking for his companions. How they became separated I can only guess."

I thought he was right, but I would not say so. The last thing Cathal needed was another reason to heap guilt on himself.

"You said you'd stolen my future." I had to speak of this, difficult as it was. "Cathal, I'm sad that Aidan is gone, terribly sad. I'm shocked and upset. To be drawn into your vision and to see that . . . I wish with all my heart that you believed there was some doubt about its truth. But, Cathal, whatever Aidan may have thought he felt for me, I didn't love him in that way. He was a suitable candidate for marriage, certainly, and for a while I saw that as a possibility. I liked him very much. I'm sad at the waste of a fine man. But I didn't love him like a . . . a sweetheart. At a certain point it became clear to me that I would never marry him. It seems wrong to say that now; it feels almost like a betrayal. But he's here somewhere, watching us, and he understands. I know it." Wherever Aidan's shade had wandered, he was no longer part of that limp body lying alone in the forest with only the dogs to keep him company. I thought of that little girl, Rathnait, back at Whiteshore waiting for a betrothed who would never come home. Would she grieve for him?

Cathal had set aside his cup and had spread his cloak over his knees with the lining outermost. He slipped a small knife from his belt and began to pick at the fabric with the point. "You believe death wipes away sorrow so instantly?" he asked. "That in the life beyond, all ills are forgiven, all guilt assuaged? I cannot share that faith. You think the shade of my mother watches this alongside Aidan, her heart full of forgiveness for that wretch who destroyed her life?"

He sounded so bitter, so angry. "Perhaps she is proud of the fine man you have become," I said. "She might well forgive your father, since without him you would not have existed. Sad though her life became, with her lover she must have had moments, blissful moments, when she believed herself the most adored, the most beautiful woman in existence. Perhaps, from wherever she is now, she can look back on that life and see that there was happiness in it."

Cathal glanced at me. "You're a rare creature, Clodagh," he said. "You're brimful of hope and compassion and love. I didn't see all that when I first met you. But I did feel a spark. I felt an affinity. And I felt desire. It trembled through me at every toss of that fiery mane. It kept me sleepless by night and restless by day. With every kind word and with every sharp one you drew me in further. That troubled me greatly. It was not only the thought that I might be my father all over again. I knew that the stronger those feelings grew, the more powerful a tool they became in my enemy's hands. As you see, I failed completely in my attempt to put you at a distance. And I worked hard enough at that; my rudeness was quite effective initially, I think. It pained me to speak to you thus. I despised myself for doing it, even though it was for your protection. But I reckoned without your ability to . . . to wrap your cloak of acceptance even around a man who had gone out of his way to be unpleasant, a man with very few redeeming qualities. We've become close and I've endangered you, as I did Aidan. If he hadn't been my friend he wouldn't be lying there in his blood, all alone." His voice was shaking. "Now that I have seen these people's complete disregard for human life, the only thing that matters is keeping you safe until you get home. I want you to put these in your pack." He cut a thread and lifted a scrap of bright cloth from the place where it had been sewn into the cloak's lining. There was a cold purpose about his movements. "From what that dog-faced being said, it sounds as if you shouldn't wear the cloak to this exchange, but only the embroidered gown and shawl. The thought that you may need to use your appearance to charm this fellow disturbs me. I want you to take these things with you. You must put them in your bag and carry it on your back."

"You mean for protection? I thought you said these charms had no such power."

He was laying each item down on the ground beside him as he severed the threads that bound it to the garment: a tawny feather, a white stone, a strip of leather. "Maybe they do, maybe they don't," he said. "You must take them anyway."

"But what about you?"

"I can look after myself." He took another object from the cloak and set it down. It looked like a tiny plait of hair. "I let them kill Aidan. I won't let them harm you as well, not if there's anything I can do to prevent it."

I watched him, finding the haunted look on his face and the furious intensity in his eyes so disturbing that I could hardly begin to absorb the remarkable speech he had just made: not a declaration of love, but more than an expression of physical desire, surely. Whatever it was, it had lit a shining lamp within me. It seemed wrong that, at the same time, I could feel the raw sorrow of Aidan's death and this warm glow of hope.

"Cathal," I said, "you say *them*. But who? An ordinary man couldn't alter his appearance like that, to make himself look almost exactly like you. You say *these people*. You mean folk of the Otherworld? The Tuatha De?" I shivered, cold with the knowledge that at dusk today I would be standing in front of just such folk to plead for my brother's release. I hesitated, then added, "I've seen someone a little like that man before. In the forest, the very first day I met you. A person in a gray cloak, watching me from under the trees. It scared me, but I came around to thinking I'd imagined the whole thing. But then, on the night before Deirdre's wedding, I saw him again. Out in the courtyard, where you were. "

Cathal's long fingers stilled, a miniature cross made from rowan wood held between them. It was bound with green thread. "Thus confirming your suspicion that I was up to no good. But you didn't report it to your father."

"It was only that, a suspicion. I could have imagined it. I did tell him later, after Glencarnagh was attacked. I'm sorry, Cathal. I thought . . ."

"You did what seemed right. I should have been honest from the first, I suppose. I feel a revulsion for this so-called talent I have inherited." He waved a hand in the general direction of the pond. "That has made me shy away from anything hinting at the uncanny. Far easier to keep well clear of such things, I thought. Yes, I believe there was someone there in the courtyard that night. Watching me. Keeping an eye on which friend was close to me, which girl my eyes fell on most often, how I might be twisted and turned."

"Who would do this? And why?"

"That I cannot say, save that they are not human forces. They have dogged me a long time, Clodagh, since I was around twelve years old. Not all the time; they choose their moments. At Whiteshore it was happening more and more often—tricks to separate me from my companions, ploys to lure me off the track. Shadowy forms; mysterious voices. Their presence gave me even stronger reason to accompany Aidan"—his voice cracked as he spoke his friend's name—"to Inis Eala. It should be far enough away from Whiteshore, I thought, to put me beyond the reach of those mischievous forces."

"And was it?" A glimmer of understanding came to me. This was what he had meant when he spoke of his presence at Sevenwaters bringing danger down on the rest of us.

"So it seemed. They never troubled me there. Folk say there is a kind of protection over the island. Johnny told me that one of your father's uncles used to live there, a man of great spiritual strength, and that the cave where he dwelt is under the watch of benign forces. It seems this influence spreads out over the whole of Inis Eala."

"So you were safe while you stayed on the island, but since you came to Sevenwaters these forces have started pursuing you again." It did not seem likely. Could he be imagining the whole thing? Had these mysterious pursuers arisen from his childhood unhappiness and made themselves real in his mind? For folk to delude themselves thus was not unknown. But not Cathal, surely. He was too rational, too capable.

"I had heard that Sevenwaters was an uncanny place," Cathal said. "Just the kind of place, I thought, where these powers would gather around me once more. And they did. That day when we rode out with the children, they drew me off the path. It wasn't my own double that lured me. It was you."

I stared at him. "Me?" I said. "But I was with the others all the time, Sibeal and Doran and . . . Aidan." Oh, it hurt to speak his name. I could see him before me, his brown eyes gentle, his smile sweet. I could hear the ringing notes of a harp.

"The girl I saw was as close to you in appearance as that assassin was to me. Good enough to deceive at a distance, though I doubt I would be taken in now. I followed, surprised to see you on your own and thinking you might be in trouble. At some point within the forest, you—or at least the girl who resembled you—vanished. It was an experiment; a test. They chose right. They learned, that day, that if you were in danger I would break any rule to rescue you."

A curious feeling was coming over me. This was like the opening of a box of surprises, with each layer that unfolded exposing another, trickier one beneath. Cathal a seer; the Fair Folk pursuing him, leading him astray, perhaps endangering all those close to him; Cathal caring enough about me to put my safety before his own future. It explained many things, but not the crucial question of *why*. Why would the Fair Folk be so interested in Cathal? What could that possibly have to do with the snatching of Finbar and my mission to bring him home?

"You were afraid," I said, recalling the shadows I had seen in his eyes as we crossed the river and as we camped in the forest at night. "If they've been tormenting you for years and years, you were crazy to come with me."

"They knew I would come," he said with frightening simplicity.

"This was what they wanted? Are you saying . . . Cathal, are you telling me it was no accident that you and I met in the forest? That the whole thing was controlled by the Fair Folk, to bring you here with me? But that would mean we were just . . . puppets. It would mean we had no free choices at all." This notion was almost impossible to accept. "Why would they do that? They wouldn't attach you to me as a protector. These folk have a facility with magic. They could make the path to Mac Dara's hall as easy or difficult for me as they pleased. Besides, you say they've been pursuing you since long before you had anything to do with Sevenwaters. What reason could there be for that?"

Cathal grimaced. "I have a theory, but I'm by no means certain it's correct. I hope very much that it isn't. It is not a thing I can speak of here. If we get back safely I'll tell you about it. Who would have thought the prospect of an honest talk could seem so enticing and so impossible?"

"Cathal."

"Yes, Clodagh?" He had finished unpicking the objects from the cloak, and now he gathered them up into a small heap.

"Are you saying you believe that even Finbar's abduction wouldn't have happened if you had not been at Sevenwaters? That he was taken in order to ensure you came here with me?" It seemed the sort of theory that would only be invented by a man with a grossly inflated idea of his own importance in the scheme of things. I might be prepared to believe Cathal deluded, misguided, but I knew he was not the arrogant person I had once thought him. Besides, I could think of no good reason for the Fair Folk to punish my parents, who had long been wise custodians of the forest and staunch supporters of the old faith. I considered the idea that my family was involved in this only because . . . because Cathal felt something for me that was a great deal more significant that I had ever believed. A man does not follow a woman into a realm where he believes he will be under threat unless he feels more for her than simple lust. *They learned, that day, that if you were in danger I would break any rule to rescue you.*

"It makes sense," Cathal said quietly. "They know you. They know your family. They had confidence that you would undertake this journey to set things right. You've seen already how these folk can manipulate our perceptions, Clodagh. I imagine they found it easy enough to ensure you recognized Becan for what he is while the rest of your family saw only a wooden manikin. Somehow they made sure you and I would meet in the forest. My instincts told me where the portal was. I cannot explain to you how I knew, only that I was quite certain there was a river in that quarter and that crossing it would bring us into the Otherworld. Those who pursue us seem to know me as well as they know you. They knew I would not let you undertake such a perilous quest alone. All the way, at every stage of our journey, they have put you in danger so I would stay by your side. Even those folk last night, who came to the gate and showed you a child just like your brother—what was that but a blatant attempt to draw you out of this safe place while I slept? If they had taken you away I would have followed, even if your trail led me so deep into the Otherworld that there was no way out. That may be exactly what they want."

I answered as I knew I had to, though the thought of going on without him made me feel sick. "When they come for me later, you'd best stay here and wait until I've got Finbar," I said. "Then we can go home together. The last thing I want is to put you in danger, Cathal. In any more danger, I mean. What can they want with you?"

But he only shrugged. "Put these in your bag," he said. "Wrap a garment around them, then stow them at the bottom."

I rolled the little items into a spare stocking and put them deep in my pack. I wondered if there was any real possibility that Cathal's bizarre theory was correct. Was my place in this whole course of events merely that of a pawn? Was it of no consequence what decisions I made, what choices I took? I did not think I could accept that. Besides, I had a nagging feeling that somewhere in my memory there was a key to all of this, a key I needed to find before it was too late. "Cathal, why did you run away from Sevenwaters when you weren't guilty of anything? Surely it would have been better to tell Johnny the full story."

"And make my affliction common knowledge?" His tone was bitter. I glanced at him. Aidan's death had put a new darkness in his eyes. If I had thought his look haunted once or twice before, it was nothing to this.

"I don't want my father's legacy," he said. "If I could wipe away the stain of him forever, I would do so. Besides, with each day that passed I was more certain that my presence at Sevenwaters was bringing down disaster on you and your family. I could not in all conscience remain there any longer."

"By not speaking out about this," I said, "you've played into these folk's hands. You've done exactly what they wanted you to do. That's if your theory is correct. One thing I don't understand is how the attack on Glencarnagh fits into this. Cathal, when you saw that vision, what exactly was it that made you suspect Illann?"

"Before I saw the attack, I was shown glimpses of other things. You brushing your sister's hair. Illann showing Deirdre a map. Illann addressing a group of men, some of whom I thought I saw later amongst those who attacked your father's property. The pieces, put together in a certain way, at least suggested the possibility that Illann might be implicated. I thought it fair to warn you, since you were a potential source of information to your sister. It may bear no relation to this other matter."

"If we're being manipulated, you and me," I said miserably, "I suppose these visions might contain whatever the Fair Folk choose to put in them. They might show us things just to stir up trouble. That old woman, Willow, said Mac Dara was mischievous, didn't she?"

Memory stirred. Willow's stories, which had seemed to upset Cathal so much: the clurichauns, Wolf-child . . . There had been something about Mac Dara, too, but when I tried to recall it, it slipped away.

Cathal bowed his head. "Aidan's dead," he said. "I can't allow myself to hope that was a lie. I know in my bones that it's true."

"I'm sorry. I didn't mean to make you feel worse."

He said nothing.

"I didn't tell you," I said, "but just before you came up to see me, the day Finbar was taken, I contacted Deirdre to tell her about the birth. And . . . and she asked me some unexpected questions. They weren't very specific, but they did concern Father's dilemma with the northern chieftains, the sort of thing Deirdre has never been interested in before. So perhaps your vision was true; perhaps she and Illann were somehow involved. If the Fair Folk have a grand plan involving you, that attack really doesn't seem to fit."

"If it's a worldly plot, Johnny and Lord Sean will sort it out between them. I hope I was wrong about your sister. That would be hard for you. Clodagh?"

"Mm?"

"I can't stay here while you go off to confront this Mac Dara. It would run against every instinct that's in me. I can't let you do this on your own." He sounded wretched.

I looked up and saw his face quite unguarded. He was white as chalk, his lips set tight, but love blazed in his eyes, fierce and uncompromising. For a moment it stopped my heart. I moved across to kneel by him and wrap my arms around him, pressing my cheek against his. "I want you to be safe," I whispered. "If they mean you harm, you mustn't come with me."

"If my theory's right," he murmured against my hair, "you won't be able to do it unless I'm there."

"Let me try. I'm a daughter of Sevenwaters, after all. There have been hundreds of years of goodwill between us and the Tuatha De. Surely that can't be erased so quickly."

"Shh," Cathal whispered. "Let's not talk about this now. Let's not talk at all." His hand moved against my hair, then traced a tender line down temple, cheek, neck, his thumb pausing where the blood pulsed close under the skin. His touch was like a bard's on his instrument, and it awakened a deep and mysterious music in my body. I sighed and nestled closer. We sat like that a long while, touching gently, not letting the spark between us rise to a flame, for now was not the time for that. If all went well, when we got back to Sevenwaters we would have all the time we wanted. A lifetime if we were lucky. I knew, as Cathal held me, that no objection anyone could raise was going to keep me from being with him. I had a good precedent: Father had approved of Muirrin's marriage to Evan, an Inis Eala man who was neither high born nor rich in worldly goods. Evan had been considered suitable because he was a skillful healer and the son of a family friend, and because he and Muirrin loved each other. That, in the end, would be the argument Father would heed most, since he and Mother had been fortunate enough to wed for love themselves.

I mustn't plan too far ahead, I cautioned myself. That was to set myself up for sorrow. But I couldn't help it. This was nearly over. By nightfall today I would have my brother back. By tomorrow or the next day, all three of us could be home again. Today there had been terrible sadness. Tomorrow there would be hope. There would be love. There would be a future. Fair Folk or no Fair Folk, I would make sure of it.

CHAPTER 13

Later we lay down awhile with Becan between us. The baby was drowsy, but Cathal and I could not sleep.

"You know that song?" Cathal murmured.

"What song?"

"The one you were singing last night, about a handsome young man. Did you find a rhyme for *tangled and wild*?"

"I thought you were asleep, or I'd never have sung it out loud," I said, embarrassed. "And yes, I found a rhyme, but you wouldn't like it."

"Try me," Cathal said.

"It's too personal," I told him.

"Go on, Clodagh. I want to hear it."

At least he was sounding more cheerful. I sang:

"Where have you wandered, my dear one, my own
Where have you wandered, my handsome young man
I've strayed in a wilderness tangled and wild
I've raved like a madman and wept like a child
And still I can't find my way home
I still cannot find my way home."

"You think me handsome?" queried Cathal.

"It's a traditional ballad," I told him. "The young men in such verses are always handsome."

"Ah, that explains it. I never thought, when you and Aidan played music together in your father's hall, that one day you would make a song about me."

"The word handsome is not adequate to describe you, Cathal. You are unlike anyone else: a rare creature. I put this in the form of a ballad because that makes a sad story easier to set down." I must not go down that track now. What we both needed was something to give us heart. "Cathal, what was Aidan like as a boy, when the two of you were growing up? Did he love music even then?" *Talk about him,* I willed him. *Talk about the good times, the happy times.*

"He liked to sing, just as you do, Clodagh. When we were out fishing or trapping he'd suddenly get an idea and start whistling or burst into song. It's no wonder we didn't catch much. We spent a lot of time out of doors. Built a tree house; camped overnight; had adventures in boats. Lord Murtagh didn't expect us to act like miniature noblemen. He let us run free when we needed to. But we had tutors as well, some to teach us our letters, others to make sure we could ride and shoot and use weapons. Aidan didn't like being second best at that. He didn't realize he had talents I could never match."

"Like music, you mean?" Between us, the baby had fallen asleep; his slight form took up so little space that I could feel Cathal's thigh against mine, a disturbing sensation.

"That, and the ability to charm folk with his warmth and good humor. He was well loved. Because of that, people accepted me despite my . . ." His voice trailed away.

"Oddity?" I suggested.

"My inability to play the right games. My failure to behave in the way people expected. Aidan was a staunch friend. Over and over I hurt him, upset him, made things difficult for him. Over and over he forgave me, stood by me. He wasn't perfect. Some things he did, I found hard to excuse." He fell silent, perhaps feeling it was wrong to criticize a man so newly lost.

"Aidan did have a temper," I ventured. "I saw it when the two of you were fighting, and it surprised me. He got jealous. And yet at other times he was such a sweet man."

"He killed my dog," Cathal said flatly. "Fleet. There's a strip from her collar in your bag, among the things from the cloak. Even as a child he got jealous. Lord Murtagh gave me Fleet not long after my mother died. I'd never had a dog before and I loved her. Aidan resented that. Perhaps he thought it unfair that his father would make such a gift to me, the bastard foster son. At any rate, Fleet was kicked in the hindquarters. The injury didn't mend. She went lame, then sickened and died. Aidan swore he hadn't done it, but he was seen. That cruel streak in him was one of the reasons I tried to warn you off."

"One of them?"

"My own feelings had more than a little to do with what I said to you." A fleeting smile played across his lips.

Now was not the time to speak more about this, though his words made my heart beat faster. "What else was on the cloak, Cathal?"

As we lay there quietly and the day passed, he told me the story of each small item: a white pebble that had formed part of a childhood game, skipping stones across the stream, then using them in an elaborate competition of throwing and catching. An eagle feather, trophy of a climb up a perilous, forbidden rock face. Aidan had wrenched his ankle; Cathal had caught a pony from a nearby field and somehow conveyed his friend home. A piece of shimmering multicolored cloth: part of a gown once worn by Aidan's mother, relegated to the scrap bag, retrieved by a small boy who had thought that this exotic fabric must surely have real magic in it. "She was kind to me," Cathal said simply.

The plaited hair was his and Aidan's, twined and fastened. "We did that when we were quite small," Cathal said. "A ritual; we swore that we'd be true friends until death." He choked over the words.

"And you were," I said softly. "It doesn't matter that you were on the run or that he had been sent to hunt you down. I saw his face as he watched us disappear on the raft. He wasn't resentful that you'd escaped him. He was sad to be saying goodbye, and pleased that you wouldn't be brought back to face charges that were based on lies." *And jealous*, I thought, but did not say it. "He argued your case to the last. But he was dutiful as well—that's a lesson a chieftain's son or daughter learns early. Johnny threatened to send him away from Inis Eala if he didn't obey the order to go after you. He had to do it."

"Perhaps I was not such a bad influence as I thought. He never learned to enjoy breaking rules." His hand came across and curled around mine. "You're such a wise person, Clodagh," he said.

"Actually, I make it up as I go along most of the time," I said, blushing. "Cathal, can you hear something?" My ears had picked up a soft rustling, a steady beat as of horses' hooves, a faint jingling beyond the safe confines of the thorn hedge. I sat up slowly, careful not to disturb the sleeping infant, and Cathal did the same.

Someone was approaching. Beyond the hedge I could see lights and movement, and I could hear voices, high and strange, calling and laughing as they neared our sanctuary. Cathal put his finger to his lips, signalling silence. I gathered up the baby and we rose cautiously to our feet. The light had begun to fade. In keeping with the oddities of time in the Otherworld, dusk was coming fast.

The gate creaked open, then banged shut. A small figure came across the grass toward us, silver mask before its face. Behind it were two others. One had something of the look of a mossy stone, the eyes round patches of lichen, the mouth a chink; the other was of indeterminate shape, changing each time I looked at it. It put me in mind of water.

"Oh dear," said Dog Mask, halting a few paces from us. Beyond the hedge, a procession was passing now, though I could not see it clearly through the tangle of thorn. There were lanterns; stately folk on horseback; a shimmer of sumptuous, sparkling fabrics; and the voices again, speaking almost as human folk would, save for a note whose strangeness jarred even as its beauty enticed. A harp rang out, its music surpassing in loveliness any tune my own world could hold, and behind it I could hear something crying, desperate, bereft.

"What do you mean, *oh dear*?" I challenged. For all the defiant words, a chill apprehension was creeping into my bones. I held Becan close. "You told us to be ready at dusk. We're ready." At least this would soon be over.

"I told you to prepare yourself. You look as if you've just emerged from a tumble in a haystack. Wash your face and comb your hair, Clodagh. Straighten your clothing. You're about to ask Mac Dara a favor. You don't want to fail for want of a little tidying."

Cathal began an angry retort, but I hushed him. There was no point in protesting. I went to the pond and knelt to splash my face with my free hand. Back at the fireside I got out my comb, but Cathal took it from me before I could start the process of restoring my curls back to the order I had achieved earlier.

"Let me," he said.

His touch was gentle. With Becan cradled in my arms, I stood watching the cavalcade pass by beyond the hedge—here a tall woman whose silver hair was studded with tiny twinkling stars, here a man of arrogant appearance with a pitch-black owl riding on his shoulder—and felt the careful movement of the comb through my hair and the brush of Cathal's fingers against my neck, my forehead, my temple. He made the simple task an act of tenderness that turned my heart over.

"It's done," he said eventually. "You look lovely, Clodagh."

"Thank you," I whispered.

"Any time," he said, and I heard the tremor in his voice.

"You must stay here," I told him. "Let me do this on my own." I glanced at the three small beings who stood in a row, watching me. "These are friends; they'll help me. Wait for me here and we'll go home together."

"Very wise," said Dog Mask. Its odd companions uttered what seemed assent—the stony one made a grinding sound and the other a liquid gurgle. "If you want our help, leave him behind. We will not walk with *his* kind. Now come, Clodagh."

Cathal had fetched my bag, into which I'd tucked the special things from the cloak, the talismans to keep me safe.

"You won't need that," said my guide. "The way home is shorter. That bag is ugly. Mac Dara won't listen if you look like a vagrant who carries all her worldly possessions with her."

"I'm taking it," I said sharply, and turned so that Cathal could help me hitch the pack onto my back. "If Mac Dara makes his decisions based on how folk look, it's time he learned there are better ways to do things."

The watery being let out a bubbling sound that might have been laughter. Dog Mask sighed. "Mac Dara's a prince," it said. "He's powerful. He's wayward. You're an ordinary girl without the least magical ability. If you won't follow simple advice—"

There was a rumble from the rocky one, and my guide fell silent. Perhaps it had been a reprimand, who knew? Beyond the hedge the last of the procession was passing. I judged that the folk in it were moving along the path and back to that broad avenue under the trees, the place that was like the grand entry to a royal hall. I heard the tinkling of little bells and a woman's laughter, high and giddy. The sounds faded. The light had turned to the purple-gray of a spring dusk and in the clearing all seemed hushed. The birds had fallen silent. Our fire had died down, its remnant coals a faint glow beneath a pile of shifting ash.

"It's time to go now," said Dog Mask.

Cathal was standing two paces in front of me, still and silent. I cleared my throat. "I won't be long," I said, trying for a confident tone.

Cathal's eyes told me he had seen right through me. He knew I was terrified. He knew I wanted more than anything to have him with me when I confronted the Lord of the Oak. I turned away quickly. He mustn't come. This was my quest, whatever Cathal believed about the reasons he was here with me. He shouldn't put himself at risk because of my weakness.

My small guardians were already walking toward the gate, the three of them forming a procession of their own.

"No," Cathal said behind me. "No, Clodagh! You mustn't go alone!"

"You can't come with me," I said, tears starting in my eyes. "They said so. Please don't argue; it just makes this harder."

"Come!" Dog Mask called from beside the gate. "The lamps are lit in Mac Dara's hall! If you would attend his audience, follow me!"

"I have to go," I whispered. Despite myself, I turned back, taking Cathal's hands in mine.

"Wait, Clodagh!" He released my hold to fumble with the pouch at his belt, reaching for something. "Here," he said, and I felt him slip a ring on my finger. I did not need to look at it to know that it was made of green glass. "It was hers, my mother's. I want you to wear it."

For a moment I was speechless. Then I protested. "You must keep this, Cathal, you've given me all the other things—"

Cathal lifted my hand. His lips brushed my palm; his fingers clung a moment longer, then let go. "I want you to have it," he said. The quiet words drifted away into the night. "Clodagh, I can't bear to see you go on alone. We don't know what you might be facing. I'll come after you. I'll keep a safe distance behind and stay out of sight unless you need me. I can't wait here while you do it on your own. That would be wrong."

My heart was filled with a confusing blend of relief and fear. Maybe he was right about unknown forces pursuing him; perhaps his theory was true, that I had been brought to the Otherworld solely as a lure to entice him after me. But Cathal was a warrior of superior ability. He was strong, brave and resourceful. He was quick and clever. He was unafraid to break rules. Without a doubt, he was exactly the companion I needed to face a foe such as this Lord of the Oak. I did not tell him all this, only laid my hand against his cheek and said, "Thank you. You've been the best, the truest friend . . . Please make sure you stay out of sight."

"Come now or your opportunity will be lost," said Dog Mask in tones of deepest disapproval.

So I followed the trio of strange guardians out through the gate of thorn, bearing Becan in my arms, and down between the rows of stately trees toward a place where the forest was lit by glowing lanterns. From time to time I glanced back over my shoulder, but if Cathal was following, it was so discreetly that he was invisible. Perhaps his cloak shielded him, even without its cargo of charms. I felt their presence in my bag, against my back: reminders of the world we had left, the world where we belonged, the world that held our hope for the future. On my finger, the green glass ring was smooth and cool.

As we walked, Becan awoke. His pebble eyes came slowly back to awareness; his twiggy mouth opened in a wide yawn. Under the shawls, he flexed his limbs, his sharp elbow digging into my chest. "*Oo-roo, little dove,*" I sang under my breath, but the lump in my throat was so big I could manage no more than that.

The avenue of forest giants opened out to a clearing neatly bordered by a circle of pale stones, each the size of a small child. Above, the sky had turned to indigo, but neither stars nor moon appeared there, and I was still oppressed by the sensation that this entire realm, trees, animals and all, lay underground. Around the perimeter of the open space, above the stones, burned lanterns of many shapes and colors, suspended from the branches. They cast a warm light over the motley assortment of folk gathered within the stone circle, so many and so varied I found myself gawking like a simpleton, unable to take the scene in. Most of these people were tall and elegant; most were clad in finery of one kind or another, though their clothing bore little resemblance to that of my own world. There was a woman in a gown of sheerest gossamer, beneath which her not-quite-human figure was clearly visible in its nakedness. It made me blush. The man with the black owl was there, speaking to another whose long robe had a patina like that of butterflies' wings—if it was real, hundreds of them must have been sacrificed to make this extravagant garment. There were some folk clad in leaves, and some wrapped in strange watery fabrics, and some in raiment of brilliant feathers. I took the taller, grander ones to be the Tuatha De, who had inhabited the land of Erin long before my own kind had come to this shore. But they were not the only beings present in Mac Dara's hall tonight. Smaller folk mingled with them, many no higher than my waist. Some were little more than wisps of vapor with strange eyes; some resembled hedgehogs or foxes or swamp hens as much as they did men or women. My head turned from one side to the other as I tried to absorb it.

"Over there," said my masked companion, pointing.

In the center of the circle, on a rise, stood an enclosed pavilion hung with silken cloth of deep green. An edging of silver glinted in the lantern light. Ivy twists and red-berried garlands festooned the uprights. It seemed this was where the Lord of the Oak would hold his audience. Huge guards stood to either side of the entry, where the fabric was looped back by glimmering cords. I could see little of the interior, save that there seemed to be a fire within—a foolish risk, I thought, but then, this place could not be expected to follow the rules of the human world. The segmented helms of the guards gave them the look of gigantic beetles. Their hands were clad in gauntlets, and they held spears tipped with gleaming serrated blades.

Trumpets sounded a ringing fanfare. I glanced down to find that my small companions were turning to leave. Panic swept through me.

"Wait!" I said. "Don't go! Where is Mac Dara? What do I do next?"

"We do not enter Mac Dara's hall." The mask concealed any expression, but the tone was flat and final. "Our kind does not mix with his kind. You must go into the circle. When your name is called, step up to the pavilion. You will be invited to enter and present your case. Once you have your brother, return to us as quickly as you can. We will guide you safely from this realm."

I watched them slip back under the trees. There was no sign of Cathal. I told myself that was a good thing. He would be safe. I could do this on my own. I simply had to walk through this intimidating throng with my palms clammy and my heart hammering, enter the heavily guarded pavilion, and make a coherent speech before a prince of the Tuatha De. "Here we go, Becan," I murmured.

I walked forward, the baby in my arms. He was hungry again; his little whimpers attracted the attention of the sumptuously clad folk and a hush fell over those closest to me, spreading quickly through the crowd. Strange eyes turned to watch us pass: elongated eyes like those of cats; glowing, faceted eyes; bulging eyes that would have suited a toad. A whispering began, but I could not understand what they were saying. I held my head high. I was a daughter of Sevenwaters. I would do this.

There was an empty space around the pavilion, as if nobody was prepared to approach beyond a certain point. I hesitated on the edge of the crowd, wondering if I should venture across this area. My instruction had been to wait until I was called. Becan began to squall, wanting his honey water. The sound jarred horribly; pained expressions began to appear on the lovely, nonhuman faces of the folk standing near me. A panicky feeling gripped me. There was something terribly wrong about this place, these folk, this whole endeavor. I could feel it in my bones.

I put the baby up against my shoulder, patting his back. I had never felt more out of place. "There, there," I murmured. "Not long now, sweetheart."

As if my words had been an invitation, folk began suddenly to crowd in around me, whispering, murmuring amongst themselves. Inquisitive fingers reached to twist in my hair, to brush my body, to poke at Becan's face. His little form stiffened in my arms. I tried to shield him with a fold of my cloak, but there were many of them and most were far taller than I. Someone pushed me. I stumbled, almost losing my balance. Someone pulled my hair hard.

"Release her."

The voice was deep and dark. So commanding was its tone that my molesters fell back in an instant, leaving me standing all by myself between the crowd and the silken pavilion. I looked toward the tent's opening and my jaw dropped. The man who now stood between the guards was tall, lean, dark-haired, clad in a sweeping black cloak. It was Cathal.

"Come forward," he said, beckoning with a long-fingered hand, and his thin lips formed an ironic smile.

For a moment I stood paralyzed with shock, and then I saw that it was not Cathal but that other man, the one in the vision. They were very alike, but this man was taller, and although he looked young, no more than five-and-twenty, his eyes were old. They were the eyes of a man who had seen so much of sorrow and loss, of cruelty and trickery and heartbreak, that nothing much mattered to him anymore.

"Come, daughter of Sevenwaters," he said, and this time his voice held a note of tender familiarity. It was so like Cathal's that it jolted my heart.

I reminded myself that this man had killed Aidan in cold blood. I could not understand what cruel trick he was playing now. I was not brave enough to challenge him in front of this crowd of whispering, pointing folk. Gritting my teeth, I walked toward him, clutching Becan so tightly he squealed in alarm. "It's all right, little one," I whispered. Then I was facing the stranger, not three paces away, and he extended his hand to cup my elbow in courtly fashion and usher me into his sanctum. I was trembling with fear.

Inside, the pavilion was much more spacious than had seemed possible from its outer appearance. The fire burned on a neat hearth of stones, making no smoke. Lamps on creature-shaped stands stood around the area: a dragon held this light, a phoenix that one, a sinuous serpent a third. There were low seats covered with what might have been wolf skins and strewn with embroidered pillows. On a small table stood a jug with a graceful curved handle and several delicate cups of colored glass, three of them filled with ruby-red liquid.

"Welcome," said the Lord of the Oak. "A difficult journey. You've been hurt." He reached out again, this time to touch the cuts on my face. The soft tone and delicate gesture might have been Cathal's. To my horror, I felt a blush rise to my cheeks and a warmth spread through my body.

"Don't touch me!" I snapped, shrinking away. "There's no need to do this, to make yourself look and sound like my friend. I know you're not him. You don't fool me for a moment. *He* would never kill a man who had shown he was ready to parley." And although I knew I should not antagonize him, for this must be the powerful prince with whom I had to negotiate my brother's return, I was proud of myself for being honest.

He threw back his head and laughed. It was a full-throated sound of unabashed amusement. "Sit down, please," he said when he was finished. "Let me offer you a drink." He moved to the table. He was a well-made creature, I could see that; even a woman of experience would succumb quickly to the charms of such a man. Could he possibly have assumed Cathal's form with the intention of seducing me? I seemed to remember that the tales of Mac Dara included numerous exploits of that sort. This prince of the Fair Folk might have been watching Cathal and me all the way; he might have spied on our most private moments. If he thought he could dazzle me with his charms, he thought wrong. There was only one man I wanted, and it wasn't this one.

"Thank you. I will not drink." I sat gingerly on the very edge of one of the draped seats, and he came immediately to settle his long form beside me, his leg almost touching mine. "I take it you are Mac Dara, the Lord of the Oak," I went on. "As you can see, I've brought back the child who was left at Sevenwaters in my brother's place. I wish to take Finbar home." Becan had quieted; he was gazing at the lamps. I was grateful for that small mercy.

"Oh, let's not get down to business yet," drawled Mac Dara, stretching his arm along the cushions behind me. "Your family, I understand, has long supported my kind in our endeavors to hold onto what little safe territory is left to us. Indeed, one or two of yours have coupled with one or two of mine over the years, or so I've heard."

Was he referring to Ciarán's mother, who had been a dark sorceress? She was the only person of Mac Dara's kind I had ever heard of in the lineage of my family. I didn't imagine he meant the Old Ones, though I knew they had a place in my ancestry. "They say that is so," I murmured. Everything about him was making me edgy. I wished he would transform back into his true self, even if that self was hideous beyond belief. I hated his being in this not-quite-Cathal form. The familiar turned subtly unfamiliar: it was the most frightening thing in the world. "The folk of Sevenwaters made a pact with the Tuatha De, long ago, to look after the forest and the lake, to keep them safe, and not to allow disbelievers to turn your kind out of their homes. We've kept to that as well as we could. The Fair Folk helped us in their turn." *But I suspect that was before your time.*

He laughed again, as if he could hear my unspoken thoughts. "So they tell me," he said. "Myself, I'm from the west. Those with whom your grandmother and her brothers dealt are gone from here, passed over the sea with a turning of the tide. You have the air of a startled rabbit, young woman. I mean you no harm."

I had to ask. "If you are a friend of Sevenwaters, why did you take Finbar? My mother has been almost destroyed by it. She so longed for a son."

"The child was a means to an end. You can have him back. We don't want him." He might have been talking about an excess of beans in the garden or a cockerel too many in a brood.

"Thank you," I said after a moment. "May I see my brother now, please? I wish to make the exchange and leave. There are people at home who will be terribly worried. I must get back."

"Calm yourself, daughter of Sevenwaters. Your brother has been well looked after; we acquired a nursemaid for him. He's had everything a human child needs. There is no cause for haste or for anxiety. That little frown does not sit well on your pretty face, my dear." I felt his cold fingers against my neck, toying with my hair. I tried not to make my disgust too obvious.

"I have another question," I said. "You killed a young man called Aidan, shot him in cold blood out in the forest not long ago. Why?"

Mac Dara shrugged. "Why does one do these things? Need there be a reason?"

His insouciant manner appalled me. "How could you kill someone without a reason?" I burst out. "That is evil."

Mac Dara shrugged. "It was entertaining. Briefly. I'm easily bored these days."

I could think of absolutely nothing to say. If the tales were true, this man had once led great armies, ruled a vast territory, held off powers worldly and otherworldly with consummate strategic skill. He might never have been a particularly likeable character, but he had been someone of influence, a leader. That such a man could fall so low sickened me. "Perhaps," I said eventually, "you have lived too long."

There was a moment's silence. His fingers tightened in my hair, pulling hard enough to hurt me. Then his thin lips formed a smile. His grip relaxed; he stood and moved to the small table, picking up a cup and draining the contents. "You're outspoken," he commented. "I suppose that goes with the flaming red curls. You have courage. No wonder he wants you so badly."

I looked at him. He gazed back at me, his dark eyes suddenly serious in his long, pale face. And if a spell or charm had banished the clue I needed from my memory all this time so that I had failed to put together the pieces of this puzzle until it was almost too late, now, in an instant, I had it. I remembered Willow's third tale: the fey woman Albha and her half-human daughter, and the tricks and maneuvering with which Albha had sought to get her back. The charm she had cast . . . Gods, the charm had everything in it, every single step of the journey that had brought Cathal and me to Mac Dara's hall. *Cross the river left then right . . . the field of time, no, thyme . . . fall so far you cannot climb . . . sorrow's pathway . . . the gate of thorn . . .*

"You're his father," I breathed. *I have a theory*, Cathal had said. *I very much hope I'm wrong.* He had hated the extraordinary scrying talent his unknown parent had passed on to him. How much more appalling would be the confirmation that he was the son of this dark Otherworld prince and only half human? "You haven't assumed his form. He looks like you because he's your son. You look young because of what you are. Cathal was right. You've done all of this, every single bit of it, just to lure him back. Why didn't I see it?"

"This is a simple transaction," said the Lord of the Oak. "A son for a son. I don't want the changeling. Take it home with you if you wish. You've more regard for it than any of my people are likely to exhibit. An excess of regard, one might almost say. You can have your little brother back. Just give me your companion in exchange. Incidentally, where is he? Somewhat remiss of him to let you come in here all by yourself, isn't it? I thought he'd been trained as an elite warrior."

I was chill to the core of my bones. Thank all the gods Cathal had not come here with me; thank every power there was that he'd had the sense to stay back out of sight. How could I have forgotten the rhyme? How could I have been so stupid? *Set your foot inside the door, you'll be mine forever more.* With those words, Albha had sought to enmesh the daughter who had fled the Otherworld to live a life as her own woman. Whether she had succeeded in the long-term, I did not know—I had missed the end of that story. All I knew was that Cathal must not come in here. I must not let him step inside the pavilion. If he did so he could never, ever go home again.

"Well?" The Lord of the Oak was sounding displeased now. "Where is my son? He is the price you must pay for Lord Sean's heir. There is a pleasing symmetry in the arrangement. You'll appreciate that, I'm sure. I'm a virile man, Clodagh. I've sired more than my share of children over the years. I have something in common with your father, Lord Sean of Sevenwaters. Each of us has an abundance of daughters. So many daughters, and only one son."

My mind was racing. I had to get Finbar and escape from here before Cathal revealed himself. I had to find the Old Ones and hope they could get us home. But Mac Dara wouldn't let me go until he had what he wanted. His eyes were full of implacable purpose. Those guards with their spears would be nothing beside his wrath if I tried to escape without fulfilling my side of the bargain. Maybe I could stall awhile, keep talking while I worked out what to do. "His mother drowned herself," I said. "Did you know that?"

"I did hear something along those lines," said the Lord of the Oak, folding his arms and regarding me through narrowed eyes. "A waste. She should have found a new man, a farmer, a fisherman, someone of her own kind. As you will do—oh, not the farmer, I expect, but a young man from your father's list, someone who will provide a suitable territorial advantage. You can't have my son. He's destined for greater things."

"It is sad," I said, "that you cannot allow him to make up his own mind. If you wanted me to turn my back on him and marry my father's choice, perhaps you shouldn't have loosed the arrow that killed Aidan of Whiteshore. As well as being a suitor of mine, he was your son's dearest friend."

"You're beginning to try my patience just a little. These matters do not interest me. Take your father's son home and he will owe you such a debt that you may marry any man you choose."

"Except one," I said.

Mac Dara nodded. "Except my son," he said. "He takes after me, no doubt, and is skilled in pleasing women. But he's not for you. His future lies elsewhere. Now tell me, *where is he*?"

Somehow, remarkably, it seemed that Cathal had managed to conceal himself from the eagle eye of this Otherworld prince, even in the heart of his own realm. But then, if he was Mac Dara's son, perhaps he had uncanny powers too, not merely an exceptional ability at scrying but all manner of other talents thus far untried. "I don't know where he is," I said. "He suspected he was being lured into a trap. He decided not to come any further. I expect he's well on the way home by now."

For a moment I saw a look on Mac Dara's face that terrified me, an anger on the brink of spilling out into such violence that I feared for my life. Then he composed himself. "I see," he said. "He won't get far; I have sentries everywhere. Forgive my ill temper, please. I have waited so long for this day. It is disappointing that I cannot yet welcome my son back. But I mustn't delay you unduly, that wouldn't be fair. You'll be wanting to convey your brother home. I'll take the changeling instead." He held out his arms.

It was too quick, too easy. He didn't want Becan, he'd just said so. This had to be a trick.

"Not so fast," I made myself say. "I'm not giving Becan up until I see Finbar. I need to be sure he is well and has not been harmed."

Mac Dara clicked his long fingers. Almost immediately a young woman entered the pavilion, a pretty human girl of perhaps seventeen, clad in a countrywoman's garments. Two women of the Tuatha De escorted her, each of them wearing a hooded cloak of gray. The girl had a baby in her arms. Her expression was curiously blank, and it troubled me.

"Place the child on the seat there," the Lord of the Oak said crisply.

She obeyed, scuttling over with her eyes downcast. The very air felt full of peril. Making myself breathe slowly, I knelt beside the infant to examine him, holding Becan with one arm as I used the other hand to loosen this child's shawl.

It was Finbar. I saw it in an instant and had to restrain my urge to snatch him up immediately. This was a realm of trickery and deception. Mac Dara was utterly untrustworthy. I must exercise caution; I must not rush something so important.

I made an inventory: copious dark hair, boldly shaped nose, rosy mouth, unusual eyes, already lighter in color than they had been at birth. A visionary's eyes. I checked that every part of my brother was whole and undamaged. I folded the gossamer-soft shawl back around him, glancing up at the girl with a smile. If she had been looking after him, she had done a good job. She gazed back at me, not a glimmer of expression in her eyes.

"We would not harm the heir to Sevenwaters," said Mac Dara. "He may be slightly changed. No human who spends time in our realm returns entirely the same."

"Changed?" I echoed, recalling what Sibeal had said about this. "In what way?"

"For the better, without a doubt," said Mac Dara, smiling. "Do not concern yourself. Such alterations are subtle indeed."

I had no grounds on which to challenge him further. My brother was here; the Lord of the Oak was offering me exactly what I had expected, one baby for the other. But something was wrong. We had reached this point far too easily. The only one Mac Dara really wanted was Cathal; I'd stake my life on it.

"Swear to me that there is no trickery in this bargain," I said, knowing that a lord of the Tuatha De did not make binding promises to a human woman. "You give me Finbar as a straightforward exchange for this baby. Your folk allow me to make my way safely home with my brother." Becan's body stiffened; his hands clawed into my gown, holding on tightly. He was staring up at me, his pebble eyes wide with anxiety. Out in the woods beyond the clearing something let out a long, mournful cry.

"Of course," Mac Dara said. "Would I lie to you? A simple exchange—that child for this. Then take your brother and return in safety to your own realm."

He sounded perfectly calm and businesslike. He sounded trustworthy. But I could not bring myself to put Becan into his arms. A man like this did not suddenly give up. A creature like this, who would kill in cold blood for no better reason than to amuse himself for a moment or two, did not capitulate without a fight.

"I don't trust you," I said in a small voice.

Mac Dara folded his arms. "Why did you come here?" he asked. "I thought it was to fetch your brother home; to stop your mother from dying of a broken heart; to give your father back the son who is more important to him than he could ever have believed possible before he held him in his arms that first time and felt a love like no other. Was not that your mission?"

"Yes," I murmured, tears springing in my eyes. "But . . ." I bowed my head over Becan, knowing I had to do it, realizing just how difficult it was going to be.

"I'll take him." This soft voice was that of the nursemaid, and when I looked up she was standing right by me, reaching out her arms. "I'll look after him, I promise." Her face was not blank now, but bore a sweet, shy expression. I wondered how she had come to be here in the Otherworld and whether she was content.

The moment had come. "Very well," I made myself say. I kissed Becan on his brow, my tears watering his leafy skin. I unfastened his twiggy fingers from my clothing—oh, so tightly he clung—and put him into the girl's arms. He began to cry, a tiny, forlorn sound. I gathered Finbar up. Though he was small, he was a far heavier burden than Becan; a warm, real human baby. And yet . . . and yet, at that moment, my heart ached fit to break for my changeling, my little one, beloved in all his curious oddity.

Mac Dara smiled. It was the kind of smile a man gives when he scents victory in a game of wits. He clicked his fingers. The nursemaid put Becan in his arms, and Mac Dara threw him into the fire.

A great scream ripped itself out of me. Dropping Finbar on the seat, I flung myself toward the flames. Mac Dara's arm came around me, holding me back. Becan's shriek pierced me like a blade. I fought, biting, scratching, sobbing, every part of me straining toward the fire.

"I'm sure that was loud enough to do the trick," observed the Lord of the Oak.

Gods, oh gods, no . . . He was burning, burning, his twigs and bark and mosses going up like a torch. I kicked and struggled, my body convulsed with wrenching sobs, until Mac Dara released me and I threw myself down beside the fire, scrabbling in the burning coals for any part of my little one that still remained.

"Careful," said Mac Dara. "Don't burn those pretty hands."

Blinded by tears, I snatched at a corner of the woollen shawl, the only part of Becan I could see, ripping it out of the flames. Something rolled with it as it came: a speckled pebble, my baby's blind, dead eye. I clutched it in my hand; its heat scorched my palm. My gorge rose, and I retched the contents of my stomach out onto the floor of Mac Dara's pavilion, splattering the embroidered gown they had made me wear for this travesty of an audience.

A commotion outside the pavilion, running footsteps, shouting, a clash of metal. I heard the Lord of the Oak suck in his breath, and then someone flung himself down beside me, setting his hand on my bent shoulder, and I wrenched myself violently away.

"What have you done to her?"

The voice was not Mac Dara's. It was Cathal's, full of cold fury. He was here. He was here beside me, reaching to support me, his arms as gentle as his tone had been hard.

"Becan," I gasped through my sobs. "Oh, Cathal, he . . . he . . ."

Cathal unfolded my tightly clenched fists, revealing the pebble and the scorched scrap of shawl. For a moment his whole body went still. Then he leapt to his feet, strode to the table, grabbed the jug and hurled its contents onto the flames. There was a sizzling. As the blaze died momentarily down, Cathal thrust his hands into the fire and snatched something out, cursing under his breath. He crouched beside me, holding what was left of the changeling. I made myself look, fighting down a new wave of nausea. Becan was scorched and broken, one arm quite gone, his face an ugly travesty of its sweet uncanny self, his body blackened and twisted. Smoke arose from the bark of his lips; inside, he was still burning. He was completely still, his remaining eye blank and lifeless. He looked exactly the manikin of forest matter that my family had believed him, a thing that was not alive and never had been. There were sounds coming out of me I had never heard anyone make in my life, racking, tearing sobs that made my whole body hurt. Cathal laid the baby down on the ground, then reached into my pack for the water-skin. Without a word, he put it in my hand.

My hands shaking violently, I took out the stopper and trickled the contents gently over the ruined body of my little one. Behind us, nobody was saying a thing.

"Clodagh," Cathal said quietly. "You must take your brother and go. Go right now. I know it's hard, but you must do as I say."

Something in his tone brought me back to reality, and in a flash I understood what Mac Dara had done. Because of him I had delivered not one, but two of those I loved to the enemy. All calculated. All planned. I gathered the pitiful remnant of my child and got to my feet, and Cathal rose to stand behind me, his hands around my arms, holding me against him. I looked over at the Lord of the Oak. Triumph blazed on his face, the face that was almost the twin of his son's, but not quite. He was the master trickster. In the end, he had outwitted us all.

"No," I breathed. "No! You can't do this!" But Mac Dara was smiling. His trick had worked. He had killed Becan without a qualm, just to make me scream. He had known my scream would summon his son; he had known Cathal could not hear it and hold back. Cathal had come to my rescue. He had set his foot inside the door, knowing that once he did so his father could keep him in the Otherworld forever. He had sacrificed his future for me.

"Welcome home, my son," said Mac Dara. "You have made this hard work. I must confess to a certain pride in the way you've managed to evade me all these years. You have indeed proven yourself worthy to be my successor." He was looking almost affable now; his arms were stretched out as if offering his son an embrace.

Cathal turned his head to one side and spat on the floor. "I have no father," he said.

"You can't go back, of course," Mac Dara drawled, "not now you've set your foot inside my hall. My spell craft is without peer; you will not break through the barriers I have set around you. But why would you want to leave? A future as prince and ruler awaits you here, a life such as the human world could never have provided for a man of your humble origins. Right now you may think you don't want it, but that won't last. You'll change. This place will change you. Deep down you already know the truth, my son. Under the surface you're just like me."

"Go, Clodagh." Cathal's voice trembled. "Take him and go."

"I suppose we could keep the girl," the Lord of the Oak said in conversational tones. "I can see you're attached to her. She's a bold little thing; I like redheads. In fact, she might come in useful for ensuring your compliance until you understand your new role here. You arrived quickly enough when you heard she was in trouble. Ah, love; what fools it makes of us! You and your little piece here; she and her wretched changeling . . . Then there's Lord Sean's heir. I had planned to send the child back, but he could still be useful to us." He turned a considering gaze on the small form of Finbar, lying on the seat where I had dropped him without a thought for his welfare.

"Go, Clodagh," Cathal said. "My brave girl. My remarkable girl. Please go now." He removed his hands from my arms. Without looking, I could tell that he was crying.

There was no choice. I must do as he said for Finbar's sake. But I would not leave Becan. He must be laid to rest kindly, with love and respect, not abandoned in this domain of cruel strangers. I slipped my bag off my shoulders, opened it up and laid him inside, on top of my folded garments. It was the best I could do for him. I put the bag back on and went to the bench where my brother lay. My breath was still coming in gasps; my eyes and nose were streaming. I wiped my face, and the cool, hard surface of the green glass ring brushed against the cut on my cheek. And suddenly, although I was near paralyzed with shock, although my heart was crushed and bleeding, deep inside I felt a little flame of courage. I picked Finbar up. His bright eyes were fixed on me, curiously aware. My kin; my flesh and blood. I made him a silent promise. *I've failed Becan; I will not fail you, little brother.* Then I turned to face Mac Dara.

"Don't think this is over," I said, and if he was a prince, in that moment I was a queen, my voice cold, hard and steady as a rock. "I'm not giving up. If you go against your word again, if harm comes to me or my brother on our way home, you will have destroyed all goodwill toward the Tuatha De Danann within the territory of Sevenwaters. Your kind will no longer have safe haven here. I swear it on the memory of my kinsman Finbar, the man with the swan's wing, for whom this child was named. I swear it on the memory of my grandmother, Sorcha of Sevenwaters, whom the Tuatha De loved and aided. As for your son, he is more man than you can ever imagine. You will not defeat us. Nothing defeats love."

Mac Dara's lips twisted. After a moment he brought his hands together in slow, derisory applause.

I ignored him. The lamps seemed dimmer now; the cursed fire had died down. The others who had been with us in the pavilion, the two robed women, the all-too-obedient nursemaid, had vanished, and in their place were armed men of the Fair Folk standing in silent rank around the walls. So many. Did this prince fear his warrior son so much? I turned back to Cathal, who stood silent and pale by the fire. He had not tried to fight. He had remembered the tales better than I did; he had known all too well what it would mean if he entered his father's hall. It was too late for resistance by arms. *Set your foot inside the door, you'll be mine forever more.* If Willow's story was accurate, he had no way out.

I held Finbar cradled in my left arm. I put up my right hand

and laid it against Cathal's wan cheek. I looked into his eyes. His face was wet with tears. "I love you," I whispered. "I'm coming back for you, I swear it. I'll find a way."

He put his hand over mine, holding it against his face, then brought my fingers to his lips. "Beloved," he whispered, and let go. "Goodbye."

I walked away. It was the hardest thing I had ever done. I left the pavilion. The guards were no longer standing by the entry but lay bruised and bloodied on the ground outside. The courage drained from me; grief and shock flooded in. My moment of strength was over. A violent trembling seized my body. I clutched Finbar closer, fearful of more cruel tricks and traps.

As I moved further away, I heard Mac Dara speaking inside the pavilion. "She won't come," he said. "Once she gets home she'll realize the utter folly of such an idea. Human women are not cut out to be heroes. All your Clodagh wants is a child of her own, and any man can put that in her belly."

And Cathal's voice, my dear one's voice, raised in a ragged, furious challenge: "Don't sully her name with your filthy lying tongue!"

The sound of a blow. "Restrain him," Mac Dara said coolly. I imagined those ranks of fey warriors closing in. Cathal was a superb fighter, but there would be no point in putting those skills to use, not if the Lord of the Oak was as powerful in magic as he had claimed. I heard Mac Dara add, "As for her name, my son, you'll soon have forgotten it. You'll be amazed how quickly the memory will fade."

I made myself walk on. I could be sure, at least, that Cathal would not die as Aidan had. His father loved him, to the extent that the Fair Folk can love. His father wanted him safe; safe under his control, to be molded into another like himself, cruel, callous, powerful, full of dark tricks. The seed of that person was in Cathal alongside the seed of the good man he was striving to be. The longer he stayed here, the more like his father he risked becoming. Because of me he was facing what he had feared most in all the world. As I stumbled across the clearing with my brother in my arms and a host of strange eyes watching me, I knew I would not abandon him to that. I owed it to

Becan, whom I had not been able to save, to prove that a human woman could be a hero. Never mind that I was neither druid nor mage nor warrior. Never mind that the rhyme said *forever more.* I loved Cathal. I would not desert him. As surely as spring followed winter I would come back for him, and I would bring him home.

CHAPTER 14

Beyond the circle of white stones, up a rise and under the huge trees that bordered the ceremonial way, the Old Ones were waiting for me: seven of them in a silent line, with two bearing torches that cast a small pool of light around them in the shadowy forest. As I approached, the uncanny voice rang out, its wailing louder now, as if its owner were drawing ever closer.

"Come," said Dog Mask, apparently impervious to the fact that I was shaking with sobs. "No time to waste. Follow me." It turned and headed off along the path. Its companions, which now included not just the stony and watery entities but a being in a feathery cape and others with animal masks concealing their faces, padded along after their leader. "So he took the changeling after all," Dog Mask added over its shoulder, as if it had known all along what was likely to happen.

"Becan's dead," I hiccupped. "And Cathal . . ." I could not continue. My lips refused to shape it: Becan falling, falling, and the flames coming up to take him. Cathal's voice, so gentle, so insistent, telling me to go. The last tender word. The last sweet touch. Mac Dara telling his son, *You'll change. This place will change you.* "He stepped inside the door, like in the rhyme," I managed. "I screamed and he came to rescue me and now he's trapped. Mac Dara has him. He'll twist him and change him, he'll try to turn his son into an evil man like himself, someone who kills for entertainment. This is my fault, all of it! I handed Becan over, I gave him up to be burned and I led Cathal straight into the trap—"

"Burned," echoed Dog Mask, and all of them halted. "Burned to nothing?"

"Not quite," I sobbed. "But he's dead, he's all scorched and broken . . . We must stop somewhere so I can . . ." The words *bury him* stuck in my throat. "So I can lay him to rest," I whispered. Finbar gave a gurgle, then stuck his fist in his mouth. Soon he would be hungry and there would be nothing to give him.

"Where is he?" Dog Mask's voice had lost its usual detachment; it was fierce and urgent. "Show us!"

"He's in my bag," I said, knowing I did not want to put Finbar down even for the few moments it would take to show them the pitiful remnants of my little one.

"Show us!" A chorus of voices now, all of them muted, for we were not so very far from the clearing with its crowd of gorgeously clad folk. We were only a stone's throw from Mac Dara's hall. They gathered around me, chittering, humming, rumbling anxiously. Strange fingers, furred, stony, watery, clawed or feathered, reached out toward the bag on my back.

"Give me your brother," said Dog Mask.

"No!" I clutched Finbar closer.

Dog Mask sighed. "Pass him to me so I can hold him while you take off your bag."

"We will help you, Clodagh," said the watery one, and its voice made each word a little rippling melody.

"Trust us," the rocky one rumbled. "Kindred aid kindred."

"And you're in sore need of help, believe me," put in Dog Mask. "Come, time is short, and we are not yet in a place of safety."

"All right," I said after a moment. "But no tricks, you understand? Stay right there where I can see you." I passed Finbar into Dog Mask's arms, realizing how unheroic I must look with my eyes and nose streaming, my clothing spattered with vomit and my chest still heaving with distress. I reached to push my hair back out of my eyes.

"Ohhh," murmured the being in the feather cape, whose mask gave it the appearance of an owl. "Poor hand, poor hand! Fire hurt you!"

"I tried to save him," I said. "I really tried. But he . . . he . . ."

"Show us," said Dog Mask.

I took off my pack gingerly—my burned hands did hurt—and set it on the ground. There had been no time to fasten it after I laid poor Becan inside. The Old Ones clustered around, peering in. I forced myself to look. My baby lay where I had placed him, his solitary pebble eye staring blankly up, his mouth twisted out of shape, the green leaves of his skin scorched to crisp brown. A little shriveled thing that could never have been alive. I reached in and lifted him out.

"Ahhh!" A great sigh of shock and sorrow shuddered around the circle of Old Ones. I held Becan against my breast, wishing from the very core of my being that he would reach out and take hold of my clothing as he once had, grasping at security. I had failed him utterly.

A little silence. Then the stony creature said, "Quick! The hedge of thorn!" and all of them started walking again, much faster this time. Dog Mask still had Finbar.

"Wait!" I made to put Becan back, but Dog Mask turned its head toward me.

"No, no!" it said sharply. "Do not relegate him to your baggage. Carry him in your arms, next to your heart. Fold your shawl around him. Talk to him. Sing to him."

I slung the bag awkwardly over one shoulder and hastened after them, the inert form of Becan cradled against me. Perhaps they were right; perhaps he deserved better than to be stowed away in the dark. As for singing, that would be more than I could bear. But I murmured as I stumbled up the path under the oaks. "There, there, my love, my baby . . . sleep sound, little dove . . ."

We reached the hedge of thorn. The gate creaked open to let us in and shut behind us with a determined snap. By the cold fire was Cathal's pack. Perhaps he had intended to collect it on the way home. Or maybe he had known all along how this would end for him. A little further away there was a white nanny goat tethered to a post.

"Milk will nourish little thirsty one," said the watery being.

"Work," the stony one said crisply. "Work to be done!"

"Pull yourself together, girl," added one of the others. "No time to lose!"

But I sank to my knees, rocking the lifeless child, my heart twisting in pain, my tears falling on his little burned face. Dog Mask settled beside me, holding my brother's shawl-wrapped form with confident ease. The others gathered close. Even those with masks managed somehow to look expectant.

"What?" I asked wanly. "What is it I'm supposed to do? He's dead. Becan's dead. He's not breathing. Anyone can see that. All I can do is dig a grave and . . ." I faltered to a halt, feeling the pressure of their strange eyes on me.

"Clodagh," said a being that was a curious mixture of dwarf and hedgehog, "you are not required to be a hero right now. All you need to do is be yourself."

"What do you mean?"

"Fix!" said the stony one with a snap of its chinklike mouth. "Match! Patch!"

"Tending, mending, gathering, mothering . . ." murmured the watery one.

"You have a reputation as a model housewife," said Dog Mask. "Tell me, if a cooking pot develops rust, do you throw it away? Do you discard your sheets when they go into holes? If your sister's favorite doll lost an arm or leg, would you tell her to throw it on the midden?"

"Of course not," I said, not understanding what this had to do with anything. "In a well-run household nothing is wasted."

"Since the changeling has not been entirely burned away, why do you speak of laying him to rest? Surely an enterprising young woman like you can do better than that?"

This was cruel. "You know quite well that Becan isn't a doll or a sheet or a cooking pot, but a living being," I said furiously. "When a child dies, it can't be put together the way you'd fix a broken toy."

"Ah!" said the hedgehog-dwarf, rippling its prickles with a

sound like grains dropping into an iron pot. "But if someone other than yourself, Clodagh, someone such as your father, Sean of Sevenwaters, looked at this child, he might say: *It is only a manikin of wood; of course it can be mended.* In the eyes of such a person that task would be relatively simple. Do you not at least wish to try it before you consign this little being on whom you have lavished such love to a dark and lonely grave?"

"But he's not breathing," I said.

"He wasn't breathing before, when you fished him out of the river," pointed out Dog Mask. "What you have done once, you can do again."

The cry rang out over the forest, a piercing lament that chilled my marrow. I had the uncanny sensation that the owner of that voice was watching us and could hear everything we said. As for the crazy idea that had just been suggested, I hardly dared hope it might be possible. "It would be risking the anger of the gods to try such a thing," I whispered. But I wanted to do it. Oh, how I wanted to.

A creature in a cat mask spoke, its voice invoking warm hearths and cozy corners in the sun. "Didn't your mother ever teach you that old rhyme, Clodagh—*Stitch and darn, patch and mend, a woman's needle is her best friend*? Did you bring sewing things on this quest of yours?"

"No," I said as foolish hope began to rise in my heart. "But I think Cathal did." The owner of that cloak was not going to travel far without the means to maintain its cargo of lucky charms. Besides, a warrior of Inis Eala was always prepared. He did his own mending on the run, so to speak. When Johnny had lived among the Painted Men as an infant, they had cut down garments of their own to make clothing for him. It was a tale Aunt Liadan enjoyed telling.

Dog Mask hissed its disapproval. "Cathal!" it said. "As if we would accept the help of *his* kind."

"If you had told me before why it was that you distrusted him so," I pointed out, "it might have helped him stay out of his father's clutches. Why didn't you explain? Why does everything need to be hints and symbols and puzzles?"

"When you face a crisis at home, Clodagh," said the hedgehog-dwarf, "what is it you need, weeping and wailing or good common sense? If you would make this right, waste no more time."

"Small, frail, broken, forsaken," murmured the watery being.

"Quick!" the stony one growled. "Act!"

Treat this as a practical exercise in household mending, I told myself. *Don't doubt yourself, just get on with it.*

As I had suspected, Cathal's pack contained bone needles and a twist of sturdy thread. I could have patched a pair of trousers or mended the fastening of a shirt with ease. But this was a task such as I had never attempted in my life. I found Cathal's second set of clothing and spread the tunic out on the grass. I put Becan down on it wrapped in my shawl. He lay stiffly, not moving so much as a finger. It was a fragile hope indeed that he could be brought back. But I must try. I rose to my feet, clearing my throat.

One of the Old Ones was milking the goat, the stream of creamy liquid spurting into a little shiny bucket. Another was laying wood on the fire. A third was filling a pannikin with water from the pond. Others had stationed themselves near the gate, perhaps on sentry duty. A torch had been placed close by us, but it was night now and sewing by such fitful light would not be easy.

Dog Mask sat cross-legged with Finbar in its arms. The mask stayed in place even when its owner could not spare a hand to hold it there. Dark eyes were fixed on me through the holes.

"Will you watch Becan while I gather what I need?" I asked. "Please?"

The creature inclined its head gravely. A moment later the hedgehog-dwarf was by my side with torch in hand, ready to light my way.

I made a picture in my mind of Becan as he had been before Mac Dara, before the fire. I would not be able to remake him exactly; certain berries, certain leaves were not present in the safe area within the hedge of thorn. But there was plenty to gather: fresh foliage from the trees and bushes, bark strips that could be taken with care, not too much from any one plant lest I wound it badly; twigs from the ground beneath. For every gift the earth gave me I murmured a prayer of thanks.

When I had gathered enough, I returned to the fire with my materials in my skirt and settled beside Dog Mask. The watery being was pouring milk into a dish; there was a cloth ready for feeding my brother. The Old Ones seemed to know what they were doing.

And then I went about mending my little one. Stitch by stitch, leaf by leaf, twig by twig I remade him, and if I watered him with my tears as I went, none of my companions uttered a word of criticism. Where I could weave or knot his pieces together without using my needle I did so, thinking that more natural. Besides, I was in danger of using up Cathal's stock of thread too quickly. Cathal . . . He was just down there, a short walk from me . . . I yearned to run back, to find him now, straightaway, to get him out and safely home this very night, for I had not forgotten the quirks of time in this place. I might come back and find a hundred years had passed. He might be an old man; his human blood meant he would not live as long as his father's kind did. He might be gone far away. I might search until the day I died and never find him. My heart shrank at the prospect.

I straightened Becan's remaining eye as best I could, stitching a patch of moss in beside it to hold it firm. I took the other pebble from my pouch and set it in place. He did not look quite as he should.

Dog Mask was feeding Finbar from the bowl of milk. Suddenly the eldritch voice cried out, and this time it sounded as if it was right outside the gate, screaming a sorrow from deep in the bone. The sound turned my blood to ice. "What *is* that?" I whispered.

The eyes behind the silver mask turned toward me. "His mother," said my companion. "She grieves."

"His *mother*?"

"She is powerless against Mac Dara's magic," Dog Mask said, squeezing milk from the cloth into Finbar's mouth. "She has followed us, watching, listening, racked with sorrow. Help her."

The thought of it filled me with horror. My own grief over Becan paled beside hers. To have her own child taken away, sent to the human world, perhaps forever, and then brought back to be sacrificed so a selfish, cruel nobleman could get what he wanted . . . It was unthinkable. And then, to see Becan burned, disfigured, lying here still and helpless . . . I swallowed hard and returned to the task, and this time I sang as I worked. Not a lullaby; that, I knew I could not manage without falling apart. I sang Cathal's song, the ballad about a man wandering lost, and as I sang I took out from my bag the stocking in which I had wrapped the items from

Cathal's cloak, his tokens of love. Into the body of my little one I wove one black hair and one brown from the twist Cathal had kept, and a red one plucked from my own head. I put in a snippet from Fleet's collar and a tiny patch from the shimmering cloth that had once been worn by Aidan's mother. *I've been to the river, I've been to the well . . .* I added a thread or two from the woolen blanket that had been almost burned away; a blanket that my mother had crafted with her own hands for her longed-for baby boy. *I've run through the forest, I've climbed up the hill . . .* I was crying again. I saw Cathal lifting Becan's scorched and broken form out of the fire, his hands gentle even in such an extreme. I heard him saying, *Beloved.*

"It's not enough," I muttered.

They gathered around me then, all of them. A clawlike hand stretched toward me, holding a golden feather plucked from an exuberant, plumy cape. Another held out a chip of stone shaped like a heart, a third a sharp spine from its hedgehog coat. Each in turn made an offering, and each gift in turn I sewed or wove into Becan's body, making him stronger and more beautiful. Dog Mask did not give me a token, but when the others were done it gestured toward Finbar, who had finished drinking and lay somnolent on the small creature's knee. I used my little knife to snip a lock of my brother's fine hair and twined it carefully in. The watery being reached out and dribbled a handful of liquid onto the changeling. "Grow, burgeon, bloom," it murmured.

All was hushed. Nothing stirred in the darkness of the forest; nothing moved beyond the safe boundaries of the hedge of thorn. The Old Ones sat in a circle around me, waiting. The mending was done; Becan was whole again. Whole, but stiff and lifeless. Not breathing. And somewhere out there, his mother was watching me.

I stroked his leafy brow with my fingers, and then I put my lips to his and breathed for him, as I had once before. One, two. A pause. One, two again. *Live,* I willed him. *There are folk here who love you. Live. Live!* As I breathed, the Old Ones sang, their voices making an eerie music that filled the safe place with its throbbing, humming, gurgling beauty. It was a music old and mysterious, a music like the heartbeat of the earth, timeless and deep. I shivered to hear it, even as I kept breathing, breathing, holding onto the thread that still bound my baby to this life. A thread of story so old it stretched to the time of our first ancestors. A thread of love so strong that not even a prince of the Fair Folk could break it. *Live!*

The song died down. I could not tell how long we had been there, I breathing, they singing, but I sensed, all of a sudden, that over at the other side of the enclosure, just beyond the gate, someone was standing in complete silence. When I lifted my head to look, Becan's chest continued its slight rise and fall. He was breathing on his own.

"Ahhh," said the Old Ones in chorus, and turned toward the gate. Dog Mask still held my brother in its arms.

The gate creaked open without challenge. She stood in the gap, a figure of about the same size and shape as myself, clad in a trailing garment of leaves and vines and flowers, with her hair cascading over it in dark, tangled tendrils. The torch nearest the gate flared. She shrank back before it, trembling, terrified. The flame illuminated wide, wary eyes in a face that was both sweet and strange, for she was no human woman, but a creature of woods and thickets, hedges and coppices, her body a lovely female shape built from all the wildest and most secret materials of the forest. To come so close to humankind must set a great fear in her. But then, I had her child. And now, so soon after I had brought him back from the brink of death, I must give him up again.

This time I did not hesitate. Her great eyes, fixed on me in terror and wonderment, filled with bright tears as I approached with her baby held against my breast. I could feel him breathing now; I could sense the life returning to his body with every step I took. His mother gave a cry, not an eerie shriek of pain this time, but a low, yearning call from deep inside her.

And Becan answered. He opened his mouth and let out the hungry, uncomplicated squall of a healthy child who has had a fright and now wants his supper. My own eyes brimming, I took my last step forward and laid him in his mother's reaching arms.

"I'm so sorry I let him be hurt," I said. "But he's better now. He just needs feeding." The lump in my throat made further words impossible.

She held him before her, examining him as closely as I had Finbar, back in Mac Dara's hall when I had still believed the Lord of the Oak capable of making an honest bargain. She looked into Becan's pebble eyes, inspected his gaping, squalling mouth, smiled with wonder at the scrap of iridescent fabric and the bright feather, the strands of hair and the soft shawl in which her son was wrapped. She bowed to me, courteous despite the fear that shook her body like a birch in an autumn wind. Then she pressed her child to her and kissed his odd little head, and her tears poured down her cheeks.

"I'm sorry," I said again. "He's a fine baby, sweet and good. He didn't deserve this, and neither did you. I looked after him as well as I could." And I thought of that young nursemaid in Mac Dara's hall and her false assurances.

The forest woman made no sound. She only nodded, then turned with Becan in her arms and moved away on silent feet. Before she reached the first rank of oaks she was lost in the shadows. For a little I could still hear Becan crying, but soon enough that, too, had faded to nothing.

"Here," said Dog Mask into the quiet, and reached up to put Finbar in my arms. "You have room for him now. Take him home; leave this place forever. Your quest is done."

The rocky being rumbled as if clearing its throat. "Wait," it cautioned, its patchy lichen eyes fixed on me. "Ask. Seek."

"Soothe poor skin," hooted the owl-masked being.

"Smoothing, salving, healing," rippled the watery one.

"By *ask* and *seek*," said the hedgehog-dwarf, making an abrupt turn toward the fire and coming perilously close to spiking Dog Mask with its luxuriant prickles, "my friend here means now would be the time for you to request explanations if you need them. Advice, too, if you believe we can help you. And you need rest. Time enough to go on in the morning."

Dog Mask shrugged, evidently outvoted, and we returned to the fireside. Finbar felt heavy in my arms; he was almost asleep. I would have to get used to the weight, the substance, the realness of my brother. Looking down into his unusual eyes, I felt I owed him an apology. *I don't think I can love you as I did Becan,* I told him silently. *But there's more than enough love waiting for you back home.*

I sat down and let the Old Ones tend to my burned hands. The watery one put on some kind of salve, its insubstantial fingers cool and light on my skin. The angry throbbing of the burns was immediately gone. The cat-masked one dabbed the same curative material on my face with soft paws, following the lines of my cuts. My heart could barely contain my sadness as I remembered the gentle touch of Cathal's fingers.

"How long will it take us to reach a portal back to my world?" I made myself ask, though the moment I had sat down a weariness had come over me that made it difficult to think straight. All I wanted to do was wrap myself up in the blankets, with Finbar tucked in next to me, and sleep. "If we start at dawn, when will I reach Sevenwaters? Finbar is so little, and—"

"You will be there soon enough," said Dog Mask. "We will provide milk for the journey home." The owl-masked creature was already filling a squat earthenware jug. "It will not be difficult. I do not believe Mac Dara will pursue you. Likely he has already forgotten you."

"But I must—" I began.

"Once you are among your own people, you and the child will be safe and cared for. You can put this misadventure behind you."

"But I won't be staying—"

"Sleep," said the hedgehog-dwarf, spreading a blanket beside the fire. Its prickles glinted fiery red in the light. Its hands were just like small human ones, save for the nails, which were long, strong and sharp, as if designed for digging. "No ill dreams tonight, only rest."

"I need to explain something first." My head was fuzzy with tiredness, but there was one thing that must be said. "After I take Finbar home, I'll be coming back here straightaway. I have to rescue Cathal."

There was a sudden, frozen silence. Then Dog Mask said, "Oh, no. No, no, no. A daughter of Sevenwaters does not associate with the son of the Lord of the Oak. Walk out, walk away, have nothing more to do with his kind. They are harmful. They are full of tricks and lies. Throw in your lot with Mac Dara's son and you face a lifetime of sorrow."

"You're wrong," I said firmly. "I love him and he loves me. Yes, he's Mac Dara's son; he carries that legacy and I'm not trying to deny it. But he is his mother's son, too. And he's tried all his life to be his own man. He is a warrior of exceptional skills. He can be a good person, I know it, he just needs to . . . he just needs to find his way home."

There was a pause, and then they sighed as one, gathering close around me in a circle. I sensed a thaw in the air.

"Oh, dear," said Dog Mask. "What is it that makes the folk of Sevenwaters love so fiercely and with such determination? We have seen it before, over and over. A foolish thing, a perilous thing. But what can we do?"

"If not for that," pointed out the hedgehog-dwarf, "the child of the prophecy would never have been born. That was not so foolish. And but for Johnny, Mac Dara's son would not have evaded his father's clutches for so long. Perhaps this is meant to be. The young man has acquitted himself well thus far."

"Strong," said the rocky being emphatically, and it thumped its chest with a fist in illustration. The sharp knocking sound made birds twitter with fright in the trees all around. "Tough. Bold."

"Twisty, tricky," added the watery one, as if these were admirable qualities.

The eyes behind the dog mask glinted with annoyance. "He is *Mac Dara's son,*" the creature said, as if it thought its companions fools.

"True love!" hooted Owl Mask. "Pure! Good!"

Dog Mask hissed softly. "Mac Dara's get can never be a good man," it said. "Blood will out."

"That isn't true," I said, remembering something. "What about my father's uncle Ciarán? His mother came from a dark branch of the Fair Folk. From what I've heard, she was just as wicked as Mac Dara. But Ciarán is expected to be chief druid after Conor. If that isn't good, I don't know what is."

There was a ripple of amusement around the circle.

"I vowed to Cathal that I would come back for him," I said, encouraged. "I won't abandon him here. But on my own I won't be able to manage the way we came in. If there's another portal I need to know where it is."

"Finding a portal is the least of your worries," said the

hedgehog-dwarf. "Do you imagine Mac Dara is going to let his son wander about freely to be found and led away by anyone who happens along? The Lord of the Oak may not believe you would willingly return to his realm, but he'll have protections in place all the same. He's been trying to get his only son back since the boy was seven years old and ready to begin learning. To win this Cathal of yours, you would have to out-trick the trickster."

"Then that's what I'll do. I've promised. I don't expect help; you've aided me a great deal already and I'm deeply grateful for it." They could have helped a lot more, I thought, if they had given me better information from the start. But it was plain that their kind despised the Tuatha De and that they considered Cathal as bad as his father. "Somehow I'll find a way."

"Ripple-green," murmured the watery being, which was stroking my hand with its cool fingers. "His ring?"

I nodded, remembering. "It belonged to his mother. Cathal gave me all his talismans. He should have kept them for himself."

"Then you would not have saved your brother, Clodagh," said the hedgehog-dwarf. "There are surprises in this story. For love, the son of Mac Dara sacrificed his own freedom. He gave up his life in the human world. A selfless act. This man is no copy of his father."

"Hah!" snorted Dog Mask. "His father read him perfectly. Mac Dara predicted what his son would do from the first moment the young man clapped eyes on you, Clodagh. Perhaps the Lord of the Oak even set you in his son's path, who knows?"

I remembered the day I had first met Cathal, when I had sensed an uncanny presence in the forest watching me, something that had sent me running out of the woods in panic and straight into Aidan's arms. "That idea troubles me," I said.

"The Fair Folk like to meddle, and some of them have great power," Dog Mask said. "They have played a part in the history of your family for more years than you could count, Clodagh. Many a forebear of yours has danced to their tune."

"But not all," said the hedgehog-dwarf. "From time to time, one will crop up who doesn't play by the rules. Your Aunt Liadan was one such. It looks as if you're set to become another. That is a surprise. I had thought you cut from simpler cloth. If you get Mac Dara's son out of here safely, you will impress all of us."

"Such a task is beyond any human woman," said Dog Mask flatly.

"Didn't Aunt Liadan stand up to the Tuatha De when she chose to take Johnny away from Sevenwaters?" I asked. "Isn't that the same?" My aunt had defied the Fair Folk to wed her Painted Man and go with him to Britain, where their child would grow up safely.

"This is not Deirdre of the Forest or her Fire Lord," said Dog Mask. "It's Mac Dara. Nobody can outwit *him*. Try it, and he will destroy you as easily and with as little thought as he might snap a twig or swat a troublesome fly. Go home, Clodagh. This is beyond your abilities. Do not inflict yet another loss on your family." Its tone was final.

"What happened to the Lady of the Forest and those others my sister used to see?" I asked. "Where did they go? Why does the Lord of the Oak rule here now?"

Dog Mask shrugged. "What do we care for the doings of *their* kind?" it said.

"Drifting, shifting, away, away . . ." The watery creature's vague gesture set a spray of droplets dancing in the air.

The hedgehog-dwarf shook itself, making a rattling sound, then said, "When your cousin Fainne went to the Islands to stand as guardian to their mysteries, the Lady of the Forest and her companions retreated from this land. I do not think they will return here before your grandchild's grandchild is an old woman, Clodagh."

"Gone, gone," said Owl Mask dolefully.

I had been told the strange story of Fainne, only a few years my elder, who had lived with us briefly, then had gone away to be custodian of a sacred cave. When he had related the tale my father had provided scant detail, and after a while my sisters and I had stopped asking questions. "Gone," I echoed. "And all that's left is *him*. That can't be right. The forest of Sevenwaters can't stay under Mac Dara's control. Our ancestor, the one who gave us the task of looking after it, would feel betrayed."

"One thing at a time, Clodagh," said the cat-being, and the elongated eyes behind its golden mask were warm. "Save your sweetheart before you take on the Tuatha De in their entirety.

Mend your broken heart before you attempt to change the course of history. Show us this ring."

I held out my hand, and three or four of them bent close to examine the green glass ring. They looked at it; they looked at each other. They turned grave eyes on me.

"What?" I asked, suddenly feeling very tired again.

"It's old," said one.

"It's very old," said another.

"It's as old as we are," added a third.

"Who exactly was this young man's mother?" asked the hedgehog-dwarf.

"An ordinary woman, low-born, a fisherman's daughter, I think. Cathal didn't say much about her except that she was very beautiful and that she waited years and years for Mac Dara to come back."

"She was from the west?"

"That's right. A place called Whiteshore, on the coast of Connacht."

"A fisherman's daughter," mused the hedgehog-dwarf. "There is a good magic in this, Clodagh, a powerful old sea magic. Your young man did well to put it on your finger before you faced the Lord of the Oak."

"If he had worn it himself—"

"No, no," put in the owl-creature. "You, you!"

"It is a woman's ring," said the hedgehog-dwarf, "and meant for your finger. As for Cathal, if you attempt a rescue you must wear this. Do not be tempted to give it back to him. He will require his own talisman of protection, and it is up to you to determine what that may be. Does this young man not understand his mother's legacy?"

"Her legacy? What do you mean?"

"Ah. He dismisses her, perhaps, as someone he loved, who failed him. If she owned this ring, she was far more than that. There is a strength in such folk that runs very deep, Clodagh. He is her son; it runs also in him. He has shown it by passing the ring to you; by ensuring your safety at the price of his own."

"All he said about his mother was that she loved Mac Dara and that she killed herself from despair when he didn't come back.

If there's more, I'm certain he doesn't know. He was only seven when she died." Seven. *He's been trying to get his only son back since the boy was seven years old.* Without being quite sure why, I felt suddenly chill. "Are you saying this could be the key to getting him out? That it is possible?"

"Possible, maybe," said Dog Mask a little sourly. "Not probable, and not at all advisable. Now sleep. Husband your strength. Tomorrow you will be home among your own."

"Will you tell him about this? If there's something he doesn't know about his mother, something he can use—"

"Our kind does not speak to his kind," said Dog Mask predictably. "Now sleep."

"But . . ." I could not bear the idea that there was a clue that might help Cathal escape, and that there was no way I could tell him about it.

"If he is what you believe him to be," said the hedgehog-dwarf, "he will seek his own answers."

I lay down with Finbar nestled against me and a blanket over the two of us. Around me the Old Ones went about various tasks, banking up the fire, checking the torches that lit the enclosure, feeding the goat. Two stayed by the gate; two more patrolled the perimeter. Beyond the hedge of thorn, all was quiet.

My last thought before I slept was of Cathal. I pictured him as he had been on the day I met him, his thin lips twisted in a mocking smile, his dark eyes dancing with mischief. From the first he had been an enigma, an irritating, intriguing puzzle of a man, full of a restless intelligence. It came to me that if anyone knew how to outwit the trickster, it might be the trickster's son, if only he did not let despair overwhelm him first.

The dawn woke me, seeping under my eyelids in a glorious wash of pale gold. Finbar was still fast asleep, a warm, damp bundle against my side. The blanket was over us and my pack was under my head. But I was no longer in the safe place within the hedge of thorn. The sunlight told me so before I sat up and saw that instead of the massive dark trees of the Otherworld a grove of graceful birches stood around the small expanse of open ground where the two of us were lying. Real sunlight; above me the sky was turning to a delicate duck-egg blue. There was a freshness in the air, an openness that made my heart lift. All around us, birds chorused their greetings to the rising sun. We were out. We were back.

I had dreamed of a long walk through narrow underground ways, secret ways, with the Old Ones padding before and behind with their torches, guiding me as I carried Finbar against my chest in the sling. That path had been nothing like the one Cathal and I had followed to enter the realm of the Tuatha De, and I had sensed it was an entry known only to these smaller folk. I had dreamed that I walked all night. And now, on waking, I realized that perhaps it had been so. I felt refreshed, as if I had slept well, but my legs were aching. I stretched, looking around me again. The area looked familiar. There was a marker stone not far up the hill with ogham signs on it. Beyond it, oaks grew. I was close to the nemetons, the well-concealed habitation of the Sevenwaters druids. It was a fair walk back home, but not so far that I could not manage it.

The earthenware jug had been set not far away, with a neatly folded cloth covering it—the Old Ones had kept their promise of providing milk for Finbar. I thought my dream had perhaps included a pause in a little shadowy cavern where I had changed my baby brother's wrappings and fed him. I'd have to do both again before I moved on.

Which way? Head straight for home, so I could put Finbar in my mother's arms myself? How could I do so, then announce that I must leave again immediately? I could imagine how Father would react to the idea of my heading back to the Otherworld to confront a dark prince of the Tuatha De. He would consider it his responsibility to stop me; to make sure I came to my senses and stayed safe. I could not go home. But Finbar must, straightaway.

So, go to the nemetons. Seek help from the druids. How would they react when I appeared? Conor was a wise and open-minded man, but I was sure he would share my father's opinion on this matter. I did not know Ciarán very well. He was the same kind of half-breed as Cathal. Whether that would influence him to help me or hinder me, I had no idea. Perhaps I could slip into the nemetons, leave Finbar somewhere safe, then disappear into the forest. No, that would be irresponsible. Even if I did not love him as I had Becan, I owed it to my brother to deliver him safely into the arms of his family.

As if reading my mind, Finbar awoke, requesting his breakfast. He was loud. If we were as close to the druids' home as I thought, his crying would soon arouse curiosity. I fed him, and as he sucked and swallowed I cast my eyes all around the area, looking for the chink or crack or cave through which I must have emerged last night more asleep than awake. I couldn't see anything. No stream or pond, no large cluster of rocks, nothing that might conceal an opening. Only the gentle birch-clad slope. And now, walking down it toward me, an old woman clad in an oddly shifting garment that might have been cloak, gown or robe. She used her staff for support, but she moved with an energy and purpose that belied her years.

I should not have been surprised. After the events of the last few days, I should have been ready for anything. "I thought you'd gone away," I said as Willow came over and seated herself on a flat-topped stone beside me.

"Where's your young man?" the crone asked, without any preliminaries. "You got the little one, I see. You did well. Was the price higher than you expected, Clodagh?"

I gaped at her. "How can you know so much?" I challenged. "Those stories you told, they were all about Cathal and the journey the two of us had to take. I know the traveling people have unusual gifts, but what you did went beyond that. It was uncanny." Even as I spoke, my mind was filling with questions I needed to ask her, things I must find out in case they might help me rescue Cathal. "My young man, as you call him, is trapped in the Otherworld. His father did it; it was just like that story about Albha and her daughter: *Set your foot inside the door, you'll be mine forever more*. There must be some way to get around that charm, but Mac Dara is so powerful, and I have no magic at all . . ." I stumbled to a halt, seeing that she was only waiting for the flood of words to abate. "Please will you help me?" I asked, struggling for calm.

Willow smiled, a map of wrinkles spreading across her face. "I don't cast spells," she said. "I don't fight battles. I'm a storyteller."

Brighid save me, this was going to be like Dog Mask all over again, a blank wall in terms of getting any useful advice. I bowed my head so she would not see the frustration on my face, and met the tranquil blue gaze of Finbar, lying on my lap, drowsy and content now his belly was full of milk. The annoyance abated as swiftly as it had arisen, and the right question came to me. "Will you tell me a story?" I asked. "I missed the end of that tale you told about Albha and her half-human daughter. I'd like to know what happened."

"If you weren't wise enough to listen the first time," Willow said, laying her staff down beside her, "that's not my fault. I've another tale in mind for this morning, and I'll keep it brief. You'll be wanting your breakfast."

"Very well," I said, for if I had learned anything about her, it was that there would be a lesson of some relevance in any story she told. I just hoped I could understand it.

"There was once a lovely young woman named Firinne, the daughter of a fisherman she was, and lived at a place called Whiteshore on the coast of Connacht. I see you're bursting to interrupt already, Clodagh, but if you're wise you'll leave an old woman to tell the tale straight through. You don't need me to remind you that time is short.

"Now, Firinne had the misfortune to lose both her parents before she was fifteen years old, but she was adept at mending the nets, and between one piece of work and the next, and one kind neighbor and another, she managed to make ends meet. There were plenty of suitors in the village where she lived, but none that took her fancy. A few years passed, and a man came a-knocking on the door, a very fine fellow in a big long cloak. So fine he was, in fact, that despite all her better instincts Firinne fell under his spell, for no woman could resist such strong shoulders, such long legs and such mischievous dark eyes. The stranger knew how to woo a woman, and although Firinne held him off for some time, eventually she succumbed to his undeniable charms. And then, to her surprise but not, I expect, to yours, the fellow was off without a parting kiss, and she was on her own with a babe in her belly and not much of a livelihood to support it with.

"Now I should perhaps have mentioned a certain ring, a plain green one much the same as that glass circle I see on your finger, Clodagh. That ring had been given to Firinne by her father, and he had made it clear to her that the simple object, passed down from generation to generation, contained protective powers of extraordinary strength. Her father had bid her wear it always, for it would get her out of all kinds of trouble, especially the kind a foolish woman might fall into should she step inside a mushroom circle or entertain the wrong kind of handsome stranger. Unfortunate, then, that Firinne had been doing her washing the day the fellow knocked on her door and had taken the ring off and set it away in a wee box for safekeeping. And once she'd clapped eyes on the visitor, she forgot about the ring until after the dark stranger had left her his unwelcome gift and departed. Now, with his child growing fast inside her, she knew how foolish she had been. For her lineage had an unusual thread in it, a thread that gave her certain instincts beyond those of ordinary humankind. She'd been duped, fooled. She'd thought that long, dark, wicked fellow loved her; she'd believed his tender and passionate words. Now, in the cold light of the time after, she realized what he was and what he really wanted.

"For she knew, as we know, Clodagh, that the Fair Folk are not good breeders. Their best chance of a child is to couple with a likely man or woman of our world. Firinne chose the dark stranger because she could not resist his charms. *He* chose *her* because she was an ideal mother for his child—she was exceptionally lovely by human standards; she was healthy; she was a simple woman from a fishing village and would be unlikely to put up a fight when he came back for his son later, should he be fortunate enough to get a boy from this coupling. Or so he thought. He never saw the ring. He never knew that somewhere in her ancestry, long, long ago, there had been one of the Sea People. That was Mac Dara's great error.

"Firinne knew her stories. She knew she had seven years, no more, no less; seven years to spin a web of protection around her child so that he could not be reclaimed by his father and taken to the Otherworld forever. For at seven years old, a boy is old enough to leave his mother's skirts and her influence and to begin learning his father's trade. That trade might be carpentry or fishing or scribing. If the father happens to be a prince of the Otherworld, then from seven years old the boy's future lies in that shadowy realm. Of one thing Firinne was quite certain. Mac Dara would be back. Not for her; for her son."

"You're telling me Cathal's mother didn't waste away for love of Mac Dara?" I asked, shocked that this tale had been turned upside down. "She didn't kill herself out of hopeless longing? How can you know that?"

Willow smiled again. "You seem to find it astonishing that my memory has anything in it at all. I hope that when you are old, Clodagh, your grandchildren do not expect you to spend all day mumbling by the fire. I do recall telling you, when we first met, that I'm Dan Walker's aunt. But, just like everyone else, I did have two parents. My father wasn't one of the traveling people. He was a handsome stranger my mother met out in the woods one night, a fellow who, from her description, looked uncommonly like that young man of yours. My mother was a bit of a wild girl. Well, she got more than she bargained for from her midnight tryst, just as Firinne did. Fortunately, nobody came for *me* on my seventh birthday. Mac Dara's only interested in sons, not daughters."

My head was spinning. "But . . ."

"But I'm an old woman?" She chuckled. "How old do you think *he* is? That man's been fathering girls since the time of ancient legend. Why do you think he places such value on the one son he's managed to get? It's taken him a long, long time. Long enough to break his heart, though it's commonly believed that he doesn't possess one. Your Cathal has older sisters in every corner of Erin, Clodagh. Of course, not all of them make use of the unusual talents their parentage has bestowed; most have no idea what they are. Now, do you want the rest of the story or don't you? We haven't long. You need to get that baby home."

I glanced at Finbar again; he seemed to have fallen asleep. "Yes, please," I said, still reeling from what she had just told me. This wrinkled crone was a daughter of Mac Dara? No wonder her tales revealed uncanny truths.

"Now that little boy was very special to his father, for obvious reasons. But that didn't make him any less precious to Firinne, and she vowed to herself that she would do everything in her power to stop Mac Dara from taking him. She swore she would not let his father turn the boy into another like himself, a man with no awareness of right and wrong. So she took the green glass ring, the gift of her unusual ancestor, and she strung it on a cord and tied it around her baby's neck. Then she went up to the stronghold of Lord Murtagh, who ruled in those parts wisely and well, and offered herself as wet nurse to his own newborn son. And when she offered, she told Lord Murtagh something of her story, but not everything, and persuaded him to take little Cathal into his household and keep him safe while he grew to be a man. She made his lordship promise to teach her son that he must never, ever go abroad without the green glass ring around his neck or carried somewhere in his clothing. Lord Murtagh was an exceptional chieftain and an exceptional man; still is. He promised to do as she asked, and offered Firinne a permanent place in his household, but she said no. Better, she thought, if she had as little to do with her son as possible, for it would be through her that his father would try to track him down."

"That must have hurt her terribly," I said, remembering how it had felt to give up Becan, who had only been mine for a few days. "Cathal thought his mother didn't care about him."

"It was an act of selfless love," said Willow, nodding. "She knew she should go away, leave Whiteshore forever, to put Mac Dara right off the scent. But she couldn't bring herself to do that. She lived for the little glimpses of her boy that she got from time to time: fishing in the river with his friend, riding through the village with Lord Murtagh and his family, and sometimes walking all by himself along the shore, staring at the waves. She tried to ensure he didn't see her watching. She thought it best if he forgot her. His new family was kind to him; she could see they treated him as they did their own sons, almost. Sometimes the best place to hide something is right under the seeker's nose, Firinne thought. When Mac Dara passed that way again, she would tell him his son was dead.

"The time came. Cathal was seven years old and, right on time, Mac Dara came a-tapping on Firinne's door again. It wasn't fun and games he wanted this time, but his own child to carry off to the Otherworld. And when Firinne told him Cathal had fallen sick and died two years earlier, the Lord of the Oak didn't believe her. He pressed her; she held fast to her lie. He used a charm to try to force the truth out of her. She fled out the back way, down to the riverbank. Exactly what occurred there I cannot tell you, for not a living soul was witness to it. I do not believe Firinne killed herself. Her ancestors were the Sea People. She would not have chosen a death by drowning. Nor do I think Mac Dara murdered her, for with her would die a vital clue to his son's whereabouts. In any event, she carried the truth to her watery grave. I believe they struggled, and that somehow in that struggle she was killed. It was a few days before the boys found her body in the water; time enough for any telltale marks to be gone."

It was almost too much to take in. "This changes everything," I said, wishing with all my heart that I could tell Cathal this news right now, for if this was a true story, it gave him back the most precious gift of all: his mother's love. "If only I had known this before we crossed over into the Otherworld. If only someone could tell him. He'll be so lonely and lost, without any love at all. What if he sinks into despair?"

Willow raised her brows. "You think him so weak?" she asked with a half-smile.

"Weak?" I was outraged. "Of course not! I just wish someone could tell him the truth about what happened to his mother. And about the powers he might have inherited from her. If she stood up to Mac Dara, if she kept her secret until death, she must have been a brave woman."

"She was," said Willow. "Cathal is her son; he, too, will be brave. But he does need you, Clodagh, so you'd best listen while I tell the rest of the story quickly. It took another five years for Mac Dara to work out where his son was. That was highly unusual. Anyone would have expected a powerful prince of the Tuatha De to discover the truth within one season at the most. Why so long? Well, it wasn't the green glass ring. That was a charm to ensure the boy's physical safety, not to keep him hidden. No, the reason Mac Dara found it hard to track him down was the boy's heritage: Tuatha De on the father's side, both human and Sea People on the mother's. Young Cathal was an explosive bundle of eldritch power wrapped up in the body of a sad, confused, clever little boy. Not long after his mother's death, he began to sense that someone was making attempts to draw him away from safety. He took his own steps to deal with it, hardly understanding what he did. He made up the sort of luck charms all children invent. Because Cathal was who he was, his wards worked. Sometimes he looked into the water and saw things that couldn't really be there. He told nobody, though from time to time he made use of what the visions revealed. He hated being different. But you know that part."

I nodded, though it was not the image of young Cathal scrying that was in my mind, but that of Firinne watching her little son as he walked alone on the beach at Whiteshore. I could feel the ache in my own heart. "So he managed to evade them for quite some years, and then when Aidan went off to Inis Eala, Cathal seized the opportunity to go with him," I said. "And then he came to Sevenwaters, and ended up sacrificing his freedom because of me."

"You are somewhat hard on yourself," Willow said. "Cathal might say that to have won your heart made up for everything else. He did give you the ring. A gift of selfless love."

There was a pause; she was waiting for me to say something. "The ring kept me safe until I could get out," I said slowly. "If I made a talisman for Cathal, something that represented selfless love, would that provide him with protection against his father?"

"Perhaps. It would not get him out of the Otherworld. But it might help. He'll need help."

I was still framing my next question when Willow took up her staff, rose to her feet and made to leave.

"Oh, please wait!" I begged her. "Tell me if there is some way that charm can be broken, the one about setting a foot inside the door—how can I possibly counteract something so powerful?"

"I told you, I'm a storyteller," said the old woman, not unkindly. "You have what you need already. And now I must be on my way. I wish you well on your journey, Clodagh." She cupped a hand to her ear. "Who's that I hear? Unusually busy in this part of the forest, isn't it, so early in the morning?" As she walked off down the hillside, I heard voices; someone was coming over the hill from the other side. I peered uphill under the birches and discerned two figures approaching swiftly. A slight, dark-haired girl in a blue gown: Sibeal. A tall, redheaded man in a hooded robe: Ciarán. By the time I turned back, Willow had vanished.

My sister was beaming. She ran the last few steps, fell to her knees and threw her arms around me and Finbar, causing him to complain vigorously. "Clodagh! You've got him!" There were tears running down her smiling face.

"Mother," I said. "Is she all right, Sibeal?"

My sister nodded, momentarily unable to speak. Then Ciarán came up behind her, inclined his head courteously, and said, "We are camped a short distance away, over the hill. When you're ready we'll take you there. We have food and water and a change of clothing for you."

I must have looked incredulous. Sibeal gave a shaky laugh and said, "We knew you were coming soon and where we'd find you. We saw it in the water, both of us. But I couldn't tell Father or Mother. It would have been too cruel to get their hopes up and then find out the visions meant something else. Uncle Ciarán told them I had to come here for some tutoring. Oh, Clodagh, everyone's been so worried about you! What are those scratches on your face? And Finbar—is he unharmed?"

For Sibeal, this was an unusually animated speech. "He seems fine," I said. "He's been well looked after. It's a long story. Thank you for being here." I glanced at Ciarán, trying to work out what he was thinking, but his mulberry eyes gave nothing away. "Uncle, I would prefer not to be seen by anyone else at the nemetons. Not even Conor. I need to explain something to you and Sibeal, something my parents aren't going to like at all. Not about the baby," I added hastily, seeing the sudden alarm on my sister's face. "Another matter."

Ciarán seemed unperturbed. "My brethren do not disturb me when I am teaching, Clodagh, and our little camp is at some distance from their gathering place. Conor is at Sevenwaters; there's a council in progress. We, too, have some news."

"A council? Isn't that rather quick? Father and Johnny weren't even—" I halted, a frisson of anxiety passing through me. "How long have I been gone?" I made myself ask.

"Nearly a whole turning of the moon," Sibeal said solemnly. "Clodagh, there's some very bad news. It's about Aidan."

"I know he's dead," I said. "Mac Dara killed him. We saw it."

"We? Who—"

"This can wait, Sibeal." Ciarán was watching me closely. "Let us walk to the other side of the hill before we exchange our news."

"A whole turning of the moon," I muttered. "So long." These tricks of time could work either way. I thought of Cathal, and what might happen if months and years passed in the Otherworld before I could reach him. *Let him not forget me,* I prayed. *Let Mac Dara not poison his mind beyond recovery.*

We moved to a neat small encampment on the far side of the hill, with a hearth between stones and rudimentary shelters for sleeping. An area under an awning housing various tools—birch augury sticks, a mortar and pestle, a copper bowl and ewer—indicated that my sister and her tutor had been working hard while they awaited my arrival. There was a pot of porridge beside the fire. Ciarán, a man economical with both words and gestures, filled a bowl for me and made me eat all of it before I told them my story.

Sibeal was surprised that Cathal had come with me on my journey. She was astonished that he had proven to be, not just a rather difficult friend of Johnny's, but the son of Mac Dara himself. Ciarán listened intently, saying very little, but none of it seemed to shock him. I had a feeling he knew a great deal already.

"And so," I said at the end, "I can't come home. I have to go back and get him out. But the Old Ones didn't tell me how to find a portal, so I suppose I'll have to wander off into the forest and look for one, as I did before." Somehow, here in my own world with my stomach comfortably full and the fire warming me and my sister sitting right beside me holding the drowsing baby, doing that did not seem quite as possible as it had before. After all, it was Cathal who had found the river; it was Cathal who had taken me across it. "I have to, Sibeal," I added, seeing her eyes widen in disbelief. "There's nobody else to help him."

After a moment's silence, my sister burst out, "You mean right now, straightaway? Clodagh, you can't! You must take Finbar home yourself! Mother's frantic with worry about you. Father would never forgive himself if something happened to you now, after you've got back safely. He's already beside himself with guilt for misjudging you over the changeling. And then there's this business with Illann—"

"You'd better tell me everything, starting from the beginning," I said grimly. If even Sibeal, the wisest and most solemn of my sisters, was babbling on as if this were the end of the world, I could imagine what kind of reception I would get if I went home and announced my plans.

"When you left," Ciarán said, "your father called both Conor and me to the house so we could advise him. Past experience has taught me that the best approach in these crises is to tell the truth. That was the advice I gave your father. So Sean went to your mother and explained what you believed about the changeling and why you had gone away. Some had thought that to hear such tidings would cause her to abandon hope altogether, since the loss of her baby had already left her much weakened in both body and mind. But Aisling is made of stronger stuff than may be apparent. Even as she feared for you, the news of your mission gave her heart. She believed from the first that you were right; that, for some reason of their own, the Fair Folk had taken her child and that you would bring Finbar back to her. For her, it was a relief to know that the baby was in their hands and not those of an unscrupulous political rival. Sean has been less certain. He berates himself, as any father would, for letting his daughter put herself at such terrible risk. But he took heart from a contact with his sister not long ago."

Aunt Liadan; my father's twin. She shared the same kind of bond with him as I did with Deirdre. Liadan had rebelled against the express wishes of the Tuatha De; she had married a man of her own choice, an outsider, and had taken their child away from Sevenwaters. It was another of the tangled family stories. I knew there were parts of it my sisters and I had never been told. There was something dark there, something that was still secret, a twist of fate that had never been publicly unraveled.

"Liadan supported your choice," Ciarán said. "Sean did not tell us exactly what she said to him, but it was her counsel that made him realize he had been wrong about a political abduction, wrong about a conspiracy, and unjust in his refusal to listen to you, Clodagh. He will be alarmed and upset if you do not return home today with the child."

I noted that he did not offer advice one way or the other. "Sibeal could take him home," I said. "You or another of the druids could escort her."

Ciarán looked at me, his strange eyes very intent.

"Or a message could be sent to my parents, saying Finbar is at the nemetons and unharmed," I added. "Father would send someone straightaway to fetch him, I'm certain. Whatever we do, it should be quite soon, because this milk will not stay fresh, and he is quite little—he needs feeding often." The next part was awkward to say. "But I must have time to get ready and leave before they reach here. I know Father would try to stop me."

"But, Clodagh," said Sibeal, quieter now, "how could you do it? And why? Cathal is a warrior; surely he can look after himself."

"Mac Dara is a creature who cannot tell right from wrong," I said. I had not told them about Becan and the fire, only that the changeling had been injured and that I had mended him with the help of the Old Ones, then returned him to his mother. I had left out quite a lot, not so much to spare my sister as because it hurt too much to put certain things into words. "He'll try to twist his son to his will. He wants to turn Cathal into a copy of himself. It's true, what Willow told us in her tales. There's been a change in the realm of the Tuatha De since their kind last had dealings with our family. The place has turned dark; the good ones have gone away over the sea. It isn't right that a heartless leader like Mac Dara should rule there. Maybe we can't do anything about that, but I must rescue Cathal. He's only in there because of me. If I hadn't rushed off after Finbar, if I hadn't accepted Cathal's help, if I hadn't screamed at the crucial moment, he would still be safe."

Sibeal turned her big, light-filled eyes on me. There was a question in them.

"I love him," I said simply. "There it is. I must help him."

"Clodagh, that would be . . ." My sister hesitated.

"Dangerous? I know that." It would be more than dangerous. There was every likelihood that I might never come home again.

There was a silence. Ciarán stared into the coals. Sibeal watched me with the sleeping Finbar on her knee. I thought about Cathal and forced back my tears.

"I spoke to Willow, just now," I said eventually. "I believe I have to make a talisman for Cathal, something that signifies selfless love. That has protective power because it's beyond the understanding of the Fair Folk. Then I have to find a portal. And then, hardest of all, Cathal and I must break the spell. Mac Dara implied that it was the same spell that was in Willow's story: *Set your foot inside the door, you'll be mine forever more.* And I can't think of any way at all that I could counter that. Mac Dara is absolutely determined to keep Cathal. And he's . . ." *Powerful. Ruthless. Entirely without scruples.* "He's strong," I said, lifting my chin. "But I have to try."

"You really are going to go," breathed Sibeal. "You really do love that strange, awkward man. Aidan seemed so much more suited to you."

"I did like Aidan. He was a fine person, for all his faults. But I never loved him, not as I love Cathal. Tell me, did Johnny bring Aidan's body home?"

"Johnny found him in the forest," Ciarán said gravely. "Aidan and the two men who rode out with him were all killed by the same kind of arrow. The make was unlike anything Johnny had seen before; it was another indication that uncanny powers might be involved in this course of events. Aidan was laid to rest at Sevenwaters; Conor conducted the ritual. A rider was sent to Whiteshore with the news. As to the matter of Glencarnagh, there are still no answers there, and it has caused grave dispute between Sean and your sister's new husband. Johnny's investigations failed to uncover any conclusive evidence as to who was responsible for the attack. He paid Illann a visit and confronted him with Cathal's suggestion that he was somehow involved. Illann denied it with some vehemence and demanded an apology, which he didn't get. As a result, there's significant disquiet among the southern chieftains."

That sounded serious; it would have the potential to reignite the territorial feuds that had plagued the region for generations. "Is this why the council is being held so early?" I asked, thinking of poor Deirdre, caught up in the middle of it all.

"Illann and Deirdre are at Sevenwaters now," Sibeal said. "The chieftains are working on a treaty, but I don't know the details. Father is grim, Illann's angry and Deirdre's furious with you, Clodagh. She told me she's been trying to reach you and that you were blocking her out of your mind."

"I just haven't had room for her," I said. "Tell me, what have people been saying about Cathal?"

"There was plenty of talk when he first disappeared," said Ciarán. "It was a mystery: where had he gone, who was paying him, how had he managed to vanish so effectively? Nobody seemed to entertain the possibility that the young man was not fully of humankind, or that his reasons for fleeing Sevenwaters had nothing to do with disputes between Lord Sean and his neighboring chieftains."

"You must tell Father that Cathal played no part in Finbar's abduction or in the attack on Glencarnagh," I said, looking from Ciarán to Sibeal and back again. "Explain what I've told you, that he was just trying to keep out of his father's clutches and to warn me about what his visions had shown him. Make sure Johnny knows that, too. Please."

"Clodagh," said Ciarán quietly, "in this matter of Illann . . . Perhaps it can wait, I don't know. How exactly did Illann come into Cathal's vision?"

"He'd have to answer that himself," I said, my heart sinking as I realized my uncle must believe it possible that Illann was in some way guilty, or he would have no cause to ask such a question. "Cathal did say that perhaps his father had been meddling with his visions; showing him certain things just to create strife. Mac Dara could have been trying to get Cathal into trouble so he would leave Sevenwaters and go into the forest on his own."

Ciarán nodded. "In time, with the right training, Cathal could learn to counter such interference. Unless and until he discovers the extent of his own abilities, I fear he is at great risk. You're right, Clodagh; you must move swiftly."

I looked at him, and so did Sibeal. "Thank you," I said quietly. "I wasn't sure you'd support my decision to go. I don't think Conor would, and I know Father wouldn't."

I could see memories in Ciarán's dark eyes, sad ones and happy ones. "This is not the first time I have found myself in disagreement with the two of them on a personal issue," he said. "When it happened before, they prevailed over me. Their decision was wrong; it led to bitter losses. I will not allow that to happen again, Clodagh. If you love this young man, you must go to his aid. I regret that I cannot come with you; there are many, many reasons why that would be inadvisable, and perhaps one day I will speak of those to you and your Cathal. But I can show you the way in, and I can provide advice that will help you."

"The way in?" I breathed. "You mean you . . ." I could not quite say it aloud.

Ciarán was suddenly grave again. "I have not entered that realm in a long time," he said. "I am one of the brethren now; my path took a twist and a turn a few years back and I have chosen a discipline that requires me to curtail certain . . . certain skills, abilities, that I once put into practice on a daily basis. I've been tempted; especially so since this Lord of the Oak made his presence known in the forest of Sevenwaters. I like his ways as little as you do, Clodagh. But there is a time for everything, and now is not the time for me to do battle with Mac Dara. If I went with you, this could grow into something far bigger and more perilous than any of us is ready to deal with." Seeing that both of us were staring with fascination, he gave a diffident smile, adding, "Enough of this. We have practical decisions to make. With your agreement, Sibeal and I will take the baby down to my brethren and arrange for a message to go to Lord Sean. Sibeal, we must ask you to remain at the nemetons with Finbar until someone comes to collect him—then you could return home and explain to your father what Clodagh has told us about Cathal and why she has not come with you. I suppose he will send for me and give me a stern talking-to. Or perhaps not. He knows from sad experience, as I do, just how much this family has lost through the machinations of the Tuatha De. We must not lose another." He glanced at me. "As for a talisman of selfless love, perhaps you need not make one."

"Why not?"

Ciarán smiled. "To return to that realm of shadows for your sweetheart's sake, Clodagh, is a breathtaking act of selfless love. I think you are the only talisman he needs."

Sibeal was already gathering her cloak, Finbar held competently in one arm. "You know that rhyme, Clodagh," she said diffidently. "*You'll be mine forever more,* and so on. There is another part to it, after that. Did you forget the story?"

My heart stood still a moment. "I was called out of the hall before Willow finished telling it," I breathed. "What, Sibeal? What other part? How can *you'll be mine forever more* not be the last line? I mean, forever is . . . forever."

"You mean the tale of Albha and Saorla?" asked Ciarán. "Oh, there are three or four variants of that one. There's always some kind of rider after *forever more,* different for each version. Sometimes it doesn't come in until the end of the tale. Which one did Willow tell, Sibeal?"

Sibeal frowned, trying to remember, and I gritted my teeth in impatience.

"Something about waves," she said eventually. "*Till waves are calmed by human hand,* that was the last line. It sounds poetic, but it's not especially useful. I think *hand* rhymed with *stand.*"

"*Till ancient foes in friendship stand, and waves are calmed by human hand,*" said Ciarán quietly. "It could be interpreted in many ways. Now we must go. You will be quite safe if you wait here for me, Clodagh. Within the boundary marked by the ogham stones we are protected by forces of nature."

My sister looked so small, standing there with the baby in her arms. "Thank you, Sibeal," I said, getting up and embracing her. "You've done so much for me already, and now you're having to do all my explaining again. I'm lucky to have such a true sister."

"It's all right, Clodagh," she said soberly. "I hope you'll be safe. I'll watch for you in the water."

While I waited for Ciarán to come back I tried to imagine under what circumstances human hands might be able to influence something as big and powerful as the sea, and failed. The other part was easily interpreted. In a realm where folk kept saying things like *Our kind does not speak to his kind,* there were foes aplenty. Changing their attitudes, it seemed to me, might be the work of a lifetime.

It was some while before my uncle returned. I refilled my water-skin at the nearby stream and helped myself to some supplies from the store of food at the little camp, packing them neatly into my bag. I washed my face and hands and changed my clothes. It was a pleasure to put on the familiar things Sibeal had brought for me—a favorite old homespun gown, fresh small-clothes and a warm shawl. I rolled the embroidered gown I had been wearing into a ball and left it under a tree. Then I sat quietly awhile, thinking of what awaited me and trying to gather my strength. My thoughts strayed over the tale of Firinne, that sad, strong young woman. If she had outwitted Mac Dara, I thought, then perhaps I could, too. There was a little thread of the uncanny in my own ancestry, after all.

I was deep in my thoughts and did not hear Ciarán approaching until he had walked right up to the encampment. Perched on his shoulder was his raven, Fiacha. The bird's plumage was glossy, his eyes preternaturally bright. The hair stood up on the back of my neck.

"A message is on its way to your father," Ciarán said, putting a little bag down by the fire and seating himself opposite me, cross-legged and straight-backed as a child. The raven fixed me with its gaze.

"Thank you." I felt ill at ease in the bird's presence and suddenly shy without Sibeal. Knowing Ciarán's story did not mean I knew the man. He was Conor's half-brother, born at Sevenwaters after Conor's father, Lord Colum, took a second wife who proved to be more than she seemed. She had spirited Ciarán away as a small child, but his father had found him and brought him back to be raised in the protection of the nemetons. My sisters and I had never met Ciarán until four years ago, when he had come to the aid of my father and Johnny in the resolution of a feud with the Britons. That was quite odd, since Conor had more or less brought him up and Conor himself visited our home often. It was one of those subjects both my parents seemed reluctant to talk about; a part of our family history that held secrets.

"We spoke of talismans earlier," my companion observed now. "I believe I was right about your presence being sufficient to protect Cathal. But it won't hurt to take this as well." He opened the bag and took out a simple strand of dark twine. On it was strung a small white stone with a hole in it.

"This is more precious to me than you could possibly imagine," he said, following my gaze. "It belonged to your father's sister Niamh." His voice changed as he spoke this name, and in that moment the mystery became plain to me, so plain that I wondered how I had not seen it before. His eyes were just the same as my cousin Fainne's, dark mulberry eyes, the legacy of the sorceress. We had been told that Fainne was Niamh's daughter by an unnamed second husband, someone Father's elder sister had met and wed far away from Sevenwaters. That was the official story. If Ciarán was Fainne's father, there was a compelling reason to keep the fact quiet; his union with Niamh would have been forbidden by laws of kinship. If he was Fainne's father, he had lost his only daughter to the Fair Folk four years ago. And long, long ago, he had lost Niamh. I said nothing.

"Take it," Ciarán went on, handing the necklace to me. "I gave it once as a gift of the heart; it was all I had to offer. Niamh gave it to the daughter who was so precious to her. In time it made its way back to me. When you find Cathal, place it around his neck. It is a reminder that love outlasts the strongest enchantments."

"Thank you," I said. "It must be very hard for you to give this up. I'll do my best to bring it back safely." I motioned to the other item he had brought, a gray stone shaped like an egg. "Uncle Ciarán, what is that?"

"You have several challenges ahead of you, Clodagh. Getting in may be quite easy. Finding Mac Dara may not be difficult, that's if he believes you are no threat to him. Gaining access to Cathal could be hard. If Mac Dara thinks there is any chance his son may still want to escape the Otherworld, he's unlikely to want him to see you. But he'll have been working on Cathal. He may use this as a test. If Cathal meets you and remains indifferent, or if he fails to recognize you, Mac Dara will know he's got his son back body and mind."

I felt cold all through. "You're saying that if I ask to see him and Mac Dara says yes, it probably means Cathal has forgotten me?"

"Perhaps. If there's one thing you should remember in there, it's that nothing is what it seems. Expect tricks, puzzles, mysteries. Remember that love is the only truth. Now let us imagine you succeed in finding Cathal, and that he wants to escape. Your next challenge is likely to be Mac Dara's capacity to see you, wherever you go. Such a one can summon whatever he wishes to the scrying bowl. He can follow you into the most secret places; he can spy on your most intimate moments. To flee from an individual who possesses such power is nigh on impossible unless he chooses to let you go."

"There was a safe place," I said. "A place of the Old Ones, protected by a hedge of thorn. I don't think he could see us there. And when I went into his pavilion, he didn't seem to know where Cathal was, even though I had left him not far away in the forest."

"You could retreat within the hedge, yes," said Ciarán, as if he knew the place. "But he would guess where you had gone. He would send his henchmen to wait for you just beyond the barrier. The Old Ones could not lead you back to their portal without venturing out into Mac Dara's territory. You would be trapped. If I could be with you, I could keep you concealed until you were safely out. But I will not go there, Clodagh; now is not the time for that. Take this, and use it only when you must." He passed me the egg-shaped stone, which felt smooth and cool in my hand. "Throw it to the ground and it will provide concealment for a time. It will not hide you long; you must choose your moment carefully."

"I will," I said, stowing the stone in my bag and trying not to look astonished. However accomplished my uncle might be as a druid, I had not expected him to be in possession of an item so like a sorcerer's charm.

"One more thing," Ciarán said. "I have never met this Lord of the Oak, but his arrival in these parts has interested me. I have made a study of him over the last few years. Clodagh, this is extremely dangerous for you. Do not attempt it unless you are fully aware of what the consequences could be, not only for Cathal, but for you as well. Your father will be appalled that I did not prevent you from going."

"I know that I could die. Just as Cathal knew, when he chose to come with me, that he was at risk of losing his future in the human world. The stakes are very high."

"You could die. Or you could suffer a different fate. Mac Dara likes women. Has it occurred to you that he may decide to take you for himself?"

"I don't think he would do that," I said, shuddering in disgust at the very idea. "He did make a comment along those lines, but he was just saying it to goad Cathal. I shouldn't think I am the type to interest him in that way."

"Maybe not," Ciarán said. "But he could have other motives. From what you tell me, he's spent years trying to lure his son back to the Otherworld. To the extent that his kind can love, he loves this only boy of his. He might assault you as a demonstration of power or to punish Cathal in some way. He's devious."

A plan had begun to form itself in my mind as he spoke, a plan that just might win me some time alone with Cathal, if I could bring myself to try it. I found myself reluctant to speak of it. To put such an outrageous idea into words might cause me to lose my courage. "Is it true that the Fair Folk can't understand selfless love?" I asked him.

"Indeed," Ciarán said, and his face was a very image of sorrow. "They don't see the point of it. For them love is tied up with power and influence. Mac Dara prizes his son because through him he can exert control over his realm for generations to come. He values Cathal as another self, a younger, fresher, more energetic one. Such a parent works hard to impart his own knowledge and his own skills; to impose his own view of the world on his child. I know it from experience. It can be hard to resist, especially with promises of untold power held out as reward. But it comes at a most terrible cost."

"And so," I breathed, frightened by the speed with which my plan was taking shape in my head, "having a son to carry on after him is what Mac Dara values most of all. He would expect Cathal, in his turn, to father sons."

Ciarán regarded me in silence. After a little, he said, "You must not make him promises you intend to break. He would destroy you."

"I won't," I said, though the plan might take me perilously close to it—I would have to stay alert and keep my wits about me, no matter what happened. Even if Mac Dara hurt me. Even if he hurt Cathal. I hoped I was strong enough.

"By all the gods," muttered Ciarán. "I wish there were some way I could aid you further."

"It's probably better not," I made myself say. "I let Cathal help me, and look what's happened to him. I do have a question."

"Ask it, Clodagh."

"That charm, the verse . . . If there are three or four versions of the story, and the last two lines are different in each one, how can I know which one Mac Dara spoke when he worked the spell over Cathal? Supposing we could make ancient enemies into friends, and somehow tame the sea, impossible as that sounds. Mac Dara could turn around and say he didn't use that version of the rhyme, but one in which the last part was something different. *You'll be mine forever more, until the stars tumble from the sky and Eilis volunteers to do the mending.* It could be anything at all."

My attempt at humor had brought a faint smile to Ciarán's lips. "If that was the story as the old woman told it," he said, "then that is the correct version of the rhyme. Willow gave you the key to undoing the charm. It seems she wished to help this much younger brother of hers. That she did so cryptically, through a tale, was doubtless for her own protection. Mac Dara's anger is greatly to be feared. Should the last part of the rhyme become true, he will be obliged to let his son go. How could an old woman know such a thing? I expect there were witnesses to the casting of the charm. If a wandering storyteller asked those witnesses a question or two, why wouldn't they answer? Mac Dara has at least one weakness. Over the years, it seems he has underestimated women."

"But," I protested, finding it almost too much to take in, "Willow told that story a long time ago, well before Cathal and I went to the Otherworld. How could she know what spell Mac Dara was going to use? And why couldn't she just explain to Cathal the danger he was in?"

"You're not thinking, Clodagh." For a moment Ciarán sounded like what he was, a teacher of druidic lore. "The spell would have been cast long ago, on the day Mac Dara first discovered his son's whereabouts. It would have hung over the boy like a doom from that day forward. Who knows, Willow may even have heard it spoken. As for explaining to Cathal, would that have made him act differently? Would he then have left you to undertake your quest alone?"

I knew he would still have come with me. "All the same, it would have helped if she'd explained it to us."

"She is a storyteller. She gave you what you needed."

"I hope I'll know how to use it." My heart was beating hard with anticipation and dread. "Now I suppose I'd better be off, if you'll show me where to find the portal. Please don't give Father too many details about what I'll be trying to do. He'd be so worried."

"Bring what you need and I will take you to the doorway. You need not travel quite alone; Fiacha will go with you." Ciarán glanced at the predatory-looking bird on his shoulder, then back at me. "He can guide you, guard you and warn you," he added. "And he knows the way home." With that, the raven spread its dark wings, launched itself off his shoulder and flew to perch on a branch of a nearby tree. Its restless stance and piercing eye said quite plainly, *Come on, then.*

I shouldered my bag. "I'm ready," I said.

"One more thing," said Ciarán as we set off down the hill between the birches. "As I said, Mac Dara likes women. My advice would be to approach him in an apparent spirit of conciliation. Ask for Cathal back, since Mac Dara would think it odd if you didn't, but do it nicely. Let him talk; encourage him to confide in you. Perhaps he is not so unlike his son as you imagine. Play his game as long as you can. My guess is that he will see this as an opportunity to test how well Cathal has learned his lesson."

"Lesson?" My voice was shaking now.

"The lesson of forgetting," said Ciarán. "You must prepare yourself for any possibility, Clodagh. Even that the man for whom you risk so much may no longer want to be rescued."

CHAPTER 15

I bade Ciarán farewell at the entrance to a shadowy passageway that opened between rocks close by a spring. I could not tell if it was the same way by which the Old Ones had brought me out of the Otherworld. Sometimes the raven flew ahead, stopping with visible impatience for me to catch up, then winging on and leaving me no choice but to scramble after him. Sometimes he did not seem so confident, and rode perched on my shoulder, his claws sharp through shawl and gown. Without the Old Ones' torches it was dark; the faint glow of fireflies, clustered here and there on the tunnel roof, barely made the journey possible. In some places I had to feel my way with arms outstretched to graze the walls. My knees were soon bruised from falling; I jarred my left hip painfully on a spur of stone. My eyes longed for the sun. Even the strange, muted light of the Otherworld would be better than this.

I stopped twice to rest and forced myself to swallow food and water. Crouched there in the semi-dark with Fiacha's eyes on me, the only thing I wanted to do was go on walking so we could be out as soon as possible. But I must keep up my strength. I would need all my wits about me when we reached the other end.

There were obstacles. At one point I teetered on the edge of a drop, a breath away from plunging down into the unknown. I stepped back from the brink and blundered about in the dimness until I found a different way. There was a narrow place where water trickled down the stone walls and pooled under my feet; I ducked through, balancing Fiacha, and came out with my skirt dripping. Later I entered a cavern tented with spider webs of monstrous thickness, their occupants invisible in the dark corners from which these sticky nets were suspended. Fiacha stopped to probe a crevice with his beak; I saw him swallow something. Several times I came to what seemed dead ends, my progress halted by impassable barriers of stone. Each time there was a path to be discovered. One was the merest slit, concealed behind a rough protrusion. Fiacha hopped through and I squeezed after him, ripping my shawl. One was a tiny aperture at foot level, through which I made a wriggling, eel-like passage. Another seemed to have no opening at all, but when I set my hand against the rock wall and sent a silent request to the Old Ones for guidance, a little door appeared, just large enough for me to step through.

Day was over when we finally emerged in the forest of the Otherworld. Now to find the way to Mac Dara's hall. With luck he would be holding another audience tonight. If I could play this game right, he would at least agree to talk to me.

I walked forward under a stand of huge old trees that somewhat resembled oaks. Beneath my feet, dry leaves crunched; these forest ancestors were almost bare of foliage. The air was chill. Berries hung shriveled and dry on the bushes around me. A mist was forming in the forest, twisting its way around the boles of the trees like creeping fingers. The woods surrounding the nemetons had been alive with spring sounds, birds singing, insects chirping. The trees had been resplendent in new season's green. In Mac Dara's world it was autumn.

I ordered myself to be calm. I would be ready, no matter what. I would do this even if years and years had passed. I had the green glass ring, I had the necklace, I had the egg stone and I had Fiacha. And I had a plan, a plan that frightened me half out of my wits, but then the very notion of confronting Mac Dara would be enough to make most young women turn tail and flee, I thought. Perhaps, to survive in a place like this, a person had to be half mad; as mad as a man who would sacrifice his future to save a friend; as mad as a woman who could love a child made of sticks and stones.

Fiacha did indeed know the way. I followed him along the forest tracks to the grand avenue where the Fair Folk had passed on the night Becan was burned. I was about to step onto that open ground when the crow let out a warning caw and edged back along the branch where he was perched, letting the shadows swallow him. I shrank against the trunk of the tree.

Down the broad path beneath the arching boughs Mac Dara's folk came in their stately procession. Lantern light announced them; their strange, compelling voices lilted over the sward, laughing and singing, and the music of a harp rang out, with a whistle adding a piercing tune that made my feet want to dance, almost. The hooves of their horses made no sound on the soft grass; the great gray hounds that padded by them did not look to one side or the other, but only straight ahead. There was the man with the black owl—Fiacha shifted on his branch—and there the woman I had thought, for a little, was Deirdre of the Forest come to help me. Her lovely blue eyes were cold as frost. There was the person in the butterfly-wing robe, and there a lady all in brilliant feathers, tossing her head as she laughed at something the man beside her was saying. There was no sign of Mac Dara, or of Cathal. A new fear crept into my heart. Perhaps they had gone away, back to the west where the Lord of the Oak had his origins. Perhaps they had gone still further, somewhere I could never reach them.

I waited until the last riders in the procession were disappearing down the avenue, lanterns held high, then glanced up at Fiacha. He winged ahead; I took a deep breath and followed. We walked the green way in silence, though it seemed to me my heart was beating so hard it must sound like a drum announcing my approach. At the edge of the open space bordered by white stones, Fiacha flew up into a tree and settled there. He busied himself with preening his feathers. It was quite clear that he was not planning to accompany me any further.

"Wonderful," I murmured, looking up at him in disapproval. He ignored me. "Make sure you're close by when I need you, then." There was no way to tell if he heard or understood. For now, I was definitely on my own.

I stepped between the white stones in my plain, well-worn gown, and out among the assembled folk of the Tuatha De Danann. I held my head high and walked straight toward Mac Dara's pavilion. The hanging that concealed its doorway was closed and there was no sign of light inside. The entry appeared unguarded. I maintained a steady pace forward. Nobody was quite looking at me, but the crowd parted to let me through.

Outside the pavilion I hesitated. Last time, the Lord of the Oak had come out to greet me. Now the silken curtains remained closed. Mac Dara's hall looked deserted. But then, I had been told to be ready for tricks. I cleared my throat. I must try to sound both confident and courteous. "I am Clodagh, daughter of Sean of Sevenwaters!" I called out. "I seek an audience with the Lord of the Oak!"

There was a silence. Behind me on the open sward, the folk of the Otherworld had hushed their talk. Then the curtains parted and there was Mac Dara in the entry, looking me up and down, unsmiling. Behind him the pavilion was in darkness. "There is no audience tonight," he said flatly.

"I will not take up much of your time, my lord," I said, making myself dip into a curtsy. "I want to see Cathal. Tell me where to find him and I need trouble you no further."

His gaze was so blank as he stood there staring at me that I began to wonder if he was under the influence of a potent herb or mushroom, the kind that sends folk into a trance. Or perhaps he had been scrying and I had interrupted him. Then he said, "Come in," and ushered me into the pavilion.

The fire was out; the lamps were dark. There was a clammy chill about the place. Something was terribly wrong here. The only light came through the silk of the walls from the lanterns outside. It showed Mac Dara's lean face as pallid and lined, the dark eyes sunk deep in their sockets. He motioned to one of the cushioned seats and sat down on the other, long legs stretched out before him. "I should offer you a drink," he said vaguely, glancing toward the small table.

The same hearth, the same jug, the same goblets . . . I saw it again, Becan falling, the flames taking him; I heard my own shriek of anguish. "There's no need," I said. I could not look at Mac Dara without seeing Cathal. They were so alike, the two of them. There was a terrible sorrow on Mac Dara's face, and in it I saw Cathal broken, defeated, despairing, somewhere out there all alone. "My lord, is something wrong?"

He gazed at me in the dimness. "Why are you here?" he asked.

I must stick to the plan; I must not allow myself to feel sorry for this man who had done the unthinkable. "I don't know if you remember me," I said. "I came here with your son, and you made him stay. It's time for him to come back now. I'm here to fetch him home."

Mac Dara got up to walk restlessly around the pavilion, his dark cloak moving about him like smoke. "You've left it a long time," he said. "Why bother now? You should have wed a nice lad of your own kind and settled down to produce a brood of children."

"My lord, I went out from here one day and came back the next, by human counting. You say, *a long time*. How many moons have passed here in your realm since I went away?" *Don't say it's years,* I willed him.

"Remind me," said the Lord of the Oak, "what season was it when you last favored us with your presence?"

As if he would forget the momentous day when he had finally lured his son across the threshold. "Spring," I said.

"And it is autumn here, as you will have observed. You are not so lacking in your wits that you cannot make a count of seven turnings of the moon, daughter of Sevenwaters. Or did you imagine it to be far longer, long enough for his little friend to have faded entirely from my son's memory? Was that what you feared?"

My mouth was dry. "I knew that was possible," I said. "That's why I turned around and came straight back. My lord, I hope Cathal is well." I fought to keep my voice steady. "Well in body and mind. I did not see him ride by with your court tonight."

His lip curled. He stopped by the table and filled a goblet, then stood with head bent, looking down at it. "This can't be what it seems," he said. "My son would not attach himself to a woman who was stupid. What is your true purpose here?"

Why wouldn't he tell me if Cathal was all right? Had something terrible happened? The plan. I must stick to the plan. "Firstly," I forced out the words, "I wish to thank you for allowing me to leave here in safety before and to take my baby brother with me. I know you didn't have to do that. I owe you a debt of gratitude. My parents will be overwhelmed with joy to see Finbar back home."

Mac Dara fixed his dark eyes on me. "And yet you did not take time to deliver him to them yourself, that's if you're telling the truth about turning straight around. Who took him home?"

"My sister, who happened to be in the forest where I came out." I must move this on; I did not want Sibeal brought into it. "So, thank you on behalf of my parents for your generosity. It shows that the goodwill between the human folk of Sevenwaters and your people is not entirely gone, even with the departure of those my family knew somewhat better than yourself."

A wintry smile appeared on his face. "You did not think me so generous last time we met."

"I don't deny that. I was horrified that you would discard the changeling with so little thought. I hated what you did to lure Cathal in here."

"You refer to the attack on your father's holding in the southwest?" Mac Dara asked idly, making my jaw drop. "You found that excessive? It did burn very nicely. Provided a stunning show, I thought. And achieved its purpose. Along with your brother's well-timed disappearance, it sent Cathal running from Sevenwaters lest he bring down more havoc on the place. Which underlined his guilt in Lord Sean's eyes, as I anticipated it would. My son shared his vision with you, didn't he? The one in which a certain member of your family appeared in an unfavorable light? I was sure Cathal would feel obliged to warn his little friend. Don't look at me like that, young woman."

"You . . ." I breathed. "It was all your doing. You burned Glencarnagh. That lovely house . . ."

"Houses can be rebuilt. Even changelings can be rebuilt, so I've heard."

"People died in that fire," I said, outraged. His response had been so casual; so careless. He had spoken of Aidan's death in just the same way. "It was completely unnecessary, even in your scheme of things. Cathal was already gone by then—" I made myself stop. I was supposed to be placating the Lord of the Oak, not challenging his actions. "My lord," I said, "I've come here for exactly the reason I told you before. I love your son. I want him back. Will you please consider my feelings and Cathal's and let us be together? He never wanted this life. All he wants is to return to Inis Eala and be a warrior. And to have a family of his own."

"I am his family." The statement was final, absolute.

"You love your son. I understand that. I saw how my own father felt when Finbar was born: as if the whole world had changed. It is a powerful bond. But a son cannot love his father if that father denies him the future he wants, my lord. What if Cathal never comes around to your way of thinking?" This was risky; I based it on what I had seen in Mac Dara's face earlier, something akin to despair. "What if he just isn't suited to being a prince of the Tuatha De?"

Mac Dara looked me straight in the eye. "You're wasting my time," he said.

"Are you afraid to answer my questions?" Inwardly, I was quaking with fear.

"They are irrelevant. My son is here. He set foot inside my hall. That ensures he must spend the rest of his life in my realm. There is no charm strong enough to break that one. There is no enemy with the power to stand against me. Most certainly not you, young woman, courageous as you are. Perhaps foolhardy would be a more accurate term. Take my advice. Go home, find yourself a suitor Lord Sean approves of and live the rest of your life."

A deep breath. "That's just it," I said. "I love Cathal and only Cathal. He is the man I want to spend my life with. He is the man I want to father my children. I will have no other. Do not dismiss this as a girl's folly, my lord. I don't want a suitor of my father's choice. I want your son."

I had seen it in his eye as I spoke, a spark, a gleam of interest. He was quick. He had picked up the message I wanted him to hear.

"What if he doesn't want you?" he asked.

"Whatever you've done to him," I said, blinking back tears, "it can be undone. I believe that. I can see you're unhappy. Disappointed. Perhaps that's because your son has been more resistant than you expected."

"That's not your concern," said Mac Dara, dark eyes intent on me. "You know you can't have him. You know who I am and what power I wield."

"You took long enough to get him back," I said before I could stop myself.

He smiled again, thinly. "My son is strong," he said. "I would think the less of him if he had not fought me, evaded me, outwitted me. I would think the less of him if he had been quickly bent to my will. He's not leaving here."

I let the tears spill. "I knew all along that you would refuse," I said, wiping my eyes. Every word must be chosen to aid my plan. "But . . . it's very hard. If I can't have Cathal, I will never marry. He's the only one in the world for me. And it chills my heart to imagine the future alone, with no husband. I can't bear the thought that I will never have children of my own."

After a moment he said, "Children are easy enough to get. And you're a comely enough woman in your own way. There'd be no shortage of takers, I imagine." I saw in his eye that he would be all too ready to provide such a service himself.

"I do want a child, so much," I whispered. "But not just any child. I want *his* child. His son."

"Who would, of course, be my heir after Cathal," said Mac Dara. "Oh, you are a clever little thing."

He had seen right through my strategy. Clever? Compared with him I had the subtlety of a newborn babe. "Thank you," I said softly, continuing to play the game since I had no other plan ready. "You know what I really want. I want Cathal as my husband, for the rest of my life. I want him to live in my world. I want us to bring up our children together." It was easy to sound convincing, since my heart was in my words.

"You know that's not going to happen," said Mac Dara. "But perhaps there is room for compromise. Would you do it? Would you bear a son for Cathal, knowing you could not remain together? Knowing such a son would be yours only until he reached his seventh birthday? For I could not agree to such a plan unless I were sure my son's son would cross to this world when he was ready to be trained in the ways of his own kind. What if you raised your boy and then, when it was time, found that you could not bear to give him up? Such a dilemma would break you. Besides," he added after a moment, "chances are you would have a daughter."

I put my chin up and squared my shoulders. "You make the bargain sound very one-sided," I said. "Don't forget what I would bring to it. Whatever you may think of humankind, you should realize that my bloodline is as fine as can be found anywhere in Erin. Not only do I carry the lineage of the chieftains of Sevenwaters, but I also bear the blood of the Old Ones from time long past." Mac Dara hissed under his breath; I saw that perhaps this had been a mistake. "My son would possess both a flawless human heritage and the powerful blood of the Tuatha De, passed down by Cathal," I added. "Imagine what such a child could become. He would inherit not only your remarkable skills in the craft of magic, but the wisdom and strength of the human line of Sevenwaters. In time, he could be a peerless leader." *But not in your realm. I would make sure of that.*

The Lord of the Oak drained his goblet. I was trembling with nervousness, my hands pressed together, my palms sweating. I had no idea what he would say.

"Let me get this right." He fixed his dark eyes on me. "You are suggesting I should *replace* Cathal? My own son?"

"No, my lord. But even if Cathal became exactly what you wanted him to be, you would still value a grandson highly, I imagine. I don't want to give you my child. If I did, I would not be much of a mother. But I want to see Cathal, and I want his baby. To have that child for seven years would be better than never having him at all."

"You have truly surprised me," said Mac Dara, and I felt a surge of hope. "I'm forced to confess that I like your style. Supposing I agreed to this. Supposing I said you could have one night with my son, one night only, to do what you needed to do. There would still be an impediment to the plan."

"Oh?" I tried to sound calm.

"A man cannot put a child in a woman's belly, willing as she may be, if he does not desire her," Mac Dara said. "Have you observed a stallion or a ram when the females are in heat? His member stands up with excitement; his body readies itself for the fray in dramatic style. It is just the same with men, though I see from your blushes that you are not accustomed to hear such matters discussed so openly. And yet, here you are asking to share my son's bed tonight. Aren't you afraid, maidenly little thing that you are? Are you sure you're not lying to me?" The edge in his voice was dangerous.

I cleared my throat. "Of course I'm nervous. I've never lain with a man before. But I want to do it. Tonight. If I cannot take Cathal home with me, I will not stay here any longer than I must."

"You missed the point," said Mac Dara flatly. "He doesn't want you. He doesn't want anyone. Don't you think I've tried, offering him woman after woman over the months he's been here? Don't you think I've done whatever I could to break through that wall of reserve? I provided him with a girl fashioned in your exact likeness. Cathal was as indifferent to her as he was to all the rest. And it's not as if you are an expert in the art of seduction. The unpalatable truth is that my son's just not up to it. If you're after a child of your own, you'd be better to let me give you one."

He must surely see me shaking; he must surely hear the terror in my voice. "It is Cathal's child I want," I said. "As for his capacity to . . . perform . . . I will deal with that when we are alone together. I wish to have this time undisturbed. And unobserved. A woman does not want others to spy on her intimate moments."

Mac Dara's brows shot up. In that moment he looked painfully like his son. "Oh, you set conditions?" he drawled. "Then I will make my own absolutely clear. On his seventh birthday your son is mine. You give him up to me willingly."

My heart was pounding. Finding the right words was like teetering along a thread. *You must not make him promises you intend to break,* Ciarán had said. *He would destroy you.* "If I conceive a son from tonight's encounter," I said, "then I will give him to you when he is seven. I promise." If the Fair Folk could not understand selfless love, then Mac Dara would never dream of the possibility that Cathal might be willing, able and enthusiastic, and might still be prepared to restrain himself for the sake of our future together. I was counting on that. My belly twisted tight with apprehension. If I was wrong, there was everything to lose.

"Tonight's encounter or tomorrow night's," Mac Dara said, sharp as a knife. "Because that is the other condition. If my son can't perform, if he's incapable of bedding you tonight, then I have you tomorrow. That way you get two chances of a child. The bargain's not ungenerous. If it's a girl, as so many of my progeny have been, you'll get your daughter to keep with no conditions at all. If you don't conceive, you can go home and put all this behind you. You won't be pristine on your wedding night, but it seems that doesn't bother you." His lips twisted in a smile that was the twin of Cathal's at its most sardonic.

I drew a deep, shaky breath. "I agree to your terms if you agree to mine," I said. If this went wrong, if I were forced to lie with this hideous man, my life and Cathal's would be forever blighted by it. If it went as I planned, I promised myself I would never, ever take risks again. I would devote myself to a life of mending my husband's shirts and cooking him nourishing soups. "You're to leave us alone tonight," I reminded him. "No spying. No scrying. No coming in the door. This is just the same as a wedding night and it's private."

He laughed. "I fear you will find it a deep disappointment. But we'll make up for it tomorrow night, I promise. As for the spying issue, I won't peep. I doubt there will be much worth seeing."

"I want your word on it. And that I will be allowed to return home safely afterward."

He looked astonished, as if it were remarkable that there existed in the world someone who might believe his word was a thing worth having. "I give you my word, then," he said. "No spying. But I'll have to leave the guards on the door. I don't trust anyone, not even those who seem too weak to be a threat. As for the other, I'm willing to spend a night with you to get a child, but I can't think of any reason why I would want to keep you. Shall we go?"

He led me out of the pavilion. It was quite dark now, a moonless night, and the sward where Mac Dara's people had been gathered not long ago was completely deserted. A chill breeze sent dead leaves tumbling across the withered grass. I wondered if the glittering company had moved elsewhere once it became clear that their lord did not intend to entertain them tonight. Or maybe time was playing tricks again, and hours had passed while I was pleading my case. I was glad that I need not endure those people's uncomfortable stares. I felt transparent, with such a tumult of feelings inside me that they must be plainly visible. Mac Dara must know that I planned to trick him. How could he not? Was I walking straight into a trap? Somehow it didn't matter anymore. All that mattered was that in a short time I would see Cathal again.

We did not walk far. Mac Dara took the lantern that hung outside his hall and carried it as we made our way across the circle, out between the white stones and along a crooked path between thornbushes. I glanced surreptitiously to left and right, back over my shoulder, up into the dark shadows of the trees, wondering if Fiacha would make an appearance and whether Mac Dara might find the bird in any way suspicious. *There is no enemy with the power to stand against me*, the Lord of the Oak had said. And Ciarán had said, *There is a time for everything, and now is not the time for me to do battle with Mac Dara.*

"Here." Mac Dara halted so abruptly that I walked into him. He put out a hand to steady me and I forced myself not to shrink away.

"Where?" I said, looking around me and seeing nothing that resembled a dwelling or shelter.

The Lord of the Oak pointed ahead. The path skirted a rock wall grown over with briars. In a curve of this wall the lantern light revealed a darker space: the entry to a cave. Something moved. I started, gasping with fright. A hooded figure stepped out of the shadows; a spear gleamed in a gauntleted hand. "All's quiet, my lord," a man's voice said.

"She can go in," said Mac Dara. "Don't disturb them before morning. Alert me if there's any trouble."

"Yes, my lord." The man retreated. I could see now that another, similarly clad, stood to the far side of the entry.

"You keep your own son under armed guard?" I asked. "What are you afraid of?"

"You're wasting time," Mac Dara said. "If you want what you came for, you'll need to start working on him straightaway. Go in."

"Remember what I said. No spying." Gods, I could not stop shaking. Cathal was in there, so close. My heart was ready to leap out of my breast.

"Do you doubt Mac Dara's word?" He sounded as if he was smiling. A moment later he turned on his heel and was gone, taking the lantern with him.

My eyes were slow to adjust to the darkness. After a little, I discerned a faint, flickering light coming from within the cavern. Ignoring the guards, I put my hand against the wall to guide me and edged through the opening.

A candle burned on a rock shelf not far inside, and another on a small table. Their fitful light illuminated a space that resembled more closely the cell of a druid or scholar than the habitation of a prince, or indeed a place of confinement. The shelf bed was narrow and looked hard; a blanket lay at its foot, folded with perfect precision. There was no hearth and the place was cold. A stone table had a stool set before it. Cathal was sitting there, his back to me, a parchment spread out before him, a quill and ink pot on the table to his right. He was clad in black, just like his father. "Go away," he said without turning.

"Cathal." My voice came out as a nervous croak. "Cathal, I'm here." Part of me longed to rush forward and throw my arms around him. A wiser part held me where I was.

For the space of a breath he went completely still. He might have been turned to stone. Then he said, "A pox on my father. Can't he think of something new? I said go. I don't want you." He could have been the Cathal of early spring, the one whose cruelly dismissive comments had so irked me.

"Cathal. Turn around and look at me."

I saw him take a deep breath before he moved, as if to fortify himself. Perhaps there had been a whole string of women who looked like me, spoke like me, pretended they were Clodagh of Sevenwaters come back to fetch him as she had promised. Then he turned, stood, and looked into my eyes.

"Go away," he said. "You're wasting my time." He looked wretched; he looked years older than before. There were deep shadows around his eyes and his face was grooved by lines of sorrow. He was so thin—not the lean, fit warrior who had done battle with such skill and flair in the courtyard at Sevenwaters, but a pallid, sorrowful wraith of a man. My heart bled for him.

I walked across and sat on the edge of the hard bed. "Then I will waste it until morning," I said. "That's the time I've been given by your father, no more, no less, and I don't plan to head back home without making best use of what little he's allowing me." I struggled for an easy tone. The sight of him wrung my heart, and I could not keep the anguish from my voice. "Cathal," I said, "in our world, the human world, only one day has passed since I left you in your father's hall. I'm sorry it has been so long for you. I thought you knew me well enough to be sure I would come back, no matter how much time it took." I must be careful, very careful. I did not for a moment believe Mac Dara would forego the chance to watch us and, if he could, to listen to every word. Such a man placed no value on promises.

"Uh-huh," said Cathal, folding his arms and leaning against the wall so his face was in shadow. His eyes were intent on me. On the table beside the writing materials, something was emitting a faint glow. Not a lamp; a flat object that I could not identify from where I was. There were a mortar and pestle there as well, and stalks of yarrow in a jar. Had Mac Dara's son taken up divination? I took heart from the fact that he had been engaged in some activity, not sitting in the dark with his thoughts. Wretched as he seemed, perhaps he was not yet defeated.

"How can I prove to you that it's really me?" I asked him. "The marks on my face from when we crossed the river on the raft and watched Aidan fade into the mist behind us? The burns on my hands from trying to save Becan? Or should I sing the song?"

"No!" he snarled. I saw him gather himself, then he said more quietly, "You are no different from the others. If not a woman of my father's procurement, changed by his arts to resemble her, then a phantom from the recesses of my own mind. A dream sent to torment me. How many times must I say it? *I will not play this game.*"

"It's not the game you think," I said softly.

"Then what is it? I can never be free of this place; I can never be free of *him*. If you were really Clodagh"—his voice cracked as he spoke my name—"and if you had spoken to that man before you came to me, you would know that he will never release me. It's in the charm, isn't it? I knew what would become of me the moment I heard that old woman telling the story."

"There was guidance in all three of her tales," I said. Best be careful with this particular thread of conversation, if Mac Dara was listening. "Clues. Answers. If I'd understood them, I could have stopped you from coming here at all, let alone stepping across your father's threshold. Even the silly tale about the clurichaun wars had a message in it." I twisted the green glass ring on my finger and saw his gaze sharpen.

The object on the table glowed more brightly for a moment, then dimmed.

"What is that?" I asked.

"Are you blind? It's a mirror. As Mac Dara's only son, I'm required to keep up appearances. No more throwing on an old cloak."

My heart did a peculiar somersault in my chest. He knew me. For all the outward defiance, it was in his choice of words, and it was in his eyes, careful as he was to mask the spark of recognition. Careful because he believed, as I did, that Mac Dara was watching every move and listening to every word. Perhaps Cathal had known me from the moment I came in here, when he had frozen at the sound of my voice. "If that's your idea of keeping up appearances," I said, "you're not doing much of a job. Why don't you let me attend to your hair, at least? It looks as if it hasn't seen a comb since last spring." I rose and approached the table.

"No!" He edged back along the wall, out of my reach. "Don't try your tricks on me!"

"Look at it this way," I said, glancing at the little round mirror on the table and seeing that this was indeed the source of the strange light that came and went. "If I'm a dream, I can't do you any real harm, can I? And if I'm not, I'm an ordinary human girl, too powerless to have any effect on you, and certainly incapable of influencing such a mighty prince as your father. All I have is what you see before you." I motioned to my own form in its plain homespun gown. "That's what I have to trade, and that's what I'm offering. Not forever; you're right about that, he refused to allow it. Only for tonight. You called me *beloved*, once." My voice shrank to a whisper, for this part of the game went very close to the bone. "For a little, I believed you thought me beautiful. Desirable. But perhaps I was fooling myself, as women do. We're all too ready to believe the words of flattery men use to obtain what they want. To father the sons they want. I see in your eyes that you are as much of a liar as he is."

His mouth tightened. It hurt me to wound him. I was by no means sure that the two of us were playing the same game, only that the intention was to deceive Mac Dara until we might evade his scrutiny for long enough to speak honestly. How might the Lord of the Oak be lulled? What would make him weary of watching us? Seeing my clumsy attempts at seduction fail, or the opposite? And how could I convey to Cathal that I, too, was playing a part for his father's benefit?

"Here," said Cathal, taking a comb out of his pocket and putting it on the table. "You may as well make yourself useful. But no tricks. I know what you are. I know why he sent you. You're doing a more convincing imitation than the ones before you, but I'm still not interested. All my father wants is to see me use a woman as casually and heartlessly as he did my mother. You speak of fathering sons. If I accepted what you seem, rather ineptly, to be offering, if I lay with you tonight in the knowledge that you'd be gone tomorrow and I would never see you again, I would prove the point you just made—that I am my father's son not only in blood, but also in character and intentions." He sat on the stool with his back to me, and I reached to gather the dark hair that came well below his shoulders now. Seven turnings of the moon? Or far longer? Mac Dara was full of lies.

"You *are* his son, Cathal," I said quietly. "That means I can never have you for my own. He told me so. As for my being a mere simulacrum of the woman you once loved, all I can say is, nothing here is what it seems." I picked up the comb and began to draw it through his hair, working out the knots. I hoped he had understood me.

"A wilderness, tangled and wild," murmured Cathal.

"It is not so bad that it cannot be set to rights," I whispered, touching his neck with gentle fingers. Careful, careful; best if Mac Dara believed his son did not know me for who I was. If it seemed Cathal thought me yet another phantom conjured from his imagination, or some other woman charmed into the form of Clodagh, his father would be less likely to anticipate what was to come.

We were still deep in Mac Dara's realm, and there were only the two of us. I must tread with the utmost caution. I combed and combed, and as I did so I laid my hand on my dear one's neck, feeling the blood pulsing beneath my fingers; I stroked his temple; I used both hands to ease the tight muscles of his shoulders and heard him suck in his breath at my touch. Now he did nothing to stop me, though his eyes, in the little mirror, were at the same time bright with desire and as wary as those of a wild creature hunted. The worst thing about it was that I *did* want him, I wanted to touch and kiss and caress, I wanted to be held and stroked and loved. Feelings coursed through my body more powerful than any I had experienced before, lovely, urgent feelings that pulled me toward him as a swift-flowing river might carry a drifting branch. To make a show of my desire for Mac Dara's sake was wrong, all wrong. Yet if I wanted to save Cathal, that was what I must do. I must convince the Lord of the Oak that I was prepared to go through with his dark bargain.

I gathered Cathal's hair away from his neck and bent to touch my lips to the exposed skin.

"Don't," he said, his tone harsh. "Don't do this!"

"He said you'd be incapable," I murmured. "He explained to me that without desire a man cannot father a child."

"*What—*" He had spoken without thinking, caught off guard, and now he swallowed his words. "You would not lie with me if he were watching, surely," he said. "Whatever you are, whoever you are, you must have some sense of modesty. He always watches. There is no way to prevent that." His glance went to the little glowing mirror and immediately away.

"So you haven't availed yourself of the women he offered," I said, trying not to stare at the disc of polished metal. "It would seem you've become a scholar instead." Ciarán's necklace was in the pouch at my belt. It would be easy enough to slip it around Cathal's neck now. But not with Mac Dara looking on. If the Lord of the Oak saw me attempting this, he would know I wanted a great deal more than a night in his son's bed.

"It's been a long time," said Cathal, "and I'm not accustomed to being idle. I've worked on certain skills of which I had only the rudiments before." He had his hands on the table before him;

his first finger moved slightly, pointing toward the mirror. "One scarcely needs them in this place, but one must do something to fill in the time. I hope, one day, to make some kind of important discovery; something new to the craft of magic. But my progress is slow. My father finds that frustrating."

"Cathal," I said, and put my arms around him from behind, laying my head on his shoulder.

I felt his body tense, but he said nothing.

"Please," I said. "Please lie with me, just this once, just this one night, that's all I'm asking. If we can't be together as man and wife in the human world, at least I will have this to remember. I love you. I want you. You must know that." And as I spoke, although it was a game, although it was a deception, I meant those words with every part of my being. My body ached for him; my heart longed for him. I heard how my desire throbbed in my voice.

Cathal shook me off, getting to his feet. "No!" he said. "I won't listen to you. You do a good job of imitating her; so good you almost fooled me for a moment. But I know you are not Clodagh. You can't be. If she were here I wouldn't be able to keep my hands off her. I would hold her so close she'd beg me to let her breathe. I'd kiss her so hard she'd plead for mercy. I'd unfasten her clothing and lie with her on that hard bed, and what was between us would be as far above the ordinary congress between man and woman as the stars are above their pale reflections in the lake below. I know you're not Clodagh because when you touch me I feel nothing, you understand, nothing at all. You might as well be a creature made of twigs and leaves like that wretched changeling she so doted on. I want you to go now. For the love of all the gods, leave me alone."

If he was acting he was doing a fine job of it. His words made me sick with anguish. He had moved into the shadows by the wall again, his arms wrapped around himself, his eyes bright with pain.

"I see," I said, and my own voice was shaking with a hurt that was entirely real. "Well, that makes your position pretty clear. But I'm not going. The agreement is that I can stay until dawn, and that's what I'll be doing. So it looks as if I'll sit on one side of the chamber and you'll sit on the other, and we'll ignore each other until it's time for me to leave. That should be a fascinating way to pass the night. When he said you wouldn't be capable I didn't believe him for a moment. But it seems it's true. Being here has unmanned you. And it's blinded you. It's as if he's set a wall between you and what's in front of you, a barrier you can't see through to the truth."

I retreated to the bed again, seating myself upon it with my knees drawn up and my arms around them, my bag beside me. On the other side of the chamber, in the shadows, Cathal gave a strange little smile. "A wall to screen out truth," he murmured. "You believe my father has the power to create such a charm?"

No, I thought, doing my best not to look at the mirror. *But maybe you do. Maybe that's what you're trying to tell me. Is that thing somehow connected with Mac Dara? He sees us through it? No; then all you'd need to do to shut him out is turn it upside down. Can it be that it shows you when he's watching you and when he isn't?* Ciarán had implied that Cathal could learn to counter his father's magic, given time. And Cathal had already possessed an exceptional talent at scrying, even before he entered the Otherworld. Could he have acquired sufficient knowledge to devise this powerful tool so quickly? But then, perhaps Mac Dara had lied. Perhaps I had been gone not months, but years. "Your father can do anything he wants," I said. "Including what you seem incapable of. He promised me that if you couldn't oblige me tonight, he will do so tomorrow."

He blanched. Eyes blazing with fury, he made to speak, then clamped his lips tight.

"He did give you the chance to demonstrate your virility," I made myself say. "But you won't even try. I hate you, Cathal. I hate that you don't know me, I hate that you don't want me, I curse the day I met you. Now stop talking and leave me alone." I bent my head onto my knees, and although my speech was all pretense, the tears I shed were entirely real.

And then we waited. I sat on the bed; he stood against the wall opposite. We tried not to look at each other, but the space between us was full of the cruel words we had spoken and the tender ones we could not speak. It was alive with my longing to touch him, to hold him, to cling to him and never let go. In the silence, I could hear Cathal's words: *I would kiss her until she begged for mercy. I wouldn't be able to keep my hands off her.* And though he held his expression cool and distant, a flame burned in his eyes. What if Mac Dara never turned away his gaze? We could not attempt an escape in full view. If morning came and we had not lain together, and Mac Dara argued that it was because Cathal could not perform the act, I would be obliged to share my bed with the Lord of the Oak tomorrow night. I could be condemned to give him my firstborn son. For that, Cathal would never forgive me. I would never forgive myself.

A long time passed. My body was strung so tight with need that it drove everything else from my mind. I tried to breathe slowly, to relax, to work out a number of plans according to what happened next, but I could not. There was only me and Cathal and the aching distance between us.

And then, much later, the glow from the mirror dimmed, and dimmed further, and went out, and the flickering candles were the only light in the little chamber. Cathal took two strides toward me. As I rose, his arms came around me, holding me so hard I struggled for breath.

"Clodagh," he whispered against my hair. "Clodagh, you're really here, you came back at last, oh gods, it's been so long . . ."

I had no words. All I could do was press close, wind my arms around his neck, surrender to a kiss that was deep and hard and searching, feel his body against mine and know, without a doubt, that what Mac Dara had said about him was quite wrong, for it was plain as a pikestaff that Cathal wanted me as desperately as I wanted him. We fell to the bed in a tangle of arms and legs and garments, our breath coming fast and unsteady, our hands urgent, our bodies hungry. The mirror stayed dark; it seemed Mac Dara had found our long vigil poor entertainment. I fumbled with the fastenings of Cathal's shirt. His knee was between my thighs, his hand pushing up the fabric of my gown.

From outside, a harsh, derisive cawing assaulted our ears; Fiacha, without a doubt.

"No!" I said, suddenly still in Cathal's arms. "We mustn't, not even if there's time, not even if we want it more than anything in the world!"

"What?" Cathal was struggling to comprehend; his breathing was ragged. He sat up, adjusting his clothing.

"Cathal! We have to go! We have to get out of here right away! You heard what I said, he's made me promise to be with him tomorrow if you can't—"

"This makes no sense," he said, but he was getting up and putting on his boots even as he spoke.

"Trust me," I said, doing up the clasps of my gown with shaking hands. "I shouldn't have forgotten myself even for a moment. Saying I wanted your child was just a ruse to get me in here, I never expected him to—that is, of course I want your child, Cathal, but—never mind, I'll explain it all later. Did I guess right? Does the mirror show you whether he's watching?"

"More or less." He slipped the copper disc into a bag, scooped in a few other items from his worktable, threw on a cloak and looked at me with his brows up. "Is there a plan?" he asked.

"Not exactly," I said with a lump in my throat. "I have some friends, and some useful things that may help. But actually I was thinking you would come up with a plan for the next part. I was hoping that once I found you, you might have enough tricks and strategies to do the rest."

Cathal looked at me gravely. "I see," he said, and his mouth quirked into an uneven smile. I wondered if he knew me well enough to guess that this, too, was part of my plan. If he could not rescue me, if he could not lead our escape, he might never regain his self-respect. He needed to defeat his father; he must out-trick the Lord of the Oak. "I'd better think fast, then. Useful things. Such as?"

We were talking in whispers, for the two guards were doubtless still on duty outside. They would be the first obstacle.

"Such as this, to start with," I said, taking the necklace out of my pouch. "Bend closer. I think it will work better if I put it on you."

He did not bend but knelt before me, his arms around my waist. His dark eyes were steadfast, solemn. There was no trace of mischief there; perhaps his long lonely wait in the Otherworld had quenched that spark completely. "I love you more than life itself, Clodagh," he said. "Whatever happens, I want you to know that.

I hope I don't regret this forever. Tonight's missed opportunity, I mean." His smile almost broke my heart.

"There will be other opportunities," I said, tying the cord around his neck. When I was done, I let my hands rest there a moment. "Better ones. In more comfortable beds. I promise."

He brought my hand to his lips. Then he stood up, and his face changed from that of a lover to that of a warrior. "Tell me first," he said, "what power this charm has." His fingers went to the necklace with its little white stone.

"The same as the green glass ring," I said. "It's a charm of selfless love; it protects you from harm." I hesitated, a little embarrassed. "Actually, Ciarán said I'm your talisman; the necklace is extra. I think that means Mac Dara can't hurt you if you're with me. But he wouldn't want to hurt you, anyway."

Cathal's smile was grim. "True. He has plans for me. Clodagh, the bird that screeched outside—is it one of these friends?"

I nodded. "He knows the way out. He'll lead us."

"Anything else I should know?"

My mind leapt from Willow's last story to my discussion with Ciarán to what Mac Dara had revealed about the attack on Glencarnagh. There was no time. "Your mother," I said, choosing the most important thing. "I heard a tale about her, a true tale. She didn't kill herself, Cathal. She died trying to protect you from Mac Dara. She sent you away to keep you safe. And she . . ." I halted, seeing from his expression that this was not a surprise. "You know," I whispered.

"I have learned much in this place," Cathal said, and gave me the sweet, uncomplicated smile that he offered so rarely. "Things my father has never dreamed of, Clodagh. I have seen a boy fishing, and a woman on a bridge with her heart in her eyes. I have seen that my mother possessed a capacity for love equal to yours, and the same extraordinary strength of will. I thought that she had failed me. I believed her weak. It was my joy and my sorrow to discover how wrong I had been." He cleared his throat and added, "We'd best move without delay. Any more surprises?"

"I have a charm that I can use to conceal us, but only for a short time. I'm supposed to save it until we really need it. Cathal, the spell—the one about setting foot inside the door—that's vital to our escape. There's another part to it." I told him the rest of the verse. "That means there is a way to break the charm, impossible as those lines sound."

He lifted his brows. "We must make them possible. But first we must reach a portal. You realize he could decide to seek us in his scrying mirror at any moment? I don't imagine he trusts you any more than he trusts me, the son who refuses to fulfill his expectations. On the other hand he won't imagine you have so many tricks up your sleeve. You wouldn't have something to disable the guards, I suppose?"

"Sorry," I said, as a mixture of excitement and terror seized me. We were really going to do this. We were going to pit ourselves against the Lord of the Oak with his power and his magic and his complete lack of conscience. "You'll have to do that on your own."

It was soon apparent that Cathal's thin, wan appearance did not reflect any fading of his exceptional combat skills. He made me wait inside the cave while he dealt with the guards. I heard muffled shouts, the scuffing of boots on the ground and a squawk, then he was back, only a little out of breath.

"That bird has a sharp beak," he commented.

"Did he hurt you?"

"Fortunately, he seems to realize I'm on the same side as he is," Cathal said. "Coming?" He held out his hand and I took it. In his other hand was a dagger that had not been there when he went out. "I won't kill unless I must," he added, following my glance. "But my father will be angry, and his anger can be formidable. We'd best run, Clodagh."

"How can we see the way?" Beyond the last reach of the flickering candles from within the cave there was now a hint of moonlight, but it barely illuminated the path.

"I can see well enough. We'll follow the bird. Keep hold of my hand."

We ran, and I reminded myself that the man I loved was only half human, and that if we managed to escape this place I would probably discover far more remarkable things about him than an ability to see in the dark.

Fiacha did not seem to be leading us back to the portal through which he and I had entered Mac Dara's realm, though I imagined that was the nearest. We splashed through a shallow stream, climbed a steep hill under beeches, crawled through a mess of prickle bushes—the crow flew over the top—and emerged, trying not to curse aloud, in front of another rock wall. From somewhere higher up, Fiacha cried out in his harsh voice. As soon as I stopped moving my legs began to shake. My breath was coming in gasps.

"It looks as if we're supposed to climb," Cathal said. "I'll help you, Clodagh. From up there we may get a useful view."

The unspoken message was clear: sooner or later Mac Dara must notice that we were gone and come after us. The more ground we covered before then, the better our chances. I clenched my teeth, found hand and footholds in the rock and hauled myself up.

On my own I couldn't have done it. Ignoring Fiacha's impatient cries, Cathal climbed close by me, helping me find my grip, murmuring advice and encouragement, keeping calm even though I was so painfully slow. We were almost at the top when the tone of the crow's call changed and so did the light. Below us in the forest torches flared, and in the air above us there was a creaking sound, as of leathery wings, and a harsh cry that set terror in me. That call took me back to the raft and those things that had dived and slashed me. My eyes screwed themselves shut. My hand slipped and I clutched wildly at the rock face.

"Here." Cathal's hand came over mine, directing my fingers to a chink. "Grab hold and pull yourself up; there's a foothold to the right. Ignore those things. The crow will see them off. You're about two arm's lengths from the top, Clodagh. You can do it."

"Torches," I muttered as I pulled myself up. "Down there."

"One more stretch . . . Cursed creature!" Cathal swiped at a diving form with one hand while clinging on with the other. "That's it, Clodagh. Lift your left foot about three hand spans and slightly to the left. Good. You should be able to grip the foliage at the top now, but don't put all your weight on it . . . Good girl, you've done it." He boosted me over the edge, where I sprawled in a heap. A battle was raging in the air above me, a screeching, creaking, flapping combat. It seemed unwise to look up. I heard Cathal hauling himself over the edge, and a moment later the noises ceased. As I sat up, a black feather floated down onto my lap.

I made myself look. In the dim light, I saw the crow perched on a low branch nearby, his wings a little tattered, his eyes as bright and shrewd as ever. There was no sign of his opponent. Or opponents. It seemed altogether likely that Fiacha was a warrior unparalleled, the same as Cathal, able to despatch several enemies with ease.

"Come on," Cathal said. "We have a momentary advantage, but only that."

There was no running here. A dense thicket crowned the rock face, and the moonlight did little to illuminate the narrow pathway down which Fiacha was leading us. We could not walk hand in hand. Cathal made me go next after the crow, with him behind me. Out in the forest there now rang out all manner of noises: furious screams, hollow cries, a spine-chilling wail like that of the banshee. And voices, shouting. The trees were so close together, the net of branches and boughs and twigs, leaves and needles and vines so intricate that the least error could cause a person to be completely lost. I hoped very much that Fiacha's way would be the best, the safest, the one on which Mac Dara was least likely to find us. It surely wasn't the quickest.

"Keep moving," said Cathal, and I heard an edge in his voice. "Maybe it opens up ahead. This can't go on forever."

He was right. A hundred paces further on the terrain changed again, dense growth giving way abruptly to more open ground. I felt grass underfoot and smelled something sweet, like curative herbs. This was oddly like a shorter version of the way Cathal and I had come in. We clasped hands again and, as Fiacha winged ahead, we ran. My mind was racing through the trials we had endured coming the other way, wondering how many of them we would have to face again, when a line of lights appeared in the gloom ahead. Fiacha flew up and out of sight. Cathal halted, looking back, and when I turned my head I saw a similar array of lights—torches, approaching—not far behind us. Cathal let go of my hand and drew his dagger.

"Did you say you had a concealment charm?" he whispered.

"Mm."

"Be ready to use it, then. Those are horses, and the riders will be armed. My father won't want me seriously hurt. But he'll have no hesitation in using you to force my hand. I think the ring will protect you, but I'd prefer not to put that to the test. It certainly won't stop him from separating us and despatching you back home. Employ your spell before it comes to that, or this will be over all too quickly. I cannot fight so many."

"All right." I tried to breathe slowly; I tried to remember exactly what Ciarán had told me.

The riders drew closer. All wore hooded robes of gray; all bore spears or swords or other weapons with spiked or pronged or serrated blades. There were scythelike cutters and stranger items that spoke of spell craft. The two lines approached in silence from before and behind. When they were a certain distance away they deployed in a circle with Cathal and me in the middle. The torches bathed us in a flickering red light.

One rider guided his horse forward, a tall, black animal with a dangerous eye. The rider dismounted and pushed back his hood. His dark gaze passed over Cathal and fastened on me. "So you were lying after all," he said. "You wanted far more than a night with my son. You lied to Mac Dara."

My heart hammered. "Didn't you expect that?" I asked. "We're in your realm, not mine. You must be used to lies."

"Perhaps she didn't tell you," said the Lord of the Oak, walking closer to Cathal. "Your little human playmate gave me a promise tonight, and I expect people to keep their promises. It's clear you didn't perform for her. That may be just as well, since your child would have been forfeit if you had. Your failure means she's mine. Lord Sean's daughter promised to bear me another son if you couldn't give her one. A backup, let's say, in case you fail to come around to my way of thinking. We've seen how much Clodagh likes babies. She's perfectly happy to rear mine for me in the comfort of her father's stronghold and give him back when I want him. Isn't that right, Clodagh?" Beneath his outrageous, gloating smile, I thought I could see well-masked pain.

I could not look at Cathal. "That's not quite what I promised," I said through chattering teeth. "What I said was—"

"The exact wording is immaterial," said Mac Dara coolly. "At the very least, you owe me one night for the trouble you've caused me. Seize her."

Two of his entourage rode forward and dismounted, but before they could step any closer Cathal had put me behind him. "Lay a hand on Clodagh and I'll kill you," he said coolly. "I'll fight you while there's breath in my body. Of course, if my father is so disgusted with me that he wants me dead, I suppose that might suit him quite well. On the other hand, if you happen to make an end of me it's possible he may get quite angry. He doesn't have his replacement yet."

Mac Dara raised his black-gloved hand. There was something in the gesture that told me he was not directing his warriors to apprehend me or to attack Cathal, but was preparing to cast a spell. I slipped my hand into my pouch and took out the egg-shaped stone. "Now," I murmured, and threw it to the ground in front of me.

Instantly a blinding mist arose, a thick white blanket blotting out trees and rocks and horses, men and women and creatures. I could not see a hand span before my own face. I stood paralyzed, all sense of direction gone.

"This way!" It was Cathal's voice, and now Cathal's hand grasped mine and the two of us were running again, running blind through the vapor as the sound of hooves came after us. *Let the portal be near*, I prayed. *Let us find it soon . . .*

We ran until my legs would barely carry me; until my head was dizzy and my eyes were blurred. Still the mist clung. We could have been anywhere. My chest hurt and my legs ached. The terrain changed again, and now I could see skeletal forms of willow and elder looming through the mist. I could feel the ground underfoot becoming mossy and damp. Somewhere nearby there was a sound of moving water. Cathal's grip on my hand was tight enough to hurt. He was pulling me after him so fast I could barely stay on my feet. Behind us in the obscurity someone was shouting.

I was hauled bodily up a rise, over rocks slick with moisture. The eldritch vapor had begun to dissipate; Ciarán's charm was losing its potency.

"Got to—catch my breath," I gasped. "Fiacha—where's Fiacha?"

"I can't imagine." Cathal sounded odd. Something was wrong. Through the last shreds of mist I looked up at him and my heart stopped. The man who had been leading me, the man whose hand I had been gripping as if my life depended on it, was not Cathal at all. It was his father.

CHAPTER 16

I clawed and kicked, trying to wrench away, but he was too strong. He simply took me by the shoulders and held me at arm's length, his brows raised, his lips twisted as if he found my desperation mildly amusing. There was only one thing I could do. I sucked air into my lungs and screamed, "Cathal! I'm here!"

There was no reply. Now that the mist was gone, the boles of the trees shone like silver ghosts in the light of a low, invisible moon. Beyond them lay a broad, murmuring darkness; surely the same river we had crossed on that rickety raft when first we entered Mac Dara's realm. On the far bank stood an ancient, half-dead willow, whose weathered branches reached out across the water as if beckoning me home. I saw no raft, no rope. There was something, all the same; a pale line spanning the water, beneath the surface.

"There's no point in calling my son," Mac Dara said, his fingers tightening on my shoulders. "He's not much of a man, Clodagh. First he shows a complete lack of enthusiasm for your tempting offer. Then he passes you straight into my hands. That was the most basic of tricks. He should have thought of it himself, knowing how alike the two of us are."

"Alike?" My whole body was stiff with disgust. "You are no more like him than a maggot-ridden corpse is like a healthy, living creature. You disgust me. Let me go!"

"Oh, I don't think so." He drew me close, wrapping both arms around me and pressing my body against his. "Why don't we make that son now? It's peaceful here. You'll be assured of the privacy that's so important to you. And we've nothing else to do until morning."

"You have no right!" My mind edged closer to complete panic. There was no chance at all of breaking free, and I had used the only tool I had; used it up too soon, and for nothing. "The agreement was that I would let you do this tomorrow night *if Cathal was incapable.* He wasn't incapable, my lord." Gods, his hand was roaming all over me, making my flesh crawl. I would not let him do this.

"I can play those games, too," Mac Dara said. "Games of truth and lies. I'll outplay you every time. Look me in the eye and tell me my son made love to you tonight." He moved me away from him, both hands gripping me by the shoulders again.

"That would be a lie," I said, and saw his complacent smile. "But he could have. He was capable. He chose not to. That means I don't have to do this."

"I don't believe you," said Mac Dara calmly. "You're fresh, delectable, untouched. What man would turn down the opportunity of being first to sample you? If he didn't do it, it was because he couldn't do it." He drew me closer once more, and I put both hands against his chest in a futile attempt to fend him off. "You're afraid of me," he said, sounding surprised. "No need for that. I know how to please a woman, even an inexperienced one." He moved his hands to cover mine and his fingers touched the green glass ring. In that instant, his whole body became still. "What's this?" he said, and there was something in his tone that made my hair stand on end.

"Nothing," I whispered. A moment later he was wrenching the ring from my finger. He held the little talisman in his long, pale hand. Then he tossed it far away, somewhere out into the darkness among the trees, and it was gone. If I had thought myself afraid before, it was nothing beside the chill that entered my blood now.

"So," said Mac Dara. "That was why an insignificant human woman stood up to me for so long. That was what gave you the courage to come back and seek out my son. Foolish girl. I don't know where you picked that trinket up, but it's led you into a situation far beyond your capabilities. And now you've put exactly the weapon I need right into my hand. We'll skip the dalliance and send you home, I think. This way. I know how much you like the water."

Don't panic, don't panic, babbled a voice inside my head. *The ring was your protection, yes. That doesn't mean you should turn to a jelly now it's gone. Cathal needs you. Breathe. Use your wits.* But against that last spark of reason was the iron-strong grip on my arm, the purposeful tread of my captor's feet as he dragged me to the riverbank, the terror his last words had awakened in me. No screams now. I could not summon so much as a terrified squeak.

"We're here," said the Lord of the Oak, halting with me held before him, both of us facing the river. "See, I'm giving you a chance to get back home safe and sound. Let nobody say the Fair Folk are ungenerous. Just walk across the bridge and you'll be there."

The bridge was a single tree trunk, the remains of a forest giant. It spanned the breadth of the flow and lay a handspan under the swift-moving water. In the deceptive light, I would be lucky to advance three steps onto it before I slipped and went under. To cross would be a challenge even to a man with superb physical skills, Johnny for instance.

"Off you go, then," Mac Dara said, releasing my arms and giving me a little push. "And don't try to run away; I might be forced to do something you wouldn't like."

"I can't—" I began, and staggered as the little push became a stronger one, and I was forced down the bank and out onto the submerged bridge. "Please," I begged, stretching out both arms to keep my balance. The water tugged at my skirt; there had been no time to tuck it up before I was forced onto the log. The wood was slippery from long immersion. My boots could not get safe purchase on it. My heart was knocking about in my chest. "Please . . ." I stood there, wobbling, an arm's length out from the bank.

Mac Dara raised his hand and pointed it in my direction. I did not hear him speak the words of a charm, but fire flared suddenly between me and the safety of the riverbank, scorching, deadly, and I shrank away from it, moving further out along the bridge. My knees buckled; I forced them to hold. Now I couldn't even see the log bridge under the dark water. One more step and I'd be gone, swept away to oblivion. All for want of a handhold, or a shorter skirt, or a little more courage. *Cathal,* said a tiny voice inside me. *I love you. I'm sorry.*

Something hurtled toward me, arrow swift and dark as midnight. I ducked, screwing up my eyes in anticipation of attack. A sudden weight on my shoulder; claws digging in. As I straightened, a dangerous beak came around at eye level, holding a little item that glinted green in the moonlight. The ring. Fiacha had brought me the ring. And as I took it and slipped it on my finger, a familiar, beloved voice from further along the bank said, "Clodagh. Catch."

He was here. Cathal was here. For one blissful moment I felt relief, then I saw Mac Dara's hand outstretched toward me, and the flame bursting forth anew from his fingers. Cathal's cloak passed through the fire on its way to me. My boots slid wildly on the log as I snatched at it. The crow winged up out of harm's way, and somehow I got the garment around my shoulders, the hood over my head. *You've got the ring. Cathal's got his necklace. We're at the portal. Don't you dare lose your balance.*

"Oh, take off the hood." Mac Dara's voice, a lazy drawl now. "Let's see that flaming hair go up." Fire on either side of me, swirling, scorching. I shrank back inside the cloak, heart thudding, and the eldritch flames sizzled into the river. "Fool!" spat Mac Dara, the mocking tone quite gone. He was not addressing me. "You would throw away the riches I lay before you for *her*? She's nothing. No great beauty even by human standards, and a meddler besides. Persist in this and I'll be obliged to show you just how disposable your little friend is."

"Clodagh," Cathal said. He was standing not far along the bank, looking perfectly calm. He had his eyes fixed on his father and did not spare me a glance. "Trust me."

"Oh, that's right," said Mac Dara. "Just as she trusted you to hold onto her the last time she fell into deep water. The little tricks you've picked up since you came here are insignificant, Cathal. Against my magic they are as candle flames to a great conflagration. I had hoped my son might be made in my mold; lover, warrior, leader without peer. How long must I wait to see that promise fulfilled?"

"You will wait forever." Cathal stood relaxed and still, his hands loose by his sides, his gaze locked with his father's. "My future lies in the human world. It lies with Clodagh. I want nothing of what you offer. I want neither riches nor power, and I have no interest at all in the craft of magic."

"No?" Mac Dara's brows went up. "I find that hard to believe. Perhaps you are frustrated that your progress is so slow, but you can learn, Cathal. You just deflected those flames, didn't you?" Was I wrong, or had a slight tinge of uncertainty entered his voice? "As for riches and power, there is no man in the world who does not desire those."

The current pulled like a wild horse. Surely the water was deeper, almost up to my knees now, though I had advanced no further along the submerged bridge. My back hurt. My legs hurt. My head felt dizzy. *You've got the ring, you've got the ring,* I chanted silently to myself. *Be brave. Be strong.* My body was seized by convulsive shivers—cold or fear, perhaps both. Despite this, I became aware of activity above me. In the trees on either bank and in the air over the bridge there was a continuous, rustling movement, like birds' wings or the passing of a breeze through leaves. It seemed imperative not to look up. I recognized purpose in Cathal's stance, intent in the way he was holding his father's gaze. I held as still as I could, willing my legs to support me just a little longer.

A surge smacked into me. Not only was the river rising, it was changing. Its smooth flow had become turbulent, its surface bouncing and splashing and spraying as if stirred by a mischievous hand. Not content with burning me alive, Mac Dara was going to drown me at the same time. The water rose to my hips, to my waist, and I could stand against it no longer. As I toppled, gasping in terror, lines dropped down on either side of me, strong, green ropes spanning the river at waist height. I grabbed first one, then the other, scrabbling to get my feet secure on the log bridge. No time to question. I clung, sucking in a shuddering breath, and felt solid wood beneath my boots. *He can't kill me if I've got the ring,* I reminded myself as trees and water and riverbank swam around me in a haze. Waves were breaking on either shore with sounds like blows; the river was as choppy as if it were coursing over jagged rocks. Spray danced around me as it grew deeper still, its embrace chilly and urgent. I shut my eyes, clutched the ropes and prayed.

Cathal's voice rang out, clear and cool. "This is over, Father." As I opened my eyes, I saw him raise his hand and gesture toward the water. It was a graceful, fluid movement, something akin to the dance of fronds in the current.

The river calmed. The eerie turbulence subsided; the surface became as still and glassy as a forest pond. I stood swaying on the log bridge, my chest heaving, my gown sodden, as the water level went down until it was no deeper than my ankles. The place grew quiet save for that odd rustling overhead. On the bank Mac Dara stood like a statue in pale marble, staring with disbelief at his son, who now looked up toward the trees on the far side of the river.

I followed Cathal's gaze. There were figures swarming in the ancient willow, running out along the branches, as nimble as squirrels. They passed and passed again, working with fingers like twigs, pale and slender. And on the near side, others performed the same work, weaving, making, throwing out ropes of vine and creeper to span the waterway from side to side. So quickly they wove! Their craft was a thing of deep magic, conjured from earth and air, and my breath caught in my throat as I watched them. In the twinkling of an eye they had a third rope across the river, and a fourth. With those supports, and with the water low and calm, a confident man or woman might reasonably attempt a crossing even by night.

I saw Mac Dara raise his arm, then lower it again as Cathal said, "No, Father. *Till waves are calmed by human hand,* remember? Thanks to my mother, that brave woman whom you so wronged, I can claim human blood. And thanks to her I have a certain knack with water. You are too late. The charm is undone."

Cathal stepped down to the riverbank. As he moved, a small figure cloaked in gray emerged from the forest higher up. One hand supported the silver dog mask that covered its face; in the other it was carrying Cathal's pack. Mac Dara did not stir as he watched the creature scramble down to stand beside his son at the water's edge. On the opposite bank, I could see the hedgehog-dwarf anchoring a rope, and the being that looked a little like a rock passing something up to the folk in the trees, and the owl-faced creature perched on a low branch, apparently giving instructions. My breath caught in my throat. *Till ancient foes in friendship stand.* Cathal had done it. He had won their trust, and he had broken the spell.

"Thank you," he said to Dog Mask, taking the pack. "Please convey my deepest gratitude to all your kind. Without your aid, and without theirs," glancing up at the folk of the trees, who were finished their work of making and now clung half-concealed in the foliage, bright eyes observant, "I could not have made my way out from this place. I owe you a debt."

Mac Dara was no longer trying to hurl bolts of fire. He stood preternaturally still, and his face was as white as chalk. His eyes were desolate. He looked as my mother had looked when we told her Finbar had been stolen. I understood, in that moment, that love is not always simple; that choices can be right and wrong at the same time. Even now, with hope springing high in my breast and home so close I could almost smell it, I knew that look of desolation would remain forever in my mind. He opened his mouth to speak, and I cringed, expecting a curse, a charm, some final malign attempt at sorcery. But all he said was, "I was wrong." Not an apology; he was incapable of that. An acknowledgment that his son was indeed everything the father had hoped he might be, and that the moment of realization had come too late. The spell was undone. There was no remaking it.

"Goodbye, Father," Cathal said. "I'll be going home now. You underestimated me. In all the long time you have held me here, I have spent every single moment preparing to leave. I have learned new skills; I have put into practice those I acquired in the human world, such as the ability to make alliances and to judge who can be trusted. And I have begun to learn the lore and craft of my mother's line. There was one thing you failed to understand. For me, hope never died." He looked up into the trees. "I won't forget how you helped me," he said, and the strange folk there bowed their heads to him as if he were a king.

He stepped onto the bridge, turning his back on the Otherworld. Our hands on the guide ropes, we walked across, and the water was so tranquil around our feet that I could see little glinting fish beneath the surface, illuminated by the moonlight.

"Farewell," came the voice of Dog Mask, but when I glanced back I could not see the little creature on the bank, only Mac Dara, black cloak, white face, lips set grim as death, and above him in the willows, the forms of the tree folk with their curious draping garments of leaves and cobweb and moss, their strange faces and drifting hair. Just for a moment I saw her, high in the branches—a creature very like myself in build, a small, graceful woman whose eyes were big and bright in the dim glow of the invisible moon, and whose body seemed made from all the loveliest fragments the forest could offer. In a sling on her back she bore a child wrapped in a woolen shawl, and as she passed she lifted a hand to me in greeting and farewell. Then she swung up into the canopy and was lost to sight.

In other circumstances I would have found the crossing terrifying, for the submerged bridge was still slippery and the vine ropes provided only flimsy support. Now I walked over with my head high and my back straight, like a warrior after a long and well-fought battle. Just before we reached the other side, I remembered something.

"Right foot first, Cathal," I said.

"Of course," came his voice from behind me, shaky now, whether with laughter or exhaustion I could not tell.

The bridge did not quite span the river. It ended at the old willow, and we clambered down, not onto dry land but into knee-deep water floored with round stones that shifted under our feet. When I slipped and almost fell, Cathal caught me. When he teetered, on the verge of losing his balance, I steadied him. As we stepped out onto the shore, right foot first, the forest before us sprang into light, dawn rays slanting sudden and golden through spring foliage, birds caroling overhead, flowers raising tiny, bright faces from the dappled shade beneath the oaks. My cheeks were suddenly wet with tears, and when I looked up at Cathal, he too was weeping.

"We're home," I said. "We're finally home."

He wrapped his arms around me, holding me close. "You know," he whispered, "I said once I'd tell you how it felt to cry with you watching. It feels good. It feels better than I could ever have imagined." A pause. "Clodagh, did you really promise my father your firstborn child?"

"Not exactly," I said shakily. "I worded it carefully. *If* I conceived a child last night after lying with you, and *if* it was a boy, I would give him up when he was seven. Your father agreed, on the proviso that if you proved incapable of the act—that was what he expected—I would lie with him the next night and give up any son resulting from that union. Don't look like that, Cathal. If I hadn't had some kind of plan, Mac Dara wouldn't even have let me see you. He certainly wouldn't have allowed us time alone together."

Cathal gave a low whistle. "What possessed you to take such a risk? You've become worse than I am. And what's all this about being incapable? Did you believe my time in that place would have unmanned me?"

"Of course not," I said. "But I thought you'd be able to show self-restraint. Knowing the story of your mother, I imagined it would be important to you that we waited until we were married before sharing a bed. All along I had faith that if I could reach you you'd be able to get us safely out."

"By all the gods," he observed mildly. "In view of our past history, your belief in me is astonishing."

"I believe in the man you are," I said, realizing how utterly exhausted I was and how many aches and pains there were in my body, yet knowing I was happier than I had ever been in my whole life. "I love that man, with all his tricks and oddities."

"It's actually not true, you know," he observed.

"What isn't?"

"That I wouldn't want to lie with you before we were married. Last night was a close shave, closer perhaps than you realized."

I found myself blushing. "I did realize, Cathal."

"But you're right, all the same," he said. "It would be correct to wait. That may not be what we want, but it's what we should do. We still have some challenges ahead of us, Clodagh. Your father . . ."

"He'll come around to the idea."

"I am the kind of man who would never be on his list of prospective husbands for his precious daughters."

"Shh," I said, halting and standing on tiptoe to kiss his cheek. "You're the son of a prince, aren't you? You're eminently well qualified. We'd best keep walking. I'm not sure how much longer my legs will go on supporting me."

Just once I looked back, but if the Otherworld had existed on the far side of that river not so long ago, there was no sign of it now. On either side of the waterway the forest was bright with springtime; on either side the morning sun shone, the flowers bloomed and the trees stood proud in their new season's raiment. Somewhere high above us a bird was singing as if its heart might burst with joy.

"Nobody to meet us this time," I murmured as we climbed a rise and looked around us for clues as to exactly where we were. "And it looks as if Fiacha's gone straight home." We reached a spot where a fallen tree lay across the path, and without saying a word we sat down close together with our backs against it. After all, there did not seem to be such urgency to walk on, to get to Sevenwaters, to explain ourselves. Right now, all we wanted was to be here, the two of us together, away from the rest of the world. The immensity of what had happened was beginning to sink in. It set a silence between us. I felt the tension in Cathal's body, and when I glanced at his face I saw that there was a struggle going on inside him.

"It was a long time, wasn't it?" I said eventually. "And it will probably take a long time to come to terms with it. Seven turnings of the moon, that was what your father said. But maybe it was more. I saw Becan. He'd grown a lot."

"It was long," said Cathal. "And I'm tired. But that will pass. Clodagh, before we move on there are some things I must tell you; some things you need to know."

"Tell me, then," I said. "You could start by explaining how you managed to be there, with the tree folk, at precisely the right time. Did Fiacha lead you? And what is he, exactly?"

"I cannot tell you what the crow is," Cathal said. "An ancient, powerful being of some kind, that is all I know. Yes, he led me to the portal, but my instincts would have drawn me there anyway, as they did the day I brought you into the Otherworld."

"As for what you did . . . I can't think what to say about that. There is one question I have to ask."

"Ask, then, Clodagh."

"If Mac Dara cast the original spell, including the part about calming the waves, what on earth possessed him to intimidate me by stirring up the river? Surely it would have been far safer to despatch me home through a tunnel like the one those smaller folk use to move between worlds. He should have chosen a place with not a drop of water in sight."

"Ah," said Cathal. He was avoiding my eye now. "I was waiting for you to ask about that. In fact, my father didn't make those waves. I did." And as I stared at him, not knowing if what I felt was admiration or horror, he added, "I'm sorry you were frightened. It was the only way I could think of to break the spell and get us out: to make the waves first, then calm them. My father wouldn't have dreamed I could do that. I never let him see me learning anything worthwhile. I never showed him I had any natural aptitude for magic. As for the other part of the charm, the ancient foes, I already had those; they had long since become friends and allies. Their capacity to conceal themselves more or less anywhere, to merge and blend, made it possible to win them over without my father's knowledge. They took the first step; that surprised me. It was on your account that they did so, Clodagh. Your courage impressed them deeply. As for the waves, there was a difficult moment when I realized you had lost the ring, but Fiacha has excellent eyes."

"It may take me a little while to forgive you," I said, managing a smile. "And you'll never be able to pretend to me again that you are an ordinary warrior, with no hint of the uncanny about you. No wonder your father looked stunned. How did you learn something so powerful?"

His grip tightened on my hand. "I had a memory, an old memory from childhood," he said, "of walking on the shore and feeling I could change the form of the waves if I thought about it hard enough. I befriended the Old Ones; it took time and patience. They brought me the story of my mother and steered me down the path to learning. But I am only a beginner, Clodagh. I never, ever intended Mac Dara to take you away. When you used the concealment charm, he was too quick for me. What he did not realize was that I could call in help when I needed it. I didn't waste my time in the Otherworld. Not only did I study hard, I formed alliances with those who were unhappy with my father's rule, and there were many. The Old Ones acted as go-betweens. Early on, the tree folk made me a promise of help; they believed they owed me, because you had cared for Becan. I fear they may pay a high price for coming to our aid. But they understood that risk. Clodagh, I can travel in new ways now; I can track my father as he tracks me. Fear gave wings to my feet, knowing he had taken you. Fiacha led the way. I alerted my friends; they came to my aid as they had promised. As for those tricks with the river . . ." For a moment he sounded very young and not at all sure of himself. "I'm so sorry you had to endure that. I had intended that we would cross together. Every part of me wanted to rush down and pluck you to safety. It took all my strength to stay where I was and to keep his eyes on me. I have to tell you that I was not certain my spells would work. You could have been burned. You could have drowned."

"I had the cloak," I said, not liking the shadow that had appeared in his eyes. "I had the ring."

"All the same." He sounded unconvinced.

"I thought the tree people were not strong enough to combat Mac Dara's magic," I said. "I'm sure Dog Mask implied that."

"On their own they could not stand against him," said Cathal. "But in the end they were not on their own. They were with me."

"Johnny would be impressed," I said in wonderment, thinking it had not been so surprising that the strange folk of the trees had looked at Cathal the way they did, with respect and awe, for he had become a prince and a leader.

Cathal smiled; the pinched, white look on his face retreated a little. "Maybe he would, though he should take some of the credit himself. Without the training he gave me and the example of character he showed us daily on the island, I would not have had the strength to endure this long ordeal. As for those unusual skills I have acquired, they could be seen as both good and bad, blessing and burden. The difference lies in the intent of the user. But I will not put those skills into practice here, Clodagh; not unless my father . . ."

"You think he'll keep trying to find you and to lure you across?" The idea was chilling.

"He won't like being outwitted. I don't think it ever occurred to him that I might befriend what he would consider to be the lesser races in his realm, despite the clue that was in his own verse. He believes them insignificant. He does not realize that there are good hearts there, slow as they may be to trust. Mac Dara has not spread his influence over all the lands and peoples of the Otherworld, though he might wish to."

I could not bring myself to say what was in my mind: that those people must surely want Cathal to come back, to stay, to stand up to his father and perhaps attempt to restore their world to something better and brighter. The idea was there, all the same, a shadow at the edge of this day's happiness. "He was angry to see us escape, certainly," I said. "But sad as well. What he said about being disappointed in you was rubbish. I expect that watching you outwit him made him proud even as it broke his heart. If he still wants you back, it's not to punish you, it's because you are his son and, in his own way, he loves you."

Cathal gave a crooked smile. "That's exactly what I would expect you to say, Clodagh. Your heart is so brimming with warmth and love that you see good even in a black-hearted tyrant like Mac Dara." He paused, looking down at our interlinked hands. "Clodagh, I have to tell you this before we walk on. I know how much your family means to you. You are dearer to me than anything in the world. But I can't stay at Sevenwaters. I can't live in the kind of household where you have grown up. It's not just that I am ill at ease in such company and unable to play by the rules. If I settled here with you I might bring down my father's anger on everyone in the place. I would certainly put you in danger. He knows you are the tool by which he can most easily control me. I only stayed out of his reach, those last few years in our world, because I was on Inis Eala where I'm screened from him. Clodagh . . ."

"I know this already, Cathal," I said, kneeling up and turning so I could meet his gaze. Gods, he looked thin and drained. "I had assumed that when we were married we would live on Inis Eala. Yes, I'll miss Sevenwaters, but I do have family on the island. I have skills that should come in useful there—I know there's no room for idle folk in such a community."

Cathal got to his knees and gathered me close. "Are you sure?" he said against my hair. "Are you quite sure you want to marry me, knowing whose son I am? He won't forget that promise you extricated yourself from, you know. If we have children—sons—they'll be at risk all their lives. We'll be more or less trapped on the island. He won't give up his efforts to recapture me, and you'll be a target because he can use you to force my obedience. It may not be much of a life for you, Clodagh."

"It's the life I want. I want to be with you, Cathal. Nothing else matters."

His arms tightened around me. "Why would you give up so much, just for me?" he asked, his tone full of wonder.

"You almost gave up everything for me," I told him. "The reason is exactly the same. I love you. It's as simple as that." I touched the necklace he wore, with its white stone. "I have to ask you something," I said. "Clearly you've developed great skill in magic, even if you do call yourself a beginner. Perhaps you could have left before, using those powers and your alliances. Maybe you were strong enough to defeat him all along."

"Not without you," Cathal said with such finality that I believed him instantly. "You are my talisman, Clodagh. To leave that place in safety, I needed you by me. I am as sure of that as I am that oak leaves fall in autumn. In all that long time of waiting, even when my spirits were at their lowest, I never lost the belief that you would come back for me. I never ceased to be amazed that you could love me, an outsider, a man who had insulted you, ignored you, caused you nothing but grief. That wonder will be with me all my living days. With you by my side I feel . . . I feel clothed in love."

My heart melted. "When you put the ring on my finger," I whispered, "it filled up my heart with happiness, Cathal. I never want to say goodbye again."

We held each other awhile, not talking, as the forest creatures sang and chirruped and rustled around us in the warming day.

"I'll have to give Johnny a full explanation," Cathal said. "I'll need to stay on the island and train others; I will not be able to accompany him on his missions. I hope he will be prepared to keep me on in view of that limitation."

"Of course he'll keep you," I said. "And perhaps, in time, the Lord of the Oak will cease to hold such sway in these parts. Eventually it may become safe for us, and for our children if we have them, to go further abroad. Even in the world of the Fair Folk time passes and the balance changes." I remembered Ciarán's words: *Now is not the time for me to do battle with Mac Dara.* To say that was to imply that such a time would eventually come. When it did, my uncle would not be wanting to confront the Lord of the Oak alone.

"If you're sure," Cathal said.

"I'm sure." We rose to our feet, but before we walked on I stood on tiptoe and kissed him, showing him that there was absolutely no doubt on the matter. His answering kiss set my body aflame. The compulsion to sink to the forest floor together, to lie entangled in the stillness of the spring morning and take our fill of each other was hard to resist. But we held back. He withdrew his lips from mine. I stepped away from him. He was flushed; my breathing was unsteady. After a moment, we both burst into shaky laughter.

"Come on, then," I said. "Let's go home. Keep your mind on that comfortable bed. Perhaps we can persuade Father to let us be hand-fasted quite soon. I'm hoping Ciarán will agree to conduct the ritual."

"I have a new verse for your song," Cathal said as we walked on. "I had been wondering, while I waited for you in that place, how it might end. I constructed several versions, but as it has turned out, this one is the most apt:

"Where have you wandered, my dear one, my own
Where have you wandered, my handsome young man
I met a young woman with hair like a flame
She laid my heart open, she banished my shame.

"And then, of course," he went on, "you'd need a new ending, since the handsome young man has found his way at last."

My eyes were suddenly full of tears. "It could be something

like: *Together we'll find the way home,*" I said. "I thought you couldn't sing."

"For you, my love," said Cathal, "I'm prepared to try almost anything."

There were no more tricks of time. We walked into the courtyard of Sevenwaters the day after my father had broken off his important council to ride at breakneck speed to the nemetons and fetch his baby boy home; the day after my mother had received her lost child back in her arms. At some distance from the keep we'd been halted by a pair of sentries, who had identified us then let us pass. They had eyed us with curiosity—perhaps it was not widely known that Cathal was with me, or perhaps it was his appearance that gave them pause. It was as if everything about him had been sharpened by that time away. He seemed taller, thinner, his skin paler, his eyes more intense. If he had been striking before, now he looked dangerous.

The first person we saw in the courtyard was Sigurd, on guard duty. "Thor's hammer!" the big Norseman exclaimed, rooted to the spot and staring at Cathal. "What did they do to you? You're a shadow of yourself, man!" He strode forward and clapped Cathal on the shoulder in hearty greeting, then sobered. "You've heard the bad news?"

"We know about Aidan," I said.

More men had spotted us; I noticed a heavy presence of Inis Eala warriors around the keep. That would be because of the council. The place must be full of people. I felt the tension in Cathal. Straight from the isolation of that little cell, the long battle of wits, the confrontation with his father, to this . . .

"My lady, there's a houseful of folk here, all sitting down to breakfast about now," Sigurd said. "You won't be wanting to walk straight into that." His eyes went back to Cathal, assessing.

"Could you slip inside and tell Johnny we're here?" I asked the Norseman. "You're right, we'd best not create a drama in front of Father's guests. We'll go and wait in the herb garden. And please make sure those other men keep quiet about this until my parents are told."

We made our way to the little walled garden outside the still-room door. It was a peaceful place set with stone benches and shaded by flowering trees, with a lovely lilac in the center. The air was full of the healing scents of lavender and thyme. *Step across the field of thyme, fall so far you cannot climb . . .* I would never feel quite the same about that smell again. Cathal and I sat down on a bench, side by side, hand in hand, and waited.

The first person to find us was my father, who stepped out through the stillroom door looking every bit the chieftain in his council attire of dark tunic and trousers, pristine linen shirt and short cloak, only to run across to me and, as I stood up, envelop me in a fierce embrace.

"Clodagh!" he said indistinctly. "You're safe! I'm sorry, I'm so sorry, my dear."

"It's all right." My reply was shaky in the extreme. "I understand why you acted as you did, Father. Mac Dara cast his net over all of us for a while. How is Mother? Is she well? What about Finbar?"

But Father was looking at Cathal now, and Cathal, standing very still beside me, was meeting his gaze steadily. There was much in that look; almost too much. I opened my mouth to offer explanations, but at that moment Johnny strode out of the house, a big smile on his tattooed features, and threw his arms around Cathal.

"You're back," my cousin said. "Thank all the gods."

"It is not the gods you should thank," said Cathal quietly, "but Clodagh. I owe my presence here today entirely to her intervention." He took my hand again; I felt the trembling in his. His uncertainty about the future was real, despite the bright welcome in Johnny's eyes.

"I'll need an account of your actions as soon as possible," Father said, his gaze still on Cathal. "We have a number of influential chieftains gathered in the house, and your return has . . . implications." Behind his words loomed not only the doubt that had hung over Cathal himself, but the issue of Glencarnagh, and the fact that it was Cathal who had called Illann's role into question.

I glanced at Johnny, trying not to make it too obvious. "We're both very tired," I said. "Most of what we have to say can wait, can't it? But I should tell you about Glencarnagh . . ." Faces, walls, bushes began to turn in circles around me and I swayed, then sagged down onto the bench. "Sorry," I murmured as Cathal came to sit by me, his arm around my shoulders.

"Glencarnagh?" Cathal queried, as if he had never heard the name before. It took a moment for me to remember that he had been away a long time.

"Father's holding that was attacked and burned," I said, seeing the baffled glances of the other men. Gods, my head felt strange. All I wanted was a bath and sleep. "Father, Mac Dara—Cathal's father—told me the attack was all his doing. I can explain more about it later. If it's still causing trouble between you and Illann, it shouldn't be. Illann had nothing to do with it."

Father and Johnny exchanged a look, then turned their gaze on Cathal, who rose to his feet.

"Clodagh and I have not had time to discuss this particular matter," he said, squaring his shoulders. "It seems so long ago. You'll be wanting me to account for my sudden departure from Sevenwaters and . . . and other things."

"Certainly, you have some explaining to do," Father said. "A situation has developed. If what Clodagh has just told us is accurate, we may now have the means to resolve it while the chieftains are still at Sevenwaters for the council. The matter is pressing."

"Welcome home, Clodagh!" Gareth had appeared in the stillroom doorway. "And you, my friend! By all that's holy, man, you look as if you haven't slept in days." He eyed Cathal with evident concern. "They've told you about Aidan, I take it. A grievous loss; I'm so sorry." He glanced from Father to Johnny. "I'll take this fellow off for a meal and a rest, shall I?"

"There is no need," said Cathal. "If you require my account now, I will give it, Lord Sean." It was a brave attempt to sound wide awake and capable, but I could hear the exhaustion in his voice and it seemed Johnny could, too.

"Sean, this can wait until later," my cousin said. "It's not every day you get your daughter home from the Otherworld. With your approval, I'll let the guests know that the full session will be delayed. They'll welcome the opportunity to sit a little longer over their breakfast, I expect. Cathal's going to be of more use to us if he's had some rest and refreshment. And you'll be wanting to take Clodagh up to see her mother."

"Yes, of course," Father said. He must indeed be distracted, I thought, if he needed such a reminder. "Thank you, Johnny. Cathal, my sympathies for the loss of your friend; he was a fine warrior." Both his tone and his expression had relaxed somewhat. "Clodagh, we'll go up the back stairs. Your mother is in the sewing room today. Your sudden departure wrought more changes than you could imagine. Come, my dear."

I did not want to let Cathal out of my sight. But he would do well enough among the men of Inis Eala. They were his comrades; they would look after him. "Go and rest," I said quietly. "I won't be far away."

Cathal lifted my hand to his lips under the eyes of all three men, holding it there a moment. "Until later," he said.

"Until later," I said, smiling as I turned away. Maybe my beloved did look exhausted, worn-out, aged beyond his years. But he most certainly hadn't lost his courage.

There followed a whirl of greetings, embraces, tears, smiles and garbled explanations. By the time Father and I reached the sewing room we had an entourage: Sibeal, Eilis and Coll. Mother was seated in a comfortable chair, the remains of her breakfast on a tray nearby. Morning sun streamed in through the window, catching the bright flame of her hair where it curled out from the confines of her veil. She was embroidering a pattern of spring flowers onto a tiny shirt. The baby was beside her in a willow basket. With her were Muirrin and Eithne, mending.

I had imagined all manner of grave possibilities for my mother's health. I saw immediately that I had troubled myself without cause. She rose to her feet, holding her arms wide, and I walked into them. After a little we drew apart. Both of us had tears in our eyes.

"Eithne," said Mother briskly, "Clodagh needs something to eat and drink; fetch another tray, will you? And ask someone to take warm water and a tub to her chamber for bathing, please. She'll be ready for that as soon as she's had her breakfast. You young ones, off with you! You'll have plenty of time to talk to Clodagh later. You're not to disturb her until she's had a rest. Go on!"

I was astonished to see my mother so remarkably restored to her old self when it was only a day since she had got Finbar back, but perhaps I should not have been. Although my double journey had encompassed only a few days by my own counting, that first absence had taken up almost a turning of the moon in the human world. I recalled Ciarán saying that hope had restored my mother to herself; the hope that I would bring Finbar safely home. It warmed my heart that she had had such faith in me.

Over bread and cheese and a jug of good mead I told the bare bones of my story. I did not tell them of the perilous bargain I had made with the Lord of the Oak, in which I might have found myself handing over my firstborn son or being obliged to share Mac Dara's bed. I did not tell them the full story of Becan. But I did make it clear that there was a new order now in the realm of the Tuatha De, and that we would all have to be wary. I did not spell out what lay between Cathal and me, but it must have been plain enough in my account of the way Mac Dara had used me to bring his son into the Otherworld, and in the fact that I had risked so much to go back for him. Father listened in silence. Mother went on sewing, asking a question now and then. Muirrin looked in turn astounded, amused and horrified.

"And then," I concluded, "we waded out of the river and found ourselves back in our own world. Fiacha flew off, probably straight to the nemetons, and we walked home through the forest. It's quite a while since either of us has had any sleep, so I hope you'll allow Cathal sufficient time to rest before he's called to account for himself, Father. He hasn't done anything wrong. He had no involvement with what happened at Glencarnagh—that was all Mac Dara's doing, and calculated specifically to cast suspicion on Cathal. Of course, the Lord of the Oak also likes stirring up trouble purely to entertain himself."

Father did not appear particularly reassured. "I hope you're right about this, Clodagh. There's the matter of Cathal's accusation against Illann; that has caused a good deal of trouble with the southern faction. We have the opportunity of securing agreement to an unprecedented treaty, with both southern and northern chieftains at the council table. Illann is refusing to sign, claiming his good name has been tarnished by the doubt that lies over him in relation to the Glencarnagh attack. If that matter can be resolved to his satisfaction and mine, we may yet get every chieftain's mark on our treaty. I'll want to speak to you and Cathal together as soon as you've rested."

Mother gave him a particular sort of look. "Clodagh's asleep on her feet, Sean," she said. "If she's said Mac Dara was responsible for the attack, then he was responsible." An unspoken message was quite clear in her eyes. *You've refused to believe your daughter once before, and look where that led you. Are you foolish enough to do it again, so soon?*

"Father," I said, "you do know, don't you, that the knowledge Cathal gave me about the Glencarnagh raid arose from a scrying vision? Mac Dara is powerful enough to alter Cathal's visions to suit his own needs. All he wanted was to get Cathal in trouble so he'd have to leave our household and go off into the forest on his own." I wondered, as I spoke, whether the new Cathal, the one who could change the moods of a raging river, would ever be tricked in that way again.

"Sibeal was at pains to explain Cathal's talents as a seer to me when I rode to the nemetons to fetch my son." Father glanced down at the sleeping baby, and his severe expression softened. "I also exchanged certain words with Ciarán, who seems to share your faith in Cathal's integrity, as does Johnny. But it's essential that we hear from Cathal himself. We need all the detail he can provide for us."

Mother set aside her embroidery and took my hands in hers.

"We owe you an immense debt, your father and I," she said. "This has been a testing time for us, but that is nothing to what you have been through; you and this young man whom I've barely met. Sean, you should probably go down and put in an appearance, just to reassure your guests that all is well. Clodagh must have a bath and a short rest now. I insist."

"Of course," muttered Father. "I'm sorry, Daughter; I've been inconsiderate. This matter with Illann has been . . . it's been difficult." He put a thumb and finger to the bridge of his nose, a sure sign that his head was aching. "In fact, I find myself wishing the lot of them would go home so I could sit here with you for the rest of the day. Yours is a most extraordinary story. You've shown exceptional courage, and I regret most bitterly that I did not listen to you from the start. Having you safely back home is more than I deserve, my dear. Your mother's right; I must go." He kissed me on the cheek, then left.

"You'll need a salve for those cuts, Clodagh," Muirrin said, turning her professional eye on my face. "I'll fetch you something from the stillroom and leave it in your chamber, shall I? And I'll check whether your bath water's ready."

When my sister was gone, Mother said quietly, "You've risked a great deal for this young man, Clodagh. When you speak his name, I see something in your eyes that reminds me of the way I felt when I grew old enough to realize that your father was no longer my childhood playmate but had become a fine man. Tell me, my dear. Is it true what Sibeal told us? Do you really love Cathal?"

"Yes, Mother. I know that in some ways he must seem unsuitable, but he is the only one for me. I hope Father won't make things too hard for him. Cathal's been through a terrible ordeal. He was in that place for a long time, far longer than it took in our world."

"If he's worthy of you," Mother said quietly, "he will have no trouble in giving a good account of himself to your father. There's been great unrest over Glencarnagh, Clodagh. I'm deeply relieved to hear that Illann had nothing to do with what happened. I hope his wounded pride will not prevent him from making peace with your father."

"Surely not," I said, thinking of Deirdre, who had not yet made an appearance.

"This has been a difficult time for Sean. It was a coup to get so many of the chieftains here so quickly and then to bring them to the point of agreement. But Illann is bitterly offended, and the other southern chieftains share his sense of outrage; they did not take kindly to Johnny's arrival at Dun na Ri with a party of warriors armed to the teeth. To add to your father's worries, Eoin of Lough Gall has never seen eye to eye with Illann, and this matter has given him an excuse to be, if not openly hostile to him, then something perilously close to it. Outside the formal discussions, the two of them need to be kept apart."

"When I left," I said, "Father and Johnny seemed at odds. And while I was in that place I dreamed that they were arguing. How do matters stand between them now?"

"Without Johnny, Sean would have been at breaking point," Mother said. "Your cousin has been staunch and steady, a rock when Sean came close to despair. I'm deeply grateful that Johnny and his men were here when this happened. I haven't always looked favorably on them—their presence reminds me too much of bad times in the past—but in this crisis I have seen them shine, despite the loss of one of their own. Clodagh, tell me something."

"Yes, Mother?" I knew what was coming.

"It's not easy to accept that Cathal is the son of Mac Dara. But it seems that is true, and that he will be in danger here. I understand from Johnny that Cathal has no resources of his own. He'll be wanting to go back to the island and to take you with him. Will he ask this of your father?"

I nodded, observing that her neat features, an older version of mine, showed resignation rather than disapproval. "Mac Dara may pursue Cathal all his life," I said. "Inis Eala is the only place where we can be safe. I'm sorry, Mother. I never thought I would be leaving home so soon. With the new baby, you'll need help . . ."

"Go off and take your bath," Mother said. "Your father owes you a great deal, but you must give him time to come to terms with your choosing this particular suitor."

"That's just it," I said. "I don't think we have very much time." I shivered, remembering Aidan falling to that casually loosed arrow. Mac Dara could step out into our world whenever he wanted to.

"Don't look like that, Clodagh. I'll speak to your father."

I hugged her. "Thank you, Mother." A yawn overtook me.

"Off you go," she said, "or you'll be asleep before you so much as step into the bath. And you could do with a wash, my dear."

Deirdre burst in while I was in my bath. "Clodagh, you're here! Are you all right? Why did you shut me out when I tried to contact you?"

I regarded her from where I was sitting in the shallow tub, knees drawn up. The water was cooling fast, but I couldn't find the energy to get out. "I'm fine," I said, taking in my twin sister's rich gown, carefully tended hair and pallid, troubled features. "Stark naked and half asleep, but fine."

"Where's Cathal? He came with you, didn't he? Has he talked to Father and explained what he said about Illann? It's caused so much trouble!"

I shut my eyes and let her words flow over me. When she eventually came to a halt I said, "If Cathal has any sense he'll be in bed fast asleep by now. And be careful what you say about him, because he's your future brother-in-law."

"*What?*" I might as well have said I was planning to wed a man-eating ogre.

"I'm marrying Cathal. We're going to Inis Eala to live. As for Glencarnagh, it's for Cathal to explain what he said. But it's all right; I have information that completely exonerates Illann. I think your husband will be receiving a few apologies before the day is out. Father just needs to talk to Cathal and me again first."

"Really?" Deirdre's tone had changed abruptly. I thought she was almost in tears. "You really have proof that Illann wasn't involved, something Father will accept? I can't believe it. This has been so awful. It's gone on so long. It's as if they hate each other. I've tried hard to fix it, Clodagh; to make peace between them. But neither of them listens to me."

"Believe me," I said grimly, "I know exactly how that feels. Deirdre, I'm nearly asleep and my hair's filthy. Will you wash it for me, please?"

"Brighid save us," my sister said, giving me a close scrutiny. "And you were always the neat and tidy one. How did you get those cuts on your face?" She found the soap and a scoop, rolled up the sleeves of her fine gown and set to work.

As she lathered and scrubbed, I gave her a brief version of the story. I said I was sorry I had not let her into my mind when she wanted to speak to me; I reminded her that she was the one who had first decided we should stop that form of communication. When my hair was clean, Deirdre wrapped a towel around my head, helped me out of the bath and into a nightrobe, then sat me in front of the mirror, in which she gazed at me critically.

"If you're getting married, you'll be wanting something to help these cuts heal and fade as soon as possible," she said. "I can't believe Father agreed to it. A man who is only half human . . . You're the last person I would expect to choose someone so—so unusual."

"Father hasn't agreed, but he will. As for the cuts, Muirrin gave me a salve. I'll dab it on while you comb my hair. That's if you don't mind doing it for me."

Deirdre picked up the comb. She was much calmer now. "I can't believe it," she muttered, half to herself. "It might all be over today, this whole nightmare between Father and Illann . . . Illann's quite proud, Clodagh. Being under such suspicion has really tested him. And the southern chieftains seem all too ready to make the whole thing an excuse for stirring up more trouble. Until Illann started to confide in me, I never realized how complicated it all is. Don't look so surprised. I am married to the man. I've tried my best to learn about that part of being a chieftain's wife, just as you once suggested I should. I thought I was doing quite well. But this . . . it's been awful. I hate to see Illann so unhappy."

It seemed I had underestimated my own twin. "Then let's hope that he and Father sort it all out today, and that everyone learns from the experience," I said. "I've missed you, Deirdre. I'm truly sorry I shut you out. I won't do that again. If you need me, I'll be there."

"Me, too," said Deirdre. "Clodagh . . . Mac Dara. You actually met him in that place. It's so strange. I mean, he's a figure in stories; it's hard to think of him as a real person."

He was real all right; as real as a nightmare and as close as the nearest shadow. "Are you nearly finished?" I asked her. "I can hardly keep my eyes open."

"Your hair's going to dry terribly curly," Deirdre said, "but I've got the worst tangles out. Clodagh, I can't believe how brave you were to go and fetch Finbar back. And even braver to rescue this man of yours. I could never have done that. I'm sorry you'll be living at Inis Eala. It's so far away, we'll hardly ever see each other."

I turned and put my arms around her. "I know, and I am sad

about it," I said. I would miss her. She would always be my twin, the sister with whom I shared a special bond. But I knew in my heart that the prospect of living on the island with the man I loved had quickly relegated the rest of my family to second place. My world had changed. Over the season since Johnny had brought Cathal to Sevenwaters, *I* had changed more than I could have believed possible.

CHAPTER 17

I had expected to fall into a deathlike slumber as soon as Deirdre left, but my thoughts kept spinning in circles and after a while, realizing I would not sleep, I rose and dressed again. I went to find my younger sisters, wanting to thank Sibeal once more for her help. Sibeal said there was no need for thanks; she had simply done what a sister should do. Eilis bombarded me with questions about my visit to the Otherworld.

"Were there people with wings, Clodagh? What kind of horses did they have? And what about the food? In the stories it's supposed to be so delicious that humans can't stop themselves from eating it and then they have to stay there forever. Or they get back home and then pine away with longing because human food tastes like ashes."

"The only thing I tried was water from a stream," I said, feeling as if I were a disappointment. "It doesn't seem to have done me any harm."

"But what about Cathal?" Eilis was insistent. "You said he was there ages and ages. *He* must have eaten the food."

"Well, yes," I said with some reluctance. "But the rules would be different for him."

"Why—oh, you mean because he's a sort of half and half?"

"That's right."

"And perhaps the reason Clodagh could drink the water safely," put in Sibeal, "was that there's one of the Old Ones in our ancestry, so even we have a little thread of the Otherworld in us."

This had not occurred to me, but alongside the other oddities of the last few days it sounded perfectly plausible.

"Did you see Deirdre of the Forest?" Eilis asked.

"No," I said. "I thought I did, but it was someone else. Eilis, it may not be a good idea to talk about this too openly, not while there are so many visitors in the house."

"Can I talk to Coll about it?"

"I doubt if you'll be able to stop yourself," I said dryly. "But not if any of Father's guests are about, do you understand?"

"Yes, Clodagh." The compliant words were belied by her cheeky grin. Well, I supposed it would be an open secret soon enough, that one of Lord Sean's daughters was marrying a man who was only half human. This would make it doubly important for Eilis to wed as well as Deirdre had, when her turn came. I wished her a man who would be suitable both in the eyes of the world and in hers.

I went out into the courtyard, wondering whether Cathal, too, had found himself unable to sleep. Strolling down toward the stables, I remembered housing Willow in the little harness room during her visit to our home. I thought again of her strange tales and how I had been so slow to understand their true meanings. The clurichauns, the magical signs hidden in clothing, the significance of green; it should have alerted me to the importance of Cathal's cloak with its cargo of talismans designed to protect him from his father. Instead, for a little I had believed it might mean he was a traitor. Wolf-child; I had seen Cathal in that tale from the first. I had recognized in it his chill awareness of being forever outside, forever different. As for the story of the fairy woman and her half-human daughter, the charm cast by Albha had been exact in its revelation of what awaited Cathal in the Otherworld. He had understood it; I had failed to do so until it was almost too late.

And if I hadn't left the hall halfway through the tale, perhaps I would have realized right at the start that even the most powerful of charms can be undone, if only one has the key.

By the stables something stirred. I squinted against the sun, trying to make it out. What was that by the door to the harness room, a shadow against the silver-gray of the weathered wood . . . a figure in a hooded cloak? A chill ran through me, deep in the marrow. Mac Dara couldn't be here, not so soon, surely. The Lord of the Oak was subtle, a plotter. If he came back in a fresh attempt to harm me or to lure Cathal—*when* he came—he would plan his mission with care. I looked again. Now there were several men there, Inis Eala warriors leading horses out to the yard. One man wore a gray cloak, but the hood was down, revealing close-cropped hair and facial tattoos. The others were in tunics and trousers. A false alarm. Probably. Later, I would tell Cathal. And I would tell Father. Mac Dara must not be given an opportunity to use my family as leverage again. And I would die before I let him take Cathal.

"Clodagh?"

I whirled around.

"I'm sorry if I startled you," Gareth said. He was standing right behind me. "I've been sent to fetch you. Cathal's ready to talk to Lord Sean now."

So he hadn't slept either. "Of course," I said. "Where are they?"

"I'll take you."

I fell into step beside him. After the fright I'd just given myself, an armed escort was very welcome even in my own house. We made our way back through the kitchen, along a hallway, up a narrow flight of steps and along a gallery toward a row of storage chambers. Father had evidently taken steps to ensure this meeting took place well out of the view of his visitors.

"Gareth?" I ventured after looking around to make sure there was nobody in sight.

"Yes, Clodagh?"

"Has there been any more talk about the succession, now that Finbar's safe? Has Father formally named his heir?"

Gareth gave a little smile. "Not yet," he said. "Johnny tells me that if the treaty is signed, Lord Sean plans to end the council by making a public declaration. They have the details worked out."

I decided to be bold, since I was going to be living on the island, where codes of behavior were somewhat less constrained than in the halls of chieftains. "Cathal told me about you and Johnny," I said quietly. "I hope whatever Father says about the succession won't make you unhappy, Gareth."

"One learns compromise," Gareth said. "What is offered me I rejoice in. What is beyond my reach I don't waste time regretting. Inis Eala is a good place. You'll be welcome there, Clodagh."

"Thank you," I said as we came up to the door of an unobtrusive chamber, where Gareth gave three sharp knocks, waited to a count of five, then rapped out the triple knock again.

"Come in." It was my father's voice.

Gareth opened the door for me. Within the small chamber was a formidable group of men—with my father were his druid uncle Conor, Johnny and Cathal. Conor was seated, a tranquil figure in his white robe. Father stood with arms folded. Johnny was by the narrow window, staring out across the courtyard below. Cathal was extremely still, arms by his sides, shoulders square, head held high. He was facing Father, his back to the door. The sight of him made my heart leap. Had we really been parted only one morning? It felt like an age.

"I'm here," I said, walking in with Gareth behind me. Cathal's whole body tensed as he heard my voice, and for a moment I was back in that little cell, seeing him for the first time after Mac Dara took him. I moved to stand beside him and slipped my arm through his. He let out his breath in a rush. I rested my head briefly against his shoulder.

Behind us, Gareth went out and shut the door.

"Welcome, Daughter," said Father coolly. "Cathal has given us an account of his vision concerning Glencarnagh, and has explained his reasons for sharing it with you. That episode caused us considerable difficulty; I can only be grateful that we seem to have the truth now. I thank the gods that this did not develop beyond a war of words. What we require now is some clarification from you. Can you tell us exactly what Mac Dara said to you on the issue?"

I didn't even want to think about Mac Dara. What I had seen—or thought I had seen—by the stables had unnerved me. I cleared my throat, and explained that Mac Dara had openly admitted causing the raid and the fire, and that he must have manipulated Cathal's vision to implicate Illann in the attack. "The only thing he wanted was to get Cathal across into the Otherworld," I said. "He anticipated that Cathal would warn me. He stole Finbar in circumstances that would place suspicion on Cathal; he knew I'd feel obliged to go after my brother. He made sure I was the only one who recognized Becan as a real baby. Mac Dara knew Cathal would insist on coming with me. He used love as a weapon; my love of my family and Cathal's love for me. He wouldn't have thought twice about what this might mean for anyone else, Illann, for instance, or you and Mother. The Fair Folk don't understand love, not the way we do. They think of everything in terms of power."

Father made no comment. Instead, he looked at Conor.

"This is entirely consistent with my knowledge of the Tuatha De," the druid said.

"And yet," said Father, frowning, "the Fair Folk have long been friends of the Sevenwaters family. Why would they suddenly turn against us, wreaking such havoc without a thought?"

"I hope you do not doubt Clodagh's word." Cathal's voice was quiet, precise and dangerous. "My lord."

Father sighed. "I will not make that error again," he said. "But this is troubling. Relieved as I am to have Illann's innocence established, it seems to me there is a threat of far greater significance in all of this."

"For that, I take responsibility." The edge was gone from Cathal's voice. "The ills that have befallen your family recently have all been caused by my father's quest to reclaim me. If I had not come to Sevenwaters, Mac Dara would have left you in peace."

"In that case it's at least half my fault," put in Johnny with a faint smile. "You argued hard enough not to come. I thought the trip would be good for you. Next time I'll listen more carefully when you put a case to stay behind."

"Lord Sean is right about a bigger threat," Cathal said. "If I remain here, my father's attention will be on Sevenwaters and he will use whatever tricks he can to draw me back into his own realm. Clodagh's decision to befriend me has put her at particular risk. We must both speak to you very soon, my lord, on the implications of that. The danger we face makes quick action essential."

In the short silence that followed, I saw on the faces of Johnny, of Conor, of my father that each of them understood exactly what he meant.

"Let us deal with matters in a logical sequence," said Conor. "Sean, it seems you owe Illann an apology. Should we call him in?"

"On that issue, I have a suggestion," Cathal said.

"Tell us," said Father. His tone had changed. While still less than warm, it had thawed considerably.

"I will apologize to Illann for all of us," said Cathal. "I will give him a full explanation. He is your daughter's husband; he should know the truth. The fault here is not yours, Lord Sean. On the matter of Glencarnagh, you acted as any chieftain would under the circumstances." I heard in his tone, and in his words, that he was a leader to the bone and would answer to no man. I heard also that somehow, without any need for discussion, he had already become family.

"An apology," said Father, regarding Cathal quizzically. "You believe you can summon the appropriate tone of humility?"

"I can summon whatever tone is required, my lord."

"Very well," said Father. "Let's do it now. I'll add a few words of my own; I cannot allow you to bear the full weight of this, Cathal. If Illann's prepared to accept your apology, we may have this treaty signed tonight, and some real goodwill come out of this wretched course of events."

That night after supper eight chieftains of Ulaid set their signs to Father's treaty, and Illann was one of them. He was looking rather withdrawn, but the rest of them seemed well pleased. The two leaders who had stayed away from Deirdre's wedding were both present, and Eoin of Lough Gall was smiling as he set his mark on the parchment. He made a little speech thanking Father for getting them all to the council table together and managing to prevent the gathering from descending into a brawl, and everyone laughed and applauded.

My sisters and I had remained in the hall after the meal to watch the signing, for the treaty was a momentous achievement by any measure. We had left the table once supper was over and now stood by the hearth as the men completed their formal business. Inis Eala guards were stationed around the hall, a presence that could never be described as discreet, since their tattooed faces and generally fearsome air must always draw attention. However, tonight it seemed Johnny had told them to be unobtrusive; they did their best to blend into the background, but their eyes were knife sharp. Cathal was not present. I had not seen him since the meeting with Illann. I hoped he was sleeping.

"Thank goodness," murmured Deirdre in my ear as Conor sprinkled sand over the treaty document to hasten the drying of the ink, and the chieftains mingled affably around the dais. "It's signed at last. Illann said Cathal apologized this afternoon. Did you make him do that, Clodagh?"

"Me? No. It was all his own idea."

"It surprised me," Deirdre said. "He doesn't seem the kind of man who would ever admit to an error. He really is an odd choice as a future husband, Clodagh."

"All the same, I hope you'll be able to stay on for our handfasting."

"When is it to be?"

Since Father had not actually agreed to our marriage yet, I had no answer for her.

Muirrin, who was on my other side, said, "I'm traveling back to Inis Eala in about ten days. It would make sense for us to share an escort, Clodagh."

Ten days. It wasn't long to arrange a wedding. But then, I didn't need the feast, the dancing and the fine guests. "That would be good," I said. "I'll speak to Father."

"It's rather soon," commented Deirdre, narrowing her eyes at me. "Is there something you're not telling us, Clodagh?"

At first I had no idea what she meant. Then I recalled that sufficient time had passed in the human world for me to have shared Cathal's bed, conceived a child and had the first indications of pregnancy. Gods, I thought, if things had worked out differently, I might have been carrying that boy Mac Dara wanted. I might have walked away from the Otherworld with Cathal's son, or his father's, in my belly and a dark promise hanging over me. "No, Deirdre," I said. "Nothing at all."

A sudden hush in the hall; the signing done, Father had stepped onto the dais and was raising his hands for quiet.

"My lords, friends. Before we retire, I wish to speak briefly on another matter. It has seemed to me that in such times of unrest, a chieftain must make known his plans for the succession within his own holding. For many years I had no son, though I have been blessed with six daughters, each of whom is very dear to me." Father allowed himself a glance in our direction. "You will know all too well, after my precipitate departure and prompt return yesterday, that my wife and I have recently been blessed with a son; a child whom, for a little, we thought we had lost. Thanks to the courage of my daughter Clodagh, Finbar has now been returned to us." He looked around the hall, his gaze gathering his audience in. "A man with only one son, and that a very small one, might be considered by some folk vulnerable," he said, and I heard the iron strength beneath the gravely courteous tone. "A person who made that assumption about me would be in serious error. My sister has four sons, two of whom are present in this hall tonight: Johnny, leader of the Inis Eala warriors, and his young brother Coll. Between these two are another two brothers, both grown men. One will inherit his father's holdings in Britain. By my count, that still leaves four eligible heirs to my chieftaincy. Let no man stir unrest, thinking our family in any way weak or divided.

"Tonight, I declare that my eldest nephew, Johnny of Inis Eala, is my chosen heir; he will be chieftain after me. His father is lord of an extensive holding in Britain. His mother is a daughter of Sevenwaters. Johnny is a proven leader, seasoned and wise. I have complete faith in him. For now, we work together. When I am gone, he will lead the community of Sevenwaters as ably as he has done his establishment in the north. As for my son, so newly with us, it will be many years before he reaches manhood. Finbar will be Johnny's heir; he will be chieftain of Sevenwaters in his turn. And now I thank you for your contributions to this council and congratulate every one of you on the agreement we have forged together. I bid you all good night."

As the chieftains stepped forward to thank Father and say their good nights, I looked at my sisters and they looked at me. "Who decided that?" I whispered, realizing how neat and wise and just a solution it was. Neither Johnny nor Finbar was cut from the succession. It removed all cause for future rivalry between them and their supporters. And it eliminated the requirement for Johnny to marry and father sons.

"Mother, Father and Johnny worked it out together," Muirrin said. Then, seeing me yawn, she turned her healer's gaze on me, shrewdly assessing. "Clodagh, have you *still* not slept? What's wrong with you and Cathal? You can't go on forever, you know."

"I should think Cathal probably is asleep," I said, "since he isn't here in the hall."

"Ciarán arrived just before supper," said Sibeal. "Cathal may be talking to him."

If he was, I thought, it would likely be out of doors where privacy and quiet were easier to find. I made my way out, throwing a shawl around my shoulders, for the evening was cool. The moon had appeared above the fortress wall, a welcome presence after those empty Otherworld skies. It bathed the ancient stone in light. Sigurd and Mikka were on duty, standing one to either side of the main gate. They were easily identified at a distance, Sigurd by his bulk, Mikka by the gleam of his hair, wheat pale in the moonlight.

I walked over. "Have you seen Cathal?" I asked.

"He went that way," said Mikka, pointing in the direction of the herb garden. "May I escort you, Clodagh?"

"Thank you, but I should be fine." There were lighted torches in sockets all around the courtyard, and the moon illuminated the path in between. I was longing to see Cathal again, see him properly this time without my father's eye on us, without even the well-disposed Johnny or Gareth as witness. I yearned to hold my dear one in my arms, kiss his weary face, remind him that I loved him and tell him how much I had admired his strength today. I wanted to whisper secrets in his ear and to hear his words of tenderness and passion. I hurried along the path, head down, shawl hugged around me. Of course, it was very possible that Ciarán would be there. I knew he would want to talk to Cathal. Ciarán would have questions, his own kind of questions. I would politely ask him to leave us alone for this evening at least.

In the archway leading to the herb garden, I paused. Cathal was sitting on the stone bench under the lilac, his head tipped back against the trunk of the tree, his eyes closed. A hooded cloak wrapped him; he might have been sleeping, or perhaps deep in thought. The moonlight played on the white plane of his cheek, the darkness of his hair.

"Cathal?" I said, suddenly hesitant. Perhaps I should let him rest. He was so still, as if enmeshed in a sleep beyond dreams. I took a step forward, then another. "Cathal, are you all right?"

Slowly he lifted his head. He opened his eyes and smiled at me, and my blood turned to ice. Again. So soon. Right inside the walls of my father's house, right inside the little garden that had once been sanctuary to my grandmother, whom the Tuatha De had loved and honored. Terror paralyzed me. I could not even scream.

Mac Dara rose to his feet, an imposing figure in his swirling cloak. Shadows moved around him as if even they were obedient to his will. He fixed his eyes on me, the dark, compelling eyes that held so many years within them. He raised his hand, perhaps to beckon to me, perhaps to cast a spell.

The stillroom door opened. Light streamed forth. There stood a tall figure in a homespun robe, his auburn hair fiery in the lamp's glow. Ciarán. In the time it took me to glance at him and to look back, the Lord of the Oak was gone. He had neither walked past me nor flown up in the air nor disappeared into a chink between the paving stones. He had simply vanished.

I breathed again. So close. Oh, gods, so close. And, after all, ten days was far too long.

Cathal appeared behind the druid. He took one look at me, brushed past Ciarán and strode across to me. "What is it? What's happened?"

"He was here," I managed, clutching onto him with shaking hands. "He was right here in the garden. I thought it was you, and then he looked at me and . . ."

"It's all right now," he murmured, drawing me close. "I'm here; I have you safe."

Ciarán spoke from behind him. "I felt his presence," said the druid. "Your father is strong; each day I am more astonished by your capacity to withstand his influence. And he is audacious. That he would come here, to the heart of Lord Sean's own household . . ." He lowered his voice, glancing around the little garden before speaking again. "You were right," he said. "The longer you remain here the greater the peril you risk bringing down on yourself and all the family at Sevenwaters." He was looking at Cathal.

"I care little for my own peril, my lord," Cathal said. "It is through Clodagh that my father will attempt to manipulate me. She and I must both leave Sevenwaters. We must retreat to Inis Eala without delay."

"And yet," said Ciarán, "if anyone is to stand up to the Lord of the Oak, it must be you. Would you leave both human folk and Otherworld dwellers defenseless against a prince who rules by cruelty and mischief? You have the capacity to end his influence forever, Cathal, if you would but use it."

"No!" I said sharply. "It's wrong to ask that of Cathal. You sound as if you think he should feel guilty about going away. And yet at the same time you point out how dangerous it would be for us to stay, dangerous for all the family at Sevenwaters, yourself included. He's not doing this. We're not doing it. What you suggest would mean putting our children at risk. It would mean sacrificing our whole future."

There was a silence. Then Cathal said, "You heard Clodagh. To overthrow a tyrant is to create chaos, unless there is another ready to step into his place."

Ciarán looked at him, mulberry eyes steady in the moonlight. He said nothing.

"I have chosen this world," Cathal said. "I have chosen Clodagh. I will not do it."

After a little, Ciarán nodded. "That is what I expected. I will help you by explaining to Lord Sean why it is so important for you to leave. I wish you joy and contentment, and I ask you to be mindful of one thing only. At the present moment, what I suggest seems impossible to you. For many years you have feared and despised the abilities that came with your father's bloodline. You are beginning to accept, I think, that his heritage is a two-edged sword: it can be employed for good or ill, though it is always perilous. I know that you developed those skills while you were in captivity and that you used them, in the end, to escape Mac Dara's control. It seems you have a particular facility in water magic. Your father most certainly had no idea of that, or he might have anticipated that you would in time learn how to break the charm that held you in the Otherworld. I do not know if you fully understand what this suggests: that you possess, or could possess, a power as great as his own. With the right allies, perhaps greater. We will speak of this again. I believe your return is inevitable."

"You're wrong," Cathal said. "But we thank you for your help, past, present and future. I have something that is yours." He untied the cord with its white stone and held it out on his palm. "This served me well," he said.

"Thank you." Ciarán's eyes held a shadow now. He took the little token and tucked it into the pouch at his belt. "She would be happy that it helped reunite lovers parted. She would wish you joy in each other."

"We were hoping," I said, "that you might perform the handfasting ritual for us."

A smile of pleasure and surprise appeared on the druid's somber features, making him look suddenly much younger. "Are you sure?" he asked.

"We're sure," Cathal said.

"Then we must ask Lord Sean if he will speak with us tonight. For I concur with your judgment that time is short."

Poor Father. Only yesterday he had got his little son back. Only today he had persuaded his influential guests to sign the treaty and made a fragile peace with his estranged son-in-law. And tonight, after first Cathal, then Ciarán explained the true situation to him, he was being asked to let his daughter marry and leave home within a few days of her arrival back from a long and perilous journey to the Otherworld. In that series of extraordinary events, the fact that my bridegroom was the son of a dark prince of the Tuatha De loomed less large than it might otherwise have done.

It helped that Cathal had conducted himself so well since our return. It helped that he had treated Father with courteous respect while at the same time contributing to the debate as if they were equals. Both Johnny and Gareth spoke up in support of him as a future husband for me. Ciarán presented the case strongly, making it quite clear that I was at immediate risk if I stayed at Sevenwaters, whether or not Cathal and I married, for Mac Dara knew his son loved me; he knew Cathal would do anything to keep me safe. That gave the Lord of the Oak a strong advantage. Conor was impressed by Ciarán's arguments, but unsure that heading north was the wisest choice for me. Perhaps he did not understand that love could be the sharpest weapon of all.

We sat up long into the night as the matter was debated. I refrained from saying what was foremost in my mind, and no doubt also in Cathal's: that, even if Father withheld his consent to our marriage, we would be leaving Sevenwaters together. Our love bound us to each other more strongly than any formal hand-fasting could; it would endure until death, whether or not we were officially husband and wife. To be married would be good, because it would please my family better than an unorthodox arrangement. The latter could make things awkward between Father and Johnny if we were living on the island. But a hand-fasting was not essential. Leaving Sevenwaters was. Mac Dara was only a breath away.

Finally, as the candles in the small council chamber were dying down to stubs and Gareth, by the door, had given up any attempt to conceal his yawns, Father said he would allow the hand-fasting provided Mother agreed to it; he would ask her in the morning. If she was happy with the idea, the ritual would be conducted as soon as his guests had left the keep, probably within two days. That would allow time to organize a suitable escort for us—it must be substantial. I was almost too tired to take in the good news. Cathal kissed me in front of everyone, and I retired to bed. I was asleep the moment I laid my head on the pillow.

I would have been happy with the simplest of weddings: just Ciarán to say the words, Cathal by my side and my family looking on. My sisters, however, saw the two-day preparation period as a challenge. Deirdre and Muirrin worked from dawn until dusk to make me a wedding dress in soft blue wool, its sleeves and hem decorated with bands of embroidery taken from a favorite old gown of Mother's. Sibeal planned the ritual with Ciarán and Conor, adding her own personal touches. Eilis wove a garland of fresh flowers for me to wear on my hair. Even Coll made himself useful, running errands and generally keeping folk in a good temper. Knowing that Cathal and I would neither expect nor want a celebration of the same grandeur as Deirdre's, Mother organized a special supper for the family, Johnny's men and our household retainers. Everyone in turn would have time off guard duty or kitchen duty to share the meal, tell tales and sing songs. It was to be a joyous occasion; we would not let the impending parting shadow our happiness. I was sad that Maeve could not be with us. Father had used his link with Aunt Liadan to tell the family at Harrowfield our rather startling news, and my absent sister had sent her love. Still, it was not the same.

Before the ritual I sat with my father in the small council chamber while, upstairs, Mother fed the baby. It was hard to believe that tomorrow I would be gone; that it might be years before I saw my parents again. I would miss Finbar's growing up. If Deirdre had children, I would be a stranger to them.

"Thank you for agreeing to this, Father," I said. "It was a lot to ask, I know. I'm sorry I won't be here to talk to you and to help Mother with everything."

He nodded, saying nothing. There was a pensive look on his strong features.

"You're a remarkable father and a remarkable chieftain," I told him. "The treaty was a great achievement. Considering how worried you were about Finbar, the way you managed everything so calmly showed great strength. What about Eoin of Lough Gall? Anyone who can make that man smile and crack a joke must possess exceptional skills at the council table."

"You still have faith in me, Clodagh. Yet I treated you so unfairly. I was cruel to you. I cannot forgive myself that."

I put my arm around his shoulders. "We are family, Father. We love each other. Besides, it was Mac Dara's fault that you saw

Becan as nothing but a bundle of sticks. Father, if anything goes wrong here, if Cathal's father causes strife again, you must send us a message straightaway. And tell Ciarán. I don't think the Lord of the Oak will continue to plague you once we are beyond his reach, but he's a trickster by nature. It could happen. I said nothing to Mother of this, but I am afraid for you."

He nodded soberly. "If I am the fine chieftain you think me to be, Daughter, I suppose I can deal with both worldly and otherworldly threats. I will be watchful. Now let us venture out, shall we? I hope this young man is as deserving as you believe. His pedigree is . . . unusual. I have been impressed by his demeanor over these last days, but I did not think to have to make such a decision so quickly."

"It's the right choice, Father; the only choice. I'm as sure of it as I am that the sun rises in the morning. And although I'm sad to be leaving Sevenwaters, I'm happy too—happier than I've ever been in my life."

"Then it is the right choice, Clodagh. May the gods walk with you, my dear, wherever your new path takes you."

On the lake shore beside a graceful birch tree Cathal and I were hand-fasted, and I saw in my dear one's eyes that he thought me the most precious thing in all his world, and that his love was steadfast and true. What was between us would endure forever, or as close to forever as a human life could stretch. Cathal would outlive me, perhaps by many years; such was his blood. Today, with my heart full of joy, I would not think of that. I would not consider the uninvited guest, the invisible presence looking on as his son wed a human woman who had proved to be just a little more resourceful than the prince of the Otherworld had anticipated. A father should be pleased to see that look of contentment on his son's face. But Mac Dara would not be pleased. He would be plotting and scheming still, determined to have his way.

When the ritual was concluded Cathal and I did not go straight indoors, but walked together to the place where Aidan had been laid to rest. Not alone; we would seldom be without a presence of guards now until we reached Inis Eala. Mac Dara's appearance in the private garden of my family home had furnished a powerful warning. So we were accompanied by both Gareth and Johnny, the two of them well armed, and also by Ciarán, whose weapons were less visible but almost certainly more powerful. Where the Lord of the Oak was concerned we needed protection beyond the capacity of a pair of elite warriors, be they Inis Eala men or no.

When we reached Aidan's grave, which lay in a clearing among birches, our three guardians stationed themselves well back while Cathal and I went to stand by the slight mound under which our friend lay. The earth was still bare, but grass was beginning to creep over it. By summer's end Aidan's resting place would be blanketed in green. Birds sang a fine song in the trees around us; it was more lively dance than lament. For Aidan it seemed appropriate.

I held Cathal's hand. After the elation of the ceremony, his mood had changed entirely. The lost look was back on his face. We had intended to offer prayers; to speak words of recognition and farewell, since tomorrow morning we would be gone from Sevenwaters. But we stood silent, the two of us. In the loveliness of the spring day, with the birch trunks gleaming straight and pale in the sunlight and a gentle breeze stirring the silver-green leaves, with the birdsong and the rustle of the forest and the great silence behind it, the death of a man so young and vital set a heaviness in our hearts.

"I do not know what to say," murmured Cathal. "I know no prayers; nor would any be enough. Yet I owe him something. He was my friend."

"Talk to him as if he were right there beside you," I said. "Wherever he is journeying now, Aidan will hear you, I'm sure of it."

Cathal cleared his throat; brushed a hand across his cheek. "You used to tell me I had a loose tongue," he said quietly. "My readiness to jest and mock often drove you to distraction. 'If you cannot choose your words more wisely,' you would say, 'then for pity's sake keep silent.'" His mouth twisted. "And now here I am, and although my heart is full, I have no words at all."

There was a pause; he wiped away more tears, but they were in his voice when he spoke again. "Any wrong you did me in life, I forgive you now. I do not know if you can forgive me, for I repaid your kindness poorly. You were slain in your prime for one reason only: that you were brave enough to be my friend." He bowed his head.

"You're doing well," I murmured.

He looked up, eyes streaming now. "We had good times together," he said simply. "In the bad times, we stood by each other. Farewell, my brother." He knelt and laid his palm against the bare soil a moment, then stood in silence.

"Farewell, Aidan," I said as the birdsong swelled into a jubilant chorus of recognition. "You were a fine man. You lived your life well. Go safely on your new journey."

Spending my wedding night under my parents' roof might once have seemed an awkward prospect to me, but Cathal and I cared nothing for that, only for the precious gift of time alone together and the astonishing maelstrom of feelings that had built and built between us. It was a night of sweet tenderness and explosive passion, of brief pain and long pleasure, of tears and of laughter. Laughter was good; it had been scarce enough of recent times. We did not sleep much, but that did not matter; there would be little opportunity for intimacy on the journey north, with our escort close at hand and the need to reach our destination safely driving us fast. With that in mind, we made energetic use of the time we had. Before dawn we rested, entwined in each other's arms, a sheen of sweat on our skin and a blissful weariness in our bodies, and felt the beating of our two hearts, as closely attuned as verse and melody, drum and dancing feet. With the rising of the sun we stirred, and woke, and readied ourselves to face the new day.

ABOUT THE AUTHOR

Juliet Marillier was born in Dunedin, New Zealand, a town with strong Scottish roots. She graduated from the University of Otago with degrees in languages and music, and has had a varied career that includes teaching and performing music as well as working in government agencies.

Juliet now lives in a hundred-year-old cottage near the river in Perth, Western Australia, where she writes full-time. She is a member of the druid order OBOD. Juliet shares her home with two dogs and a cat.

Juliet's historical fantasy novels are published internationally and have won a number of awards. Visit her Web site at www.julietmarillier.com.